THE WAYWARD HAUNT SERIES

THE
FOUR
REVENANTS

CAS E. CROWE

Author: Cas E. Crowe

Editor: Kristin Scearce, Hot Tree Editing

Book Cover Design: Miblart

Title: The Four Revenants

Paperback ISBN: 978-0-6488765-2-6

Hardback ISBN: 978-0-6488765-9-5

Ebook ISBN: 978-0-6488765-3-3

THE FOUR REVENANTS

Book Two

THE WAYWARD HAUNT SERIES

CAS E. CROWE

CAS E. CROWE

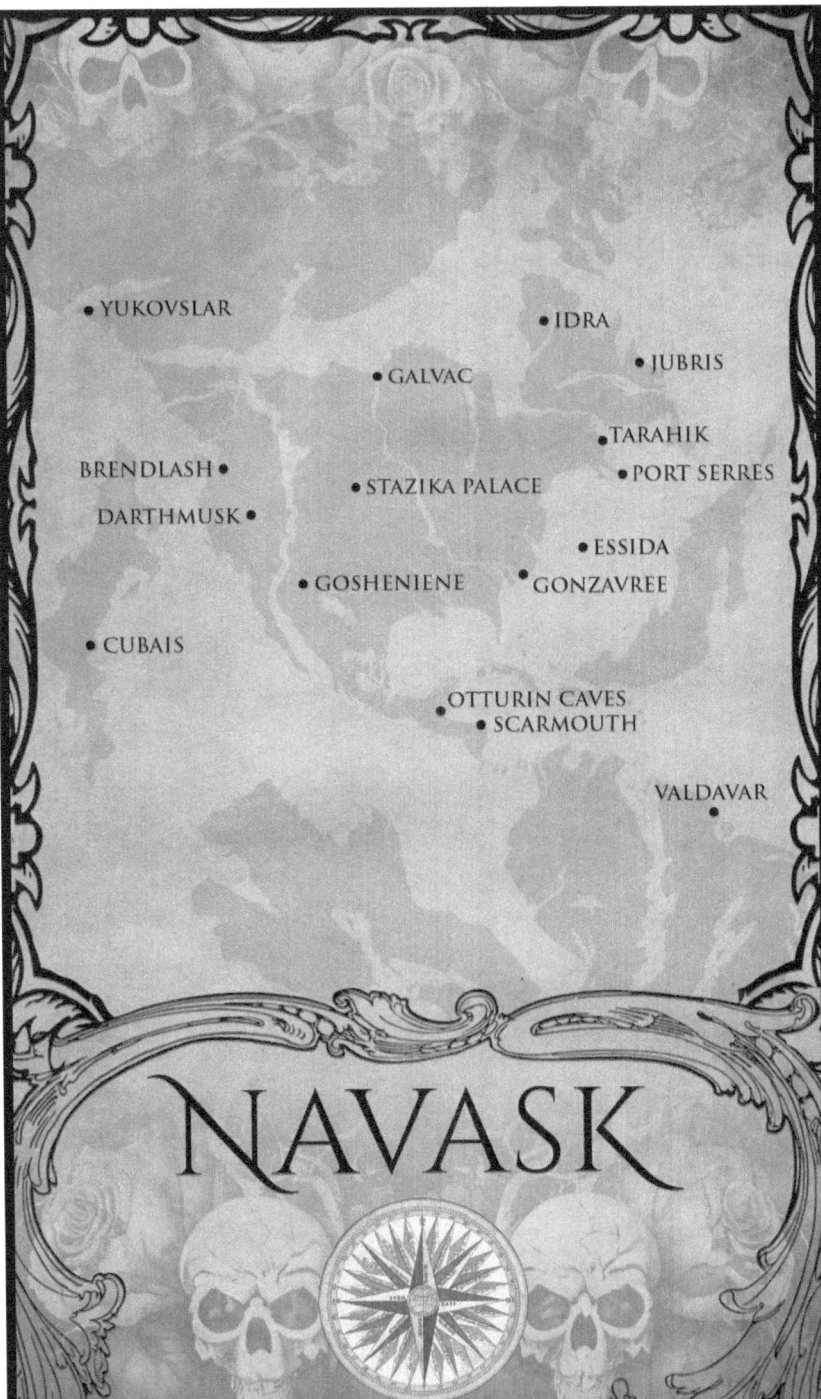

CHAPTER 1

Even before I opened my eyes I sensed danger.

I woke gasping for air. Volumes of water spilled from my mouth, my lungs spasming in my chest. Relentless waves pummelled my body.

Where am I? Where has Macaslan sent me?

I didn't know how long I'd travelled through the portal. Minutes? Hours? Days? Time was anybody's guess. One thing that was certain was the portal had teleported me somewhere dangerous. Submerged rocks scraped my body. Seawater stung my blisters and cuts. There was no point trying to swim. A large breaker spun me like a propeller blade, my arms and legs twisted around in a way an acrobat would be proud of. The surf washed me onto the shore, retreating as though I were pollution the ocean had rejected. The sun beat down and dazzled me blind. Seagulls squawked. They reminded me of a flock of hungry vultures circling above.

For a long time I lay on my back, painful tremors racking my body. I blinked away the haze that clouded my mind and rose to sit. Cliff faces obstructed the beach from either side. Behind me, white hot sand travelled to the edge of a thick and overrun rainforest.

Where am I?

This landscape was nothing like Tarahik.

Was I even on the Navask continent?

Thunder rumbled in the distance, bursts of chain lightning magnificent against the roiling dark purple clouds on the horizon. The storm travelled like an explosion as it rushed across the sky.

Drops of panic trickled into my stomach. *Galactic storm!*

Galactic storms were caused by stellar explosions near the Earth's atmosphere that advanced with alarming speed. In the provinces, they knocked out power grids, warped radio waves, and threw off compasses, causing communication to become complicated and erratic. Casters had no choice but to hunker down when these terrible storms occurred.

Which left me with one terrifying question.

What am I going to do?

I rose to my feet, my legs heavy.

I have to find shelter in the rainforest.

My progress was slow up the beach, the wind fierce as it endeavoured to rip the flesh from my bones. The sun dipped in and out of the black clouds, the light fading fast. My rapid pulse grew more frantic as my situation became more apparent.

How am I going to survive this?

All I had was my daypack—a soft canvas haversack that was soaked. I had no food. I had no weapons. I didn't know who or what lurked in the rainforest, which no longer looked lush and tropical but rather a dense maze where every shadow, sound, and unseen animal hinted peril.

This is madness. Why would Macaslan teleport me here?

Or had something gone wrong?

Surely this couldn't have been Senator Kerr's and Macaslan's plan?

Which meant one undeniable truth.

I'm screwed.

Something cold stroked my arm. The touch sent icy shock

waves across my skin. It was the sensation I had whenever I was in close proximity to a wraith. I inhaled a breath and forced myself to turn around.

She was fastened to a stake, her wrists crossed above her head in a mark of surrender. The rope had cut into her now greyish skin, leaving welts and bruises that had long been feasted on by small bugs, the exposed skin lifting in little flutters. Her legs were bound, but the damage to them was concealed by fabric that made a poor excuse for clothing. It flapped like a loose sail in the wind, giving the dead girl the illusion of movement.

Her head drooped, dank hair a curtain over her face. When the wind blew it back, it revealed an ugly burn on her forehead. On closer inspection, I realised it was the United League of Dissent's insignia: a circle with a dissent swastika in the centre, held by an eagle and griffin. It had been branded into her flesh.

I stumbled backward. It was a good thing my stomach was empty because the stench was rancid. It reminded me of fish left to rot in the sun. How long had she been left out here, the water submerging her over and over again? Days was my guess.

My body turned feeble, my necromancy revealing what could not be seen by the normal eye. Men and women were tied to stakes as far as the coastline stretched, their bodies slimy and malleable. My heart became a ticking bomb. I clambered past the broken bodies, desperate to get to the cover of the forest. My legs moved in slow motion, my boots unable to grip the sand.

What the hell is this place?

What nightmare had I been thrown into?

I ran blindly into the trees. I didn't care that branches scratched my arms and clawed my clothes, or that I tripped on gnarled tree roots. What mattered was distancing myself from the beach.

The galactic storm had doubled in strength and speed. Rain and meteoroid fragments lashed the forest, snapping trees like toothpicks. Their impact sent up explosions that were quickly conquered by the teeming deluge. The forest floor became a waterslide of running mud, leaves, and loose vegetation. I had no idea how this part of the world operated. I'd been dropped into a prehistoric time capsule where no caster had dwelled, the landscape primitive, untouched, and unforgiving.

Shelter. Search for shelter.

Something large and bone-pale appeared in the white streak of lightning ahead. I stood before the ruins of an ancient temple. The structure had been devoured by the forest, the walls swathed in moss, the monuments broken and covered in lichen. Vines entangled it like the arms of a lover.

There has been habitation here… but how long ago?

It's shelter, Zaya. Get a move on.

Inside, the temple smelt of neglect, the air stale and musty. The ground was strewn with wet leaves and twigs, a slippery trip hazard that proved difficult underneath my wet boots. Lightning ripped across the sky, illuminating beautiful but debauched carvings along the walls. They depicted some kind of creatures that were half bird and half caster. I wished I'd paid more attention in geography class back at Brendlash Orphanage. It would have been useful to identify the figures. It could have provided a clue to my whereabouts.

My arms trembled, but not from cold. Circles and crescents meant to symbolise Earth's twelve moons had been carved into the stone ceiling. The roof sloped too sharply to the right, propped up by a single column, as though the temple was an old, arthritic caster using a cane to support itself. It was a reminder that while I was safe from the storm, what I stood beneath wasn't a sound structure.

I sat among a collection of rocks and attempted to process the information in my fragile brain, but there wasn't much to go on. Every time the storm unleashed another blinding bolt of electricity, the ruins would appear ghostly pale, reminding me of the terrible faces I'd seen on the beach.

Don't think about them.

But it was becoming impossible not to.

4

Who were they?

I kept seeing the ULD's insignia burned into their foreheads.

A horrible realisation dawned on me.

I'm in ULD territory.

Which led me to my next troubled thought.

I searched through my trouser pocket and took out a gold locket, a beautiful rectangular pendant with a half sphere in the centre designed to resemble the moon. Inside was Jad's picture, his face bruised and battered, his eyes communicating a world of pain. His prisoner ID—1685302—ran across the bottom of the image.

Jad's alive. In a labour camp.

The memories of what had occurred at Galvac Tower the day I lost him surfaced like bubbles from a deep pool, raw and painful. I wished I knew where he was, but there'd been no time to find out. Commander Macaslan and Colonel Harper had been desperate to get me out of Tarahik and away from the clutches of General Kravis. Macaslan had pushed me into the portal, throwing me into a dark void that had brought me to this dangerous and unknown place.

How much time has passed? And where are Macaslan and Harper now?

Marek?

Lainie?

Talina?

Jad?

I collapsed onto the ground, giving in to overwhelming emotion.

I was lost.

Alone.

Broken.

CHAPTER 2

Morning arrived with a soft, steady drizzle. Back at Tarahik, I found the pattering of rain soothing, but all it did was make the air humid and the landscape hazy. My clothes hadn't dried. They clung to me like I'd fallen into a swimming pool. Pain pounded in the back of my head. My stomach screamed at me for food.

When was the last time I ate?

I was desperately worried about Jad. The ache that had taken up residence behind my eyes flared at the thought of the possible horrors he underwent. I missed my friends too, but the need for food was my prime concern. I couldn't do much for anyone if I had no strength.

Find food. Then figure out where you are.

Maybe there'll be fruit and berries somewhere.

I grabbed my soppy haversack, surprised by how heavy it felt. I turned the bag over. A pair of training clothes, toothpaste, and a brush fell onto the leafy ground. Another object landed with a heavy clang on the moist pebbles. My eyes caught on a familiar onyx blade, plain and narrower in width than most daggers I'd encountered. Strange runes marked the weapon—runes I recognised but did not understand.

Neathror.

A whirlwind of emotion swept through me. I'd lost the blade in Galvac Tower after General Kravis had the building hit with a missile. The dagger had fallen, lost in the ruins of the tower—or so I'd thought.

I knew this was no illusion.

I lifted the athame-sabre. Its power tremored like a disembodied pulse in my fingers. It was strong, capable. Just holding it seemed to give me purpose.

"How are you here?" My voice was a whisper in the subdued light.

I didn't trust sudden and strange sorcery, but Neathror gave me options now. I could hunt. I could sculpt wood into a weapon. The most important thing—I could defend myself.

Let's see what I'm up against out there.

My progress out of the temple was slow. Thanks to sleeping on a bed of rocks, pain spasmed in my lower back. I walked through the forest, careful not to trip on the tangles of vines and their colourful blossoms. The constant light shower of rain made the journey more laboured than I'd hoped. Judging by the position of the sun, it was around mid-morning by the time the grey clouds rolled away. The heat climbed. Sweat or rainwater—I wasn't sure which—ran down my scalp and lower neck, my hair a matted mess past my shoulders. The rainforest hadn't made a great impression on me during the storm, and it hadn't improved in my observation now. The ground was moist and spongy, the air thick and hot, like I was swimming in a bowl of soup.

I'd drunk some of the rainwater, but it hadn't quenched my thirst. The earth swayed in and out of focus more than once. No matter what direction I took, the trees seemed to close in on me, strangling, clinching, squeezing. I closed my eyes as another wave of vertigo swept past.

There has to be food somewhere.

The sweet chorus of birdsong filled the rainforest. I craned my neck toward the canopy.

Cobaltkeets.

Their water-blue feathers shone in the green tree line. I'd read about them in Gosheniene—the labour camp I'd been sentenced to—and had forgotten the bird's natural habitat was rainforest. But something that hadn't lapsed in my memory—so many cobaltkeets congregating in the trees meant there was a spring somewhere close. The parrots flew from branch to branch, their birdsong a melody in my ears. I followed, my energy renewed by hope.

I came out to an idyllic spring, the water cool and inviting. Dignity be damned, I submerged my face and drank. Water had never tasted so good. I washed my arms and face, massaging the aches out of my neck. It wasn't paradise, but it was a reprieve from desperation.

Fish swam ahead. They mocked me with their tranquillity as they gently lapped through the ripples. For a long time, I sat there cemented to the ground, watching them like a cat scanning a fish-bowl. I hated the taste of fish, but my stomach rumbled with such intense hunger that delicious longing crept through me.

Neathror.

I could throw it into the water and spear the little suckers.

Or was that too optimistic? I was decent with cast-shooters, but throwing knives were out of my element. That had always been Jad's thing.

Jad.

I bit my lip to hold in a sob.

Don't think about him. Get your strength back first. Find your way out of here.

I tightly clasped Neathror's hilt. Drawing a sharp breath, I shifted my stance, my right leg forward and my left leg behind, my spine straightened the way Jad had instructed me to do in training so many long weeks ago.

Here goes.

I threw Neathror. The blade sliced its way through the air with a resonance that sounded like singing. It dove through the water and impaled the fish. I drew back in surprise. This wasn't beginner's luck or any unforeseen talent on my part. Neathror knew what I wanted.

The decision part of my brain was split. On the upside, I had food. On the downside, hesitance soured my stomach. There was more to the blade than met the eye.

I RETURNED to the temple that afternoon with enough dry wood to make a fire. I gutted and cooked the fish, which took several attempts, and enjoyed if not a tasty meal, at least a filling one. Finding clues about my whereabouts was priority, but exhaustion clouded my momentum. I slept on and off, adrift in waking concern for my friends and nightmares about Jad. So much for not thinking about him. Around dusk, fatigue pulled me into deep, empty darkness.

But it didn't last.

The dream began, if that's what it was, in the dirty confines of a dungeon. The ceiling was well lit and cast a sickly tinge on the stone floor. Furniture, though not fancy by any stretch of the imagination, had been brought in to make someone's stay more comfortable. A stabbing itch quivered in the back of my throat, my eyes assaulted by heat. Steam hung in choking clouds. It clogged my mouth and nose, my upper lip beaded in sweat. The aging stone walls were damp with moisture. In an odd way, it made the dungeon appear like it was crying.

Hunched among a desk of tangled wires, beakers, and distilling columns, a gaunt woman prodded at an unknown specimen—something with legs like a spider's but the length and flexibility of a snake. Despite the humid air, the woman's hair remained straightened in a sleek bob, streaked black and white so the natural colour couldn't be defined. She wasn't young or old. Her skin was still youthful but chalk white, her green eyes lively as she worked. She hummed a ghostly tune as she limped through the lab, her hip sticking out like the sharp crag of a peak. I wondered how she'd broken it. Or was it a natural deformity? She rummaged through drawers, snapping up scalpels and scissors. I stepped back when she extracted a jagged-tooth saw.

My insides spasmed.

What the hell is she going to use that on?

Strange, scale-clad creatures preserved in jars of formaldehyde were positioned along the walls as trophies of medical triumph. The specimens seemed to watch the woman with trepidation. A shudder crawled over my skin. It reminded me of... *him*. The first time I'd laid eyes on Morgomoth, he'd been a lab rat in Galvac Tower. Preserved in a glass tank, Morgomoth had floated between life and death as thousands of wires, cables, and cords drank his power and converted it to energy for the Athnik region. I'd believed Morgomoth had fallen to his death when the tower had been destroyed, but that wasn't the case. I didn't know where Morgomoth was or who had him. General Kravis? Vulcan? Neither option warmed my heart.

I shimmied against the wall as the woman approached. Steam separated us, but through the thick vapour, I saw her body tense. Slowly, she reached a hand out. Her thin fingers were only inches away from my face. I pressed my lips together to keep my breath lodged in my throat. Despite the heat, a cold feeling prickled up the back of my neck. If she took a step forward, reached just a little farther—

The steam parted.

Her eyes centred on mine.

My voice was about to break out in a hoarse cry when the strangest thing happened. She examined my surroundings, right where I stood, but she seemed to look straight through me. Mumbling what sounded like an expletive, she shook her head and brushed past me back into the wafting steam.

Relief exhaled from my lungs.

She can't see me.

But did that mean I wasn't really here?

Was this real? A dream? Or something else?

I tiptoed closer to the woman. She was bent over a benchtop, picking at something with one of her incredibly wicked-looking instruments. My legs nearly buckled at the sight. A body was fastened to a surgical table, arms and legs tied down by shackles. I couldn't tell if the caster was dead or alive. There was no movement in them. My pulse hammered, every nerve in my body disabled.

What is this? Some kind of twisted experiment? In a dungeon?

A knock, powerful and authoritative, struck the steel door. Before the strange woman could answer, the person on the other side let themselves in.

A world of anger exploded behind my eyes. I could hardly breathe. Vulcan Stormouth wandered into the laboratory with an air of indifference, his irritating superiority still evident in his narrow eyes. Hatred, burning and painful, ignited inside me. I wanted to punch his teeth out, strangle him with my bare hands, slice him with my newly acquired blade. Anything to wipe that heinous smile from his lips. He hadn't changed one bit since I encountered him at Nekros Manteia, His bone-white face, curtained by waves of dark hair, and immaculate suit were exactly the same. Only his eyes had changed. They were wild and sadistic and fuelled by retribution. I had ruined his plans at Nekros Manteia, and as payback, he'd taken Jad. Even in this out-of-body experience, rage settled deep in my bones.

The woman crossed her arms. Her cat eyes examined Vulcan with the intensity of a stalking lion. "I thought I made it clear it wasn't safe to enter. These experiments... we have no idea what they may do to him." Her voice was elevated and nasal. A scream from her would be like the piercing wail of a banshee.

Vulcan grinned. It wasn't a pleasant smile. "I have faith you can make it work, Hadar. It worked on the other bodies."

"Those bodies were not subjected to the same number of potions. This could kill him." Hadar hobbled around the surgical table. The heels of her knee-length boots clicked against the stone floor, which I now realised sloped down to a drain directly under the operating table. An involuntary whimper escaped me. It was a slot drain for blood.

Hadar placed her bony hand on the test subject. "Making the ultimate warrior requires sacrifices… and patience. If you want this to work on him, then I suggest you find me new guinea pigs. Let's see how the magic affects them first before we make any long-term commitments to this subject."

Screams rang out from somewhere deep in the building.

The muscles in my throat pumped.

There are others… trapped here?

Hadar twisted her hands together, her knuckles white with agitation. Her voice erupted in a cry so piercing even the deaf would hear it. "Quiet!"

The screams ceased.

Vulcan tipped his head. "How many test subjects would you need?"

"Half a dozen should do it." She fiddled with her surgical scalpel. Her finger skimmed dangerously along the edge. "Just consider the positives. If the experiments work on each subject, you'll have more warriors to add to your army. Warriors that cannot be injured or killed."

Vulcan nudged his head toward the strapped figure on the l table. "As long as he is the strongest. When this is over, I want him by my side… always. Do you understand?"

The eerie light cast thick shadows on Hadar's face. The hard edges reminded me of the goblins I'd read about in human folk tales. "I can't guarantee that this experiment will wipe his memory. He will be conscious in there, but he won't be able to refuse a direct order."

The corners of Vulcan's mouth twitched. "That is just how I want it. I want him to remember his former life. I want him to remember *her*." He circled around the operating table, chin tilted proudly as he inspected the scientist's work. "Your test subjects will be rounded up and brought to you within the hour. Don't fail me, Hadar. Just remember that you are not here as my guest. You owe me." He pointed a reprimanding finger at her. "You are not in a position to play your tricks and witchery."

A vein pulsed in her temple, but her smile was cool and unflustered. "My accommodation has shown me I am no guest. Now leave me so I can work."

He studied her with mild amusement, but I didn't miss the aggression that flared in those black eyes. Vulcan's footsteps were fast toward the door. "We are running out of time. I expect results."

He disappeared beyond the door, which slammed with a resounding boom.

A wicked smile latched onto Hadar's lips. Her voice practically purred. "And you will have them… and much more than you can fathom."

She leaned her good hip against the table and caressed the face of her subject.

I drew closer, disgusted by the motherly attention she placed on her victim. The steam coiled up into vents in the ceiling, giving me a clear view. I crammed a hand to my mouth, but my scream bled through regardless.

The unconscious figure was Jad.

I woke with a cry.

My scream had cut through my dream like a knife.

No. Not a dream.

A vision. Something that was real.

Somehow, I'd managed to manipulate space and time and cross...

What?

Dimensions?

The reality was I didn't know what had occurred, but I knew what I'd witnessed had been real.

Had I been... a ghost? Invisible to the eye but taking everything in?

I tasted grime on my lips, the same grime that had been in the dungeon. Even my hair smelt of smoke.

I buried my face in my hands.

Jad, what are they doing to you?

Not only was he a prisoner but a lab rat in a twisted experiment—one his father was subjecting him to.

I had to get Jad out of there.

But where is he? What is that place?

And what experiment is Hadar about to put him through?

The woman's sadistic smile surfaced from my memory. *"If the experiments work on each subject, you'll have more warriors to add to your army. Warriors that cannot be injured or killed."*

Beads of sweat dampened my brow. Vulcan and Hadar were creating an army too powerful to be overthrown. And who better to lead an army like that than a captain who'd inspired men and women of the Haxsan Guard, and who'd earned respect and loyalty among those forces? Turn those qualities around, and Jad would be a supreme killing machine, unconquerable and merciless.

I saw all the evil in Vulcan's plan.

Helplessness rushed at me. Jad could be a world away. How was I ever going to find him when I didn't even know where I was?

It could take days to get out of the rainforest, maybe weeks… and providence help me if I had to survive on fish that entire time.

How can I ever—

A scream burst through the trees.

My jaw clenched as panic set in. It had sounded too close to the temple for comfort. The cry had been slow and harrowing, like a wolf and a large predator cat combined.

What creature could possibly make a noise like that?

Every part of me shook. Hot sweats and cold shivers attacked my body at the same time. I kicked dirt onto what was left of my fire and was pitched into darkness. A soft, scuffling noise broke outside the temple. My fingers curled around Neathror. Was it hooves, pawing at the ground, slow and temperate so as not be to be heard?

I stilled. What if this thing was sensitive enough to pick up a body's heat signature?

It could be staring at me right now.

I waited.

And waited.

It was silent again, but I didn't dare breathe.

I crawled to the entry and snuck a peek outside.

A beam of light swerved erratically outside the temple. It shifted over the trees, searching the forest… hunting something.

CHAPTER 3

A sigh of relief was out of the question. I huddled in a corner, my underarms damp.

What was that thing?

I didn't dare peek outside the temple again. Frantic thoughts flashed through my mind. Jad was in more danger than I ever could have imagined. And something was hunting me.

I was certain that was what the creature outside the temple had been doing.

Should I move on? Find another place to sleep?

I weighed the options. Whoever or whatever had searched the ruins hadn't found any evidence that I'd been here. They weren't likely to come back. I was better off remaining at the temple, at least until the sun rose, when it would be safe to travel through the forest.

I strained my ears.

Is that…?

The wind had distorted the sound, but I knew what it was in a heartbeat.

A drum?

And not just one drum. Many drums.

The volume increased, sending a tremor through my entire body. Was it a martial composition? Something used to synchronise the march of soldiers? Or the eerie sacrificial music of a cult?

The more I listened, the more my mind teetered toward the latter.

I snuck a tentative glance outside the temple. There was a flash of movement between the trees, bright and burning. Flamelight.

My eyes adjusted to the dark, unsure what to make of the scene in the foliage. A line of casters, guided by torches, moved through the trees. The way they strode reminded me of a funeral procession. There was no coffin. Instead there were cages filled with… people. Unconscious people. The captives were transported along what must have been a temporary conveyor.

A sleeping hex. That was the only way so many prisoners could be locked inside without complaint, crammed inside like bodies in a mass grave.

I scrambled onto my feet, caught in a moment of curiosity and… alarm.

Where are they taking the prisoners?

Before common sense could catch up with me, I darted into the forest. I hid behind an outcropping of rock, waiting until the procession was a safe distance away to follow. Flames scattered intermittent light through the trees, the shadows providing me enough cover to track the convoy without being seen.

The procession came out to the beach. I ducked behind a fallen tree and glanced through its elaborate web of low-hanging roots. Moonlight rippled from the eerily still night, providing me a clearer view of the spectacle. Tribespeople garbed in white linens, bones, and seashells danced around the cages. Humming and chanting, their eyes had rolled so far back into their heads that only a white orb remained in their sockets.

My stomach soured.

Are these people… possessed?

A woman decked in a flamboyant red dress with silver and gold amulets sashayed across the sand. She turned and faced her entourage. Her creamy brown skin was radiant in the torchlight. The pearls in her black hair glittered, a testament to her affluence. She was exotically beautiful… and cruel. Her eyes reflected the flames as though the pupils themselves were on fire—a tribal chief with nothing to lose and everything to gain. Her presence brought an electricity in the air, an excitement that was both powerful and disturbing.

The woman raised her hands, a gesture that sent the tribe into a frenzy. They swarmed the cages, snarling and gyrating, their movements neither human nor caster but something monstrous. The prisoners instantly awoke, released from whatever spell had kept them lifeless. They cried and fought against the metal bars. Tears and confusion glistened in their panicked eyes as the tribespeople, who now resembled a pride of hungry lions, snatched the prisoners out of the cages and dragged them across the hot sand. I watched with breathless horror. Each prisoner was carried to a stake. Their ankles were tied first, followed by their arms, their wrists raised above their heads and crossed. Two tribespeople brought forward a cauldron of fire. Metal sticks poked out.

Branding irons.

I covered my mouth.

No! They couldn't.

Horrible, bestial screams tore across the beach as the captives' foreheads were marked with the red-hot instruments. The scent of sizzling flesh wafted in the air. A coppery taste filled my mouth. The tribespeople spun and raved in frivolity, chanting in time to the drums that boomed thunderously across the sands.

This is some kind of twisted sacrifice.

The woman in charge of the macabre ceremony took her place among the tribe and addressed the throng in a ceremonious voice. "Behind me. Quickly. The ritual will now commence."

Her dancing clan scrambled into formation. They linked their arms, forming a barrier between the beach and the rainforest. The whites of their eyes stared out toward the sea, which was strangely calm in comparison to this nightmarish event. But it didn't last. The moon, in its silver-white glory, illuminated the placid waves and seemed to awaken something in the vast darkness of the water. The sea was... bubbling. Geysers shot into the sky. Steam billowed from the water. I blinked, struggling to come to terms with what I knew shouldn't be possible. Thousands of fish floated to the surface. The creatures had been boiled alive in the rapidly bubbling waves.

The tribal chief stepped forward, her dress flapping against her slender legs. "Four Revenants, I summon thee. We gift to you fifty undercasts, sacrificed blood and flesh in return for Scarmouth's prosperity. These men, women, and children are an illness that needs to be purged. Take them, and you will have Scarmouth's eternal gratitude."

I didn't want to watch, but my eyes were fastened to the beach, unable to look away. Desperation sank into my gut. There was no possible way I could stop this. Not without being caught. I squeezed my eyes shut for a moment, surprised by the guilty tears that trickled down my cheeks.

The deepest, cavernous rumble ruptured the night. It sent birds squawking from the trees. Panic sweat broke out on my forehead. The ground trembled, the sand beneath my feet moving like it was shaken from a salt grinder. I looked out to the sea, my brain taking a moment to comprehend what it saw. The ocean defied gravity. It roared to life, a towering wave rushing toward the beach in devilish swiftness.

No one ran. The tribespeople continued to chant, their spell increasing the strength and height of the massive wave. The captives screamed and struggled against their bonds, but it was too late. The wall of water smashed onto the beach, the surf spiralling across the sand.

In the roiling waves, four figures appeared on horseback, clad in dark riding cloaks, faces concealed by hoods. Each held a weapon in their hands—a scythe, a sword, an axe, a mace.

The Four Revenants.

The waves swept over the prisoners, drowning their cries in an instant. The torrent approached the tribespeople next. It was going to wipe out the entire rainforest. I leapt onto my feet to run, an unexpected weight in my legs.

The wave. It's going to take us all.

But before the rainforest could be steamrolled by the surge, the water came to a halt, as though it struck an invisible wall. As quickly as it had come, the sea drew back. A minute later, it had returned to tranquil waves. My gut gave an unpleasant twist. The Four Revenants were gone. The captives were gone. There was nothing left but wet, empty sand.

The tribal chief turned around to face her kin. She bared her teeth in a wolfish smile—a smile Vulcan would be proud of. "The Four Revenants have accepted our sacrifice, but our duty to the United League of Dissent is not complete. There are still undercasts among us in Scarmouth. Find them. Round them up. Together, we will purge the human filth from our caster blood."

A ceremonious cheer burst through the tribespeople.

Dizzy, I turned from the macabre scene and broke into a run. What I had witnessed had spooked me. The rainforest, which had seemed wild and beautiful today, was now a sprawling, stretching nightmare of shadows. Hanging vines tugged on my arms. Densely compacted roots appeared to unleash themselves from the mossy ground to trip me. Every dark corner, every dark space between the trees now looked like the gaping jaws of a monster.

Something heavy sprang from the side and tackled me to the ground. A scream burst from my throat but was crushed by a hood placed roughly over my head. It was a scratchy fabric with a lingering, rotting odour. The smell weakened me, my arms and legs immobile. I couldn't see. I couldn't breathe. The only thing I detected was the person's—or thing's—weight pressing down on me. Their excited exhales breathed through the fabric to tickle my ear.

It was the last thing I remembered before my world plunged into darkness.

CHAPTER 4

I woke with a panicked flinch. An itchy sensation crawled over my skin, every nerve ablaze. The memory of what had occurred slammed back into my conscious. I tore off the hood and struggled out of the blanket that had been wrapped around me. Hot sun burned my face. There was moisture above my upper lip and a salty, metallic taste in my mouth.

I shifted into sitting.

Where the hell am I?

The fog that clouded my head parted. I was in a cart filled with potato sacks. Around me, wooden structures with side-gabled roofs tilted, so old and heavy it was as though the buildings were like ancient trees growing out of the ground. Their peeling paint and rotting wood facades, their stooping porches and narrow crooked windows were sunbeaten and battered. The entire street was... odd, derelict, dusty. People congregated at what was undoubtedly the town square. They were quiet and grave, their heads bowed.

Is a frigging funeral happening?

At least, that was how it appeared.

A woman saw me. Her troubled eyes connected with mine

before she quickly averted her gaze. There was something timid in that look, as though she hadn't been sure to shout me out or not.

A nervous jig danced in my stomach.

This is bad. This is very, very bad.

I climbed out of the cart. Thank providence I still had Neathror with me. I tucked my athame-sabre into my sleeve, prepared to use it if I had to. These people were… unconventional, and that was putting it nicely.

I snuck away with cautious steps, but where was there to go? Creepytown wasn't exactly a place where you could lodge in a hotel. Thin, dusty clouds bordered the end of the street. Beyond the town were cornfields, harvested wheat, and rainforest.

Shit. Shit. Shit.

This place really was in the middle of nowhere.

I spotted an alley, a narrow path where the air was cooler and the buildings provided cover, but froze, my feet embedded to the ground. An awful fluttery sensation rippled on the tips of my fingers. On the wall was a wanted poster—with my face.

ZAYA WAYWARD, KNOWN TERRORIST.

THE INSIGNIA for the United League of Dissent was marked in the corner. The details beneath my picture claimed there was a reward in an exchange for my capture.

Oh shit. Double… triple shit.

This had to be the work of Vulcan.

But how did he get my picture?

Air left my lungs. My throat tightened.

The traitor at Tarahik. They'd have access to my records.

I tore the poster down and marched ahead into the alley. I hadn't made it halfway when a hand latched on to my shoulder, twisting me around like I was a spinning top. A scream burst from my throat, my voice bouncing off the walls into the vast sky. Before I could throw a punch into my would-be-captor's face, their hand slammed over my mouth, holding in my cry.

"Are you mad?" The man was hooded, but his voice was familiar.

I instinctively reached for my athame-sabre, but my assailant was too quick. He pulled me against him, his chest to my back, my wrist locked in his.

"Keep that hidden, and keep your head down." His tone wasn't threatening. It was anxiety tinged with bitterness. He was afraid. I sensed it in the way his breath tickled my ear.

Tickled... my... ear.

I recognised that frantic breathing now—the same breathing from the rainforest.

Him.

The man who'd captured me last night.

I drove my elbow backward into his gut, hard enough to make him tip over and retch. He was probably a master criminal, someone who was familiar with the wanted poster and was going to hand me over for the reward.

Not today, arsehole.

But he was stronger than I'd anticipated. He leapt at me. The impact knocked me off balance, giving him the opportunity to grab my neck and pin my head against the brick wall, his gloved hand over my nose so that I was forced to breathe through my mouth. Too late I realised what he planned. He brought a vial to my lips. The liquid was acidic and burned its way down the back of my throat. I blinked, trying to force the dizziness away, but it crept in regardless. My arms went limp. My knees lolled side to side.

I struggled to speak. Even my voice sounded muted, choked. "What's... happen... ing... to... me?"

My sweaty fingers lost their grip on Neathror, but before it could fall to the ground, my captor caught the athame-sabre and pocketed the blade in his cloak.

He drew a rocky breath. "I gave you an antispasmodic spell. It's used to relax the muscles. If you double the dosage, it paralyses the victim. Don't worry. It'll leave your system in an hour, maybe two, if I'm lucky."

If he was lucky?

He slung me over his shoulder like a rolled-up carpet. My voice was entirely gone. I couldn't scream. I couldn't move. No one was going to save me. I imagined in a place like this, kidnapping and slavery were commonplace.

My captor carried me out of the alley and across the dry-mud-caked street toward a dilapidated farmhouse. It had a broken chimney and a sloping roof, the small windows sticking out like inquisitive eyes. We entered the house through a back door. The rooms were mostly empty except for a few pieces of tattered furniture scattered about. I tried to crane my neck to get a clearer view, but it was as though my head had been filled with rocks, heavy and leaden.

My captor's boot came down on a small china doll that had been discarded on the floor. Its delicate face crumbled into fragments, its last remaining eye seeming to watch me as we meandered down the hall.

A doll?

The more I fought to keep my eyes focused, the more I realised this wasn't an abandoned house that my captor was going to hide my mangled body in. It was a remnant of a house. A ghost of a place that had once been a loving home. Children's toys were strewn across the bedrooms, mouldy and yellowed by the sun. The sheets on the beds had been pulled back, still waiting to be made. The dining table had been set for a meal that would never come.

A chill swept across me.

What is this place?

My captor carried me into a room that appeared to have once

been a library. Instead of tossing me onto the remains of a thread-bare couch, he approached a bookcase and tapped a spine. There was a faint click, followed by a grating rumble. The floor beneath the bookcase popped free, opening to a hidden world. He trod down the stairs, almost quiet, seeming not to disturb something that waited below. It frightened me that his hands gripped tighter onto my waist, as though he was afraid too.

Where is he taking me? What is he going to do?

Because he definitely wasn't handing me over to the United League of Dissent.

A light blazed on.

A small, inquisitive voice piped up from a shadowed corner. "Daddy?"

The unmistakable pitter-patter of a child approached us.

"Quiet." My captor's voice had issued a command but was not unkind.

He dropped me onto a couch, something that was in far better shape than the furniture upstairs but was still old. I bit down on my lip—the only thing I could manage—waiting for whatever horrors were about to befall me.

A tiny elfin face appeared, her eyes wide and curious. "What's wrong with her?"

"Nothing." The man had his arms folded. The cloak still obscured his face. "Go and get a blanket. The spell will make her cold."

The small girl ran off into the dark. When she returned, she wrapped a thick, woollen blanket around me. "You'll want to keep warm, but don't worry. Once the spell wears off, you'll be all right. It gets really hot down here."

I tipped my head. Or tried to. The girl must have been about nine or ten. She had fiery red hair and a smattering of freckles on her white face. Living in such a hot climate would be lethal on her delicate skin.

Is that why she's down here? She can't go out into the light?

She smiled, tender and fairylike, but it didn't calm my nerves.

"My name is Livel. Over there is my brother, Sarith."

Sarith was seated at a table, colouring in what looked to be a children's book. He stared, unsure what to do, and went back to his colouring. He had the same wavy red hair, pale skin, and slight features. Twins.

The man cleared his throat. "Once the antispasmodic spell has worn off, give her soup and some bread. I'll return soon."

He darted back up the stairs. A second later, the trapdoor grumbled to a close. If it weren't for the oil lanterns, we'd be in total darkness.

My neck was still in no way working normally, so I examined what I could see, my eyes roaming back and forth. From what I could tell, the basement had been converted into a small kitchenette and living area.

Why is there a secret compartment in this house?

One with no entrances or exits except for the hidden trapdoor?

By the far wall were two single beds, one covered in dolls and the other crayons.

My voice shook in my throat. "Do… you… live… here?"

Livel watched me with childish fascination. "Yes. Daddy is afraid of the ULD. He said if they know about my brother and me, they'll take us away to the beach. The beach was always a nice place to go. I don't know why Daddy's so scared of it."

Even though my head was warped and my body felt supple as water, an overwhelming urge to protect these kids took charge. Livel didn't know what was happening on the beach, or the town for that matter. I wasn't sure what was really going on, apart from some twisted act of racial cleansing—and I sure as hell wasn't about to let her in on that.

Livel took my hand and laced her fingers between mine. "Don't worry. Daddy is going to make sure no one working with the ULD saw you. He's been very worried. He was expecting to find you two days ago."

"Two… days… ago?"

Expecting to find me?

Livel laughed. "Your voice sounds funny." Her smile dropped when she saw how serious I was. "Yes. Uncle was able to sneak a message in. He told us you were coming and that you had to be hidden. Daddy searched the rainforest all of yesterday trying to find you."

Something that wasn't quite hope and not quite fear—rather a mixture of the two—churned in my gut. "Who… is… your… uncle?"

Livel's face was enveloped in a large smile. "Uncle Darius."

CHAPTER 5

"Your uncle... is Darius... Kerr? The... senator?"

I closed my eyes tight, then opened them again. The brush of good news made me dizzy with relief.

Livel smiled. "The very one. We don't see him often anymore. He's very busy. And we're stuck down here, so that doesn't help."

Sarith stood from his chair and glared from the table. "Livel, shut up." He was a stiff imitation of his sister, his shoulders hunched, his eyes watching me with wary interest. "Just because Daddy brought her here doesn't mean we can trust her. You can't trust anyone in this town." His voice grew louder with each sentence, his fist tight on the crayon. It snapped in his hot little hand. "Come back and colour with me."

Livel stroked her fingers through her red curls and stuck her tongue out at him. "You shut up. I can talk to whoever I want."

Sarith kicked his chair. "No. Come back here."

Oh boy. I wasn't qualified to deal with adults at the best of times, let alone children.

Livel smirked at Sarith, then smiled angelically at me. Her voice was a poor attempt at a whisper. "Don't mind my brother. He's an idiot."

"I am not. You're the idiot."

Livel rolled her eyes. "Sarith doesn't trust anyone since—"

"Stop it." Sarith's voice cracked, deep, raw, and too painful for a child of his age.

"Since... what?" I prompted.

Thoughts ran wildly in my head.

Was this house... these people... the destination all along? Not the rainforest? Not the beach?

But what is this place? What is Scarmouth?

I tilted my head against the armrest. I didn't have full mobility, but the antispasmodic spell was wearing off faster than my captor predicted. I cut my gaze to the trapdoor.

If the spell wears off, can I reach it?

Livel leaned forward, her lips close to my ear. "Sarith doesn't trust anyone since our mother cursed this place."

I swallowed, the only thing I could manage.

Cursed this place?

While I lay there stunned, the trapdoor opened with a low, deliberate creak, and the twins' father appeared. This time the cloak was absent. I guess I expected him to resemble Darius, but his brown hair, unshaven jaw, and sunburnt face couldn't have been more opposite. Stress lines worked their way across his brow. His hands clenched and then spread, over and over. He must have had too much adrenaline and didn't know what to do with it.

I recognised the look in his eyes. Agitation. Guilt. Despair. I'd seen the same thing in the soldiers at Tarahik. Battle. Killing. Survival. It psyched up the body and wired every muscle. It was a hard sensation to calm, and a harder one to let go.

I watched this man now and realised he'd killed. Recently.

He moved into the kitchen and took out a drink from the fridge. He tore the bottlecap off with an aggressive twist. The sound reminded me of a neck snapping. He took a long swig. "Livel, don't smother our guest. Go back to your colouring."

Livel slipped away to join her brother. The children were focused on their artwork.

Their father walked toward the couch and perched on the opposite armrest. He looked down at me, his gaze wary but attentive. "My children can't overhear us now. There's a spell on that colouring book. When they draw together, it blocks the world out. A nice little hex my wife did so she could have some quiet time to herself, may she rest in peace."

He lifted his bottle and drank greedily.

Great. He's self-medicating.

He looked at me for a long time. "Why are you here, Zaya?"

Was he frigging serious?

I'm here because you drugged me and brought me here.

He must have seen the cynicism in my eyes, because he rephrased his sentence. "I mean, what is it that my brother-in-law has sent you here to do?"

"I have... no idea." My voice didn't sound anything like my own. "Why... am I here? Who... are you?"

He smiled, but it didn't reach the corners. "Clorenzo is my name. Clorenzo Sujik. I'd shake your hand, but obviously in your predicament, that's a bit of a problem." He stole another greedy sip. "Welcome to my home. Or what's left of it." Another swig. "You're here because my brother-in-law thought you could help Scarmouth. I mean, has he seen this place?" A giddy laugh. "He sent you to your death, you know. The ULD have Scarmouth surrounded. Lycanthors patrol the rainforest. The ULD come every night, knocking on people's houses, running tests on blood. If you don't meet their criteria, you're taken down to the beach."

Clorenzo's haunted eyes wandered to his children. His shoulders gave in to what appeared to be an involuntary shudder.

Livel and Sarith mixed crayons and colours, creating a childish mess on the table, unaware of our conversation. It seemed incredible that people could think killing innocence like that would amount to something besides murder. It was no wonder their father hid them.

Clorenzo's words seemed to hang in the air. *"The ULD comes every night, knocking on people's houses, running tests on blood."*

The antispasmodic spell was doing all kinds of strange things to me, because my body became tense all over and, simultaneously, as fragile as glass.

Clorenzo rubbed a hand across his tired face. His fingernails were filthy, dirt embedded in the creases of his knuckles. "The ULD are rounding up the people they deem to be unfit. Casters who possess traces of human DNA. They've got our mayor in on it. She and her brainwashed fanatics go to the beach every night and celebrate the sacrifice. That woman is a nutcase."

My frown deepened. "Sacrifice… for what? I saw the… Four Revenants come… out of the sea. What's… really going on?"

Why has Darius sent me here?

I remembered what Commander Macaslan had warned right before she tossed me into the portal that had teleported me to the beach. *"Something has changed out there. Macha has seen visions of the Four Revenants, otherwise known as the Four Horsemen of the Apocalypse. They are meant to signal a change, an unbalance in magic… an omen that terrible things are about to happen. I believe it means Morgomoth will return."*

Sweat flushed my body. I stared at the ceiling, aggravated at how useless I was lying on the couch. If Darius had sent me here, it was because I was meant to be out there doing something, surely?

Clorenzo scratched his cheek. His eyes took on a hardened edge. "This happened because of my late wife."

I sucked in a breath. Something that felt like a spring stuck in my back. Sensation was returning, along with my snarky attitude. "Explain. Now."

Clorenzo flipped his palm up. "Steady on. Darius warned me about you and your… temper. Before you get all judgemental, you need to hear me out. You need to understand why my wife did it. I think it's why Darius sent you here. To end what she foolishly began."

"And what did she begin?" I had a very bad feeling I knew where this was going.

"Sarith doesn't trust anyone since my mother cursed this place."

That's what Livel had said. But what did it mean?

Clorenzo looked away for a minute. He shut his eyes, as though the strain was too much for him to bear. "My wife helped raise the Four Revenants."

CHAPTER 6

"S he did… what?"

Anger overrode my alarm, but all I could manage was some outraged wriggling.

Raised the Four Revenants?

The words struck home. "But that means… your wife sided… with the ULD?"

I stole a glance at Livel and Sarith. Did they know their mother had joined a sadistic insurgence who were equally as fascist and authoritarian as the Council? The same people they were now hiding from. Sarith didn't trust anyone, but I didn't think it was because he knew the truth. He was simply frightened, the way any child would be who was forced to live in a basement.

Clorenzo squeezed the bridge of his nose. "It's not like that. Violetta made a mistake. She was troubled. She thought—"

I snapped at him before he could finish. "And that's the… problem. Your wife… wasn't thinking. We're… all troubled."

Raised the Four Revenants?

How could anyone do something so foolish?

Clorenzo turned on me with pent-up rage. His eyes shone with tears. "Are you going to let me tell the story or not?"

I blinked, astonished to find I was shaking—with fury. The antispasmodic spell had worn off, and judging by the surprise that flashed across Clorenzo's face, it had happened faster than he'd hoped.

I sat up. That sensation I got—the one that made me afraid and confused, which in turn made me angry and impulsive—was back. I pressed my lips together to keep it at bay. Commander Macaslan had sent me here thinking she was delivering me to safety. She'd trusted Darius. *I'd* trusted Darius. And he'd dropped me smack bang into danger. My only intent was to find Jad. How was I meant to stop the Four Revenants? I didn't fully understand what the four disciples of the apocalypse even were.

Clorenzo squeezed his eyes shut and shook his head. No matter how hard he set his jaw, a wistful note leaked through his voice. "It was my fault. Our youngest child drowned. Oli was caught in a rip. I was meant to be watching him. I swam... I tried my hardest, but I... lost him. We never found his body."

He rubbed his fingers under his eyes. A choked, forlorn sound escaped his throat.

My gaze travelled to Livel and Sarith. It must have been hard for them losing a sibling. "I'm sorry."

What else was there that I could say? It was never easy to comfort someone who was in pain. The loss of a loved one was agony. I recalled the heartache that had gripped me when Jad had fallen into the yawning hole at Galvac Tower, toppling farther away until the darkness consumed him. The helplessness was the worst part—the inability to do anything, no matter how hard you tried. I knew exactly what Clorenzo must have gone through watching his youngest child sink away into the sea.

Clorenzo's face tightened with pain. He didn't look like he had the strength to hold his shoulders straight. "Violetta was obsessed with trying to get Oli back. She knew from Darius that necromancy existed. She didn't care how far she had to go, didn't care what kind of dark magic would be required. She was determined to bring Oli back to life. Darius wouldn't hear of it. He told Violetta that she needed to give in to the grief. Let it win. Only then would she find it in her ability to move on." His gaze held mine. "As you could imagine, that didn't go down well with Violetta." He set his empty bottle on the floor. "I actually think Vi went mad. She'd made friends with the mayor of Scarmouth, a toxic, scarlet-wearing monster of a woman. If the devil existed, she'd be the first one he'd invite over for dinner."

I recalled the woman on the beach in the vibrant red dress— the colour of blood—her creamy brown skin catching the moonlight like a river at night. She'd been beautiful, yes, but dangerous and wild. She'd reminded me of a large secretive lion gracefully stalking her targets. The mayor sacrificed innocent casters—her own townspeople—to the Four Revenants. I questioned how "friendly" this bond between the mayor and Violetta really was.

Clorenzo shifted on the armrest. His sunken eyes made him look like he'd been deprived years of sleep. "Mayor Saana Belov, a favourite among her people, until she let the ULD occupy our town and offer us as sacrificial lambs."

The facts merged together in bitter pieces. "Why did the ULD occupy this town specifically?"

Clorenzo looked sideways at me. "Why do you think? This town was the last known sighting of the Four Revenants. Centuries ago, it's said five caster women, all with the last name Kerr—my wife's maiden name—bound the Four Revenants to a watery grave in the sea off the coast of Scarmouth. It was nothing more than a story to be whispered to town visitors at night, a thrill for people passing by. At least that's what I thought. Turns out that's why the United League of Dissent came here. They got Mayor Belov on their side, not that it would have been difficult. She always was an evil vixen."

An unpleasant shiver latched on to my spine. "Blood magic, right? The Kerr family bound the Four Revenants, meaning only blood magic could unbind them."

Even in the lantern-lit basement, where the shadows closed in like approaching spirits, I saw a flicker of amusement in Clorenzo's eyes. "You're smarter than you look. There's curiosity all over your face. I see why Darius likes you. But you assume incorrectly. Well, partly incorrect."

I wanted to point out that you couldn't be partly wrong. You were either right or you weren't, but Clorenzo's dark feelings had boiled over the pot again, so to speak, his anger more vivid with each mounting second. "The ULD needed my wife's blood to find the exact location of the Four Revenants. Mayor Belov told Violetta that in exchange for her blood, the leader of the ULD would raise her son from the dead. Oli would be returned to her. Vi jumped at the chance. I told her it was madness, that she needed to let Oli go. She needed to accept that he was gone." A muscle pulsed in his neck. "One evening, when I was called up to do the nightshift in the wheat fields, Vi went down to the beach with Belov. The ocean was calm that evening. Vi cut her wrists and let her blood flow into the waves. The locator spell worked. Her blood floated out to the sea—a red glowing beacon on the surface above where the revenants were confined."

A moment ticked by before my mind wrapped around his words. "She was tricked?"

"The leader of the ULD never raised Oli from the dead. Violetta died from the blood loss. I never found her body. I believe Saana Belov just left her to be taken by the tide."

Emotion scraped at the back of my throat. "Vulcan Stormouth doesn't possess necromancy. He's a vindictive, manipulative monster. Your wife was fooled. I'm so sorry."

Vulcan was the current leader of the ULD—at least while Morgomoth was indisposed in a sleeping curse. Did that mean Vulcan was near Scarmouth?

Is Jad close?

Clorenzo gave me an incredulous look. "Vulcan Stormouth?"

"Yes. He's the leader of the ULD." I searched his face for familiarity. "The person who made a deal with Saana Belov, right?"

I was right... wasn't I?

To my astonishment, Clorenzo blinked. His eyes settled on mine with confusion. "Vulcan Stormouth isn't the leader of the ULD. He's its lieutenant. You know very well who the leader is."

I stared, lost for words.

But Morgomoth is... asleep. He's bound between the world of the living and the dead.

My memory had been sketchy at best over the last few days, but now icy premonition struck through the haze.

Larthalgule.

I recalled the events that had occurred on the night leading up to Morgomoth's near-resurrection. Nausea churned in my gut as hot bile rose in my throat. The larthalgule blade had consumed the blood of a trickster, illusionist, telepath, and clairvoyant. When it had fallen into the tank that contained Morgomoth's body, had the magic transferred into him? Was the ritual to bring Morgomoth back half complete?

Clorenzo rubbed his thumb and fingers down his jaw. "Zaya, I suspect the ULD have Morgomoth. He's still asleep, but his mind is awake, trapped inside his body. I work in the wheat fields, and I've been hearing whispers among the dissent rebels who patrol the grounds. Morgomoth is somehow linked to Saana Belov." He tapped his head, indicating the pair were psychically linked. "Everything Belov is doing, it's under *his* command. She's under Morgomoth's control."

"She's his puppet." The words tasted coppery in my mouth. Vulcan was psychically linked to Morgomoth, as Melvina had been before I killed her. There was no reason why Morgomoth's power couldn't extend to Saana, which meant—

No one can be trusted.

Clorenzo's mouth twitched, strain evident across his jaw. "My brother-in-law warned me what Morgomoth really is. Darius suspects Morgomoth is using Saana until he can break himself free of the sleeping curse. He'll raise the Four Revenants using necromancy. The revenants have awoken, but Morgomoth's not strong enough to unbind the creatures from the sea yet, not without his own physical form. But for now he's doing the next best thing."

"Next best thing?"

Clorenzo snorted, but not with amusement. "Morgomoth is feeding what he calls 'undercasts' to the Four Revenants. I don't know why. Not even Darius can explain it. It must have something to do with making them stronger and breaking them out of the sea. Once that happens, Morgomoth becomes their master. He'll have unlimited control over them."

A lather of sweat formed beneath my underarms. "Feeding undercasts? You mean those sacrifices taking place on the beach?"

"You've seen them?"

"They were hard to miss."

I sensed from the strain on his face that there was more Clorenzo needed to say, but he remained tight-lipped.

A horrible realisation settled in my mind. Clorenzo spoke of his wife's suicide like it had been some time ago. Sacrifices had been happening on the beach every night. People were hiding in their homes. My wanted poster had been yellowing from the sun and torn at the edges. My guess was it had been out there for months.

The incident at Galvac was three weeks ago.

Right?

But if Morgomoth had achieved all this in three weeks....

Panic clawed at me. "When did all of this start happening in Scarmouth?"

Clorenzo's shoulders sagged. The question didn't seem to surprise him. "Darius told me to prepare for this. He said you wouldn't be happy."

"How long?"

He stared, eyes full of pity. "You've been asleep in the portal for three months. Things have changed, Zaya."

CHAPTER 7

Three months!

I'd been knocked into a spell-induced coma and tele-ported around in a portal for three frigging months.

Which meant Jad had been a prisoner all that time. What had happened to him? Was he still the same person? Or had Vulcan torn his mind and body apart? Would he even recognise me if he saw me again?

Jad must think he's been abandoned.

Talina?

Lainie?

Marek?

Something hot and sticky rose in my throat. "I think I'm going to be sick."

I vomited onto the floor, my palms enveloped in cold sweat.

Clorenzo grunted in disgust. "Next time, aim for the bucket." He kicked a wooden container in my direction.

I wiped my mouth and collapsed back onto the couch. I was cold all over. Sweat now encased my entire body. Pearls dripped from my forehead.

"You're in shock." Clorenzo's voice might have been impassive, but there was real concern on his face.

Despair sidled through me. *"You're in shock."* I remembered when Jad had spoken those very words to me after I witnessed Tejor's death in Essida. There'd been a moment between us. At least, I thought there'd been.

I took the golden pendant from my pocket now. Jad's photo was still secure inside. I looked closer at his eyes, at the deep pools that seemed to flow endlessly into darkness. Eyes were meant to be a window into the soul.

So what does this mean for Jad's soul?

This photo was more than three months old. I was terribly afraid that Jad was broken beyond repair. There might not be any chance of saving him.

I caught Clorenzo staring. He raised his eyebrows. "Boyfriend?"

I put the photo away and shoved the pendant back into my pocket. "No."

"Ah. Unrequited love." He walked over to the kitchen, dabbed a hand towel in the sink, and returned to rest it on my forehead. "Well, whoever he is, forget him. The ULD have spread beyond Scarmouth. They're everywhere in this province. They test caster blood, and if they deem you have too much human DNA, you're branded an undercast and brought to Scarmouth to be sacrificed. There's a ritual on the beach every night—about fifty casters murdered each time. Exactly a hundred and forty-eight galactic storms have hit this area, and two hundred and twenty-one men, women, and children have given up hope and joined the ULD. Things are bad here, Zaya. So you need to rest and then find a way to keep the Four Revenants in the sea."

I swallowed against the sticky film that lined my mouth. "And how am I supposed to do that?"

I watched his eyes absorb my question. "You're a necromancer, aren't you? I wasn't sure at first, but why else would Darius send you here? Pity he didn't think of sending you before my wife made a deal with the devil."

"Listen, I'm not here to get mixed up in your family matters. I need to find someone." The words rolled off my tongue without any forethought.

What Clorenzo revealed had sparked mixed reactions in me. On the one hand, what was happening in Scarmouth was terrible. But on the other, I had people I needed to find. I had someone who needed saving.

I lowered my head, strained by guilt and exhaustion. I'd been playing Sleeping Beauty for the last three months, yet I was still tired and lacked energy. "I don't know what kind of spell Morgomoth used to raise the Four Revenants. I'd never be able to reverse the magic, not in a million years."

"We don't have a million years." Clorenzo knelt down on the wooden floor and tossed a shabby black rug aside. There was another trapdoor, small enough for a child to hide below.

How many secret hideouts are in this place?

Clorenzo opened the door to expose several dusty volumes. "The Kerr family grimoires. Forbidden magic according to the Council. That's why Darius had the books hidden here. It was the Kerr family's responsibility to make sure the Four Revenants were never found. There must be something in these books, some hint of the magic required to reverse whatever Morgomoth did. And you're going to find it by the next celestial event. We can't risk the Four Revenants being fully restored."

My skin prickled. "Celestial event?"

"Yes. Violetta's suicide took place on a full moon, which meant Morgomoth needed to harness the power of the moon to awaken the Four Revenants. I'm guessing the same must happen for the reverse effect."

A sloppy, unpleasant grin spread over Clorenzo's face. "Now, you're going to eat the soup I make you tonight, have a good night's sleep, and tomorrow you're going to start your research." He tapped one of the grimoires. "My children and I are getting out of Scarmouth. You're not leaving here until you break the spell."

I SLEPT ON AND OFF, but never for long. I was fatigued, shattered, drained, but still my troubled mind wouldn't shut off. I lay on the couch, listening to Livel's and Sarith's breathing as they slept like sedated babies. For all I knew, their father could really have sedated them. Clorenzo wasn't getting a Father of the Year award any time soon, that was for sure.

I strained my eyes to see in the dark. The basement was ridiculously cramped with kids' toys, stockpiles of food, and what looked to be emergency survival kits. Suitcases stuffed with clothes had been placed in a corner, ready to be grabbed in a quick getaway. I wondered where my own canvas haversack was. Neathror too. Clorenzo had likely locked them away in a secret hidey-hole. I'd have to make a covert effort to find them in the morning.

A flashlight and bottled water were on the stairs leading to the trapdoor. There was a compass, an extra set of batteries, and something that appeared to be a miniature radio transmitter with a microphone.

Despite the humid air, a shiver of apprehension coursed through me. Clorenzo had this well planned. He knew at any moment there was a chance he and his kids would have to make a run for it. That scared me more than anything else. I'd had a brief glimpse of Scarmouth on the surface, but lying down here in the hot, stuffy basement confirmed that things above were far worse than I'd perceived.

I closed my eyes and let the darkness crawl back in. The worst part was the stillness—the absolute nothing. I turned on my side, agitated by the heat on my clammy skin.

It was past midnight when an ice-cold feeling struck my gut, the sensation I got whenever I was in the presence of a—

I sat up abruptly. She was staring at me, right next to me. My stomach rioted. I shook so hard my teeth clacked. The wraith watched me with deeply unsettling eyes. Her skin was more blue than white, shrivelled and grooved like a dried-out prune. Wet tangles of dark hair spilled over her back, her soaked dress dripping on the floor where it disturbed the dust. She must have drowned, but then I saw the incisions in her wrists, the blood so old and crusted it appeared black.

I swallowed. "Violetta Sujik?" My voice sounded clogged in my throat.

Formerly Violetta Kerr. Darius's sister. The woman who'd wanted her youngest son resurrected. The woman who'd been tricked into helping raise the Four Revenants by slitting her wrists.

She lifted a wrinkled finger to her mouth, urging silence. Her eyes travelled to the ceiling.

Pound. Pound. Pound.

Impatient, thunderous raps struck the front door upstairs. Livel and Sarith woke. They squeezed themselves against their headboards, their tiny fingers digging into their arms, faces white with fright. They couldn't see anything in the dark. Thanks to Violetta's ghostly manifestation glowing like a will-o'-the-wisp, I could see perfectly. In fact, I wondered if she had been the reason I'd seen through the basement so clearly before.

Livel started to cry. Sarith mouthed something nasty to her, his hot little face scrunched in panic.

The hammering on the door continued. "Open up. Standard inventory. Open up."

I peeled my blanket back and ran to Livel. She cuddled up to me in the bed, her sobs loud in the silent basement.

"You need to be quiet," I whispered in her ear.

Sarith lost his mean face and scooted over, his hand searching through the dark as he felt his way between the beds. I grabbed his arm and tugged him next to his sister.

The last thing I needed was for them to burst into tears. "Don't cry. You'll give us away."

Up in the house, the front door swung open.

Clorenzo's sleepy voice broke the still air. "Evening, sir. What can I do for you?"

"How many residents are in the house?" Strict. Brusque. Straight to the point. The dissent rebel sounded like a man on a mission. I imagined he'd caught many fugitives hiding out in basements and attics. He probably had a tally going.

Was that a slight wavering I heard in Clorenzo's voice, or were my ears playing tricks? "It's just me, sir. I live alone."

"No wife? No kids?"

"Not anymore."

"Then you won't mind me taking a look around, will you?"

There was a scuffling upstairs. The ceiling groaned and complained. The floorboards creaked as the rebel stalked the homestead. His footsteps grew loud, then faint, and finally loud again as he did a loop around the premises.

He's searching everywhere.

One of Livel's tears fell on my hand. I tucked her hair behind her ear, hoping it would calm her. Sarith didn't move at all. I wondered if he was even breathing.

Low groans indicated furniture had been shifted upstairs. The rebel wasn't taking any chances. "What's that over there? Beyond that door?"

Clorenzo's voice was subdued but civil. "That's an old gully kitchen, sir. This is a very old house. I use the kitchen for storage now."

"Just the kitchen? This entire house looks like it's been used for storage. When was the last time you cleaned the place?"

No response.

"Take me to this old gully kitchen. I want to see it."

The floors above us rasped. I fancied I could hear even the nails pop.

I shut my eyes, trying to remember how I got into the basement.

Did Clorenzo carry me through a gully kitchen? Are we close to being caught?

I fought to remember. That damn antispasmodic spell had done more than paralyse me. It had made a smokescreen of my memory.

Come on. Think. Think.

I recalled a bookcase.

A library, then.

Clorenzo carried me through a library.

It was the first easy breath I'd taken all night.

"Right," the rebel spoke. "Outside, then. We need to run through a few routine tests and check your blood."

Clorenzo's panicked voice floated through the floorboards. "I've already had my test. I was negative."

"Then you should have nothing to fear the second time, should you?"

The conversation becomes muddled as it drifted farther away.

They're going outside.

I craned my neck, wondering if I could glimpse anything through the floorboards.

Something moved at the corner of my eye.

I jumped, my heart doing somersaults. Violetta sat beside me, her eyes focused on her children with heartless indifference. If she was sad for them, she didn't show it. Her cold, shrivelled fingers tapped my shoulder.

"Come with me," her voice echoed in my head.

I tugged Livel's tiny hands off me. "I'll be right back. I promise."

Innocent, childish tears streamed down Livel's cheeks to bunch in the corners of her lips. "Don't go. Please, don't leave."

"I want you both to close your eyes and think of your mother."
I shot Violetta a stern look, then focused my attention back on the
kids. "As long as you stay here and think of her, nothing bad will
happen to you. I promise."

"Zaya." The warning in Violetta's voice bordered on dangerous.
Her eyes were hollow with no trace of motherly intention. She was
dead, empty, devoid of emotion. It was, after all, the grief and
despair of losing a child that had made her a ghost in the first
place, and now that she was dead, she didn't even appear remotely
interested in her kids.

I guess there's irony even in the afterlife.

Reminiscing about their mother worked. Livel's and Sarith's
breathing slowed. No more tears ran down their apple-shaped
cheeks.

My words rolled automatically off my tongue. "Whatever you
do, don't open your eyes."

I tried to keep my face as blank as possible as I left the bed and
tiptoed across the basement, but inside, guilt plagued me. I didn't
want to leave Livel and Sarith any more than Violetta had wanted
to leave Oli, but I had to know what was going on outside. I had
to make sure Clorenzo was safe, because the worst thing for these
kids right now would be to become orphans.

Violetta directed me to the stairs. She turned to me with those
dark, sinister eyes, the skin around them black and soggy. She
tilted her head to the side. All I could think about was how similarly she resembled a corpse with a snapped neck, body hanging
loosely from a noose. I'd seen one before at Gosheniene. It terrified
me then, and it terrified me now.

My breathing sounded loud in my head. "Violetta?"

"It's beneath us."

"What is?"

"Keys come in all shapes and forms."

Before I could comprehend her elusive message, she opened
her mouth in a cavernous scream so piercing I expected it to

shatter my ears. A torrent of black water spewed from her throat. The smell was abhorrent, like seawater, fish, and rotting carcasses combined. Water poured from her body onto the floor. Violetta released a final wail of anguish and exploded into a puddle of ichor and blood. What was left of her sank through the floorboards.

I stood there for a moment, my head fluctuating between fight and flight.

And the point of that horrifying display was…?

A dark, oily stain remained on one of the boards. I bent down and saw what it was Violetta was trying to show me.

Geez. You couldn't have just told me this was here?

I knew ghosts liked to work in mysterious ways, but mysterious ways could be a real pain in the arse.

Or had something else occurred? Had Violetta been fighting something evil inside her to show me what hid beneath this small strip of wood?

The board had a tiny gap in the corner, perfect for a finger to curl under. I tore the floorboard up. Underneath was my haversack —and my athame-sabre. The blade had been cleaned. I didn't think this was Clorenzo's doing. I didn't believe he had cleaning products period. No, the blade had cleaned itself somehow. It had given itself new life and vivacity.

I lifted it from the dusty alcove. As soon as my fingers made contact, light burst from the runes, silvery and glittering. I felt stronger with it in my grasp. More determined. Less afraid.

I am getting out of this basement.

The adrenaline in my legs propelled me forward. I hurried across the basement and up the rickety stairs, so old and shabby the wood had rotted in places. At the landing, I tried the door. It was locked, of course. Clorenzo wasn't stupid.

Violetta had said keys came in all shapes and forms.

If Neathror is a key for destroying life, what if it's also a key for…?

I pressed the tip of the blade into the keyhole.

The door clicked open.

It worked!

I cast a tentative peep back at Livel and Sarith. They still had their eyes shut. Violetta was sitting at the end of the bed, her chin tilted upward in my direction, her eyes dark pools, the skin around them veined. A smirk grew deep around her mouth. She might look after her children. She might kill them. With wraiths you could never be certain.

I shot her a warning with my eyes. *"Don't you harm them, Violetta. If you do anything to them, I will become the worst wraith slayer you have ever met. I will send you somewhere far worse than this purgatory."*

Violetta didn't say anything, just turned her long neck and gazed over her children, still and silent.

I entered the house. Mother and children were safe for the moment. Now I had to find their father.

CHAPTER 8

Thanks to having been paralysed and partially concussed when Clorenzo carried me into the farmhouse, my layout was vague and imprecise. I inched from corner to corner, monitoring the halls and abandoned bedrooms. The windows were open. Damp, muggy air blew onto my skin. It had been humid and unbearably hot all night, but now there was a brisk change in the temperature, an abrupt calm before the—

Shit. There's a storm coming.

I tasted it in the air. The tiny hairs on my arms rose as the electrical shift in atmosphere crept over my skin.

Please don't be a galactic storm.

I'd have no choice but to go back down into the basement if it was. What would happen to Clorenzo?

No. I can't leave him to that fate.

From what I'd heard, it was obvious that dissent revel wanted Clorenzo to suffer. It wouldn't matter if the father of two tested positive or negative. Something terrible was planned for him tonight.

I snuck through the scattered furniture and into a living room that overlooked an outdoor pergola. The alfresco entertaining area would have offered a nice reprieve from the heat once, a place where family could sit together to drink lemonade and discuss the events of their day—if families in the provinces ever did that. I could imagine everyone playing cards and admiring the rainforest, marvelling at the scale of the wheat fields and how they seemed to travel farther than the eyes could see. What a pleasant dream... because that's all it was. The pergola was a ghost of a memory. Crumbling, splintered, and falling away from the house, it was like an old Greek ruin fighting to remain upright.

I hid behind a tattered old couch that smelt of mothballs as I stared out through the long windows that were vine-covered and dusty. I was right. A storm was brewing on the horizon. The clouds reminded me of black cotton candy as they stretched across the sky, illuminated by bursts of lightning.

But that wasn't what scared me the most.

Cries reached my ears in a hazy, delayed reaction. On the road ahead, dissent rebels closed in on a crowd of men, women, and children. They used batons to beat their prisoners into lines and forced them into some kind of retrofitted high-tech truck. The captives were crammed inside like caged hens in an egg farm. Most of them were still in their nightwear, their faces strained by fear. The rebels stripped them of their clothes and forced the captives into rough shifts that resembled potato sacks.

There wasn't enough room in the truck. The prisoners who could no longer be shoved inside were chained together, wrists and ankles bound so no one could flee. The end of the chain was tied to the vehicle. My stomach shrivelled into the size of a peanut.

The rebels are going to drag them behind the truck.

My hand instantly tightened on Neathror. But what could I do? I couldn't take on armed dissent rebels by myself.

Is Clorenzo inside that vehicle?

Livel and Sarith would never survive without him.

A voice, cool and imposing, swept through the muggy winds. At first it resonated from every direction so that I had trouble detecting the source, but then Mayor Saana Belov appeared wearing another vibrant dress decked with seashells and pearls. "Have you thought about our agreement?"

I blinked. Every fibre in me itched to do something.

Clorenzo was on his knees by her feet. His hands were tied behind his back, and his nose bled. He spat at the ground. "There is no agreement, you daft cow. You tested my blood a month ago. And the week before that. And all the weeks before that one. I'm not going to magically acquire human DNA. Now let me go so I can pretend to live a better existence than I do."

The mayor stepped into the light, her russet brown skin glowing against her black hair, her beaded dress dancing in the breeze like wind chimes. She resembled a goddess straight from the Aztec world, a creator of death, despair, and chaos. The more I looked at her, the more I realised there was something unnatural about her eyes. They didn't seem to be attached but rather sitting in the socket, unmoving.

Morgomoth.

Clorenzo was right. Somehow Morgomoth had linked his mind with the mayor's and controlled her.

The blade in my hand responded with a quiver. The runes blazed alight and threw a kaleidoscope of patterns across the pergola. It didn't burn me. Its magic protected my skin, but sweat ran in rivulets down my fingers regardless.

Did the athame-sabre... sense Morgomoth somehow?

Providence help me. They're going to see this light.

My panic climbed about a hundred notches in the space of a heartbeat.

But Saana and her band of torture-happy dissidents didn't react to the aurora display occurring at the pergola. The rebels continued tormenting the townsfolk with their weapons and threats, and Mayor Belov had her attention focused solely on Clorenzo.

They can't see this. Neathror's light is invisible to them.

My relief was short-lived.

Saana's laugher erupted into the night, a kind of whoop, groan, and giggle that made every part of me cringe. That sound would send even the most vicious hyena scampering away like a dog with its tail between its legs. "I'm talking about the proposal I offered you, Clorenzo. Let's not play dumb. Violetta's blood was riddled with human DNA. Which means your children have a very high chance of possessing the same inferior blood. Tell me where you have hidden them. We can test their blood. If their results are negative, they're free to live how you see fit. If it's positive, however, then we'll have to—"

"Kill them." Clorenzo's tone was deadpan and matter-of-fact. The only thing that indicated he was truly afraid was the rapid rise and fall of his chest.

Saana's smile expanded. Her pearly white teeth shone in the torchlight. "Not necessarily. The ULD are open to experimentation. They wish to know more about this toxic human DNA that is diseasing our caster blood. Perhaps your children can be of some benefit with that."

"No they can't. My children are dead. Why can't you believe that? They were tossed into the mass grave in the rainforest, like so many others who never survived the galactic storms."

"Speaking of which, there's a storm on its way, so we better hurry this up. Where are your children?"

"Dead."

Saana's eyes drifted skyward. "There are celestial shields all around this town and the rainforest, which means you haven't been able to sneak them out of Scarmouth. I wonder where they could be?" She raised a hand, lifting a finger with each deliberation. "Are the children hidden in the rainforest? A tunnel underground perhaps? Someone could be hiding them for you, but we've searched all the houses, so that's unlikely." She danced on her feet. "Oooh, you've glamoured them, haven't you?"

Clorenzo just stared at her. His lips remained tight.

Saana feigned disappointment. "No, of course. A ridiculous

assumption. You aren't clever enough for magic like that. No, if I had to guess, I'd say your children would be somewhere nearby. Somewhere you have access to them." Her eyes roamed back to the farmhouse.

I ducked. Neathror probably shielded me from sight, but I wasn't ready to put my entire trust into the blade yet. I snuck a tentative glance around the couch.

Clorenzo made a strangled noise. "Give it up, woman. My children are dead. What do you get out of torturing me like this?"

Saana lifted her long neck and flashed a thrilled look at the two dissent rebels who stood behind her. They must have been her security escorts. "I think Mr Sujik needs a reminder about what happens when I don't get what I want. Kindly teach him."

She leaned down and whispered into Clorenzo's ear—something that made the father of two tense, as though the bones in his body had become taut as wire. Gripping him by the hair, Saana tossed Clorenzo aside with more strength than I would have thought possible for a woman of her slight frame.

She turned to her rebels. "I'm going to the beach. I want to get this sacrifice over with before the storm hits. Do with him as you wish, just don't kill him. That will come later."

She sashayed away in the direction of the truck. The vehicle drove at a crawl toward the rainforest, the prisoners dragged behind barely capable of keeping up. Their naked feet disturbed dirt and dust. I imagined how painful the cuts on their legs must have stung as they trudged over the road, the chains from their shackles dragging with an unpleasant abrade. All it would take was one prisoner to fall and they'd all topple, lugged like dead carcasses behind the vehicle.

Angry tears threatened to spill. I knew their fate, but there was nothing I could do for them. Not now. Not ever. Not unless I managed to reverse the Four Revenants curse, which I started to believe was impossible.

At my side, Neathror's light dimmed. The blade had returned

to cold, dark metal. I'd have to put some research into it and find out what was going on. Actually, I'd have to find out what Neathror was, period, because it was definitely more than a "bringer of death."

Clorenzo's voice brought me back to reality. "Get off me, you filthy excuse for a caster."

One of Saana's security escorts was holding him down by the shoulders. The other had his fist raised, ready to punch a few of Clorenzo's teeth out.

I wasn't a match against an entire troupe of rebels, but against two? Game on.

I dove out of the pergola. My feet slammed onto the ground hard, my heartbeat so loud it made my eardrums throb. I reached the rebel that held Clorenzo and performed an effortless karate chop to the side of his neck. The blow hit the pressure point, and he fell into an unconscious heap on the ground.

Clorenzo took his chance. He tackled the other rebel into the dirt road and slammed his head back once, twice, three times until the caster finally lost consciousness.

Clorenzo spat on his body. "Pig."

I rolled my eyes. "I could think of a more offensive word."

I offered Clorenzo my hand to help him up from the road, but he slapped it away.

He rose on shaky legs. "How did you get out of the basement?"

"With this." I lifted Neathror.

Surprise flashed in his eyes, but then all the hard lines in his face scrunched up in aggravation.

"And I had help from Violetta. It turns out she's haunting your basement."

The veins in his neck throbbed. He grabbed my arm and wrenched me back to the house. His attitude didn't improve inside.

"You shouldn't have left my kids."

Seriously?

My temper flared. "A simple 'thank you' would suffice. I did just save your life."

"You saved me from a beating. Nothing I haven't handled before."

We reached the trapdoor.

I tugged my arm free. "I didn't do it for you. I did it because your children need you. And yes, I'll do what I can to reverse the spell. I'll try and keep the Four Revenants bound in the sea. But you're going to help me do it, and it will be as equals. I will not be your prisoner."

I didn't sound anywhere near as confident as I'd hoped. My voice had been shrill and cracked, but the message got through.

Clorenzo's face softened, but only for a moment. "What's the catch, hothead?"

"You seem like a capable man. You're going to get cosy with the mayor and her little ULD minions."

Clorenzo crossed his arms. "And why the hell would I do that?"

I took the gold locket out of my pocket and opened the clasp, then shoved the picture right in front of his nose. "Because you're going to help me find someone."

CHAPTER 9

It took Clorenzo a few days to come around to my proposal. It wasn't easy to convince him. Most days I sat in the basement with Livel and Sarith, colouring in picture books in our quaint little bubble, assuring them the horrors of that night would never occur again. Every time I said it though, a lump as hard and grating as a rock formed in my throat, because of course, I couldn't promise such a thing. I feared the hold the ULD had on Scarmouth. I feared for Livel's and Sarith's safety more than they feared for themselves, because I knew the truth. I'd seen the level of cruelty the dissent rebels possessed—the hunger they had to see others suffer and perish. If they found Sarith and Livel... well, I hoped it would be quick.

Maybe that's why I forgave Clorenzo's tetchy behaviour whenever he returned to the basement after a gruelling nine hours of forced labour. Every caster who'd tested negative to human DNA was given the privilege to live. I figured that would be a win in some people's eyes, but there was a drawback. Unless they swore allegiance to the ULD, these casters were obligated to fulfil seventy-four hours a week of forced labour, and for Clorenzo that meant harvesting wheat by hand and picking potatoes. Whenever he returned to the basement, his fingers bled and he'd lost another nail, his face sunburnt and blotchy. He'd complain of severe headaches that not even the strongest spells we had could overcome, but that didn't prevent him from writing in the strange leather-bound journal that he kept on him at all times. He'd sit by an oil lantern, probably straining his eyes as he wrote. Some nights he wouldn't even come down to see us. I knew he was upstairs. The whines and creaks of the floorboards gave him away. I wondered if he was secretly crying in a dark corner somewhere. It made me feel sorry for him, but only for a moment. Whatever Jad was suffering was a hundred times worse than any punishment Clorenzo could ever face.

Technically, I was a full-time babysitter while Clorenzo was away. When he did return to find me playing with his children instead of reading the grimoires, he'd assess me with his dark brown eyes, aggravation evident in the way his body became as rigid as a board. I was no fool. I *had* been searching through the Kerr family grimoires to find a counter curse to the Four Revenants, but I let Clorenzo think my attention on the task was non-existent. The deal was that he would find something about Jad first. Only then would I help him. So far, Clorenzo hadn't delivered, so I continued to be apathetic. I was all smoke and mirrors though. Inside, I was frantic that I hadn't discovered anything concrete about these apocalyptic wraiths.

Clorenzo and I were at an impasse, both of us refusing to give in, until I had the audacity to show Livel the picture of Jad. She was curious about him, wanted to know why he was in trouble. She thought he was very handsome and believed he was my boyfriend. And of course, being the sweet, kind-hearted, and loving child she was, I watched my scheme fall into place like a jigsaw piece. She begged her father to help me find Jad—and what father could refuse his daughter?

Late one evening, Clorenzo returned to the basement with, if not ease, then purpose in his step. The wood groaned under his weight as he walked to the sink and poured a glass of water. He wiped his face with the back of his sleeve and refused to look at me. I was tired, but the way Clorenzo behaved made me instantly wary. Livel and Sarith were asleep. I was sitting on the couch pretending to read a cheesy romance that probably belonged to Violetta, but inside the book I'd hidden a grimoire.

Clorenzo looked different tonight. Cleaner. Neater. His hair was pulled back, his shoulders straight. He wore new boots that were polished. Even the blisters and sores on his hands were healed, only a few bruises remaining to indicate there'd been any injury there at all.

Someone had healed him.

A flicker of unease grazed my spine. "Did you find anything?"

My voice sounded loud as it rolled between us, swallowed up by the basement walls. Livel had explained to me earlier in the day that a spell prevented sound from travelling beyond the basement. No one could hear us in here. That extra level of security didn't prevent the noise from outside sounding excessively ominous though. It was a neat trick—proof that Clorenzo was nifty with magic. It made me question exactly what he was capable of.

He meandered toward me, his gaze cantered on his children. The corners of his mouth twitched into a reluctant smile. There was a strange expression in his bottomless brown eyes—a kind of reluctance and relief at the same time. "I found out a few things."

I lifted my chin. "Care to elaborate?"

He drew up a chair and sat opposite me. "I joined the ULD."

"You did what?" I bit my lip to trap an expletive.

Discovering information about Jad meant Clorenzo would have to think of a creative way to infiltrate the ULD and Mayor Belov's cronies, but I didn't think he'd go to such extreme lengths.

His eyes pinned me in place. "If they think I'm one of them, then I avert their suspicion. I can be a spy and find out information. I might actually be able to help a few casters if I know who they're targeting."

My jaw dropped. "And do what? Get them out of Scarmouth? In case you've forgotten, this entire area has been fortified with a celestial shield. It's the reason why your children are asleep in the basement this very moment. No one can get out of Scarmouth."

"Keep your voice down." Clorenzo's eyes darted to his children and back again. His whispered voice was tense. "I'm not doing this entirely for you. I've been ordered."

He took out his leather-bound journal and flicked to a page. He handed it to me to read.

CLORENZO,

THE ULD FORCES have moved into the Esqua, Buliviesk, and Ravdarn provinces. It has been reported that they are overtaking towns and imprisoning casters. Expect more captives to arrive in Scarmouth in the coming days. The Council has deployed the current Haxsan Guard forces from the north in the Athnik region to assist, but I am certain they will not make it in time to be of any use. The damage has been done—the bad egg cracked and its contents left to fry, so to speak.

As to your request, I have done what I can to find Captain Arden's whereabouts. I am relieved to hear he is alive but fear that, in his current predicament, he is truly beyond our help. Only a select few in my office know this information about the captain. We will ascertain what information we can, but please do not give Zaya hope. If we do find him, there is little chance we can salvage him from a ULD labour camp.

Zaya is an intelligent girl and resourceful. Do not underestimate her. If she is unable to find a counter curse in the family grimoires, rest assured she will find a way on her own. In that I have confidence.

The appearance of the Neathror blade is concerning. This is out of my realm of experience. I can only assume the blade has linked itself to her in some way. I have arranged for a friend of mine who I believe

may be able to help to contact you in the usual way, tomorrow night at
8:21 during the quarter moon.

Clorenzo, thank you for joining the ULD. I will never doubt your
loyalty to this family or our cause. I know that it must have been diffi-
cult to look Mayor Belov in the eye and submit to her rule, but now
that you are in their ranks, you must find out what it is they want
with the Four Revenants. I am afraid these sickening rituals are just
the beginning.

Write back anything you have learned as soon as it is safe to do so.

Darius

A WHIRLWIND of emotions spun through me. I browsed through
the journal. There were entries spanning months, Clorenzo's on
one page and Darius's returned message on the next. They'd been
writing to each other, passing secrets and knowledge. This journal
must have been linked to a daybook or diary that Darius possessed.
It was how they'd been communicating all this time.

I read the message again, grasping at every detail.

"The Council has deployed the current Haxsan Guard forces from
the north in the Athnik region to assist, but I am certain they will not
make it in time to be of any use."

The last I'd heard, Marek, Talina, and Lainie had been sent
from Tarahik to the Athnik region to support the recovery and
reconstruction of that province. My friends had wanted to help the
people who had lost their homes to the mega tsunami—a tsunami
caused by Kravis's selfish and idiotic desire to destroy Galvac Tower
and its dam. A fat lot of good that had done. It hadn't destroyed
Morgomoth. His sleep-cursed body was missing. And now we
faced a bigger crisis: Mayor Belov and the Four Revenants.

Are my friends currently on their way to...

I looked at the journal again.

... Esqua, Buliviesk, and Ravdarn?

They had to be going to one of the provinces.

I squeezed my eyes shut for a second. Marek had no idea that his best friend was alive. He'd be devastated to know what had become of Jad.

My eyes scanned the next passage of the message.

"I am relieved to hear he is alive but fear that, in his current predicament, he is truly beyond our help."

It seemed incredible to think that a practical, quick-witted, and capable man like Jad was beyond help. But I had seen him in that vision... dream... whatever it had been. I'd witnessed how broken he'd become. Unthinkable experiments were being conducted on him. How did anyone recover from something like that? Was it possible Jad's mind was so warped by now that he wasn't the same person? Was that what Darius had meant by "he is truly beyond our help"?

Is Jad a lost cause?

A rebellious tear dripped down my cheek. I shook it off, but the damage was done. Anger worked through every vein in my body. I was light-headed. Disconnected. Ripped apart. I didn't understand what I was really going through.

Clorenzo took the journal out of my hands. "It's nearly time."

My eyes flew to him. "Time for what?"

"8:21 p.m."

He strode across the basement to the stairs where junk, broken toys, and other useless knick-knacks had been stored, dusty and covered in cobwebs. I wondered how long the house, everything inside it, and its occupants had been falling apart. Violetta had died three months ago, but my guess was the Sujiks had abandoned their home chores the moment they'd lost their youngest son.

Clorenzo swept aside a beige cloth to unveil a full-length mirror. It was nowhere near as classy or impressive as Commander

Macaslan's gold-framed mirror, but I immediately recognised what it was. "A portal."

Clorenzo tugged on his ear irritably. "Afraid not. Trust me, if this was a portal, none of us would be here right now. No, this is what's called a bridge-interface. It works similarly to a portal, but instead of transferring the person, it transfers the image and sound. The dissent rebels uncovered all bridge-interfaces when they ransacked houses. They burned them all on the edge of town. This is now the only one that exists—in this province, at least."

He carried the mirror across the room and set it beside the couch. The surface was smooth and bland. It didn't appear to have been used in a while.

I stretched my hand out to touch it, just to make sure it was real. "Why haven't you and Darius been communicating through this?"

Clorenzo sat down and propped himself up with a cushion. He might have looked tidier, but worry lines still creased his face. "Bridge-interfaces draw on a celestial event to work. That means one of the twelve moons have to be in the sky… quarter, half, full. There are times when I need to communicate with Darius at a moment's notice. The journal simply works better for that."

"Who are we meeting?"

I thought back to the journal. *"I have arranged for a friend of mine who I believe may be able to help."*

Besides Commander Macaslan and Colonel Harper, I didn't think Darius had any friends. My insides did a tiny twist in anticipation.

Clorenzo rubbed his hands over his face. The red in his eyes indicated he was in desperate need of sleep. "Someone you know."

Right on cue, the mirror's surface changed. The silver glass rippled, the undulation like water swelling in a fountain. An image appeared, distant at first, but then grew sharper and focused.

My heart hammered in happy surprise—a first time in a long time. "Macha."

My astonishment elicited a chuckle from her. She was exactly the way I'd remembered, robed in a dark cloak, her grey hair spiralling out from the sides in a frizzy mess. The deep lines around her mouth, the warts on her nose, and the crow's feet etched in the corner of her eyes made her haggard and witchlike, but honestly, after everything I'd been through, she was practically an angel.

Her large crow, Bartholomew, was perched on her shoulder. The bird's inquisitive eyes studied me with curious interest. Macha had no pupils or irises. Her eyes resembled large opaque marbles, colourless and milky white. There were casters out there who shared a unique bond with animals—seeing, hearing, and feeling through their linked creature. Macha was blind. That I was certain of. Bartholomew was the obeahwoman's eyes. She saw everything through her bird.

Macha's rumpled lips curled into a smile. "I'm glad to see you finally made it to your destination. Three months of you in that portal had us all in a head spin, but it couldn't be helped. The ULD raised the barrier around Scarmouth. It's a strong celestial shield, but lucky for us, the last galactic storm penetrated its field and the portal delivered you safely."

If that was delivering me safely, I'd hate to see what a dangerous landing would be.

There was so much I wanted to know that I grappled with what to ask first. "Your sister? What happened to her? And Colonel Harper?"

The last I'd seen, they'd been captured and taken away by Kravis's forces. The memory still left me reeling.

Macha's smile faded. "They are prisoners in Yukovslar. It's a stronghold notable for housing famous prisoners. My sister is well suited to it."

"But is she okay? What's going to happen to her?"

In my opinion, Macha was far too calm for her sister's current predicament.

"I daresay she will be executed. Colonel Harper too. According to the Council, they harboured and assisted a terrorist, something the ULD jumped on, in case you didn't notice all the wanted posters around the continent."

"I've only seen one."

All around Navask?

Macha shrugged. "I am not worried."

"But... she's your sister." My voice sounded flat in my ears.

The obeahwoman opened her mouth, closed it. "There is time to save her. And Harper. I mustn't forget him. Elspeth isn't a nobody. This scandal will make news for months. They'll want to draw it out as long as they can. It will be years before my sister goes to trial."

I flicked my startled gaze to Clorenzo, but he watched on, impassive.

Surely Macha couldn't be serious?

I returned my attention to the obeahwoman. "Then what are you concerned about?"

Macha squeezed her eyes shut for a moment. "I am worried about the ULD's rising power and their interest in the Four Revenants. I am distressed knowing Morgomoth has a psychic hold on the mayor. But what I fear the most is Neathror."

At my side, the athame-sabre heated, as though it sensed it was being discussed and disliked what it was hearing.

I blinked in confusion. "But Neathror has protected me. It came to me. It can do... amazing things. Unlock doors. Warn me when danger is near."

How could that be a bad thing?

Macha's face softened. "Zaya, Neathror is a necromancer's blade. Its magic links to a necromancer."

"Yeah. That makes sense. I'm a necromancer."

What am I missing?

Bartholomew rolled his eyes, a behaviour I resented.

The obeahwoman clasped her hands together. Her fingers were skeletal and bony, the skin stretched thin on the backs of her hands. "Zaya, Neathror feels power. It has been wielded by necromancers in the past. Necromancers who chose for their magic to become dark. The blade sucks that energy in, getting stronger, binding itself to that caster and using them."

"Wait." A creepy tingling feeling crawled over my body. "What are you saying?"

Macha's expression slackened with defeat. "I believe Neathror is trying to corrupt you."

CHAPTER 10

I stood there, my jaw hanging open and my mouth wide. "Excuse me?"

Neathror had come to my aid. There was no way it could be trying to… taint me.

The temperature down my side where my sheath was lodged was like an oven. For any other caster, the blade would be roasting their leg. Neathror didn't like what it was hearing. Was that because the truth had become known? Or because the athame-sabre was misunderstood?

Great. Now I'm trying to defend a blade like it's a real person.

Macha crossed her arms. The heavy lines in her face twisted into a complacent "I told you so." *"You're protecting the blade. That's a good indication it's holding a strong influence over you already."* Her voice resonated in my head. It had been a real shock to me when I'd learned necromancers and obeahpeople could communicate telepathically.

I flinched. "Don't read my mind. It's rude."

"Don't make it so easy,"

Frustrated, I flipped my palms up in surrender. "Fine. If you're so insistent that the blade isn't good for me, what do you want me to do with it?"

Macha was an intelligent woman with a shrewd intellect for magic. If she suspected Neathror wasn't what it seemed, she was probably right.

"Hand the blade over to Clorenzo for safekeeping." Her voice was more demanding than I'd ever heard it before. "Until I can learn more about Neathror, I think it's best we keep it out of your reach."

Her words rolled across my mind in a scary afterthought. *"Or keep you from its reach."*

My mouth pressed into a severe line. The idea that Macha thought I wasn't in control of myself but rather under control was maddening.

I set my eyes straight ahead, refusing to meet Clorenzo's eye as I handed the blade to him. He had put on gloves so that no surface of the athame-sabre would touch his skin. As soon as Neathror departed my fingers, my entire posture went stiff. A sudden chill in the air made my skin prickle. I wrapped my arms around myself, teeth chattering. The cold had become almost painful. Tremors ran through my legs, my palms and skin clammy. I blinked, but it didn't stop the dizziness from closing in. Glittering shapes obscured my vision. They flew forward like a storm of snowflakes. Neathror offered warmth. It offered shelter. Without it, I would surely die from the cold.

Macha's posture was rigid in the mirror. "How do you feel?"

"I'm fine." The lie crept easily out of my throat.

But I was far from fine. My heart throbbed, and sweat leaked from my skin.

Macha looked at me like I was an addict who'd lost their stash. "You did the right thing, Zaya."

Clorenzo stepped away. This time he wouldn't hide Neathror in the basement where his deceased wife or any other ghost could reveal its location. He'd hide it somewhere far away, or keep it on him at all times.

Maybe Neathror will come back to me, the same way it appeared on the beach.

I squeezed my eyes shut, the lining in my mouth acrid. I had just hoped the blade would return. My hands trembled at my sides. Macha was right. Neathror had some kind of hold over me. Its magic *had* influenced me. I tried to overcome the irritable sensation that I was vulnerable without the blade, but I was like a dog on a leash, unable to pull through no matter how hard I tried. I'd been strong with Neathror. Capable. Tough. Now, I was nothing without it.

Macha's voice managed to infiltrate the blood that roared in my ears. *"Don't be ridiculous."*

Her words brought me back to reality. "Hey, I said don't read my mind."

"That is the blade's influence talking. Not you." She shot me a look of disapproval, her voice quiet and strained. "You will undergo withdrawal symptoms over the coming days. It is best you distract yourself. Keep your mind occupied. Focus on finding a counter curse to the Four Revenants." She released a slow breath. "You should never have touched that blade in Nekros Manteia."

Now it was my turn to fume. "I'm sorry. I was only trying to destroy the worst dictator in caster history. Next time, I'll let Morgomoth's resurrection go ahead."

"It did go ahead, Zaya. It's half complete. All that is required now is your blood. If the ULD obtain it, Morgomoth returns. No one knows where his body is. The ULD could be hiding him. The Council could be hiding him. Look at what he has already achieved by linking his mind with the mayor. What will he achieve if he is fully resurrected?"

A sob swept into my throat. "And what am I supposed to do in this basement? I'm over colouring in childish picture books and playing with toys."

As much as I enjoyed spending time with Livel and Sarith, if I saw another doll or soldier figurine, I would scream.

I wanted out.

I wanted my friends.

I wanted Jad.

Macha's colourless eyes pinned me in place. "You could start researching the Four Revenants and the counter curse. That would occupy your mind."

I narrowed my gaze on her. "I will. I mean… I am. I started days ago."

Clorenzo shifted in surprise. "You did?"

I debated a snide remark, but I was too fatigued to pull it off. "Yes, which means you better keep your end of the bargain and find Jad."

He eyed me shrewdly. "You saw the diary entry from Darius. It's being done."

"Yeah, but now that you're all cosy with Mayor Belov and her chums, it's in your ability to find information too. And you know what else?" I pointed a nasty finger at Macha in the mirror. "You're going to do more to help Commander Macaslan and Colonel Harper. And you're going to find a way to get Livel and Sarith out of here. Those are my conditions. Got it?"

Every part of me was shaking. Confusion, sadness, and rage took control. I gulped air, but I couldn't get enough in my lungs. It was as though my windpipe had cinched into a knot, no longer open for business.

"Zaya," Macha's troubled voice echoed in my mind. *"Calm down. We are doing what we can to save Elspeth and Harper. And of course I will get Livel and Sarith out of Scarmouth when and if it is safe to do so. Did you honestly think Darius hadn't asked me to rescue his niece and nephew?"*

I forced my mind to communicate my thought. *"How will you get them out?"*

She didn't answer.

"You don't have a way, do you?"

She rubbed her temple. *"Not yet."*

This time I didn't bother with the mind speak. I wanted to be heard. "What about Jad?"

Macha didn't respond for a moment. *"We will try, but, Zaya… do not hope for the impossible."*

Those last words chilled me. It was pretty much what Darius had written in his diary entry. There was no hope for Jad. I believed Macha, Darius, and Clorenzo would do what they could, and, despite my irritation, I had total faith they wouldn't give up until there was nothing left to go on.

My entire body seemed to tighten. As much as we all cared for Jad, the inevitable truth was that it was out of our power to save him.

Tears stained my vision, but I wiped them away.

I won't give up. Not yet.

Macha's voice drifted through the mirror. "Sit down, Zaya. Let me tell you about the Four Revenants. The more you know about them, the stronger chance you have of finding clues in your research."

I dropped onto the couch, too much of an emotional wreck to do anything but obey. I curled into a ball and leaned my head against the cushion.

The obeahwoman frowned. I couldn't have looked very aspiring at that moment. On her shoulder, Bartholomew flapped his enormous black wings and squawked. She petted the bird. "The Four Revenants not only symbolise the apocalypse, as most casters believe, but signal a change. A sudden unbalance in magic. I sensed their awakening the moment Morgomoth's curse was partially lifted. They are linked to him. How? I am unsure. I assume Morgomoth dabbled with necromancy in the past and made a connection with them in the otherworld. Each rider represents a different facet of devastation. War. Famine. Pestilence. Death. Legend has it that the Four Revenants decide when and which of these events will occur, a way to balance what is unbalanced. They feed off tragedy and despair."

Macha shivered, guardedness etched in her expression. "I believe Morgomoth has offered the Four Revenants something in return for assisting the ULD. It is the only reason he would be desperate enough to link his mind with the mayor in his weakened condition. He is keeping a close eye on things in Scarmouth, which means whatever he is up to is important enough that he will not leave it in the hands of his lieutenants."

A nervous sweat flushed my body. "He's feeding them."

I knew it was the truth the moment the words left my mouth.

Macha dropped her hands. "Excuse me?"

Even Clorenzo tipped his head. He sat on the armrest, his arms crossed. "Feeding them?"

I pushed myself forward into sitting, my attention focused solely on Macha. "You said the Four Revenants feed off tragedy and despair. Morgomoth wants death to all humans and any caster with human DNA. Don't you get it?" My eyes darted between the pair. "The sacrifices on the beach are Morgomoth's way of feeding the Four Revenants."

A chilling silence ensued.

Macha let out a short, unamused snort. "That makes sense. But it still does not tell us why."

My curiosity—partly mixed with fear—rose. "He's making the revenants strong enough to break free from their prison in the sea."

The obeahwoman raised her eyebrows, the same way a teacher did when a student stated something surprisingly clever. "That is one theory, yes."

I bit my tongue to conquer a snide comment. "It's the only theory we have."

"Then I suppose we must use it and see if it fits with any more clues."

"Daddy." Livel's tiny voice stretched across the basement. She rubbed her eyes and sat up in bed.

Clorenzo went to her. The moment he pulled away, I experienced a tug so strong and sharp it was like I had an invisible cord tethered to him.

"It's the blade." Macha's voice was direct and straight to the point in my head. "It will take time to sever the hold it has on you. Keep your distance."

I braced my hands on my hips. My tolerance had reached its limit. "Why are you so convinced that Neathror was... is trying to corrupt me? I nearly killed Morgomoth with it back at Galvac Tower. That doesn't strike me as a bad thing."

Macha stroked her chin. On her shoulder, Bartholomew cocked his head as though to say "joke's on you."

Bloody bird.

The obeahwoman's lips twitched. "Why do you think Neathror was on that sarcophagus in the first place?"

She was referring to the coffin both Vulcan and I had assumed housed Morgomoth's sleep-cursed body in Nekros Manteia. What a shock we both received when we'd discovered the sarcophagus was a diversion and *very* empty.

I shrugged. "Because all magic needs to be balanced. Larthalgule returns life. Neathror wields death."

"Wields death," Macha repeated.

"Yeah." I had no idea where she was going with this.

"I told you that Neathror had been in necromancers' possessions in the past. That its magic unites and grows stronger with the caster it binds itself too." She approached closer to the mirror. Her body took up the entire frame. "Who do you think was the last necromancer to possess it?"

I wasn't able to look away from the grave expression on her wrinkled face.

This can't be true. Can't be real. The blade helped me. It couldn't have belonged to—

The obeahwoman's voice rolled loud and clear in my head. *"Morgomoth."*

CHAPTER 11

I couldn't sleep that night. The couch was uncomfortable, the basement hot and damp from the rain outside. Thunder rolled in the distance. Another thunderclap answered in response, much closer and louder. The storm must have been over the water, the rumblings and cracks echoing across hundreds of kilometres of sea. In a strange way, it reminded me of whales when they communicated, determined to find one another. I shivered in my flimsy nightdress, not because I was cold—it was far too humid in the basement for that—but because I didn't like to think what would happen if the two storms united.

I rolled onto my side. I sensed Scarmouth was on the outskirts of the storms' wrath. Wind thrashed at the house. The plantation shutters groaned in their frames upstairs. The front door trembled against the breathless whistling of the gale. It seemed to me as though the entire house constricted and shuddered like a frightened child curled into a ball, fearful of what was to come next.

I craned my neck toward the two beds in the corner. Livel and Sarith were asleep, their red curls swept over their foreheads. Selfishly, I wished they were awake, only so I wouldn't be alone.

I tossed and turned. Dark and frenetic thoughts spun through my mind. It was the memory of Macha's words that cut the deepest. *"I told you that Neathror had been in necromancers' possessions in the past. That its magic unites and grows stronger with the caster it binds itself too. Who do you think was the last necromancer to possess it? Morgomoth."*

I kicked my feet against the armrest, frustrated that I'd been deceived. Had Neathror appeared in the rainforest in the guise of aiding me when really its aim was to sabotage me?

Belonged to Morgomoth?

Would Neathror *have* killed Morgomoth that night at Galvac Tower when I'd intended to destroy him forever?

Probably not.

I'd been running a fool's errand that day. And because of that, I'd lost Jad.

I stirred, every part of me restless. I ached to find the blade. It's hold on me was all-consuming, but now that I understood more about its past—about its previous owner—I fought every grappling craving to find it. Besides, discovering the blade would be impossible. Clorenzo would have hidden it in the farmhouse. A part of me was angry about that, but that was my addiction to Neathror talking. The real Zaya—the Zaya who knew deep inside that Macha's warning was true—was grateful the blade was at a safe distance.

My eyes focused on a patch of dim moonlight in the basement. Somehow the light had managed to leak in through the cracks in the upper floorboards. It disappeared the moment the deluge started. It was another reminder that I was on a tight schedule. I had until the full moon to find a counter curse to the Four Revenants, and so far, the Kerr family grimoires had divulged nothing.

I chewed on my lower lip. Flipped over. Punched my pillow. Nothing worked. My brain wouldn't switch off.

Maybe the answer wasn't in the grimoires. Maybe it was... somewhere else.

Violetta.

She had known the locator spell to find the Four Revenants. At least, that's what she'd thought she'd known, when really she'd been duped into taking her own life to awaken the vile creatures. Perhaps Violetta knew more in her afterlife.

Perhaps I needed to... summon her.

The idea sent an unpleasant shiver across my bones. Besides Lunette, I'd never deliberately conjured a spirit. Back then, it had been a matter of life or death.

Here goes nothing.

I inhaled a deep breath, closed my eyes, and tried to envision a perfect copy of Violetta's face. In my mind I saw waterlogged skin, squelchy and sodden to the touch, small marine life living in the grooves of her flesh. I wished I'd seen a photo of Violetta when she was alive. It would have made this process much easier—and less scary.

Violetta? Are you there?

The air changed around me. The basement suddenly reeked of damp and rot. Something cold and wispy touched my face. Tendrils of wet hair? Whatever it was, it left fat drips of water along my mouth. It tasted salty. It tasted... like the ocean.

My jugular pulsed in my neck.

Don't open your eyes. Keep them shut.

Because I knew if I opened them, I'd be staring into Violetta's lifeless ones.

She's here.

I sensed her floating above me, ready to lash out at any moment. I summoned Violetta for help, but ghosts didn't always work that way. This wasn't like the time with Lunette. I sensed anger coming off Violetta in waves. I imagined her gnashing her rust-icicle teeth. There was probably an entire ecosystem growing in her mouth.

Please. I need your help. If not for me, for Livel and Sarith. How do I reverse the curse? How do I make this right?

Violetta's voice seemed to seep from every crevice and recess in the basement. *"Noooooo. I will not tell you. I will show you."*

A sonic boom split the walls. My eyes burst open in time to see water gushing into the basement. It spilled through the cracks in the walls and seeped from the basement floor. I leapt from the couch as the water rose fast. It was already up to my waist.

What the hell is happening? What is Violetta playing at?

She's going to drown me.

No. Us!

Because this wasn't a torrent of rainwater. It wasn't even a wall of water from the sea. The basement was sinking like an elevator descending the levels of a doomed vessel.

I thrashed in the rising torrent, my voice unable to overcome the roar of the water. "Livel! Sarith!"

The children's beds had been swallowed by the rush of dark water. I kicked my feet, trying to swim in their direction, but the current had other ideas. Polluted with algae and slime, it wrenched me the other way. I fought to keep my head above the surface, but that proved impossible when it lifted me right to the ceiling.

I called out desperately one more time. "Livel! Sarith!"

They must be underwater by now.

I gasped my last breath. The water rose over my head. Something wrapped around my leg, pulling me farther into the murky dark.

I'm going to run out of air.

I couldn't help it. I opened my mouth, expecting agony to greet my lungs, but... nothing. I no longer had to breathe.

This can't be real.

I recalled how Lunette had teleported me across dimensions into the otherworld, showing me clues about the mystery of her death. Was that happening now? Was Violetta somehow manipulating time and space and taking me to a place that shouldn't be real or possible? Because this didn't feel like a submerged basement anymore. The current had changed. The pressure in my ears was different. I was somewhere else. Judging from the swell and feel of the water, I was in the sea.

Violetta, what are you doing?

An anxious shudder racked my chest. I was afraid Violetta was taking me right to the scene of her death. The unrelenting force on my leg continued to drag me down.

My eyes adjusted, but it took several seconds to make something of the shaft of moonlight—at least I hoped it was moonlight —that spilled onto the sea floor. I had reached the seabed, my legs free. A hauntingly beautiful image appeared in the reef ahead. Statues of four horsemen were set on a large concrete block. Around them stood thousands of underwater statues, their faces positioned to stare at the horsemen in awe. It looked like an underwater graveyard. Fish swam tranquilly in and around the sculptures. The figures would have been lifelike once but were now algae infested and covered in coral. They had become part of the marine life. I wondered how old they were and who had built them.

I swam closer. There was something deeply unsettling about the way the statues were set together. Their faces amazed me. The shape of the mouth, nose, and eyes, even the ears were just so—

An underwater scream tore from my throat. In the centre of the figurines' foreheads was the insignia for the United League of Dissent. They all had the insignia, burned deep into their marble foreheads—only now I didn't think it was marble. I kicked and thrashed, desperate to put all my weight against the current.

It's them. The people from the beach.

These were the undercasts Mayor Belov had sacrificed.

As I stared in horror, a statue's eyes popped open and connected with mine.

CHAPTER 12

The eyes were fiery orbs and glowed like molten lava. The scream in my head seemed to drive higher in frequency. The more afraid I became, the more the swell fought me. Movement in the water made everything expand, contract, and blur, making it impossible to tell what direction was the surface.

The statue's hand shot out in one smooth motion. Its fingers latched on to my throat.

"You shouldn't have come here."

Its voice reminded me of rocks ground together.

"You need to leave. Before they realise you are here. Leeeaaavvveee."

The creature opened its cavernous mouth. A shout loud enough to make my eardrums throb flung me through the water like a torpedo. The force made every bone in my body feel brittle enough to shatter. All my organs floated and fell in response to the endless underwater waves.

Please. Let this stop.

I broke through the surface, but not in the literal sense. The ocean was gone. There was no beach. No coastline. No rainforest. I blinked the water out of my eyes, my body sopping wet but not cold. There was too much heat in the air for that.

Heat?

This wasn't the warm, high temperature of a tropical night. This was the intense heat of an inferno.

Around me, buildings were alight. The blazes inside grew into an uncontainable fire. Flames burst through windows. Gabled roofs collapsed and gave way with a horrendous crash of timber and soot. I grimaced and covered my ears. The flames leapt from building to building, the night cast in a crimson glow.

I wasn't alone. People were trying to save themselves. They cried and shrieked in panic, their faces soot covered and their hair sprinkled with ash. There didn't seem to be any way out of this burning town—if that's what it was. The place had been badly devastated by the fires, its identity no longer recognisable. The exits were cut off, the roads that led out of town obstructed by flames.

This has been coordinated.

A girl tripped on her long nightgown and landed near my feet. I reached down, but my hands went straight through her.

What the fu—

I leapt back in shock.

The girl scrambled onto her feet and ran. She hadn't seen me.

I'm not here. I'm not... real.

"You're as real as I am." The voice was the sound of a woman drowned, watery and clogged. Violetta emerged from the smoke. Her wet nightdress dripped slimy puddles on the ground. The embers floated right through her. Her smile curved high, her fish-bitten face pulled so far back the bone was visible beneath her cheeks

Fear bubbled inside me. "Why did you bring me here? What are you playing at?"

Violetta's opaque eyes drifted to the end of the road.

A man concealed in a black cloak was torching the buildings with the tip of an athame-sabre. Just as Neathror had connected with my magic, this athame-sabre had linked itself with the caster who wielded it, intensifying both their powers. If this man and the blade were setting the town alight, that meant he was a fire wielder.

My eyes regarded him with equal parts fear and amazement. Whenever one of the town's men tried to stop him, he reacted by cutting them down, his sabre slicing through flesh. He butchered arms, legs, and torsos. He was unstoppable. Five... seven... ten deaths in seconds. The ground was soaked in blood as much as it was in ash. He deftly dodged arrows and caster-fire. A brave man with scraggly blond hair swung an axe, but the cloaked assailant ducked the blow and effortlessly slammed his elbow into the man's nose. The blond guy cried out and stumbled backward. His scream was short-lived, his neck seized in a headlock and twisted. The terrible crack reminded me of a twig snapped. I raised a hand to my mouth, holding back my horror as the victim's body slumped to the ground.

He has no mercy. No empathy. He's... a monster.

I watched in sheer terror as the concealed man drew near a child, a little boy who was crying.

No. No. No. No.

The man raised the athame-sabre.

I didn't think. My feet took the lead without any direction from me. I ran forward, afraid I wouldn't be able to prevent the death that was only seconds away from happening. I forgot in that moment that I was a caster girl and fragile too. I knocked the child out of the way at the same time the blade came down.

It was an odd sensation, an object going straight through you. I expected it to burn. I expected it to be painful beyond anything I'd experienced before—but there was nothing. Not even a mark. Why I could knock the boy out of the way but still be incorporeal was a mystery to me.

My cloaked companion let out a roar of hostility. He grabbed me by the sleeve of my nightdress and wrenched me forward. At the same time, his cloak came down. A piercing cry ran through my head. It took me a second to realise it was my own.

Shock. Betrayal. Longing. They each swept through me in a confliction of emotions. He looked exactly the same as I remembered. Tanned skin. Athletic build like a swimmer. Dark, chin-length hair that curled rebelliously beneath his jaw. Slender pianist hands covered in cuts and blood. The only difference about his appearance was his eyes. Once they'd been as black as midnight. You could get lost in those eyes. Now they were red-ringed and inflamed.

From the way his eyebrows drew taut, I knew he recognised me. Light from the fires highlighted the ruthlessness in his expression, his handsome face twisted and unrecognisable.

What has Vulcan done to him?

This wasn't Jad. This was an empty shell possessed by something evil. It had to be.

A ghost of a smile stretched his lips. "Hello, Zaya."

It was his voice, but I'd never heard it spoken with such cold amusement. It made my scalp prickle.

He brought his face close to mine, his breath warm on my lips. It only took a heartbeat to realise he'd remembered everything about me but didn't care. His lips, which I always thought were perfect, now contorted with rage. "You're in my way."

He threw a punch into my stomach. The force catapulted me into the air. I smashed through a window and landed in the living room of a burning house. Flames licked the curtains. Sparks rained down, the furniture alight. I couldn't see anything beyond the little room and the towering smoke.

"Jad!" I couldn't tell whether I was screaming or whispering. The roar of the fires distorted everything.

I stretched my hands out and crawled to find my way through the smouldering debris. Every pore in my body sweated. My eyes felt like they might shrivel up and melt.

A figure appeared in the haze ahead. Violetta stepped out of the flames. Her hands were alight. Fire danced off each of her fingertips. She grabbed me by the shoulders and lifted me from the floor. Flames descended onto my body. I screamed.

In my head, her voice was as cool and cold as the Arctic. *"This is what he is now. Give up. You'll never get him back."*

The floor dropped away beneath us. I tumbled down... and down... into the unknown... into darkness... to the end.

CHAPTER 13

The first things to appear were colours. Then a musky scent that was not entirely unpleasant greeted my nose. Pinpricks of water touched my forehead, soothing and gentle. Rain.

I blinked my eyes awake, trying to force myself back into reality, but whatever this was—a hallucination, Violetta's ghostly sense of humour, or just sheer madness on my part—it had other ideas.

I stood in a vast moorland that overlooked a colossal cliff face —a sheer vertical drop into the sea.

No. This can't be real. I'm still held in Violetta's spell. Where has she taken me now?

Low-lying evergreen shrubs dominated the landscape to the west, a sea of purple flowers softening the otherwise rugged scenery. Crags and boulders stood out like icebergs. Fog swirled around them, reminding me of the drifting spirits I'd seen at Gosheniene. I shivered. Rain bit into my skin. My feet sank into the mud-soaked ground.

What are you doing, Violetta? Where am I?

The sky was dark. The clouds whipped into eddies. A storm brewed on the horizon.

"Hello."

I spun around.

A young man barely past adolescence stood before me. He had dark, mid-length hair that curled around his ears in the rain. He had a handsome face, the jawline and shape of the nose familiar. At this distance, his eyes were a cryptic, puzzling black. I imagined that up close, they would reflect beautiful bands of colour like oil slicks. Something inside me broke. He could have been Jad's twin brother.

The boy tilted his head, his mass of dark hair caught in the wind. "Do you think it wise to be out of town? They are saying this weather could form into a galactic storm. It would be a good idea to return to Cubais and be safe behind the celestial shields."

I wasn't sure how to respond.

He can see me? I'm really here?

I opened my mouth, but no words came out. Literally. I couldn't talk. I had no voice. There was nothing in my throat but air.

"Then why are you here?" a voice responded behind me.

I turned to see a girl sit up from the heather. Her white-blonde hair stood out among the purple blossoms, her white dress dirty from the rain and mud. She reminded me of the nymphs I'd read about in folk tales, a beautiful maiden unafraid of nature but embracing it, alive and enriched.

The boy smiled. I realised he'd never been talking to me. He'd been looking right through me at the girl.

I'm not here. I'm not real.

The boy strode through the heather and sat down beside the young lady. He looked out at the sea. Lightning streaked through the plum-shaded clouds. The boy didn't flinch. He crossed his arms over his knees, loose and relaxed. "I've seen you here often. It's brave to venture this far away from town. Aren't you afraid?"

The girl's smile came easily, her lips the colour of peaches. She let out a silky laugh. "No. The storm won't reach us. It'll turn east soon. We're perfectly safe. I can always tell what the weather will do." She leant forward playfully. "It's part of my charm."

The boy's lips formed into a slow grin. "You're a tempestarii. A weather-maker."

She gave a lazy shake of her head. "Not quite. I don't make the weather. It does what it pleases, but I sense what the weather is going to do. I feel energised being out here. The rain on my skin. The wind in my hair. It's never felt more perfect." She lifted her head and leaned back, as though tanning herself at the beach and basking in sun rays. "Don't you feel alive out here?"

"I feel cold. What's your name?"

The girl kept her eyes shut. "Octavia. What's yours?"

"Octavia what?"

"Octavia Partrez."

She didn't see how the boy watched her. He studied her with his head tilted to the side. In the heavy rain, the light in his eyes was pent-up energy, the hard lines around his mouth more prevalent. He no longer looked handsome or friendly.

I crept forward, evaluating the scene. Something wasn't right. Brewing behind that boy's handsome face was something dangerous.

His lips hinted at a smile. "Before I tell you my name, can you promise me one thing?"

She rolled onto her side to face him. "That depends on what it is you're going to ask me. You know, I've seen you here a few times too. It makes me wonder for what reason. Because you like watching storms? The beauty of the moors, perhaps?"

His eyes settled on hers meaningfully. "I'm here for a different kind of beauty."

A blush rose in her cheeks. "Then in that case, let me hear what it is you want me to promise."

He drew closer. His voice held smooth authority. "Go out with me?"

She inhaled a breath. "And why should I do that? I don't know you."

"Because I have great prospects, and… well, look at me. You'd be mad not to." He said it with a deliberate, haughty arrogance that I didn't think was entirely fake. He really did think himself superior and something to be marvelled at.

I wished Octavia would get on her feet and run away, but her eyes betrayed her excitement. She couldn't see what was happening on a deeper level.

Was this what all ghosts experienced? Seeing the truth of a situation but powerless to do anything about it?

The young man laughed softly, but to me it sounded harsh. "My father is influential in the Council and on good terms with the Sovereigns. Once I complete my military service, I'll be a member of the Council. I'll probably be a senator. All the men in my family have been in the past."

Octavia hid behind her hair to conceal a private smile. "Well, all of that would impress my father."

"It's not your father I'm trying to impress."

My hands knotted tightly. This entire charade was making me sick. Why couldn't Octavia see what I could? She was glowing and blossoming from his attention. She'd wilt and wither once he was through with her. I knew *his* type.

"Okay." She dipped her head, unable to hide her delight any longer. "I'll go out with you. Now what's your name?"

The young man took her hand and kissed it. "Vulcan Stormouth."

I LEAPT FORWARD, desperate to break them apart, but all I was successful in achieving was slipping right through them. I spun around, but Vulcan and Octavia had disappeared in a veil of white fog. The haze devoured the landscape. The crags had vanished. The purple heather had frozen over, ice droplets on their delicate petals. The mud and rain had thickened into slush. The wind embraced me with a chill that froze the marrow in my bones.

This is no normal behaviour for the weather.

"Violetta, where are you? What is this?"

In response, the ground lurched under my feet. I tried to steady myself, but there was nothing to hold onto. The soft terrain beneath my feet collapsed. I tumbled into a yawning hole. My hair leapt around my face in a multitude of directions, making it impossible to see what I was plunging down to. My ribs shook from my pounding heart. I braced myself for the long descent into a world unfamiliar and unknown but instead face-planted into dirt. The impact juddered every bone in my body.

I groaned inwardly.

Why are you doing this, Violetta?

Was she trying to tell me something in these twisted mind games? Or was her aim to hurt me?

I sat up. My hand scraped along a coarse surface I suspected was stone.

No, not stone.

I scrambled onto my feet. The floor, walls, and ceiling were made from skulls. Hollow eyes and toothy grins stared at me from every angle. A horrible image of the skulls snapping their jaws struck my mind.

On one side of the wall was a sleeping shelf. On the other, a bucket for the toilet. A single torch provided inadequate light, sending a flicker of shadows along the grinning skulls. This place wasn't a dungeon. It wasn't even a torture chamber but rather a pitch-black pit —a place to drive its inhabitant mad. I could imagine the effort a prisoner would have to go through to keep the torch from blowing out. Not only was it a source of light but the only source of warmth.

Who is kept in here?

A hidden door creaked open in the wall. A shadow extended across the floor, and a voice barked from the passage beyond, "Get him inside."

The door was thrust open, a body that looked to be only half alive tossed inside. Whoever he was, he lay on the floor not moving. The scent of blood and sweat saturated the air. His clothes were partially burnt, his hands bruised and swollen where he'd taken a hit—or instigated the blow. The man's body slackened the same way a person's body released after death. I stepped closer, afraid of what I might see. The man groaned and clutched his stomach. Judging from the way he was positioned, there were more than a few bones broken in his body. His dark hair covered his face, wet and splayed at different angles, so I couldn't get a decent look at him, but it wasn't necessary. I knew who he was.

The lining in my mouth tasted sticky.

Honestly, Jad would have appeared more at home in a coffin.

Someone entered the prison and kicked him. There was a crunch that suggested a bone had given way. I flinched at the horrible sound. The assailant leaned over Jad, his face captured in the subdued torchlight.

Sweat drenched my palms.

Vulcan.

Not the boy I'd seen in the previous dream… memory… whatever it had been but the *real* Vulcan. The Vulcan who had turned into a monster. The Vulcan who was obsessed with the idea of racial cleansing. The Vulcan who was smiling down at his son the way I imagined a tiger looked down at its prey.

If I punch him, will anything happen?

Or will I float right through him?

The mad impulse to try swept through me. I leapt forward with the intention of striking him down.

His voice caught me off guard.

"You did well tonight. I'm proud of you."

I froze. For a moment I thought Vulcan had been talking to me, my mind lost in a black fog of shock.

Vulcan knelt down to stroke the hair out of his son's eyes. "Trajan. It's time to come back now. Wake up."

I brushed my hands over my wet cheeks in a useless attempt to dry them.

Trajan?

Not Jad?

I recalled the way he stood amid the burning ruins of the town he'd torched, his face transformed in a lethal smile. That hadn't been Jad. The Jad I knew would never have acted that way. This person I stared at now was beyond help.

The realisation robbed me of breath.

I looked down at father and son with pity and disgust.

CHAPTER 14

Trajan was utterly quiet.

Vulcan turned his back to the torch. Shadows crept over his shoulders, which made all the hard edges in his face that more apparent. His eyes were devoid of concern. "Your injuries won't last the night, Trajan. Already your lycanthor blood is starting to heal you. It won't be long now. Soon, you won't feel anything. Physical or emotional. Those people in Cubais—our ancestral home—were hiding Haxsan Guard soldiers and needed to be taught a lesson. They brought shame to us. You did the right thing burning that place to the ground."

A strangled noise broke from Trajan. He propped himself up to sitting, his voice lashing out with cold vehemence "You made me kill those people… innocent people."

I stilled. A strange tug of hope jerked my body.

Jad?

Vulcan's hand clamped hard around his son's throat. "Listen to me. There was nothing innocent about that town. You were performing an execution that was justly deserved. Do you think I enjoy using spells on my son so he can witness first-hand that what the ULD is doing is right? It's the only way, Trajan. Open your eyes."

The red in his son's eyes dilated with rage. "It's Jad."

Vulcan smacked the back of his hand across Jad's face. The impact made a wet thumping sound. "Get up. Show some dignity."

I bit my tongue to refrain from shouting. A red welt had sprung across Jad's cheek. It was the hardest I'd ever seen someone hit. For anyone else, the blow would have smashed the side of their face in, maybe even broken their nose.

Jad rolled onto his side and spat out blood. His eyes pinpointed darkly on his father. "I hate you. One day I will kill you."

The venom in his voice stunned me.

It must have astonished Vulcan too, because he backhanded Jad across the jaw again. "You do not talk to me in that way." His flare of anger went up like a bonfire. He zeroed in on the door and screamed down the passage, "Hadar! Get in here now."

Hadar's decrepit form appeared in the doorway. The shadows were severe against her pale skin, which started to appear sicklier in the insufficient torchlight. Her eyes swept from Vulcan to Jad. She seemed to take the scene in with boredom.

Vulcan's nostrils flared. "You told me the spell would wipe his memory. You said he would forget everything but *her*."

Hadar leaned against the wall with her arms crossed. "For a normal caster it would, but you forget your son has lycanthor blood. The spell wears off. He has the strength to overcome it."

Vulcan's shoulders shook in small fits of rage. "Then make the spell stronger."

Hadar flicked a rebellious strand of her hair behind her ear. Her black-and-white bob remained amazingly straight amid the cool, damp air of the dungeon. "I'm working on it. It will require time. Besides, I thought you wanted to torture your boy."

"I want him to be on my side."

"Then hold him down. I'm not risking life or limb for this."
She took a syringe from her pocket.

Vulcan grabbed the back of Jad's neck and drove his forehead
into the ground. Jad's nose bent at an unnatural angle, and there
was a grotesque crunch. He writhed in pain. His hands curled into
fists as convulsions racked his body. I couldn't look away from the
blood that seeped over the floor beneath him.

I can't watch Jad suffer like this.

I dove forward, but my incorporeal body went straight through
Vulcan.

Hadar jammed the needle into Jad's back. He let out a cry as
his spine arched straight. Whatever Hadar had injected into him
wiped his strength. He collapsed into a spell-induced sleep, his
hands now slack at his sides.

The scientist passed an impish smile at the lieutenant. "It's like
flicking a switch in the brain. When he wakes up, he'll be the
massacring psychopath you cherish. Happy?"

A muscle twitched in Vulcan's neck. "I'd be happy if he
remained that way. I'm warning you, Hadar—"

"And I'm warning you." She moved in front of him with calm
resolve. "The more magic you experiment with on your son, the
more damaged he becomes. You want a supreme killing beast. A
soldier who does not think but obeys. A creature that can't be
killed because it's already dead inside." She jabbed a finger into
Vulcan's chest. "Be careful what you wish for, Lieutenant, because
if that wish does come true, you might not be able to control him
at all. He'll be pure monster."

She spun around for the door. "He'll be awake by morning.
The spell is already working. You'll find a much more *willing*
henchman."

She slipped away into the passage. The *click-click* of her boots
faded into the dark.

Vulcan rested his head in his hands. It was the first time I'd witnessed something in him that bordered on weariness. Maybe even concern.

But I was wrong. A vexed scream tore from his throat. He smashed his fist into the wall. The impact shattered skulls with such force they fragmented into dust. He marched out of the cell, his face flustered and red. The door slammed behind him. A moment later, the unmistakable click of the lock resonated from the passage.

Alone, I tiptoed toward Jad. He remained motionless on the ground. For one horrifying moment I believed he was dead, but then I detected the gentle rise and fall of his chest. His breathing wasn't consistent, coming in soft, wheezing spurts. My insides rioted. Swollen, yellowish lumps protruded around his eyes. His cheeks were split and bleeding. Painful-looking welts made bracelets around his wrists. At some stage, someone had tied Jad with rope.

I sat there for a long time, not knowing what to do. I wasn't really here and couldn't help.

Or could I?

A small, strange hitch escaped my throat. "Jad?"

He opened his eyes.

I stared.

Did he hear me?

"Jad?'

"Zaya." His voice was feeble and shook. He tried to move but succeeded in only causing himself more pain. His head lolled to the side, his lips strained in a tight line.

I held his hand, afraid my fingers would slip right through his, but my grasp remained firm.

How is this possible?

I wiped a fresh surge of tears out of my eyes. "I'm here."

The muscles in his battered face were drawn taut in pain, but he managed to turn and look at me. He uttered a shaky laugh. "Go away. You're not real. You're never real."

My legs became as feeble as straw. "I'm here. I'm real."

Emotion swept through his eyes. His wet lashes bunched together in fine points, almost like stars. I knew from the way he shivered and turned away from me that he thought I was a figment of his imagination, something brought on by his broken mind. "Go away. You're not real."

I wiped my hand on the back of my nose, afraid of giving in to hopeless despair. How many times had Jad hallucinated me? He was totally cut off from the world. Totally alone and on a downward spiral of loneliness. Mix that with manipulation, mind control, and the nightmarish medical tortures he underwent, and was it possible the real Jad would never return again?

"*I am relieved to hear he is alive but fear that, in his current predicament, he is truly beyond our help.*"

I knew what Darius meant now. I had witnessed first-hand what imprisonment had done to Jad.

I closed my eyes to rationalise my thoughts. I had to remain strong. Otherwise I'd break down. Vulcan would win.

There's only one thing for it.

I punched Jad in the shoulder, funnelling all my strength into the impact. His eyes locked on mine in surprise. I guess none of his hallucinations had ever used physical force on him before.

I stroked his damp hair out of his face. "Listen to me. I'm here. I'm real. I will get you out of this place. I promise."

The briefest spark of hope outweighed the confusion on his face. He gently touched my cheek. His fingers were caked in mud and stained in ash. I was startled by the feverish heat of his skin.

"*Promises mean nothing here.*"

Startled, I craned my neck over my shoulder.

Lunette Collins emerged from the dark. When I'd first seen Lunette as a ghost, her skin had been painted in frost. White crystals had streaked through her hair, her throat packed with snow. A gash had ripped through her torso. I remembered it vividly. It had plagued my nightmares for days. What the black-veined woman had done to Lunette had been gruesome, wicked, and evil. But now that Melvina had been vanquished by yours truly, Lunette's ghost had moved on from the trauma that had inhibited her soul. She appeared just as she had when she was alive.

Lunette watched me. Her lingering stare was full of sorrow. *"You can't be here, Zaya. Violetta is doing this to you, and the longer you let her, the more control she'll have over you."*

Colour flooded up my neck. "What?"

"Wake up. You shouldn't be here."

My hand instinctively clutched Jad's tighter. "No. I can't go. I can't leave him like this."

Lunette's gaze softened, but in her eyes, there was determination and… fear. She glanced behind her into the dark, which started to look more like a long, shadowy tunnel. The darkness spun into a vortex. There was something foreboding about the way it moved. I imagined it sucking a person whole, forcing them to drift downward into an eternal abyss.

I swallowed. "What is that?"

Lunette shook her head. *"Violetta is not what she seems. Do not trust her. Do not summon her. Do not let her near the Sujik family. You have to leave, Zaya. You have to leave now."*

"Zaya?"

Jad's feeble voice stirred mixed reactions inside me. I couldn't leave him. He needed me to be strong. I had to be strong.

I shook my head. There were no words for a moment like this.

Lunette hovered forward. She gripped my arm, her strength surprisingly solid for a ghost. *"This isn't your place. Go back to your body. Wake up."*

Jad lost consciousness and collapsed to the ground. His cheeks glistened where the tears remained, his breathing a shallow, irregular rhythm.

When he woke, would he even remember that I'd been here?

Lunette's icy hand burned cold into my wrist.

A lump rose in my throat. "Let me go. I'm staying."

The walls and ceiling began to dissolve around me, dripping away like an unfinished oil painting. My world—whatever this place was—was collapsing. It was being sucked into the darkness.

No. I'm *being sucked into the darkness.*

Jad slipped farther away. I reached for him, but the shadows closed in.

"Wake up, Zaya."

Lunette's voice was the last thing I heard.

My eyes opened.

CHAPTER 15

I sat up with a jerk. A tight sensation seized my chest, my arms weak and cold where Lunette had grabbed me.

"Hey, calm down. It's okay."

Someone wiped sweat off my brow with a damp cloth and forced me to lie down. My neck ached, and my head throbbed. I stared at the ceiling and tried to get a sense of where I was. My surroundings swirled in and out, my eyes stinging. Slowly, everything morphed into focus. The basement. I was in the Sujiks' basement. Livel and Sarith were asleep in their beds, unaware that storms raged outside. Rain still pummelled the house. I could hear the shutters groan and slam against the windows. The timber planks creaked and constricted, which made me think of old shipping vessels in rough seas. I was the little sailor hidden beneath deck.

"Zaya?" Clorenzo's sunburnt face appeared. His eyes grew increasingly troubled the longer he studied me. He still held the damp cloth in his hand. "That must have been one hell of a nightmare you were having. I was afraid you'd wake the children."

Nightmare?

If only.

It wasn't sleep that had tugged me into the depths of raw, unconscious thought.

What had that been?

I'd summoned Violetta, but somehow she'd gotten the better of me, throwing my mind into places I neither wanted to go to nor, as it turned out in the end, wanted to leave.

And what had happened with Lunette? How had she been there? Why had she pulled me away from Jad?

Jad!

I left him in that place!

"You can't be here, Zaya. Violetta is doing this to you, and the longer you let her, the more control she'll have over you."

That's what Lunette had said. If Violetta had been the cause of everything I'd witnessed, did that mean none of it had been real?

No. Jad had been real.

What I had seen in that dungeon had *definitely* been real.

I focused on Clorenzo, my voice weak and strange. "I need to talk to Macha. Right now."

We HAD to wait for the storms to pass before we could communicate with Macha. When there was enough moonlight in the sky to make the connection, Macha materialised in the bridge-interface. Her face was pinched and drawn from disturbed sleep, the shadows beneath her eyes making her appear haggard. She wore a pink dressing gown and nightcap, and her fluffy grey-and-white hair resembled a bird's nest. I was surprised to see her in colour. Bartholomew squawked on her shoulder, probably unhappy to be woken. I wondered what time it was in Tarahik.

Macha folded her arms. "What is wrong, child? You look like you have seen…." She shook her head. "Never mind."

I explained what had happened. I hoped—expected—her to

rationalise a reason, but she just stared. Or Bartholomew stared. Macha's white, pupil-less eyes simply reflected the oil lanterns in the basement.

She ruffled her hair with her bony fingers. "It sounds like you stuffed up."

I pursed my lips, not sure if I heard her correctly. "Sorry?"

"It is quite simple. You summoned Violetta, but you did not hold control. You are far too inexperienced. She was easily able to take command of the situation."

"Command of what situation?"

Clorenzo sank into the nearest chair, alarm evident in his voice. "You summoned my wife?"

I opened my mouth, but the words escaped me.

In the mirror, Macha's brows pulled together. "A poor attempt you made of it, Zaya. Violetta took control of your powers."

My heart accelerated, tension building through my shoulders. "But I summoned Lunette once, and nothing like that happened."

I recalled the night Lainie, Talina, and I had been trapped in a burning morgue, or, to be precise, an oven designed to incinerate everything inside. I had called on Lunette and urged her to teleport us through dimensions back into the safety of Macha's kitchen. It had been a strange evening.

The inclination of Macha's head showed that she understood my confusion. "Lunette did that willingly. You must understand that not all ghosts are enthusiastic to answer a summoning. The fact that Lunette intervened and broke the connection between you and Violetta is concerning. Yes, very alarming indeed." A frown creased Macha's forehead.

An involuntary shudder crept down my neck. "Okay, let's lose the doom-and-gloom approach. Mind elaborating?"

I'd hate to undergo therapy with this woman.

Macha drew herself upright, appearing much taller than I'd ever seen her before. "It seems Violetta could be vengeful. Pitiless. Vindictive. That can happen when the soul is tricked into death. It is unnatural and a wicked act. The soul becomes corrupted. It is a good thing Lunette intervened when she did. I can only assume Violetta showed you those terrible scenes to break your tenacity and leave you weak and afraid. Ghosts can possess a body easily when the person is emotionally distraught."

A pensive silence followed as I considered what Macha said. I had conjured Violetta's ghost with the intention of finding a counter curse to the Four Revenants, but instead she had shown me nightmarish scenes and memories. It left me reeling, breathless, and dizzy. Violetta had led me to the Neathror blade, which I now realised wasn't an athame-sabre to be trusted. Had that been intentional too? What games were Violetta playing? What reason did she have to haunt the basement? It wasn't because her children were here. That night I'd ordered her to watch over them... well, she'd looked like she'd wanted to rip her water-stubbed teeth into their flesh. Dead or alive, no mother would want to do that to her children.

Macha was right. Something was wrong with Violetta's soul.

Macha started to fade in and out of the mirror. "It is nearly daylight here. The moon's magic is waning. Soon our connection will be lost." She leant forward. "Zaya, if you see Violetta again, stay away. Do not interact with her. Do not give her a reason to try and communicate with you. Understood?"

I nodded.

Understood? How could anyone understand any of this?

The connection vanished, the mirror a silver reflective screen again A weird mix of feelings entwined themselves in me. I had answers, but the answers had led to more questions. I was on a carousel of enquiries with no chance of jumping off and landing on any solid conclusions.

Clorenzo cleared his throat.

Guilt crushed me. It took a moment to get my voice working. "I'm sorry you had to hear that."

My apology didn't seem to move him at all. His weary gaze

flicked between his children and me. "Do you really think Violetta would be capable of something like that? Harming Livel and Sarith?"

I wrapped my arms around myself. "I don't know. I never knew her. Macha seems to think so." I offered him a sad smile. My own frustration diffused in the face of his despair.

He dragged his eyes back to the corner of the basement where Livel and Sarith slept. "She was a dedicated mother. She loved her children. She loved us. When Oli died, we lost Violetta too."

"She was depressed." I didn't know what else I could say.

"Yes, but there was a madness that started in her too. It's what led her to trust Mayor Belov in the first place." He leaned forward in his chair, elbows resting on his knees. "You're not going to think highly of me when I tell you this, but when Violetta died, there was just this sense of… relief. I was relieved that it was over. She was short-tempered all the time. She would watch Livel and Sarith sleep. At first I thought it was because she was scared of losing them like she had lost Oli. I thought she was being overprotective. But then she would start to pinch and hurt them. Livel and Sarith don't remember any of it. I bought a memory spell from the apothecary and made sure they had no recollection of their mother that way." He dropped his head into his hands. "I knew even before that fateful night at the beach that Violetta was going to die. I think I had already accepted it… wanted it."

I was seized by a jolt of alarm.

He flinched at my shocked stare. "She would have taken her own life eventually. She couldn't overcome the pain. Every moment of every day was torture for her. She was always agitated and doing risky things. I just knew."

"Knew what?"

"That it was her plan to die. I just wanted it to be over too."

I shuffled my feet on the wooden floor, uncomfortable from the dark direction our conversation had led. "Did you try to help her?"

He didn't answer for a long moment. "In the end I accepted that she didn't want my help. Sometimes, you just have to learn to let someone go."

My hands gripped firm together. The statement shook me.

"Sometimes, you just have to learn to let someone go."

Violetta's story was sad, but was her fate inevitable for Jad too?

CHAPTER 16

There were no more surprises from Violetta. Every day became the same. I'd wake in the morning. Eat breakfast with Livel and Sarith. Research the Kerr family grimoires until lunch. Exercise what I could in the afternoon—which consisted of me jogging laps around the basement and doing sit-ups—followed by more research, dinner, bed. Sometimes I'd play dolls with Livel. Sarith was never keen for me to get close to his toys—something about girl germs. That was fine. I found his homemade spider and lizard figurines creepy. If it weren't for the small clock on the wall, I'd have lost track of day and night.

Time became my biggest enemy. Every day that passed without learning something new about the counter curse added to my misery. I grieved for every moment I'd lost in the outside world.

My evenings were invaded by nightmares. In them, I'd be standing on the beach, breathing in the sea air and gazing at the horizon. Warm sand submerged my feet as I ventured to the water's edge. Jad would be there, his eyes crinkling at the corners as he smiled. He'd reach out for me and—

The dream would fall apart. My eyes would open, my consciousness returned to the humid air in the basement, my heart grappling with hollow disappointment. I couldn't blame Violetta for these dreams. These nightmares were solely mine. How Livel and Sarith were still sane and managed to sleep was a mystery. They'd been living in the basement far longer than I had. I supposed when you're a kid, your imagination could take you places. I envied that childish innocence.

My withdrawal symptoms from the Neathror blade hadn't lessened over time as Macha predicted. They had intensified. My headaches were severe. My hands often shook, my fingers and toes numb. Paranoia escalated each night the moon strengthened, a constant reminder that time was against me. It became a fight not to give in to the dark stretches of despair, but the more my symptoms increased, the more I fell into depression. I feared I would never truly get out of the basement.

On the morning of the full moon, I woke as anxious as a person about to commence their first bomb disposal. Clorenzo changed his shift with a newly recruited dissent rebel to work alongside me. We had only hours left to find any scraps of information on the revenants. It pained me that more casters signed up with the ULD every day. The people of Scarmouth had lost so much that they'd decided to join the enemy rather than have their lives taken by it. Either way, they'd lost.

Clorenzo and I sat together on the floor, surrounded by grimoires. I tried not to let the exasperation show on my face, but with every minute that ticked by, my apprehension increased. What would happen if I didn't find a counter curse? Something bad. I sensed it in my bones—in the very air I breathed. It was the same intensity that built up before a storm, as though the world knew something dangerous was about to occur and it cringed tighter in response.

Clorenzo narrowed his eyes. He twitched a finger on a page. "Found anything yet?"

I scowled. My heart pounded double time whenever I peered at the clock. "No. Not a damn thing. I've looked at all these grimoires twice. There's nothing in here."

What the hell am I going to do?

Clorenzo shook his head absently. "Let's stop for lunch."

I ate a little food, which only made me nauseated, and went back to studying. Providence knew what was wrong with Livel and Sarith in the afternoon. Sarith screamed at his father. He threw his toys against the walls and stamped his feet, a little temper tantrum that pierced my eardrums. Livel wouldn't stop crying. She curled up into a ball on her bed and scratched at her arms and legs. My concern increased when she drew blood.

Clorenzo had abandoned the grimoires for his diary, probably writing to Darius in the hopes of obtaining some last-minute information. He dropped his book and glared at his children. "Enough. Sarith, pick up your toys and stop shouting. Livel, stop hurting yourself."

Sarith's face broke into an ugly scream. "Nooooo. I want out of here. I want to go to the beach. I want Mum."

Livel pulled the bed sheets around her small legs and kicked and thrashed. "I want Mummy too. I want Mummmmmyyyy."

I had to cover my ears for that one.

Clorenzo flew toward his children in a blur. "She's gone. You both know this. Stop this ridiculous behaviour now."

He had his back to me, but I could imagine flames in his irises. I shifted around and focused on the grimoires. The Sujik family dispute was really none of my business.

One hour.

Two hours.

Three hours passed.

Still, I'd found nothing.

Exhausted from their tantrums, Livel and Sarith had fallen asleep in their beds. I had no idea how Clorenzo had managed it. He sat at the table reading a grimoire.

How can he be so... calm?

Me? The more I looked at the clock, the more panic swelled inside me.

Four hours.

Five hours.

It would be growing dark outside soon. The full moon would be a silver coin in the sky, illuminating the world into a new period of darkness.

"Zaya is an intelligent girl and resourceful. Do not underestimate her for a second. If she is unable to find a counter curse in the family grimoires, rest assured she will find a way on her own. In that I have confidence."

That's what Darius had said in his journal entry.

Thank you, Darius, for the tremendous amount of pressure.

I threw my mind into another grimoire. There were celestial spells, divination magic, candle charms, and ancient invocations, but nothing about counter curses... or the Four Revenants. I slammed the book shut.

Six hours.

The nocturnal chorus of cicadas and katydids reached my ears. The damp air in the basement dropped a few degrees as the night closed in. I would have found it beautiful once, a reminder of summer and all the wonderful things the warmer weather brought in the evenings, but now it was an announcement that my time had ended.

I've failed.

My mouth went dry. I was dizzy with the need to be sick. "I haven't found anything. Clorenzo... I have nothing."

He peered up from his book. I expected him to be angry, afraid, reproachful, but all he did was close the grimoire. "Come sit with me."

My butt and legs ached from sitting cross-legged on the floor. In a daze, I wandered to the table and sat. I stifled a groan. "I'm sorry. I couldn't find anything in the grimoires. I have nothing."

My gaze flicked to Sarith and Livel asleep in their beds. My hope to save them from the horror that surrounded Scarmouth came crashing down. Clorenzo had every right to be furious with me. It was possible the Four Revenants would be resurrected tonight. Mayor Belov would have complete access to them, which meant Morgomoth would have control. If this were a game of chess, he had us at checkmate.

Clorenzo tipped his head up to the ceiling. "It will be okay." His voice was flat and held no conviction. "We've survived this long… and we don't even know for sure if anything will happen tonight. Everything so far has been guesswork."

I pinned him with a dark stare. "That doesn't inspire my confidence."

"Maybe this will." He passed his open journal across the table and pointed to a passage. "It seems Darius has managed to drive some sense into the Council. The Haxsan Guard are just beyond Scarmouth with orders to break the ULD's celestial shield down. Your friends aren't far."

My pulse jumped with something I hadn't experienced for a while. Hope.

Marek.

Talina.

Lainie.

My friends were close.

My brief optimism crumbled when a more sinister thought crept in my head. "If the Haxsan Guard are here, it will make the ULD more desperate. They'll raise the Four Revenants that much quicker."

Then there was the problem with the celestial shields that surrounded Scarmouth. They couldn't just be broken down. It took an incredible amount of magic to rip them apart, strength not even an army possessed.

That meant my friends were in danger. I hadn't only failed Clorenzo and his children but Marek, Lainie, and Talina too. The

Haxsan Guard would be the first casters Mayor Belov ordered the Four Revenants to destroy.

Clorenzo shot me a weak smile. "I have other news. It's been said among some of the officers in the ULD that Vulcan Stormouth is frequenting a place called Darthmusk. It's a fortress of some kind, rumoured to be built out of the skulls and bones of humans." He swallowed audibly. "I'm telling you this because… perhaps that young man of yours is there."

What I felt after Clorenzo shared that was what I imagined explorers experienced when they found gold. Darthmusk had become a piece of hope in the puzzle, small and fragile but something to go on.

I squeezed his hand. "Thank you."

"I hope you find him." Clorenzo rubbed at his eyes, the black under them more profound. "My children have been so unlucky. They've lost their brother, mother, and grandmother to the sea. I don't want to see anyone else experience loss."

I eyed him oddly. "Grandmother?"

Clorenzo hitched his shoulders. "Yes. Didn't I mention it? My mother-in-law, Edith, died three years ago. She walked out to the sea and just… disappeared. No one saw her again. Her body was never found. Sometimes I think this family is bloody—"

"Cursed." I had a very, *very* bad feeling about this.

All the thoughts in my head gathered for a crisis meeting.

Three deaths in the sea. That isn't just a coincidence. There's more to it.

I shut my eyes and tried to evoke a memory from a month ago.

"Centuries ago, it's said five caster women, all with the last name Kerr—my wife's maiden name—bound the Four Revenants to a watery grave in the sea off the coast of Scarmouth."

That's what Clorenzo had told me.

And I'd said, *"Blood magic, right? The Kerr family bound the Four Revenants, meaning only blood magic could unbind them."*

I peeled my eyes open. I couldn't believe how frigging stupid I'd been.

"Clorenzo." I grabbed his arm and forced him to look at me. "I don't think Oli's death was an accident."

He stared. His eyes were vacant. He looked... sleepy?

"Clorenzo. Think." I slapped his face. "Clorenzo, this isn't the time for a nap. Listen to me."

What is wrong with him?

"Yeah," he answered in a sleepy drawl.

I yanked on his sleeve. "Five caster women bound the Four Revenants in the sea. It makes sense that five sacrifices from the same bloodline are needed to wake them. Edith, Oli, Violetta. I bet they each died on a full moon."

Which meant....

My gaze wandered to Livel and Sarith.

Five sacrifices.

Two more blood relatives are required.

I launched off the chair. I had to get Livel and Sarith out of here. Their father had to hide them somewhere else.

Clorenzo dropped to the floor. The glass of water he'd been holding smashed into fragments. The sound was sharp and excruciating in my head. I crumpled onto my knees. An ache throbbed from my ears all the way down to my toes.

This isn't normal. This is....

All the details in the basement went fuzzy around the edges.

I'm under some kind of... spell.

I turned to the beds where Livel and Sarith slept. My stomach gave a shudder of repulsion. "Stay away from them."

I tried to blink the fog away, but I didn't have to see clearly to know who was there. Violetta stroked Livel's tiny face. The little girl woke, her eyes wide and terrified. She scrambled back against the headboard with a scream.

Violetta's water-soaked face, curtained by tendrils of dark hair, remained close to her daughter's. Somehow, the ghost had made herself corporeal. *"Don't be afraid, honey. I'm here."* Blood seeped from the fish-bitten marks in her neck. Fat drops of blood dripped onto Livel's bed.

I scrambled onto my elbows and knees, but I couldn't find the energy to crawl. "Livel. Get away from the bed."

Violetta brushed the soft red curls from her daughter's face. *"Wake your brother, sweetheart. We're going to the beach."*

The last thing I saw was Livel climbing out of bed, calm and robotic, under a trance.

"Livel. Don't. Run. Get away from her."

The swell of emotion constricted my throat.

My head hit the wooden boards.

Darkness closed in.

CHAPTER 17

I woke to the smell of dust. The sensation that my head was as fragile and heavy as glass dulled my focus. I was flat on my stomach, my neck crooked at a painful angle. I blinked to push through the grogginess. Tiny details fluttered in and out. Floorboards, aged and rutted. A ceiling with soggy water damage. Children's toys scattered across a grimy floor. Empty beds.

Empty beds?

Distant recognition stirred inside me. I struggled onto my hands and knees, my vision see-sawing up and down.

Clorenzo rested by the table, his eyes closed and his mouth slack. His lower lip hung like a lopsided grin.

Clorenzo?

Everything felt disconnected, surreal.

I crawled toward the vacated beds.

Empty beds.

Clorenzo on the floor.

Empty beds.

Violetta.

My insides did a queasy tap dance.

Violetta!

She's responsible for this!

The spell detached itself like a dog shaking off water. I was finally able to think clearly.

Livel! Sarith!

Violetta had taken them.

I struggled across the floor to Clorenzo. "Wake up. Wake up, you moron. I need you awake."

I slapped his face to rouse him. He didn't move. Violetta's spell had him heavily sedated. He was a male version of Sleeping Beauty.

How the hell could a ghost do this?

It was further proof that no matter how far I advanced with wraiths and necromancy, I was still a novice.

And on my own.

Violetta was taking Livel and Sarith to the beach at this moment. She might already be there.

How did she get the kids out of the basement?

I cast a hasty look around. My eyes stopped at the wooden stairs, the trapdoor open. I got onto my feet and leapt up the steps with hurricane force. Inside the house, eerie grey light leaked in through the windows, casting foggy apparitions in the corners of my eyes. The farmhouse was as much a tomb as it was a home, a place to protect Violetta's ghost and provide her with a dwelling for the afterlife.

Outside, the landscape was abandoned. Wind swept through the wheat fields, the night sky a calm black sea. The moon was a large waxy sphere that made the stars barely visible. Everything was deceptively quiet. I got the distinct impression that this was the calm before the storm.

I dashed across the road toward the rainforest. The tension in my muscles multiplied as the sound of gravel under my shoes became painfully loud. The air was warm and heavy with moisture, my clothes already clinging to me with sweat. Ahead, the lush tropical terrain remained its perfect, dubious picture of tranquillity, it's evergreen and kapok trees offering cool relief from the heat. But I knew better. I also knew the rainforest was the most direct way to the beach.

Just my luck.

Inside the rainforest, my feet struggled against the spongy undergrowth. I wished I had Neathror to cut through the vegetation. Scarmouth and the surrounding areas had received copious amounts of rain in this last month, and the rainforest seemed to have grown twice its size. Sharp, twisting branches scratched my arms and face. A network of tree roots dipped in and out of the ground in what appeared to be a deliberate trip hazard. My lungs burned, but I never slowed down.

Livel and Sarith must be so frightened.

Their behaviour all day had been uncharacteristic, which had seemed strange at the time but now made perfect sense. It was the spell. Violetta had been weaving her ghostly magic even then.

She's their mother. They'll trust her.

I was so preoccupied by my thoughts that I failed to see the tree branch in time. It whacked me so squarely in the chest, my body was thrown like I'd been hit with an electrical charge. I lay on the forest floor, the pain taking too long to subside.

That one's definitely going to leave a bruise.

Deep staccato beats ricocheted through the trees.

Drums.

The sound was haphazard, then prolific, a tribal rhythm that became a fast, furious throb in the rainforest.

I was on my feet again, not giving my body the time it needed to recover. I come out to the beach, the warm sands lit by torchlight. The tribespeople I'd encountered a month ago danced and frolicked in a circle, their heads tilted up to the moon, eyes rolled back into their sockets. This time they had no undercasts to sacrifice. They were celebrating a very *different* kind of ritual.

The image sickened me.

By the shoreline, Violetta led Livel and Sarith into the water.

She held their small hands, the three of them moving in slow unison, as though they were in a funeral procession. The waves gently lapped at their feet, then their knees.

She's going to drown them.

My chest burned from having run so fast, but I sprinted across the sand. "Livel! Sarith! Stop! Stop!"

No matter how hard I shouted, the children continued into the water.

Why won't they turn around? Are they... in a trance?

The water was up to their chests now. Soon, Livel and Sarith would be submerged.

I ran into the waves. "Livel. Sari—"

Breakers swept over me. The salty water stung my eyes. Was the ocean trying to prevent me from reaching the kids? I kicked off from the sand with each dip and rise until it became too deep even for that. "Violetta, stop this."

She turned. The cold twist of her mouth curled into a dangerous smile. Parts of her features were washed out. She was like a porcelain doll smoothed and rounded by the waves.

I kicked to stay afloat. "Don't do this."

The ocean was putting up a fight around me, but for Violetta and her children, it was calm and smooth. The trio turned and walked deeper into the sea. A moment later, Livel and Sarith vanished in the waves.

Mounting tension cut through my throat in a scream. I dove into the wave, refusing to be washed backward, propelled by adrenaline.

I broke through the surface into the calmer waters. "Violetta."

She spun around. This time her razor-thin smile vanished as I smashed my fist into her mouth, the bone-splitting crunch hinting that I'd knocked some of those stubbed teeth out. She hissed and rose like some kind of monstrous sea serpent.

In front of her, Livel and Sarith burst through the waves. They coughed and wheezed. I couldn't tell if Livel was crying or blinking water out of her eyes. She reached for me with her small arms. I held the children, determined to get them away from the creature that wore their mother's guise, because I was convinced now that this was no longer Violetta. This was something else entirely.

"Livel! Sarith!" a voice screamed from the shore.

Clorenzo. He must have woken from the spell not long after I had. The knot in my stomach unravelled. I had never felt such relief.

My fingers latched tighter to Livel and Sarith. "We're going to swim to your dad, okay?"

They both nodded. I think they were too exhausted or scared to do anything else.

Clorenzo waded into the water. I remained behind the kids, using my strength to push them closer to the shore. This time the waves worked in my favour. The ocean's surging energy ripped Livel and Sarith from my hold, washing the pair onto the beach where they were immediately embraced by their father. But the water had other ideas for me. The waves smashed into me with downward force. My body spun around in a maelstrom. I couldn't swim to the surface. I didn't know where the surface was.

Something tugged my leg.

A reef?

No.

It was more solid than that. More animated.

I twisted around, greeted by a face that was as much slime as it was flesh. The figure's jaws opened like a basking shark's, the leg joints bent outward as it scrambled in a spider-crab motion toward me.

My lips parted in a watery scream.

Violetta wrenched me along the sea floor, farther into the deep.

CHAPTER 18

Violetta was one seriously pissed-off wraith. She'd drowned in this peninsula. It made sense that her body remained here, half submerged in the sea floor or entwined in the coral. I knew from resurrection experience with Lunette that a ghost possessing their own body was unnatural. From what I'd witnessed, it was an incredibly painful experience for the soul. Violetta was willingly putting herself through torture by occupying her decomposed body. She really wanted me out of the picture.

And she was going to drown me to achieve it.

Her long fingers—fingers I imagined once played the piano but were now wrinkled meat on bone—wrapped around my neck. Pressure burned in my throat. When she looked at me, all I saw were empty black sockets where her eyes should have been. The sea had taken those too.

The current wrenched us back and forth. Powerful undulations slashed Violetta's arms and legs, tiny pieces of her floating away for the fishes.

Blood pounded in the back of my head. My body had lost its final store of oxygen. Every muscle gave out to exhaustion.

This is it. The end.

I'd never thought it would be from drowning.

I sank onto the sea floor. Nothing bothered me anymore. Calmness took over, a blissful nothing. Even the pain had evaporated.

Realisation drove through me.

If I die, there's no one to save Jad.

There's no one to save Clorenzo or his children.

I knew what had to be done to thwart Morgomoth's plans and ensure the Four Revenants weren't raised. It would come at great personal cost, but that was the sacrifice that had to be made.

Neathror, I need you!

I really could have benefited from the blade's help about now.

Something solid materialised in my hand. It quivered like a disembodied pulse to zap new energy into me.

I opened my eyes. Neathror. I'd summoned the athame-sabre.

"Neathror feels power. It has been wielded by necromancers in the past. Necromancers who chose for their magic to become dark. The blade sucks that energy in, getting stronger, binding itself to that caster and using them. I believe Neathror is trying to corrupt you."

Corrupted or not, the blade was here.

Defying what was possible underwater, the sabre became weightless in my hand. I struck at Violetta, the weapon moving with a mesmerising yet unearthly glow. It cut through her wrists. She howled in pain, which surprised me. I didn't think a dead body would feel anything. Her hands floated away into a thick cloud of bubbles.

The blade must have lent its power to me, because suddenly I had the energy to kick to the surface.

Please, please, please, let me make it.

Beneath me, Violetta waved her arms to prevent sinking, but without her hands, she had a difficult time propelling herself upward. She sank into the dark, leaving only a few bubbles behind before they too disappeared.

I broke through the surface, the air ecstasy to my lungs. The surf threw me like a cartwheeling rag doll, over and over until it discarded me on the grainy sand. For a moment, all I could do was lie there and breathe. Neathror still pulsed in my hand, but the energy had faded. It had done its part.

"Zaya."

The tiny voice drew my attention.

Livel's eyes were inflamed and bloodshot from crying, her red hair a wet tangle that curtained her face. Clorenzo was kneeling between his children, his arms wrapped tight around them. Water stained his trousers. He didn't move. None of them moved. That struck me as odd, until my senses caught up with me. My eyes lingered on the cast-shooter levelled at Clorenzo's head.

The tribespeople had us surrounded, their clubs, bows, darts, and spears all aimed on me, which seemed a tad overboard. Their cheeks moved in impossible little flutters, as though insects ran beneath their faces. But there was something else that wasn't right about them. Their heads lolled on what appeared to be broken necks, their arms and legs bent unnaturally.

They're possessed.

These casters were marionettes, tugged by an invisible puppeteer. They were as trapped as I was, only they didn't know it.

How long have they been dead?

Unlike Violetta, who had full and conscious possession of her corpse, these dead casters were soulless zombies, free labour to carry out nefarious tasks.

Who has the power to do that?

"Hello, Zaya."

The voice was smooth and assertive, but beneath the surface was something toxic.

Mayor Saana Belov appeared from behind the tribespeople. She smiled at me like we were long-lost friends. Wickedness worked its way across her beautifully exotic face. She wore a vibrant ruby dress, just as exquisite and magnificent as the last one I'd seen her in, only this one moved and flapped in the wind like flames from an uncontainable fire. It gave the impression that Mayor Belov was the devil.

She surveyed me from head to foot. "So, you're the little necromancer I've heard so much about." Her delicate feline features studied me with a lion's grace.

Neathror was still in my hand. Either through me or the situation, it sensed a threat. The blade's power resurfaced, invigorated by its own strength. No way would I let the mayor throw Livel and Sarith to the sea. Not after everything I'd endured to save them.

"Don't do this. They're just kids."

Saana dissolved into peals of laughter, girly and throaty. "Don't be ridiculous. The children had to willingly sacrifice themselves for the curse to be complete, which, thanks to your part in this, isn't going to happen now." She lost her smile. "I worked for months on their mother. She was my vessel, my way of spying on the children. Violetta was meant to drown them."

A mix of fear and disgust burned inside me. "You killed Edith and Oli too, didn't you? Five sacrifices from the Kerr bloodline are required to raise the Four Revenants. Edith. Oli. Violetta. You possessed them with magic. You murdered them."

And Livel and Sarith were next.

Clorenzo's eyes widened with baffled horror. If it weren't for the cast-shooter pointed at his head, I knew he would have lunged forward and ripped Mayor Belov apart with his bare hands.

Livel and Sarith started to cry.

Saana pointed an enraged finger at them. "You. Quiet." Her eyes focused on their father, her dark cloud of hair floating behind her. "Do not worry, Clorenzo. You will have vengeance on Mayor Belov soon."

I started at that.

She's talking about herself in third person? Vengeance... on herself?
My grip tightened on Neathror.
Something is very wrong here.
Saana saw the blade. A hint of a smile crept along her face. "I

see my athame-sabre has found its way back to you. I think it's feeling conflicted about its allegiance."

I hid the blade behind me like a kid concealing a lolly from a parent. My brain went into overdrive.

Her blade?

Macha's warning flared bright in my head. *"I told you that Neathror had been in necromancers' possessions in the past. That its magic unites and grows stronger with the caster it binds itself too. Who do you think was the last necromancer to possess it?"*

My horrible train of thought exploded on impact. It left one impossible yet coherent answer in its wake. "Morgomoth."

The name tasted foul on my tongue.

Saana uttered a heinous laugh. "Finally."

Something about the mayor's eyes had always bothered me. Dark and perceptive, they'd never seemed to fit with her delicate features. Now I understood why. Morgomoth had never linked his mind with Saana's. He *was* Mayor Belov.

The eyes that were not Saana's pinned me in a listless black gaze. Her complexion, the shape of her face, the healthy nourished skin—it started to change. What transformed in its place was a skeletal facade with stretched skin. Veins matted together under decomposing flesh. Wind gusts carried its foul odour to me. I covered my nose, every nerve inside me assaulted by the stench. Shadowy mist hovered around the decrepit figure. No, not mist. Locusts. They swarmed around the body, a single dark entity that oozed together and moulded into a new form until the shell of Mayor Saana Belov was gone.

I stood numb with fear.

In her place stood Morgomoth.

CHAPTER 19

The air didn't seem to reach my lungs as questions ricocheted off every surface in my skull. *Has Saana been dead all this time? Or was she a host? How can Morgomoth be here, inside her like an intestinal worm? How has he been possessing her when he's meant to be cursed into an eternal sleep? Or was that a lie too?*

My eyes darted to Clorenzo. He stared at the creature before him. Sweat beaded his upper lip as his arms tightened around his children in an endeavour to shield their eyes. Livel and Sarith buried their faces in their father's chest, but it did little to hide their sobs. My heart burned from racing. There was still a gun trained on Clorenzo's head. How was I going to get the Sujik family out of here?

"Zaya."

Morgomoth's voice was a callous, grisly rasp—the wretched hungry breathing of a creature that shouldn't exist. His body erupted into a rioting, fluttering swarm of locusts again, reappearing as Saana... or at least in her form.

She smiled, but the predatory look remained in her eyes. "Zaya, Zaya, Zaya." She shook her head with feigned disappointment. "You ruined my resurrection plan at Galvac, and now you ruin my plans for the Four Revenants. You have left me partially hexed. My mind is awake, allowing me to possess this magnificent vessel." She lifted her arms, showing off Saana's sculpted perfection of beauty. "But my own body is still cursed and rotting in a casket."

Her voice, or rather Morgomoth's voice, rose to a scream inside my head, multiplying into a crescendo. A veil of black spots swept over my vision. In the corner of my eye, Clorenzo and his children squirmed from the same affliction. Morgomoth—even when he wasn't in his true form—was still powerful. Misery crushed me.

Saana laughed a quiet chuckle that lacked humour. "The Larthalgule blade revitalised me to some extent, but I still need your blood to fully restore my body."

Her gaze slid from my face to my hands. Her eyes lingered on Neathror with greedy anticipation.

The blade pulsed. Did it sense danger? Or could it hear its true master calling for it?

I swallowed the knot in my throat. "Why are you here, Morgomoth? What do you want with the Four Revenants?"

Saana tilted her head to the side. "I'm here to finish what I started. Destroy the Council of Founding Sovereigns and purge the world of humans." Her eyes lit up with pure homicidal delight. "With the Four Revenants at my side, I'll achieve it."

I flinched. Whatever semblance of calm I had was overcome by desperation. "I just stopped you from doing that."

"No. You prevented Violetta from sacrificing her children." Saana wagged her finger at me. "I don't think Violetta's heart was truly in it. I often had to conjure her soul and manipulate her into doing my bidding. There were times when she nearly did work her way out of my spells, but I caught her again, just in time... every time."

I recalled the night I'd summoned Violetta for help. She had taken me on a long, confusing journey through time, showing me the Four Revenants and their sea of victims. For reasons I didn't understand, she had carried me to the past, introducing me to Vulcan as a teenage boy. She'd taken me to Jad. At the time, I thought Violetta had been messing with my head, torturing me with her ghostly psychological games. But now I wasn't so sure. Had Violetta been trying to show me something else? Were there clues in the places she'd taken me to? Had Violetta been trying to reach out for help?

My blood foamed like a can of shaken soda. I wanted to scream or cry or throw myself in front of Saana. I wanted to beat Morgomoth out of her. "What are the Four Revenants? What do you want with them?"

Saana had been staring at the ocean. She turned to face me. "I want my blade back."

My eyes widened. Neathror slipped out of my hand. It soared across the beach straight into Saana's, the hilt snug between her fingers. In her grasp, the black dagger looked twice its size.

I stared, unsure what to do. My weapon to defend myself—if it even had been mine—was gone.

Saana's eyes narrowed into slits. "I need the Sujik family blood to resurrect the Four Revenants. You will not stop me."

She raised the dagger, the slender end aimed in Livel's and Sarith's direction. The runes along the athame-sabre blazed alight, throwing a kaleidoscope of patterns across the beach. Livel and Sarith screamed. I tossed a hand over my mouth. The skin along their arms slashed open. Somehow, Neathror's magic tore into their flesh, as though the children were cushions to be ripped apart. Blood spilled from the wounds. The tribespeople had wrenched Clorenzo away and held him down against the sand. He struggled and cursed. I worried they might kill him right there and then.

Uncontainable rage overwhelmed me. The scream that burst from my throat was otherworldly. It was thunder and the roar of the sea combined. It was earth-shattering and eruptive. A ringing in my head detached me from every other sensation. All I could identify was the single word that spilled from my mouth and the fury that encompassed it. "Stop."

The tribespeople went utterly still. They didn't blink. They didn't breathe, though I suspected under Morgomoth's control they hadn't been breathing for some time. Clorenzo tore out of their grasp and gathered his children together. He stared at me with conflicted horror, his face pale and damp. He turned Livel's and Sarith's heads away to prevent them from seeing me. I distinctly heard the words "Don't look."

Saana laughed, but this time it was underscored with a hint of panic. "Finally embracing the darkness inside you. Maybe you're better equipped to join the ULD after all."

I looked down at my hands. Terror dangled over me. My skin was grey and rotting, my fingers nothing but bones with a few meaty bits of flesh. They looked like they'd been pecked at by vultures. I flailed my arms, trying to shake the illusion off, because surely that's what it was. My hands morphed back into their regular shape. I touched my face, my neck, my hair. It all seemed normal.

Had that illusion been all over me?

Saana snapped her fingers. "You lost control of your power, Zaya. But that little display of necromancy won't stop me. You're too late."

She held a glass vessel. Inside was a red liquid that resembled—

"Blood." Saana lifted the vessel higher. "I have the last of the Sujik bloodline right here. You will not stop me from raising the Four Revenants."

Confusion pressed down on me. Somehow, she'd managed to transfer Livel's and Sarith's blood into the glass. I drew in a deep, frazzled breath. "The bloodline has to willingly sacrifice themselves."

What is Morgomoth playing at?

She brought the glass vessel to her lips, offered me a short toast, and drank. Watching her guzzle it down made me want to bend over and retch. Some of the blood missed her mouth and ran down her neck to soak into her dress. When she finished, her teeth were stained red and dripped.

She stepped into the water. The moonlight cast a cloud of silver-white across her tanned skin. She stared at the moon. "The bloodline willingly sacrifices themselves."

Too late I realised what Morgomoth intended to do. I sprang forward, but I couldn't stop Saana. The athame-sabre gleamed like a glistening set of stars. She dragged the blade across her throat. Her eyes bulged in surprise. I think Morgomoth may have departed her body then. He was finished possessing her. To him, Mayor Belov had reached her expiry date. She stared at me, as though she wasn't sure of who I was or what was going on. Horrible gurgling sounds worked their way up her split throat. She was drowning in her own blood.

The ghastly image burned into my eyes.

Saana dropped into the water. Her blood floated around her.

No.

Not her blood.

Livel's and Sarith's.

Sujik blood.

A cry welled up inside me.

I've failed.

Morgomoth succeeded.

And that means….

The sand beneath my feet quivered. The entire beach lurched, the force tossing me to the ground. Over by the cliffs, loose rocks and boulders fell into the sea, causing a tremendous explosion of water to jet into the sky. The trees in the rainforest bent at unnatural angles. Some of them uprooted and pitched. Even the sky grew darker, the stars and moon closed off.

I climbed onto my feet and fought to stay upright. "Clorenzo. We need to leave. Now."

When I reached them, Clorenzo lifted Livel into my arms. He

took up Sarith. Neither child complained. They knew it was far safer to be in adult hands.

Panic sweat broke out on my face. "We have to get to higher ground."

Clorenzo's voice was stiff, frozen. "What about the house? We could go back there."

I shook my head. "Scarmouth's done for."

And if we didn't hurry, we would be too.

The sea had already drawn away. On the horizon, an ocean monster rose. A churning, whirling storm of water was coming toward us.

CHAPTER 20

"Run!" I screamed. "Run!"

We broke into a sprint, desperate to put distance between us and the water. Our boots fought for traction on the sand. Damp, muggy wind tore at our clothes to hamper our momentum.

Providence, please, please, let us make it.

Livel locked her small fingers around my shoulders. Her panicked cry sent a dart of pain through my ears. She'd seen the wall of water. There was no reasoning with Livel now, no little assurances that we would be safe. She wasn't stupid.

Clorenzo's stride was faster than mine thanks to his height, and he made easier progress up the beach. I stepped where he did to make quicker headway. When we reached the rainforest, I stole a glance behind me to see how far the surge was. The tribespeople stood assembled together facing the colossal wave. They looked like tiny figurines in comparison. I imagined their eyes still glazed, not seeing the reality before them. I honestly had no idea what was wrong with the tribe, or if it was even fair what was about to befall them, but their fate had been sealed. The wall of water was a vertical line as far as the eye could see. Nothing could be done for the coastline. This was not something anyone could fight—only evade.

Livel's squeal of protest snapped me back to my senses. I plunged ahead into the rainforest. The forest floor trembled and bucked. Tree trunks upturned. Branches crashed into broken, scattered chunks around us, setting an obstacle in our path.

High ground. We need to find higher ground.

I had been locked away in a basement for the last month and had no recollection of Scarmouth's layout.

The temple ruins. We could go there. No, not high enough. And it would force us to run parallel with the water, not away from it.

My chest tightened. Each mouthful of air burned my lungs rather than revived them.

We could climb a tree.

Impossible again. Judging from the height of the wave, the entire rainforest would be underwater.

Renewed by fear, the adrenaline inside me worked double time in my legs. I caught up to Clorenzo. Sweat dripped off his nose and chin. His hair was soaked, the muscles in his arms taut as he strained against Sarith's weight. I knew how he suffered. Livel felt like she'd doubled in size since we'd left the beach.

Something hit me hard on the side. I could barely keep my hold on Livel as the little girl screamed. Her arms clung tighter to my body. The thing that had collided with me kicked and bucked. No, not a thing. A very frightened pair of brown eyes made contact with my own before the okapi ran through the underbrush toward safety. We were not alone. Monkeys howled in the trees, and lizards scurried through the leaves on the forest floor, their senses sharp and their movements faster than we could ever hope to be.

Follow the animals.

Clorenzo had the same idea, and we trudged up the track in pursuit. The smallest flare of hope blazed inside me. Scarmouth was on higher elevation than the rainforest.

Maybe... maybe we'll be okay. Maybe we'll—

An ear-splitting roar enveloped the earth. It sounded like a formation of fast-approaching fire-crusaders, but I knew the truth. The wave had smashed on the beach, destroying Scarmouth's coastline.

It's coming through the forest.

The town's warning sirens blared ahead, the alarms intensifying the closer we approached.

When we arrived in Scarmouth, chaos had already ensued. Screams doubled in volume as sleepy residents left their houses, their eyes suddenly wide and alert, their faces pale as realisation dawned on them. They ran in haphazard directions. Some headed for the hills that on a normal night would have sheltered the town from southerly winds. Others hurried to the forest to climb the trees. I wanted to shout that it was useless, but my focus was on keeping the Sujiks from harm. There was no time to help the misguided.

A gunshot erupted. I twisted around and searched for the culprit. It was followed by another. And another. Dissent rebels fired into the crowd. They screamed and spat orders. "Get back! Get back! Inside your houses. Now! Get back!"

They think this is a false alarm. They think someone deliberately set off the warning to break curfew.

The crowd became a formidable force of confusion. More gunshots were fired. A woman barrelled into Clorenzo. He lost his balance and toppled, his cry indicating something worse had occurred than a scraped knee. Sarith scrambled out from underneath his father. The boy was covered in blood. Horror replaced my distress. Sarith wasn't hurt, but his father was. Clorenzo lay on the ground bleeding. My stomach dropped. He'd been shot in the upper thigh.

There's no way he can run now.

Dizziness swept through me. I hadn't been prepared for such a bad stroke of luck.

I plopped Livel on the ground and pointed to a narrow road between two dilapidated houses. "Help me lift him. We're taking him over there, in the laneway."

Clorenzo's eyes were pleading as he struggled to talk. "Take the kids and run. Climb onto the roofs if you have to. Leave me."

It had crossed my mind, but compassion smothered the thought. "Shut up, Clorenzo."

I was beyond fear now. Beyond the thought of my own safety. Beyond the thought of dying. Livel and Sarith were all that mattered. They had lost their mother, brother, and grandmother. I wouldn't let them lose their father too. I wouldn't let them lose their lives.

Please. Please let this plan work.

We carried Clorenzo through the hectic crowd. His weight became a struggle the more he slackened. By the time we'd slipped into the laneway and set Clorenzo on the ground, he'd lost consciousness. His head lolled to the side, his pale face splotched yellow and feverish.

Livel's voice broke into a short gasp. "Is he going to die?"

We're all going to die if I don't get you out of here.

I swallowed too quickly to be believable. "No. He'll be fine. Now I want you both to take your father's hands. Can you do that for me?"

They sat beside their father and interlinked their tiny fingers with his.

"Good work. Now keep your eyes closed. No peeking."

Hot tears trickled down their cheeks, but they did as I instructed.

I tossed the panic in my mind aside to invoke a level of calm.

"Lunette. Violetta. Adaline. Please, are you there?"

I hadn't thought about Adaline in weeks, but she had been a strong presence in my life back at Tarahik. Her death linked us, and now I needed her help. I needed all their help.

I had no idea if this would work, but I had to try. Something had happened to me on the beach. Something I had never experienced before. There hadn't been a chance to contemplate what it meant, but there'd been no denying the power that had coursed through me when I'd appeared... dead.

Alarm rippled inside me. Even now, I sensed a force in me writhing to get out.

"Lunette. Adaline. Violetta. I invoke you to come forward."

The roar of water approached, only this time it was accompanied by the crash of everything and everyone—uprooted trees, wiped-out houses, screaming people. It was water and thunder and destruction, accelerated to drown Scarmouth.

"Please. I need your help."

This was treading on dangerous ground, both physically and spiritually.

"Please. Please."

A high-pitched hum filled the air.

"Zaya?"

I opened my eyes. They were standing there, three angels of glory and beauty. Light glimmered from their translucent skin. It was impossible not to be awestruck. No longer under Morgomoth's control, Violetta inched toward Livel, her soft fingers brushing red curls from her daughter's face. Livel probably thought it was just the wind.

The ghosts weren't wearing their death wounds, though I knew at the slightest annoyance they could change into three goddesses of death, swift to bring punishment and destruction. Something I'd learned about ghosts—they excelled at being unpredictable.

Their eyes were luminous, but their faces lacked expression.

"Please. Take us away from here. I know you can do it."

I was a necromancer. They had to obey me. Right?

I recalled Lunette's words at Valdavar Tower. *"All you need do is ask. I can't ignore a necromancer's demands."*

So why weren't they doing anything?

Blind, hot rage erupted inside me. Power I could no longer control expanded from my body. The ground lurched. The windows along the alley burst in cascades of glass. Even in the house next door, the light fixtures burst. Tremendous pressure built in the laneway, but it was my voice that drowned out every other noise. "Do it now!"

Lunette and Adaline took hold of Livel and Sarith, their fingers wrapped tight around the children. Violetta knelt beside her husband and rested her head on his. I was seeing the true Violetta, the woman who loved her children and husband dearly. I wondered if the Sujiks could feel the presence around them or if this was a miracle only I witnessed.

Lunette's blue eyes locked with mine. *"Where are we taking them?"*

There was only one place we could go. "Weeping Hollow. Take us to Macha."

Macha would be able to protect us. Livel and Sarith might even be able to leave the house and explore the grounds—supervised by Macha, of course. They'd have the chance to be kids again. Clorenzo would get the healing and care he needed. I could start my real mission and find Jad. It was a perfect plan and something I wished I'd achieved a month ago. Stupid damn powers.

Lunette reached out to me. *"I'm sorry, Zaya. Three wraiths. Three casters. We do not have the power to cross dimensions with all four of you. Your magic is what gives us strength, and at this moment you are too weak."*

A claw of ice cinched my heart. "Okay. Get them out of here. Now! Please."

Lunette's water-blue eyes filled with sorrow. She turned away from my gaze.

Wind whipped through the lane, tiny spits of water blown in like we were in the midst of a rainstorm, but I knew better. The wave was close.

The wraiths faded away to empty space. A moment later, the

Sujiks receded, as though they too were smoke vaporised by a breeze.

Leaving me to face the wall of water alone.

CHAPTER 21

My throat was dry with terror. Jad's face was the one clear thought that drummed in my mind.

Survive for him.

I broke into a run, imagining the gigantic tidal wave smashing windows, tearing brick from mortar, crumbling walls like they were made from sand. I pictured water flooding my mouth and nose, filling my lungs to suck the oxygen away like a vacuum.

My feet slammed against the ground hard in a desperate bid to live, but my mind had already accepted the inevitable. There was no way I could survive. That point was proven further when I crossed into the street. My cry bounced off what was left of Scarmouth's remaining buildings. The water was coming from both directions.

"Zaya."

Lunette's voice flowed thick and fast through my mind.

She was here?

"Zaya, let me in. Before it's too late."

Dark waves rolled across every surface of the street, a swirling vortex of blue and white that raised its ugly head like a striking cobra. And in the midst of it, the most unlikely thing. Horses. Black. Sleek. Muscular. Definitely not the size of any ordinary horse. The creatures' hooves traversed through the waves, the water having no impact on their strong legs. If anything, the surge seemed to dip and eddy around them, fuelling their strength and speed.

Transfixed, I watched the four riders approach, their faces beautiful, commanding, and severe. It was impossible not to be awestruck by the two men and women. I'd heard old human fables about angels and how they embodied glory and power. For the first time, I believed it. Sunlight seemed to glisten off the male riders, their skin luminous and their faces handsome yet cherubic. They were astonishingly attractive with their perfect cheekbones and symmetry. The women were like the Amazon warriors of old, long braided hair floating behind them, their bronze-coloured skin illuminated with golden light. These were not the four riders I'd seen depicted in the monument when I'd first arrived at Tarahik. They had been draped and obscured in death robes. This was something else. Was this the Four Revenants' true form or just the way they wanted to be perceived?

"Zaya, it's not real. It's an illusion. Let me in. Let me in."

Lunette's voice floated to the edge of my mind. I couldn't prevent my eyes from absorbing the Four Revenants' supreme beauty.

"Zaya, let me in. If not for yourself, for Jad. Let me in."

Jad!

The spell broke. The scene ahead transformed, the glamour torn away. The Four Revenants were terrible in aspect. Exposed bone broke through their skin, the chunkier parts of their flesh slimy and scaled. The clasps and buckles which had held their rich garments before were not ornamentation and clothes at all but seaweed, seashells, and—I swallowed—bones. When they saw my frozen gaze, they grinned with malevolent pleasure, revealing jagged teeth.

"Let me in, Zaya. Now is your only chance."

I didn't know what that meant, but I agreed to it. "Yes."

A rush of energy coursed into me. The strange force expanded through every muscle and vein until it had immersed even my skin. When I looked at my hands, they were no longer my own. When my eyes travelled down my body, it wasn't *my* body. Lunette hadn't been speaking figuratively when she'd said *"let me in."* She was me. Or I was her. She was possessing me. We had become the same person.

Her voice echoed inside my head. *"Stay calm. This may feel a little strange."*

I looked up—or we looked up—just in time to see a hand reach for my face, the talon nails about to sink in my cheeks.

But I didn't have to duck or dodge the Four Revenants. I felt myself peeling away, slipping into a place where there was only grey cloud and smoke.

And then it was completely dark.

MY EYELIDS FLUTTERED OPEN. A briny scent invited itself into my nostrils. Warm light streamed through the clouds, the air muggy. Rain must have been on the horizon. It was a pleasant sensation lying there, but something wasn't right. In that half-conscious moment, the memory of what had occurred stung with striking clarity.

The Four Revenants!

Lunette... possessed me!

We'd disappeared into... what?

I sat up too fast, my surroundings taking a moment to settle into focus. I was on a flat stretch of rock that overlooked a vast estuary. The water wasn't blue but brown, thick and dark as tar in some places. Uprooted plants, trees, and debris floated on the surface.

"It's Scarmouth."

I jumped at the voice right beside me. Lunette's eyes seemed to mist over. She wasn't corporeal, flicking in and out like an image on a hologram screen, her movements static. *"I came back. I couldn't leave you to that fate."*

My eyes wandered back to the devastation. I had failed Scarmouth. I had failed to find a counter curse. Morgomoth had raised the Four Revenants, and he'd done it while asleep in a comatose body. If he could possess the likes of Mayor Belov, he was more powerful than anyone had realised. He was more powerful than I had allowed myself to acknowledge.

Lunette shifted beside me. Sadness stretched over her pixie-like face. *"You need to leave this place, Zaya."*

I winced. The air was humid, but somehow my feet and hands tingled with what I imagined were the first symptoms of frostbite. I gritted my teeth against the cold. Had the blood inside me turned to ice?

Lunette stiffened. *"It's all the death that has occurred around you."*

I crossed my arms tight over my chest to preserve the warmth I had left. "But I witnessed death on a massive scale at Galvac when the dam collapsed, and I never experienced anything like this."

"That's because your necromancy wasn't as powerful back then. You accepted your magic tonight. Now you're more in tune with it. You saved the Sujiks. You should be proud."

"I'm not proud." I wiped my hand across my cheek. "I'm scared and tired and cranky. I don't understand any of this."

"All you need to understand is that necromancy is no longer a potential magic inside you. It is you. From now on, you will feel death just as you feel the wind and the sun."

I gave her a flippant stare. "Thanks, you're really selling it. You should work in marketing."

Lunette covered my hand with hers. *"Leave this place now. The Four Revenants are hunting you. Morgomoth wants you found."*

She pointed in the direction of the mountains. In the sunlight, the mountain ranges had never looked more treacherous or inhabitable. The foothills were a maze of tropical jungle, the uppermost level covered in bare rock so high in the sky it was covered in snow. The peaks disappeared into the clouds. I imagined glacial ice and blizzards.

Lunette squeezed my fingers, something I didn't think was possible for a ghost. Or was it because I had changed that she could now achieve physical touch? She peered down at the polluted estuary. *"The Haxsan Guard have made camp at the bottom of the mountains. Go there. Find your friends and leave."*

"But the celestial shields... I can't pass them—"

"The celestial shields are gone. They were torn apart with the rise of the Four Revenants." Her fingers tightened on mine. *"You can't stay here. Once you find your friends, head to Port Serres. There are smugglers there. You'll be able to board a ship out of here to Vukovar."*

My spine tingled. "Vukovar is a different continent. You're asking me to leave Navask?"

"Yes, thank you. I know my geography." She stared with determined resolve. *"The Four Revenants can't be stopped. Morgomoth can't be stopped. Everything has changed now. He has won."*

Cold sweat broke out along my hairline. "He's only half alive. There must be a way to put the Four Revenants back into the sea, or wherever they come from."

Lunette shook her head. A mournful look dulled her eyes. *"Not anymore."*

The cold seeped in. Goosebumps popped out along my arms. "If I need to get out of here quickly, can't you just possess me again and take me to my friends?"

"No. You're not strong enough for another possession. At least not any time soon. I barely got you away from the Four Revenants. This was as far as my strength could take you."

Lunette tipped her head. She became as intense as a dog with raised hackles. Her voice was the thinnest whisper in my ear. *"They're not far. Follow me to the mountains. And be quick."*

CHAPTER 22

Hunted.

Lunette insisted I move faster. That was easy for her to say. She could glide through trees and float across rivulets with no worries. Me? I struggled against vines, fought to keep my footing on the leaf-strewn ground, and hit my head more than once against low-hanging branches. To make matters worse, Lunette's terrified eyes would roam our surroundings. It made me think the Four Revenants would jump out at any moment to snare me like a spider.

The only good thing was the cold had gone. Now that I was away from Scarmouth's devastation, death no longer held its icy grip. I was free to experience the sticky, damp air of the rainforest.

At first glance, the mountains hadn't seemed so far, but now the jungle was widespread and never-ending. Cicadas buzzed. The chorus of birdsong gave the impression of serenity, but deep inside I sensed something dark and vile approach. The jungle was no match for the horror that came for me.

"*Zaya.*" Lunette's voice hovered in my mind. "*Don't go near water, no matter what it is. Sea. Creeks. Rivers. Don't go near it. Understand?*"

I blinked sweat out of my eyes. *"What do you mean?"*

My mind-speak sounded fuzzy in my head.

Lunette hovered above the edge of a creek. Her keen eyes inspected the water. The ripples bubbled and ebbed, resembling the frothing undulations in a spa bath. The closer I approached, the more it boiled and jetted in geysers.

"Stay back." Lunette's voice sent a spasm of fear through my legs. *"Something isn't right. The water is strange. Don't go near it. We'll have to move farther east. It will delay us by an hour, but I'd prefer doing that than crossing this creek."*

We hiked for a long time. Sunlight dipped in and out through the canopy, making a slow trail across the sky. Lunette had to stop and wait for me to catch up, her arms crossed, eyes narrowed in impatience. If she hadn't been floating a few centimetres off the ground, I could have imagined her tapping her foot like an angry mother. No matter how fast I attempted to move, my feet remained graceless and heavy. My head was drowsy, my body exhausted. I'd used far too much power in Scarmouth and had drained my energy. Each time my eyelids drooped, Lunette's voice would climb to unimaginable levels in my head, forcing me to be alert.

As nightfall closed in, a blinding flash of light halted my step.

Lunette and I stared at each other. Our eyes communicated the same thought.

Lightning.

The next second, torrential rain broke from the sky. It caused a mini mudslide beneath my feet. Thunder bellowed between the grey clouds. The moon was blotted out, the jungle swarmed by monstrous shadows.

"Zaya." Lunette was beside me, her lips the same bloodless blue as the night she'd died. *"Run. The rain will continue and flood this forest. The Haxsan Guard camp is about a kilometre that way."* She pointed in the direction beneath the steep incline. *"You're so close. Run, Zaya. Run!"*

She vanished.

My heart thrashed against my ribs.

Okay, thank you. Wish I could just disappear like that.

Wait. Flood?

The rain teemed harder. I watched with horrified fascination as water crept over the land, spilling across the earth to form ponds. In under a minute, the rainforest resembled a swampland.

I drew in a rocky breath. Lunette's previous warning rose up from the deep niches in my mind. *"Don't go near water, no matter what it is. Sea. Creeks. Rivers. Don't go near it. Understand?"*

I ran, or tried to. The ever-increasing water swallowed my legs. Endless rain and gloomy vapour made visibility poor. I beat my way through the compact foliage. Wet branches slapped my face, my boots and socks drenched. Fear seized me. My feet had been coated in a thick lather of sweat for the entirety of the day. They'd stung and itched. Now that the rain had soaked in, trench foot was a real possibility.

Ahh!

My foot must have slid over a submerged rock, because in an instant, I was flat on my back and riding downhill on a natural waterslide. The ground went out beneath me. I plunged in a perfect diving acrobat—at least it felt that way—slicing into an incredibly dark pool. The water was icy the deeper I sank. Bubbles floated around me, almost relaxing. I could have pretended I was taking a dip in a deep swimming hole at the end of a summer day... until something scraped my leg.

Were there... faces in the water... all around me? Pale and rotting. Cheeks torn away. Eyes mucus-covered and cloudy.

"Don't go near water, no matter what it is. Sea. Creeks. River. Don't go near it. Understand?"

I kicked to the surface, sensing that something heavy and bloated reached for me from the depths. I scrambled to the water's edge, half expecting to be wrenched back into the deep. Fighting the haze of shock in my mind, I forced myself to crawl through tufts of long grass. Nothing pursued me, but that didn't mean I wasn't being watched.

There were bodies.

In the water.

How?

I gasped in happy relief. Not too far from the treeline was the makeshift military camp. The tents swayed, the shelters struggling to stay intact in the heavy rain. The Haxsan Guard wanted me just as much as I was hunted by the ULD, but I no longer cared about being seen. Anything to get me away from the water.

Ahead were a handful of communication trucks, sandbag barriers to fortify positions, and armoured personnel on watch. Hopefully they would see the wave of floodwater coming toward them and forget about shooting me.

Find the medical tents. That's where Talina and Lainie will be.

For the first time, I was grateful for the heavy rain. It provided the cover I needed to climb the sandbags and drop unceremoniously on the muddy ground. I kept low and manoeuvred my way past the sentinels who were perched high on a makeshift viewing platform. The storm had intensified. They wouldn't be seeing anything no matter how strong their binoculars were.

The campsite was a ghost town. Anyone who wasn't on duty had no doubt decided to stay put in their tents. I weaved through the labyrinth of inflatable shelters, searching for a medical cross.

What if Talina and Lainie aren't on duty?

Was Marek at this camp? Where would he be stationed?

He's in love with Talina, so a good guess is right at her side.

Darting around what I assumed was a large accommodation shelter, I arrived at the medical tents. All thirty of them. A long line of expletives erupted in my head. My friends could have been in any one of them—and only if they were on duty.

I shut my eyes. Lunette had said necromancy was a part of me now. It was time to test that theory. I ignored the rain, the lightning, and the thunderclaps, and focused on nothing but my breathing and heartbeat. I sensed movement. Gentle whispers of the dead flowed into my ears. I didn't know who they were, but somehow I knew they belonged to the rainforest from long ago. They were as old and ancient as the trees. Wise and accepting of their fate. It was almost as though… they'd become part of the rainforest.

"Please." I fought hard to keep my voice projected and calm. *"Tell me where my friends are. Where are Talina, Lainie, and Marek?"*

Whispers swept over me in a cold breeze. *"Tent 22."*

I opened my eyes. The spirits were right. The tents were numbered.

The rain pelted harder, nature itself against me. I sloshed through the mud to tent 22. My heart leapt in nerves and excitement. For so long I had been alone. For so long I had sat in the Sujiks' basement feeling unworthy and isolated. Even though I'd had Livel and Sarith, even Clorenzo on occasions, their company couldn't detract the pity, self-loathing, and despair that had struck me night and day. The world had moved on, and I'd been stuck, forgotten. I had missed Talina, Lainie, and Marek so much. It seemed incredible that the only thing dividing us now was polyester composite.

I slipped through the tent flap, astounded by what I saw on the other side.

CHAPTER 23

The mobile medical unit was deathly quiet. Except for the rain outside and the metrical whistling that rose and fell as ventilators cycled, there was nothing. Sedated patients were strapped in blankets on hospital beds, tubes hooked to various parts of their bodies as liquid spells worked their magic. These were Scarmouth's survivors—or what was left of them. I crept among the beds, which had been arranged in six neat rows. The patients had been cleaned, but the odour of rainforest and seawater lingered around them. I wondered if that smell would ever disappear.

Few nursing staff were in attendance, which was good and bad. It meant those on duty were too busy to take any notice of me, but it also meant there was every chance my friends weren't here.

"Excuse me, are you lost?"

I turned. That voice was… familiar, only I was used to the tone being gentle and calm, not directed at me with suspicion.

I nearly cried. Talina was in her nursing scrubs, her blonde hair braided in what would have been dedicated precision by her but had become unkempt from a rigorous shift. That's what I'd missed most about her. Her pride in her appearance and the way she forgot about it when it came to helping others. The absence of make-up made her appear fragile and young, tiny freckles evident on her cheeks. I wasn't even aware she had freckles.

She raised her hand to keep distance between us. "Did someone send you in here for treatment? Are you hurt?"

She looked at me as though I were a deranged person in need of serious medical help.

She's probably not wrong.

The smile that had worked its way across my face vanished. "Talina, it's me."

She studied my mud-sodden skin, matted hair, and filthy boots.

Fair point.

Her eyes widened in recognition. "Zaya!" Despite my filthy clothes, she embraced me in a bone-crushing hug. "Zaya, where have you been? What happened to you? Were you in Scarmouth? Did you... were you caught in the wave?"

Before I could respond, she ushered me out of the medical unit into the pouring rain. She gazed around the camp, her brow scrunched with wariness. "Zaya. Everyone is looking for you. The Haxsan Guard say you're a terrorist and a spy for the United League of Dissent." Panic climbed in her voice. "You can't be here. I have to get you out of this camp. If you're seen—"

"Stop." I grabbed her arm before she could turn away. "We can't stay here. Morgomoth unleashed the Four Revenants. That tsunami that wiped out Scarmouth... that was them. The Four Revenants are on their way."

A blank expression crossed her face. "The four what?"

Oh right. I have explaining to do.

Her eyes turned wide and afraid. "Wait. Did you say Morgomoth?"

Dread swirled inside me. "Listen. I'll explain everything, but first we need to get out of here. Where are Lainie and Marek?"

Heavy footsteps approached. An elongated shadow appeared around the tent.

The taste of fear flooded my throat.

Talina linked her arm with mine, and we dashed through the rain, kicking up mud, which soaked into our trousers. I could feel it running down my legs to turn into a cold puddle in my boots. Talina's nursing scrubs were ruined. Her long braid flew out behind her as we weaved through the rows of medical tents. The anxiety of the past twelve hours had zapped me of energy. My legs strained to move. All I craved was a shower and a warm bed to sleep in.

"In here." Talina unzipped a heavy-duty canvas flap and pushed me inside. The tent was designed for sleeping and nothing more. Sitting in a circle cross-legged on sleeping mats, Marek, Lainie, and Edric played cards. The trio looked up from their game, aghast at seeing what no doubt appeared to be a homeless beggar in their tent.

My eyes started to tear up. "It's me."

Lainie dropped her set of cards. "Who the fuck is 'me'?"

Finally, someone who speaks my language. How I've missed you, Lainie.

She rose to her feet. Except for being a little thinner in the face and arms, she hadn't changed. Her black hair was set in a stylish bob, the red streaks highlighted by the camping lantern. Dark, puffy skin made her eyes roundish and small, as though she spent her evenings crying into her pillow while everyone was asleep.

Marek scrambled to his feet. Recognition dawned in his eyes. His hair had grown longer since I'd last seen him. In the lantern, it was mousy blond. He was taller than I remembered too, or maybe his promotion to lieutenant had given him confidence and he simply stood straighter now.

Disbelief filled his eyes. "Zaya."

Lainie spun around to take a closer look at me. She darted forward, wrapped her arms around me, and then struck me on the arm with a nasty slap. "Never disappear again. We didn't know if you were alive... if the ULD had you... if the Haxsan Guard were hiding you in a prison somewhere. Why didn't you let us know you were okay?"

Talina intervened. "Now's not the time. We have to leave this place."

Marek shot an uneasy stare in my direction. "What's going on?"

I explained what had happened in Scarmouth, the reason I had been there in the first place, and what was now on its way for the camp. "There's something unnatural in the rain. Something... dead in the floodwater."

The news sent their already alarmed faces into a bleached-white pallor. Edric was the only one who remained calm, his legs crossed on the floor as he stared at the discarded pack of cards without interest. His blond shoulder-length hair hung limp, his face haggard and drawn. When I'd last seen Edric, he was receiving help for shell shock. The fact that he was here meant the treatment had been discontinued. I knew after the atrocities committed in Essida, guilt and shame had burdened Edric. He'd broken off his engagement to Lainie and, from what I could see, had completely withdrawn from everything and everyone. Maybe the pair had tried to remain friends, but they wouldn't look at each other.

Marek ran his fingers briskly through his hair. "There are celestial shields around the camp. Nothing passes the celestial shields."

I shook my head. "I was able to enter the camp. Somehow the Four Revenants obliterated the temporary shields at Scarmouth. They've done the same thing here."

The fine lines around his eyes tensed in frustration. "If these... Four Revenants are coming, I have to warn the captain."

But it was too late. Horrible screams erupted outside. My stomach clenched and churned. The awful smell of bog water drifted in the air.

Talina visibly shook beside me. "What's happening out there?"

She went to undo the tent zipper.

I jerked her hand away. "They're here. We have to leave. Now!"

Marek already had his camo rucksack on his back. He strapped a second one around Talina's shoulders. Lainie tugged Edric onto his feet, tossed a rucksack into his arms, and quickly threw one against her own back.

She plucked up another pack from an empty mattress and flung it at me. "Here. Use Mica's."

I caught the rucksack. "Won't she want it?"

"Mica's dead. Stood on a mine a few days ago."

I swallowed emotion in the back of my throat.

What have my friends been through?

Marek helped me strap the rucksack on. "We keep extra food, clothes, and blankets in the bags at all times. You never know when there'll be an emergency."

I breathed in deeply in an effort to steady myself. "We should head for the mountains. We have to stay on high ground. These things came from the sea. Somehow they can manipulate water. We can't go near puddles, ponds, rivers, or creeks."

Lainie flicked on a flashlight. "What about the rain?"

I stiffened at the question. "I think rain is okay. At least before it hits the ground."

I hope.

The screams outside intensified. A series of short blasts resonated through the rain, and then the never-ending staccato boom of cast-shooters and gunfire erupted. Not even the tent's thick canvas could hide how the night outside turned bright with the glow of hexes and explosions.

Marek was at the back exit of the tent. He signalled for everyone to hurry. Edric went first, followed by Lainie and Talina. When I reached the exit, Marek caught my arm. He tilted his head so the others wouldn't hear us. "Zaya, the only way out of here to the mountains is through the marshes."

The marshes?

But that meant... water!

A roar pierced the night, like some huge firework had been let off. The ground shook from the ripple of detonations.

Summoning my courage, I tried to sound more confident than I was. "Then we'd better run through the marshes. And fast!"

CHAPTER 24

I flung my arms against the blades of grass that grew in two-metre-high tufts around us. The marsh was overrun by thick, heavy reeds, which made it difficult to get any understanding of our course. If it weren't for the mountains—Marek told me they were called the Kanzina ranges—we'd have no sense of our destination. Marek ran in front. I went second, followed by Talina, Lainie, and Edric. There was a mutual unspoken understanding between us—*stay in line, follow the person in front, and keep up.*

Nature had other ideas. Rain sent streams of ankle-deep mud over our feet. Running turned into walking, which turned into wading. Each time I stepped into the marsh's spongy surface, I felt as though I had concrete blocks strapped to my boots. Every second, every step, every breath became harder.

My stomach cramped at the sound of Lainie's loud expletive. "This is impossible, Zaya. We can't move fast enough."

Keep your voice down. Keep your voice down!

Marek's eyes caught mine with alarm.

I tried to keep my voice low but level. "It's not much farther. We have to push through. We can't remain here... not with the water rising around us."

Lainie gestured grandly at the marsh. "And what exactly do these creatures do to the water? Because as far as I can see, it's just rising."

Is she serious? Is Lainie actually second-guessing me? Does she think I made all this up?

I was spared answering by a blood-curdling scream. Something tramped through the marsh ahead. The reeds swayed and thrashed in the rain, not giving us a clear indication of what was coming. None of us dared move. Something approached, its gait startlingly zombielike.

Marek took out his cast-shooter, his finger poised on the trigger. The pressure inside me inflated. A yearning desire for Neathror swept through me.

What I could do with that blade.

No. Don't think like that. Don't think about Neathror at all.

I shook my head clear. Even in the face of danger, I couldn't sever the blade's hold on me.

The creature made a low grunting sound in its throat as it lumbered through the reeds. My heart rate soared, then dipped as recognition dawned. I knocked Marek's cast-shooter aside. "Don't. They're one of us."

He was covered in mud, but I could just identify the insignia for the Haxsan Guard below his shoulder. He must have been on duty and fled when he knew there was no hope for the camp. He didn't appear injured, but he was breathing hard. He looked like he'd fallen head first in the water a few times. He crossed his arms and stashed his hands under his armpits for warmth. The way he stood, he resembled a patient in a straitjacket.

The cloud cover that coasted over the sky parted. The moon lit our surroundings.

I stepped back. "Crawley?"

Private Crawley was one of the first soldiers I'd met from Tarahik. He'd assisted Jad and Marek with my transfer from Gosheniene to the military base and hadn't been kind during the process. I recalled him nodding off to sleep and letting Marek and Jad do all the work. He was a bully, a coward, and idle at his duties. He must have fled the camp as soon as he detected conflict —not that I really had any right to judge him on that.

Marek recognised him too. This time I leapt in front of the lieutenant to stop him from using his fists.

A voice shouted from farther in the reeds. "Crawley? Where are you?"

It was followed by another, more feminine voice.

Someone came loping through the tall grass and nearly barrelled into Edric. I swept my eyes over the panic-stricken young man. Tusk Monahan, Tarahik's superficial jock, stared back at me with poorly disguised horror. I had broken his nose during a late-night gym session back at Tarahik, and it had never quite healed. The slight crook was more noticeable with the rain running off it. It wasn't entirely clear whether he found me or the thing he'd been running from more frightening.

The female voice that I vaguely recognised shouted in the night again. "Tusk? Crawley?"

Half a second later, a blonde girl in tight-fitting trousers and a soaked pink sweater appeared. Make-up ran down her face. The red in her eyes indicated she'd been crying. For a moment I was sorry for her, but then I saw who she was, and my compassion boiled into an inferno.

Indree Raminorf made a whimpering sound of relief when she saw us. She ran straight into Marek's arms.

Typical princess bitch needs rescuing.

She clung to the lieutenant's shirt. "Those things are coming. Whatever attacked the camp is in the swamp."

"Marsh," I corrected, then immediately scorned myself for my petty jealousy.

What had Jad seen in her? To actually be *engaged* to her? It was a mystery I would never understand.

Another pinch of misery cinched my chest. Indree didn't know Jad was alive. Neither did Marek. Eventually the time to announce that their supposed dead best friend and fiancé was actually alive and imprisoned in a labour camp would arise, but for now it would have to wait.

I thumped a hand on Marek's back. "Keep moving. And you"—I shot a nasty glare at Indree—"step in line and shut up. You've made so much damn noise you've probably led those creatures right to us."

I had only wanted to scare her, but it turned out there had been total truth in my words. Grisly, slimy popping sounds whipped at the reeds behind us. It was exactly what I imagined a giant squid would sound like as its tentacles glided over a surface, suckers latching with a watertight seal.

Something shifted in the water ahead.

No.

It didn't.

The water changed.

It rose and moulded shape.

It morphed into a new....

Indree screamed.

The creature had definitely been a caster at some point. That much was identifiable. It was covered in slimy mucus, its skin and face feasted upon by sea bugs and hagfish. My heart gave a terrified shudder. I had a terrible feeling we were looking at a servant of the Four Revenants—at one of the "undercasts" who had been sacrificed at the beach. Morgomoth had done it. Somehow, the sacrificial ritual had made this caster into... a zombie. I remembered the old human folk tales about the undead. Boy, had they gotten those tales wrong. This thing was reanimated by necromancy, but it was also partly monster.

And it could become water.

And we were surrounded by water!

The creature opened its jaw. Long, thready mucus hung from the tentacles around its mouth. It snapped and snarled, its gaze heavy and hateful. I recalled the first evening I'd slept in the ruins in the rainforest. A cry that had sounded part animal, part monster had woken me. Now I knew what creature had been on the hunt that night. The undead had been scavenging around Scarmouth for weeks.

The water around the creature's feet bubbled. We stood transfixed as a second creature emerged.

Then two.

Three.

Four.

"Go! Run! Run!" I cried.

No one needed to be told twice.

The undead tramped in the water behind us. We beat back the reeds that clawed at our arms and clothes. Marek did his best to make a clear path through the tall grass. We really could have done with a machete about now.

"Keep moving," I insisted.

The marsh was sprawling and confusing. More of the undead came in from the sides. I was amazed at how Marek kept his focus single-mindedly on our escape, weaving us in and among the grass and shooting any creature that sprang forth to hinder our way. Each time he shot the undead, the creatures would erupt in a fountain of innards that dissolved into the black water, but then the slimy, bubbling mess would merge together, and the transformation would take place all over again.

These things can't be stopped!

They closed in like a pack of wild dogs, grunting and snarling.

We're not going to make it. They're going to rip us apart.

Marek shoved his way through the tufts of grass into a clearing.

A clearing!

I was out of breath and plagued with fatigue, but I knew stopping wasn't an option. Not when it meant certain death.

We didn't stop running until we were some distance from the marsh and the rain had eased. When I snuck a glance behind me, the black water in the marsh was still, reflecting the silver moonlight with tranquil deception.

I shivered and hurried away.

CHAPTER 25

We stayed in a cave that night. It was reasonably dry, but cold air from the wet seeped in, sending us all into a shiver frenzy. My cheeks stung and my ears were numb. None of us dared suggest lighting a fire or even switching on our flashlights. Thank providence we had our rucksacks with spare clothes and sleeping bags or we'd freeze. For once, I looked forward to the humid air that suffocated this terrain during the day.

We took turns showering at the mouth of the cave where it was private. My heart thumped double time when I suspected a puddle was forming around my feet, my body tensed for some heinous, undead creature to emerge. It wasn't a luxurious shower by any stretch of the imagination, but it served its purpose.

In the cave, we sat huddled on our sleeping mats. No one spoke. Shock and disbelief still held a firm grip on us, and everyone flinched at the mere hint of a rustle in the trees outside.

Talina drew herself into a ball and wrapped her arms around her knees. "What do you suppose those things were out there?" It sounded as though she struggled to get her voice past a whisper.

Tusk evaluated her with quiet disgust. "Pretty frigging obvious, don't you think? The fucking undead. Things that shouldn't exist."

I opened my mouth to yell at him, but Marek beat me to it, only his voice was level and calm. "They're called chak-lorks. The waterfaring dead. They're myths... or at least I thought they were. They have the appearance of the undead, but they can manipulate and travel through water. Drains. Pipes. Plumbing. None of that matters to them. So long as water is around, they can get in."

Indree made a whimpering sound. Apprehension crawled over her face. "What do we do for drinking water?"

I glared. Even though it was a good question, my envy made me petty. "They can't affect the rain, at least not till it becomes a puddle on the ground. We have enough water to drink for two days."

Marek and I had taken everyone's drink bottles outside and filled them with rain. We had looked at the canned food that was mandatory in rucksacks and calculated we had enough for a week. Water was going to be our biggest issue. It rained frequently in the rainforest, but with these creatures around, water was both our best friend and our biggest enemy.

"Two days?" Indree's gaze jumped from Tusk to Crawley to Marek, as though hoping someone would contradict it. "Why not just go back to the camp? The attack would be over by now." There was a waver in her voice which I knew meant she didn't quite believe it herself.

Lainie whistled and rolled her eyes. "There'd be nothing but bodies left there, bimbo... and chak-lorks feasting on them. Do you really want to go back there?"

Indree gulped. "Why can't we just call for help? Tarahik would have sent more Haxsan Guard soldiers. They'll be on their way. We have flares. We can signal that we're here."

It was Crawley who lashed out at her, his lips pulled back in an ugly sneer. "You are so bloody stupid. Look at her." He pointed at me. I stared. *Me? What have I done?* "She's a known terrorist to the Haxsan Guard. And they're her frigging friends." His fingers swept in the direction of Marek, Lainie, and Talina. "They're not going to hand her over, idiot."

Marek's face was flushed with concern. "You're right on both accounts. The Haxsan Guard will be on their way… and we're not handing Zaya over." He focused his attention on Indree, Crawley, and Tusk. "If you three want to wait for the Haxsan Guard, that's fine. But I suggest we all stay here until the morning. At dawn, we leave."

No one said anything, which to me meant there were no objections. Talina settled into her sleeping bag. Lainie dug into her rucksack and pulled out a can of vegetables from her field rations. Edric remained on his feet in a nonchalant, disinterested stance. His shoulders were so badly hunched—they always were now—that permanent damage must have been done to his spine.

Lunette's warning flared bright in my head. *"You can't stay here. Once you find your friends, head to Port Serres. There are smugglers there. You'll be able to board a ship out of here to Vukovar. The Four Revenants can't be stopped. Morgomoth can't be stopped. Everything has changed now."*

I sucked on my lower lip. *Should I say something?*

Edric interrupted my thought process when he gasped and clutched his stomach. The next moment, he tumbled onto his knees and vomited onto the cave floor, his face pale and blotchy.

Lainie rushed to his side. She brushed back his hair and wiped the sweat from his brow. The rest of us took a step away, as though Edric had caught an infectious disease.

Lainie held on to Edric's shoulders as he continued to retch. "What's happening to him?" She glared at me. Her eyes demanded an answer.

I threw my hands up. "Don't look at me. I have no idea."

Edric cried sharply. "It's my hand. Something is wrong with my hand. It's burning. It's on fire."

Marek swept past me to kneel beside Edric. He inspected the private's palm. "We have another problem."

I moved forward. Dizziness closed in at the sight of Edric's hand. When we were first enrolled as cadets at the Tarahik Military Base, we were made to cite the pledge of allegiance to the Council of Founding Sovereigns. The Infinite Eye—a triangle with a hexagon-shaped eye in the centre—had been branded into the palm of our left hand. It was a magical contract, a mark to bind us to the Haxsan Guard and serve the Council. Now, Edric's mark was covered in red blisters that oozed pink liquid. It reminded me of pork cooked in a frypan.

A sickening wrench played tug of war in my gut. "Everyone for the Council. No one outside the Council. No one against the Council."

Everyone looked at me.

I wiped my nose on the back of my hand. "We just fled. We defied our oath. The mark is punishing Edric."

In her sleeping bag, Talina appeared small and fragile. Her wet hair clung to her face and cast shadows over her eyes. "I hate to say it, but Zaya's right. My palm hurts, and I have an awful headache."

Lainie helped Edric into his sleeping bag. She rested her hand on his brow. The private's eyes closed. He was asleep in an instant. Lainie's ability as a harmonist still surprised me. She could inflict different moods on her subjects. This time, she had made Edric drowsy.

Wish she could do that for all of us.

I knew better than to ask. Lainie hated being treated like she was a doctor with a magic touch. Worse, she hated being treated like she was everyone's personal therapist. She'd repaid people with nightmares for asking for a lot less.

After she watched Edric sleep, she brushed the last of his matted hair from his face, then tore toward me. "If Edric's sick and Talina's feeling the side-effects, then we can only assume we're all going to get it."

Again, why was she directing her anger on me?

Marek squeezed the bridge of his nose. "Okay. We each have a first aid kit in our rucksacks. We take painkillers and sleep it off. We'll be fine by the morning."

I didn't miss the hesitation in his voice.

Indree sashayed forward in her muddy pants as though it were the latest trend on the catwalk. She folded her arms moodily across her chest. "Are you serious? We didn't abandon the Haxsan Guard. We fled for our lives. Because of her."

My breathing come out a little faster. "You didn't have to follow."

I wish you hadn't.

She flipped her hair off her shoulders. "I never broke any oath to the Haxsan Guard or the Council."

I tried on a sympathetic face, but it became more of a grimace. "In the eyes of the Council and the Haxsan Guard, leaving the camp meant we defied our pledge of allegiance."

She exhaled a long, pouty sigh. "We had to because of you. You brought those *things* to the camp."

"Those *things* are called chak-lorks, and they were already on their way."

I could have ripped the hair off her pretty little head.

Marek caught me before I could make good on my plan. "That's enough. Now is not the time to fight. Everyone take a painkiller and get some sleep. Understand?"

No one said anything. Marek had sounded so much like Colonel Harper. It was kind of nice to have someone take the responsibility for a while. I was exhausted, and my eyes were threatening to close. A sleeping bag had never looked more appealing—for both sleeping and smothering Indree.

The lieutenant peeled himself away from the rest of us. "I'll be on sentry duty for the next two hours. We need to keep a lookout. Crawley, you take the next shift."

Crawley stared up from his sleeping bag, mouth open in a perfect circle of surprise.

Marek ignored him and disappeared toward the mouth of the cave.

Everyone took a painkiller and settled in for the night. I pretended to pop a pill. I didn't think now would be the right time to tell them that my mark had disappeared weeks ago, especially when I'd experienced no pain. I wondered why that was.

Sleeping on the cave floor wasn't comfortable by any stretch of the imagination, but my exhaustion knocked me out. Strange, disjointed images swirled in my mind. I saw Jad swing his athame-sabre, slicing through casters who dared to oppose or resist him. His eyes were the same bloodthirsty red as the first night I'd dreamt of him. He lit houses alight, cut down the people who tried to flee, and bit down on their necks like a feral animal.

The dream changed.

Jad lay flat on his back, barefoot and shivering. The floor was soaked with blood. His eyes had returned to the colour of velvety night that I was so familiar with, but they were vacant and broken. A mad impulse to shake him took hold of me, but I couldn't. I couldn't touch anything. I was there, but I wasn't. There was no saving Jad from the anguish that consumed him.

"He's running out of time."

I jumped at the voice right beside me.

Violetta.

She wasn't wearing her death wounds. She looked beautiful. Her long black hair flowed out behind her, her skin intact and shimmering. Her lips were delicate and red. There was no sign of the nightmare she'd once been—the drowned corpse with a face full of sea maggots. Violetta had moved on. She'd found peace.

"The spells and experiments are weakening him. Soon, he'll be entirely monster. The captain you remember will be gone."

Sweat broke out on my skin. "How long."

"I can't tell exactly, but soon."

Her eyes met mine. *"You saved my family. For that I am grateful and willing to exchange my knowledge."*

I waited for the catch. Rule one with ghosts—their knowledge came at a price.

She caught my hand. Icy fingers pressed tight aagainst my skin. The cold swept through my entire body. *"There is a portal in the Otturin Cave on the other side of the mountains where you rest. That portal can take you anywhere. You may have a chance to save your captain."*

"Otturin," I repeated, ensuring I'd remember the name. "What does the portal look like?"

"It isn't your average portal. You'll know when you see it." Her eyes drifted back to Jad. *"Leave as soon as you can. He needs you."*

The dream started to fade. Colours swirled in and out, washing away like floodwater.

My eyelids flew open.

I had to talk to Marek.

CHAPTER 26

I cy tension crept up my spine. Jad was in trouble. I had to do something. There was no way he could be left to that fate.

Everyone was asleep. I tiptoed past, my eyes growing accustomed to the dark. The bleak moan of the wind and rain outside swept through the cave, producing a howling effect that gave me the creeps. Raindrops crept down the cave walls. It soaked into the soil but was not thick enough to form puddles—just enough to be alarming. I shivered and moved along.

I approached the jagged mouth of the cave and found Marek sitting on a rock that jutted out from the wall. He was using the moonlight to examine a map but kept himself hidden in the shadows.

His mouth twitched when he saw me. "Can't sleep?"

"Bad dream. What are you looking at?"

He patted the rock beside him.

I sat down.

He leaned in to reveal a mapographic, a hologram display projected out of a tablet. Each time he moved his fingers, the map shifted too to exhibit new terrain. He studied the topography with a deepening frown. "No matter what direction I look at, it's going to take us at least three days to get out of here. Maybe more if the rain keeps up and we have to hide from chak-lorks."

My eyes travelled over the landscape. After we'd escaped the marsh, we'd made some progress up the mountain. The view tonight was a never-ending display of lush green plant life, spectacular waterfalls, and fog sliding in and over the canopy. Parts of the rainforest appeared almost ghostly where the moonlight leaked through the clouds and rain, and despite the air being warm with moisture outside, inside the cave it was cold and dank. I couldn't stop shivering.

Shivering from the memory of the dream.

Shivering from Violetta's warning.

"Marek." I forced the words out of my mouth. "I need to go my separate way."

He looked up from the mapographic. It hurt to see the shock wave of betrayal run through him as he scrutinised my face. I wouldn't let him speak, not until he heard what I had to say. "I need you to take Talina, Lainie, Edric, and the rest of them, if they want to come, to Port Serres. From there, you can find smugglers who'll take you to Vukovar."

He didn't say anything for a long time. I grew increasingly uncomfortable the longer he stared. He dropped the mapographic on his knees, his tone curt but forced. "The ghosts have something else they want you to do, don't they? Or are you working on another secret mission for Senator Kerr?"

I flinched at his hostility—so very unlike Marek—and then his words settled in.

He knows.

I wasn't fast enough to hide my surprise. Marek exhaled a frustrated sigh. "Talina told me. I caught her snooping one evening on a tactical briefing. She was trying to learn information about you and your whereabouts. I knew something strange had been going on with you at Tarahik. It didn't take much convincing for Talina to spill everything: necromancy, Morgomoth, the plan Darius Kerr cooked up with Commander Macaslan to take down the Council."

I kept my face expressionless, but inside I was reeling. "That's because Talina trusts you."

"Yeah, well, I wish Jad had trusted me with this. I was his best friend."

"He was protecting you."

"Protecting me! If I had known, I could have prevented his death."

I let out a miserable laugh.

This is so not going the way I hoped.

Marek had been shaking with barely controlled anger. Guilt and pity flashed across his expression. "We just got you back. We can't—*I* can't—let you wander out there alone. We're out in the provinces. Jad would never have forgiven me if I did. He'd—"

"Just stop." My heart rate climbed. Telling him what I was about to divulge went against everything Darius and Macaslan had instructed, but I needed him to understand. "Listen to me. Morgomoth isn't fully resurrected, and look what he's already managed to achieve. He's raised the Four Revenants. They have an army of chak-lorks. Their purpose? Probably to murder who they deem inferior casters. Humans too." Emotion clogged my throat. "A ghost told me to leave for Vukovar. I want you to take our friends to Port Serres and head for the new continent."

He closed his eyes. Both reluctance and surrender reflected on his face. "If the ghost wants you to leave, it must have good reason. So why are you staying? I know it's important, or you'd be straight with us to Vukovar."

How am I going to break this to him?

Wind tangled my hair across my face. I brushed it back with my fingers. "Jad is alive."

The scowl faded from his face. His eyes pinned me in place. "What did you just say?"

"Jad's alive." The words sounded funny in my ears.

I took out the locket with Jad's mugshot. Marek's entire posture stiffened. I told the lieutenant everything, the visions, the dreams, Jad's true identity and the unfortunate circumstances of his lineage. Each secret revealed lifted a weight off my shoulders. I had no idea until now how much this had plagued me.

Marek didn't say anything for a long time. Shock. Despair. Relief. It all danced across his face before it finally settled on resolve. "No. You go to Vukovar. *I* will get Jad."

My tolerance reached its limit. "You don't even know where Jad is." The determination in Marek's countenance was unmistakable. This was going to be a hard fight to win. "Plus, I don't even know if you can save Jad."

"What do you mean?"

Anxiety cracked in my voice. "There's a portal. It's in the Otturin Cave on the other side of these mountains. I think it's a portal only necromancers can take."

Marek focused on the mapographic. He scrolled in on the mountains and the surrounding landscape. "It's not quite a day's journey from the Kanzina ranges." His eyes went wide with concern.

"What? What is it?" Blood pounded in my head again, my legs jumpy.

He looked up from the mapographic. The hologram sent flickering colours across his face. "The Otturin Cave is a sea cave."

I stared for an absurdly long moment. The sea. The place we were told to avoid. If chak-lorks originated from the sea, the chances were they'd be more powerful near it. Life wasn't playing fair… again.

Marek cradled a compass in his hand. He found north and pinned our location on the map. "We're going to have to risk it. Tomorrow, we head that way." He pointed somewhere off in the mountains. "It's not the most direct route, but there are fewer creeks. The river runs to the east, so we avoid that too."

I flinched. "Wait. What?"

We're going to have to risk it?

His mouth hardened at the edges. "No one is leaving anyone behind. It's too dangerous. We go together. We rescue Jad, and then we head to Port Serres."

"Didn't you hear what I said about the portal?"

"I heard every word."

"Then you know—"

"Necromancers can teleport the living with them."

An icy tingle shimmied up my spine. "Excuse me?"

His eyes sought mine. "Talina told me you transported her and Lainie once. We're going with you." The faintest smile crept across his mouth. For the first time, he looked like the Marek I remembered.

"That was an accident. I never intended to bring Talina and Lainie with me."

"Then it's a good thing this time you'll know how to do it for real."

I choked on the thought. I was still recovering from the last summoning with Lunette, Adaline, and Violetta. What if this portal succeeded in taking us all to Jad's prison but required too much of my magic and wore me out? We had no idea what we would face on the other side. Darthmusk could be a fortress, a tower, a military base. It was far safer if only one person snuck in.

"Besides"—Marek's focus sharpened on the mapographic —"Indree will demand coming once she hears Jad is alive."

Indree.

I gave an ironic snort. Of course she'd want to come. She had every right to. More so than me.

Marek's probing gaze watched me close. He must have seen something on my face, something that gave away my thoughts. "Why is it important for you to save Jad alone?"

I looked away to dodge the question. Sadness and longing fluttered inside me. I imagined my cheeks burning the colour of a flashing beacon, my embarrassment lit up for the entire rainforest to see.

Marek shifted his glance. "I'm an omniologist, Zaya. I read languages, including body language. I've suspected your feelings for a long time. Jad was fond of you. There's no denying that. But he thought of you as a little sister. Indree was... *is* his fiancée. When we rescue Jad, he'll be with her."

My throat locked up. "I know that. Jad saved me, and I owe it to him to bring him back. That's all this is about."

You total liar. Never play poker, Zaya. You'd suck at it.

Admitting it to myself was hard. For a long time, I'd put Indree on the back wall in my mind, preferably where I could throw figurative darts at her. I couldn't do that anymore. She was more part of this than me.

Marek took stock of our surroundings. The rain teemed harder. Fog crept in from the sides, the wraith-like tendrils curling around us. Soon, it would obstruct our view. "Go back and get some rest. Crawley will be here soon to take sentry duty. We'll discuss the plan in the morning with the others."

I made a casual sound of agreement, but inside I was fuming.

At the world.

At myself.

At my stupidity.

My feelings for Jad were unrequited. I needed to get that cemented in my head, even if it did make me sink like a stone.

I wandered into the cave. Marek never did hand me back the locket. Somehow, its absence was worse than anything else.

CHAPTER 27

In the morning we woke to the stench of wet, rotting vegetation. Judging from the subdued light in the cave, it was early sunrise. Already the humidity had risen, the muggy air providing an escape for the reek of decaying plants and wood. At least it was no longer raining. It meant the threat of chak-lorks would be minimal. Still, my mind conjured images of water-bloated bodies creeping through the rainforest.

Thanks to the painkillers, everyone had slept soundly, but the grim, uncooperative faces that surrounded me hinted that the Infinite Eye brand still burned.

After breakfasting on canned fruit, Marek laid out our plan. There was shock, surprise, wonder at the revelation that Jad was alive, and agreement on Talina's and Lainie's part to make our way to the Otturin Cave and find the portal. Edric shrugged. I didn't think he cared where he ended up. It worried me that he was so indifferent to everything and everyone. Indree insisted we pack our things and leave immediately. She didn't seem to understand what she was really getting herself into. I wondered if she'd still be enthusiastic after three days of waving away mosquitos and tramping through the forest in soggy boots.

Crawley and Tusk wanted to stay behind and wait for the Haxsan Guard. I had no problem with that. What surprised me was Talina's reaction.

Her green eyes evaluated the boys with mixed emotion. "Remaining in the cave, just the two of you, means more exposure to any lurking chak-lorks. And there's no guarantee the Haxsan Guard will accept you with your Infinite Eye brands missing. To them, our loyalty is in question. You'd be much better off coming with us."

I could have slapped her. I wished Talina had been more inclined to sugar-coat the facts, but she was right. Leaving Tusk and Crawley behind meant certain death. The Haxsan Guard would abandon them the moment they realised the Infinite Eye brand was damaged. They would have preferred everyone died at the camp than flee.

I sucked in an aggravated breath. There was no way we could let them stay. They had to come with us. Based on the hard, measured glance Marek directed at me, he'd come to the same conclusion.

We packed our rucksacks and left our hideout. The jungle's warble of birds and colourful plants was lost on us. The ground dipped and rose, making our trek arduous. Indree complained about her feet, which fuelled my resentment. There were times when I wanted to spin around and slam my fist into her perfect complaining mouth, but Talina always grabbed my arm, sensing what I was about to do.

Many times we had to stop so Talina could apply ointment and bandages to our cuts and scrapes, which took time and effort we couldn't afford. We stopped for lunch—beef jerky that failed to satisfy my stomach—then continued to crest one wooden slope after another.

Some hours later, an orb of sunlight leaked through the canopy and made a slow trajectory across the sky until it sank in the west. We made camp but didn't dare light a fire for fear we'd attract chak-lorks. As it turned out, we couldn't have lit a fire even if we wanted to. Purple-grey storm clouds stretched across the sky. Rain plunged down in torrents. Sitting in my two-person tent, I panicked about the fast-moving water outside. We'd settled our camp on a hill in case it rained, which meant puddles or streams wouldn't form around us, but still an alarmed flutter upturned my gut. I listened to the rain trickle down the canvas, my imagination projecting horrifying scenarios in my head. I half expected the tent to collapse under a surge of water, the Four Revenants reaching out with skeletal limbs, their chak-lorks wrenching me into the water like some kind of wild hunt.

The water isn't all bad.

It should wash away our tracks.

Hide our scent.

I hunkered down in my sleeping bag, hoping a dreamless sleep would evolve.

In the morning, the air was hot and moist. Sweat filmed my back. My scalp was itchy with it. A tingling ran up my arms where the mosquitos had used me as a blood bag throughout the night. I craved a burger. I craved a warm shower. Even a sink with fresh water. I loved sleeping under the stars for sure, but preferably five stars.

My stomach screamed at me. Was it eating itself in there? I stretched my legs to examine my bruises, wanting to do nothing more than to curl up in a ball in a nice comfy bed.

Jad!

We're doing this for Jad.

Every time desperation or hopelessness closed in, I reminded myself that we were doing this for him. It didn't animate me like a clock with a new battery, but it gave me the small oomph of determination that I needed.

I was fairly certain that was what kept Marek going too. After we packed up the camp, he led the way with the mapographic, monitoring our direction and changing course whenever we came too close to a creek or stream for comfort. I was grateful he'd taken it upon himself to be our leader, but even he was tiring. It was recognisable in the way he slouched his shoulders and dragged his feet.

I scrambled after him, which took more effort than my tired brain wanted to acknowledge. "Hey. Want me to take over for a while? You could hang back with Talina. I'm sure she'd like the company."

The tiniest smile inched across his lips. "I know what you're trying to do. I'm fine. Besides, I don't think anyone is in the mood for talking."

I looked back at our line-up. Forget being chased by the living dead. We *looked* like the living dead.

Marek raised his arm and sheltered his face from the pools of sunlight that slipped through the foliage. "Not that I don't trust you, but I'm the best qualified caster to read the map. And lead the team. No offence."

I frowned. "Why would I be offended? But just to let you know, I am capable of reading a map. Indree, on the other hand… we'd probably be going in the opposite direction by now."

Marek shot me a disapproving stare. "Leave her alone, Zaya. She's going through a rough patch."

And I'm not?

His eyes reverted back to the mapographic. "It's not that I don't think you're capable. I've had better training, and I know what to look out for. For instance, were you aware that we had a jaguar stalking us for an hour this morning?"

I flinched. "What?"

My eyes scanned the landscape, my body braced for a wildcat to leap out at any moment.

Marek smiled. "It lost interest. Too many of us. But that's what I mean."

I waved it off. "Okay, okay. You're more qualified to steer the ship."

And I'm damn happy about it too.

I'd been responsible for so long that it was kind of nice to sit back and have someone else take the reins for a while—at least until we reached the portal. Then the accountability would be back on me.

Marek inched closer. His voice barely surpassed a whisper. "Tusk and Crawley aren't buying our story."

My back ached from the weight of my rucksack, but my spine stiffened at the revelation. "I thought they were too dumb to have minds of their own."

"They've been asking questions. Last night, when the three of us were on sentry duty, they asked me how you were made aware of this portal and its ability to take us to Jad."

Anxiety whittled through me. "What did you tell them?"

Marek, Talina, Lainie, and I were the only ones who knew about my power. I planned to keep it that way, but how would we achieve that if half our company were snooping for answers?

Marek's eyelashes fluttered, his frown uncomfortable "I said you heard it in passing."

"In passing? As in I heard it in the Tarahik cafeteria while I waited for coffee. That kind of passing?"

"Tarahik doesn't have a cafeteria."

"I know that. We need a lie that's believable."

No wonder Tusk and Crawley didn't buy it. All day they had been passing me tentative looks.

I bit my lower lip and debated my next plan. "If they ask again, tell them I punched a dissent rebel for the information."

Marek stroked his chin. "That does sound like you."

"Then we're in agreement. That's the cover story."

I directed a fleeting glance over my shoulder. Only it wasn't Tusk's and Crawley's eyes that I'd felt burning into the back of my head. Indree's sparkling blue eyes reflected poorly disguised distaste, her blonde eyebrows narrowed with loathing. A blush rose in her cheeks when her gaze met mine. She looked away, but not before I caught the real motivation behind that glare. Animosity, definitely. But suspicion too.

My heart pulsed so fast it was as though there was a bird fluttering inside my chest. We all knew Indree was the queen bee and that Tusk and Crawley were her minions. If the boys doubted me, it was because she'd put the notion in their heads.

I resisted the urge to slam her face into a tree and turned to Marek instead. "What are we going to do about Indree?"

Marek snorted. "You sound like you want to murder and bury her. Indree's just after Jad. That's all that matters to her."

That made two of us, but it didn't make us a team.

I wasn't afraid of Crawley and Tusk, but they were under Indree's influence—and what Indree wanted, she received. If she knew the truth, I worried what she'd do once we rescued Jad and reached Port Serres. She was loyal to the Haxsan Guard and quick to blame others. I had the upper hand in the rainforest, but once we reached civilisation, there were opportunities for Indree to hand me over to the Haxsan Guard in an endeavour to be reprieved.

Marek stopped walking to study the wet leaves that dangled like emerald jewels in the sunlight. "It's going to rain soon."

"How can you tell?"

He checked his mapographic. "There was mist early this morning. It rises throughout the day and transforms into rain clouds. We should find high ground and make camp. We're not going to make our destination in time."

"But it's only 3:00 p.m."

If we stopped to make camp now, it would take two days to make it out of the Kanzina ranges, and I wanted to be out of here tomorrow.

"We'll start tomorrow at dawn. Sorry, Zaya, but we can't risk water and chak-lorks." He spun around to announce the plan to the group.

An hour later, we'd set up camp in a large hollow tree, wide enough that a vehicle could have fit inside it, and flung our sleeping mats down. Everyone slept, too exhausted to eat. Talina and I took the first watch.

Marek was right. Thirty minutes into our watch, the first drops of rain fell. It beat down furiously. A stream of fast-moving water rushed down the slope, almost forming a waterfall. Marek had chosen the peak of the incline. He'd been right to do so. It was colder up here and the vegetation sparser, but at least it kept us away from water.

Talina shivered beside me. She blew warm air into her hands and shoved them beneath her armpits. "Is this plan going to work? Or are we trying to do the impossible?"

I crossed my arms, my body trembling. After sweating all day, the cold spell took its toll. "What do you mean?"

She chewed her lip. "If we find the portal and go through it, we don't know what we're going to discover on the other side. We don't know where we'll end up. It could be… dangerous."

"It's bound to be dangerous, but we can't abandon Jad."

Her face fell. She made a deflated sound. "I worry that this will be too much for Lainie and Edric. He's… depressed. He hasn't gotten over what happened in Essida. And Lainie's… she's heartbroken. She's still mourning her brother's death, and now her breakup with Edric is just making her mood… unbearable. Can't you feel it? That sense that everything is…."

"Lost?" I raised my head to the thunderous sky. "Yes, I feel it." *It's been pissing me off for a while now.*

As a powerful harmonist, Lainie didn't always have control of her emotions. They'd been leaking out of her, the rest of us catching it like an airborne contagion. It was partly why we were all exhausted.

Talina stuffed her hands in her pockets. "I just hope we're doing the right thing."

An irate breath slipped between my clenched teeth. "We are."

But in the back of my head, a tiny voice nagged that it wasn't entirely true.

CHAPTER 28

The next day, late in the afternoon, we emerged from the rainforest into a rugged peninsula of volcanic rock. Cliffs and jagged outcrops overlooked the ocean in a steep vertical drop. We walked for an hour on the glossy basalt, smoothed by millions of years of rain and salt spray. It was a moon-like environment. Hollowed-out dips caused trip hazards with our ankles. If we hadn't kept a constant eye on our footing, deep crevices would have swallowed us whole. The headland spanned to the horizon and probably much farther. This massive volcanic cliff, with its streams of once molten rock, was alien and strange.

Marek led ahead with the mapographic. He stopped and scanned the area, his squinting eyes alerting us that something was wrong. "It should be here. The Otturin Cave."

Lainie kicked a rock. She blew hair out of her eyes with a huff. "Maybe you read the map wrong."

The lieutenant rubbed his hand along the back of his neck and checked the mapographic again. He made a strangled noise. "Not possible. This isn't your average map. The cave has to be here. Somewhere close."

He was right. Mapographics were accurate. They were powered with magic. It was impossible for them to lead you astray.

I tried not to let my exasperation show on my face. "Okay. This place was once volcanic terrain. The cave might be an old lava tube. Everyone look for it."

Half an hour passed, and still we were out of luck. The sun set in the west, the light fading fast. After days of being trapped in the Kanzina ranges, the tangerine glow of the sunset, the pastel purple colours of the sky, and the briny scent of the sea was a welcome reprieve. But it couldn't last. We were out in the open, and there was the ocean to worry about. The sea was deceptively calm with its creamy surf, but deep in its depths, I wondered if chak-lorks loomed. Could they even climb the cliffs?

I tipped my head up to the sky. Stars were visible in the twilight. No sign of rain. At least we had that in our favour. "I think we should head back to the rainforest. We can't find the cave now. We're too tired. We need to make camp in the rainforest where there's shelter and resume the search tomorrow."

It was bad news. I wanted to find the portal and locate Jad as soon as possible, but I couldn't risk all of us to the exposure of chak-lorks. It wouldn't help Jad if we were torn apart by water-bloated corpses.

Indree choked out a laugh. "Are you serious? The rainforest is an hour away. I'm not walking back there. Not at night."

A murmur of agreement met her outburst. Dark smudges ringed everyone's eyes, their skin bleached like an old photograph left out in the sun. Even their hair was matted from dirt and sweat. I was deliriously hungry and tired. I wanted to rest too, but we couldn't do it. Not out in the open.

An awful tension coursed through me. My arms and legs became taut, my head light with worry. It was necromancy. My power was telling me staying here was a bad idea.

A pained expression crossed Marek's face. "I agree with them, Zaya. We can't go back to the forest. We can't see at night. You saw the size of some of those fissures. And we can't use flashlights. If there are chak-lorks out there, it will attract attention." He stared at the ocean as though it could solve all his problems. "I think we should make camp here."

My bubble of hope burst. It was seven against one. I didn't like it, but I wasn't about to become narcissistic and demand everyone head back to the rainforest.

I just prayed that my instinct was wrong.

WHEN CRAWLEY LEARNT he'd be taking the first night watch, there was hell to pay. He swore at Marek, called Talina horrible names, and glared at the rest of us like this was entirely our fault. I didn't trust Crawley. Honestly, I had to get away from him before I punched his teeth down his throat. He and Tusk had done nothing but complain through the rainforest. We had listened to *"My feet hurt… I'm hungry… I have a headache… Are we nearly there yet?"* more times than we could count, each obnoxious comment more infuriating than the last. Indree had been just as bad. She'd cried when we came across spiderwebs, used me as shield whenever she mistook a tree root for a snake, and scowled at me whenever she had a chance.

I sensed my emotions brewing into a war inside me. I left the camp before I'd say anything I'd regret—or worse, do something I'd regret. A torch wasn't required. The Milky Way was a hazy band of purple colour in the night sky, providing enough light for me to see my way.

Too dark to walk back to the rainforest, my arse.

I didn't venture too far, just enough to get away from the three complainers. I spotted Edric by the edge of the cliff. He looked down at the long drop into the sea. Something about the way he stood screamed… *wrong.*

Alarms went off in my head. I dashed toward him, afraid he'd seen a chak-lork. "Edric? Are you okay?"

He didn't answer. His eyes remained on the crashing waves below, his expression blank, like the world had left him and there was nothing inside but an empty shell.

"Edric?"

Is he... here with us?

I followed his gaze. The rough crags were covered with twisted branches of dead coral. In a strange way, it resembled skeletons climbing out of the sea. The howling wind and cold spray from the ocean sent an icy flutter through me, but it didn't affect Edric in any way. He stood there, perched at the edge of the cliff, not seeing anything.

I patted his arm. "Edric? Are you okay?"

He flinched, as though waking from a dream. His expression clouded. His eyes took on a hard, glittery edge. "I'm fine. I'm just... tired."

But it was more than that. Edric had been somewhere else, trapped with only his tormented emotions for company. Talina was right. This journey was too much for him. He'd been going through the motions, walking, eating, sleeping, but with a detachment that was concerning.

I took a firm hold of his arm, worried by how close he was to the edge. "Why don't we go back with the others and get some rest? Lainie will be able to make you sleep. Have you eaten?"

Canned fruit, vegetables, and meat wasn't exactly five-star dining, but it was better than nothing.

He shook his head, reluctant to be led away at first, but then plodded along beside me with his head down.

Edric's experience in Essida was miniscule compared to what Jad had been through. If Edric was suffering like this, how was Jad surviving?

Warped dreams played games in my head. Swift, choppy, and unexpected, the images bore me along like driftwood in rapids. I saw Hadar torture Jad with scalpels and scissors. Only, when I took a closer inspection, it was no longer Jad but a vicious, blood-curdling chak-lork with oily black eyes and bloated skin. I saw teenage Vulcan kissing Octavia at the altar. Her eyes were as dark as bruises in her white face, and her belly was swollen with the first signs of pregnancy. She didn't resemble the confident, sassy girl I'd seen in the previous vision. She'd lost weight, practically skin on bone except for the baby bump. Not even the make-up she wore could hide the black-and-purple discoloration in her face, no doubt achieved with a fist. Vulcan cupped her chin in his hand. It wasn't sweet or gentle but firm and possessive. Light bounced off a brooch on his lapel. The gold-plaited pin was adorned with the ULD insignia.

The dream changed. The tender image before me brought a warm sensation to my chest. Octavia was holding a newborn in her arms. Midwives patted the beaded sweat on her forehead and brought clean towels and linens. Octavia couldn't stop smiling. In the doorway, Vulcan leaned against the architrave with his arms crossed, his shadow elongated across the floor. He watched his wife and son, his fists clenching and unclenching. A shrewd smile that was entirely unpleasant crept along his mouth. In a few quick strides, he was across the room and snatched the baby out of Octavia's arms.

A new image appeared. A boy no more than five with curly dark hair, peach-coloured cheeks, and eyes so dark they appeared obsidian played with a wooden toy soldier. He sat on the floor in a drawing room. The Victorian-style wallpaper was peeling and aged, the room large and airy. Furniture was rotten and broken. Most of the windows were smashed, the glass scattered across the floor. It looked like a bar fight had taken place. The house would have been a grand residence once, but the people who lived here did so in decay.

A lump stuck in my throat at the sound of screams. Deep, tortured cries broke through the walls. Five-year-old Jad looked up. He ran to the door on his tiny feet, but no matter how often he slammed his fists against the wood, pounded his feet, it wouldn't budge. He was locked in. He screamed for his mother. His tormented cries were the worst sounds to my ears.

The image faded. New scenery rolled in. Octavia carried a frightened Jad in her arms. He couldn't have been older than seven. Octavia paced down a dark tunnel, her torch casting just enough light to illuminate the path before her. The weak radiance revealed one horrifying truth. Her boots kicked up red splashes as she traversed across bones and skulls. Some of them still had meat attached with teeth marks in the flesh, while others were so old they'd crumbled into a wet paste

My stomach plummeted.

Lycanthors.

Monstrous, wolverine-like creatures loped after Octavia, snarling and snorting as their powerful feet stomped through the deceased. Huge drops of saliva dribbled from their jaws, their blood-red eyes focused intently on their prey. One of the creatures bit into Octavia's ankle and dragged her down. Jad scrambled out from beneath her and managed to run, but his gaze couldn't help but wander back. He witnessed everything—his mother secured in the teeth of a lycanthor, dragged and carried away like a rag doll, her hair trailing in the dust.

Violent sobs swelled in my throat.

"Zaya, wake up."

The voice interrupted my nightmare.

No.

Not a voice.

Voices.

"Wake up. Run."

The whispers of the dead called to me, urgent and demanding.

"Run to the Otturin Cave. There is a large fissure north. Run to it. It is the entry to the cave."

My eyelids broke apart, my head woken and alert. Something wasn't right. There was an electricity in the air that was thick and charged. A sweet, pungent zing filled my nostrils—the scent of earth, rain, and dust. The wind was so intense, it almost blew my sleeping bag off my legs.

What is going on?

I turned to Crawley to ask if he'd seen anything peculiar. My insides slammed together. He was asleep. The slimy, worthless coward was meant to be on watch. He'd endangered us all. I unzipped my sleeping bag and kicked him with my boot.

Dazed and half asleep, he blinked at me. "What the hell?"

"You were meant to be on watch. You stupid—"

An unfathomable rumble tore across the sky.

The ground lurched and bucked. Lightning veined through the clouds.

My anger at Crawley dissipated the moment I saw it. A roiling storm of dust, boulders, and fire approached from the sea like a lava tsumani. I stared, transfixed by the monstrosity.

It was a galactic storm.

And galactic storms were impossible to outrun.

CHAPTER 29

"R un!" I screamed. "Run!"

Marek snapped awake. When he saw the wall of fire churn and thicken, and realised it was heading directly our way, he roused the others. "Grab your rucksacks and leave everything else behind. Run!"

It was damn unlucky that we couldn't pack our sleeping bags and mats, but there wasn't time as the storm approached swiftly. Celestial shields protected the Free Zones. They'd sheltered Gosheniene and Tarahik, even Scarmouth to a certain extent, but out here in the provinces, we were fair game.

Thrown from sleepy bliss into full-scale panic, we scrambled over rocks and craters. The ground swayed beneath us. Boulders plummeted into the sea. Bolts of white-hot lightning streaked overhead.

To hell with hollow-dips that could trip our ankles.

To hell with fissures large enough to swallow us whole.

That would be a mercy compared to the horror behind us.

Heat snaked over my back and shoulders, so intense I imagined blisters boiling all over my skin. The worst part was the taste of ash on my lips and the sizzling cinders that clogged my airway.

It made me fuzzy in the head, my movements coming across as slow and uncoordinated when really I ran at breakneck speed. When I risked a look over my shoulder, the earth was fried to a blackened char. Bolts of pure pristine white erupted in jagged streaks, sending shock waves of explosions across the ground. The scorched earth was catapulted in multiple directions. I shoved Talina out of the way as a massive boulder sliced past us, most of it consumed in fire.

When I stole another look behind me, my stomach turned in circles. Crawley struggled with the difficult terrain. He hadn't put the effort into training like the rest of us, and it showed.

I waved for him to hurry. The storm was nearly upon him.

My heart rate soared.

Providence help us. He isn't going to—

A fireball exploded beside him. The burst of energy from the explosion knocked Crawley flat on his stomach. He looked at me at the same time the embers set him alight. His scream of agony was short-lived against the howling wind and thunder. There was a blinding flash where everything smelt of copper and ash, and then I was staring at a body that looked like it had been dipped in black tar. No hair. No skin. No eyeballs. Just an oozy mess that soaked into the ground.

It elicited screams from the rest of us. We zigzagged to avoid the spray of dirt and rocks that rained down on us, the image of Crawley—or what was left of him—fresh in our minds. At least, it was fresh in mine.

We're not going to make it. Where is that fissure? Where is the cave? The spirits said it was north of here. How much farther?

I searched frantically along the ground.

The entry has to be large, right? It's a fissure. We couldn't have missed it. We can't end up like Crawley.

Large objects flew by in the scalding wind. Trees from the rainforest. Scorched stones and rocks. Sticks that spun over us like projectiles. We were lucky no one was skewered. The splitting thunder left a ringing in my ears that exceeded sensible decibels. My head couldn't take it anymore. Communication in my brain went numb.

That's probably why it took me so long to see the dark crag ahead.

I dug my heels into the dirt as though tapping an emergency brake, my hands stretched to counter my balance. Marek caught my rucksack and heaved me backward, saving me from a dangerous fall into a volcanic fissure. It was a deep crack in the earth that reached into eternal darkness, too wide for any of us to jump. The others watched with open-mouthed horror.

The lieutenant covered his face with his hand and let out an anguished cry. "Shit."

It was the first time I'd heard Marek swear. Rightly so. He didn't know that this fissure was our ticket out of here—our ticket away from being scorched alive.

I teetered toward the edge. "We have to jump."

Lainie's eyes were bright and fired up. "We can't jump. We don't know how deep it goes. It could kill us."

Dust and ash crusted in my eyes. I wiped at them furiously. "It's the entry to the cave. You stay on the surface, you die."

And before any of them could argue, I leapt into the dark.

THE FALL WAS ENDLESS. Or at least it seemed that way. I landed with a heavy thud, the sickening swell in my throat slamming back into my gut. I groaned. The painful, terrible sound echoed in the dark, farther and farther away until it was just a mere sound in the distance.

Great. How big is this place?

I shifted into sitting. My eyes were greeted with black. Black to my right. Black to my left. I felt as though I were drowning in the dark. The air was cool and smelt earthy, a nice reprieve from the flames I'd escaped from. Whenever I dared move, my hands scraped against something hard and notched.

Screams resonated above. I scrambled away as heavy thumps, moans, and cussing broke through the stillness. Relief rippled in my chest at the realisation that my friends had decided to take the plunge.

"Damn it, that hurt."

"Where the hell are we?"

"Are we dead?"

"Of course we're not dead, you idiot."

"Crawley is dead. Did you see? He's dead!"

"Everyone calm down."

Someone turned a flashlight on, bright and stabbing. Wherever the light touched, the surface reflected stone dry as rotted bone. Large basalt columns gave a cathedral-like atmosphere. In the middle, huddled close, were my friends. We'd barely escaped the galactic storm, and it showed. Our hair and faces were covered in ash, our clothes partly seared where embers had landed.

One by one, we stood and lit our flashlights. More features emerged from the gloom. The rock formation was a natural archway of long cylindrical tunnels. Stalagmites protruded from the floor like the crooked teeth of a monster. From what I could see, it was an endless maze of passages that wound and twisted through the bedrock.

Marek extended his flashlight. The storm raged above the fissure. It was like looking at a backward version of reality—hell on the surface and life below ground.

Marek chuckled a soft, disbelieving laugh. "If I had to hazard a guess, that was a volcanic conduit we just fell through. Maybe about seven... eight metres."

Lainie fixed him with a seething glare. "No shit. What the hell was that? We lost our sleeping bags... most of our supplies." Her angry eyes spun in my direction.

Colour sprang into my cheeks. Was she really blaming me for this? "Crawley was meant to be on watch. He was asleep. He risked our lives."

She flashed me a savage grin. "Sure. Blame the dead guy who can't defend himself."

"I'm telling the truth. What's your problem, Lainie? You've been nothing but a total bitch since we left the Haxsan camp."

There. I'd said it.

Her eyes narrowed, her voice dangerous and low. "My problem is you. Ever since you arrived, there's been nothing but problems."

My jaw dropped. "I got you out of that camp. Would you have preferred I'd left you there to be ripped apart by chak-lorks?"

"I'm not talking about the camp. I'm talking about your arrival at Tarahik. You've completely messed up my life. Talina's life. Edric's life."

The tension in the cave became more toxic than the surface. Marek watched the escalating argument with wide eyes. Talina was crying. Tears streamed through the dirt on her face. Tusk was restless, squeezing his hands into fists as though he were training in the ring for a boxing match. Indree had a vindictive gleam in her eyes. She enjoyed the fight no doubt. Edric stood there, eyes lacklustre and face bored.

I opened my mouth to respond, but Lainie wasn't finished. "Everything that's happened is because of you and your stupid necromancy."

My insides spiralled to my feet. She had revealed my biggest secret to Tusk and Indree, two people I didn't trust. They stared. A million questions swam in their eyes, while my own started to water. Why had Lainie betrayed me like that? She was meant to be my best friend. She, Talina, and I had a pact, a sisterhood—and Lainie had destroyed it.

She tipped her head back and spat a rueful laugh. "Our Infinite Eye brands are gone. No one is going to help us out in the provinces. We're outcasts now. We have no place. It's fine for you and

Marek. You have no family. You can make a new life in Vukovar. But what about the rest of us? What must our parents think? Dead, that's what. They think we're dead. They've probably already held funerals for us."

My resentment bolstered. If she was going to be brutal with her honesty, so was I. "I never wanted any of you to come with me. I wanted to save Jad on my own." I jutted a finger at the lieutenant. "Marek insisted we stick together. I don't blame him. It's sensible. And you're right. I didn't think about your families. I acted and did what I could to save you. If you want to hate me, fine. If you want to part ways after we rescue Jad, be my guest. But never"—I latched at her collar, so angry I almost lifted her body off the ground—"blame me for saving your life."

It was Marek who pulled me away from her. "Okay. I think you've both made your point. Everyone needs to calm down. Arguing like this isn't going to solve our problem. We'll make camp here. At dawn we'll hold a short service for Crawley. It's the least we can do for him. Then we'll resume our search for the portal."

There was no disagreement from anyone, but Lainie and I continued to glare at each other like feral cats in a stare-down, ready to claw and rip each other apart.

We made camp. People drifted to sleep, their breathing heavier. I couldn't sleep. Our fight had changed things on a massive scale, perhaps on an irrevocable scale. Tusk and Indree knew about my necromancy. The possible implications sent a chill through my body that iced my core.

I shifted, surprised to find Indree staring at me. She shut her eyes, but not before I witnessed the intensity in her gaze. It had been filled with curiosity, wonder, and—my heart compressed in a nasty squeeze—satisfaction.

CHAPTER 30

We didn't talk much as we traversed the tunnels. Since the argument, there'd been a drift in our group. Marek and Talina walked beside me. Lainie, Edric, Tusk, and Indree followed behind. The only sounds were the swishing of our clothes and the soft treads of our footsteps.

I think that's what unnerved me the most. Not our obvious rift but the eerie stillness. The caves had a haunted tomb feel. The rock was drab and dark. Whenever I passed my flashlight along the walls, runes and other ancient cave paintings flared alight. The symbols were spookily similar to those I'd seen on the Neathror blade and—I remembered with a shudder—Morgomoth's vacant sarcophagus in the Asrath cliffs. It should have given me hope. If necromancer symbols were here, we were getting close to the portal. But instead I was tense, alert, afraid. I couldn't deny the acute sensation that we were being watched.

The hours dragged on. Turn after turn. Tunnel after tunnel. Our flashlight beams crisscrossed left and right, scattering along the ground ahead. I knew what everyone was thinking. *"How come the necromancer hasn't found the portal yet?"* But after the tension of last night, no one dared speak. It did make me wonder though.

Why hadn't the spirits communicated with me? Shouldn't they be here, telling me where to go? After all, they had warned me about the galactic storm.

I wasn't concentrating—at least not on where I was going—and my leg collided hard with a stalagmite. The serrated stone cut through my trouser into my calf. It made a horrible, bloody mess. I bit back a curse. Tears filled my eyes, but I wiped them away before they could spill down my cheeks.

Marek raised a hand to the rest of the group. "Stop. We need to heal this. Everyone take five."

I wouldn't allow it. "It's a scratch. We don't have time to stop. We need to find that portal."

Jad depends on us.

Marek reluctantly agreed, but the frown on his brow indicated he thought otherwise.

After twenty minutes of limping, the back of my trouser pant was so damp with blood, it made awful, wet slapping sounds against my skin.

Marek made the call, the authority in his voice final. "Everyone take a moment to rest and eat. We'll resume the search in half an hour."

My head buzzed with impatience. "Half an hour? That's too long."

There was a simultaneous groan at how *short* the break was, but Marek ignored all of us. "We're on a time schedule, and an urgent one at that, but we need some respite. Too long or too short—I don't care. Thirty minutes is what you have."

My face grew accustomed to scowling. "You'd make an excellent drill sergeant."

The lieutenant studied me for a moment. "Thank you."

"It wasn't a compliment."

I hobbled away with the best cold stare I could master.

Marek just rolled his eyes.

We settled on the ground to eat canned beans and tinned stew from our field rations. I sat away from everyone else, alienated, angry, and confused. The feeling that we were being watched still lingered deep in my gut, but I kept it to myself. It was probably just curious, wandering ghosts my necromancy picked up on. Nothing to worry about.

To my surprise, it was Indree who sat beside me with a first aid kit. Even sitting down, she was still half a head taller than me. She made sure to position herself higher—a queen peering over her subject. "Not who you were expecting?"

I wanted to spit food at her. "I'd hoped for Talina."

Indree tipped her head so her long platinum-blonde hair would shine past her shoulders, a tactical move I'd seen her employ at Tarahik when she'd wanted to express superiority in front of others, only this time it didn't work. Her eyes grew wide. She slapped a hand to her hair, her perfect little mouth open in revulsion. When she pulled her hand away, dust and ash smeared her fingers. "This is in my hair!"

From the way she'd reacted, you'd think someone had zapped a razor across her scalp.

I managed a not so coy smile. "Welcome to real life, Indree."

A sense of satisfaction at seeing her sassy attitude destroyed lit me up like sunlight inside. That was until I saw Jad's locket around her neck. Marek must have given it to her. I folded my clammy hands together or else I'd rip the locket away and wouldn't have cared how much hair I took with me.

She's his fiancée. She should have it.

My head aimed to be sensible, but my emotions refused the order.

Indree opened the first aid kit and began assembling bandages, cloth, and antiseptic potions. "Let's take a look at the cut." She sounded less than enthusiastic.

I inspected the line of ointments and spells. Tyreinorol potion for pain. Ibufonix tonic for disinfectant. Calamintis herbs for swelling. All common spells for dealing with deep cuts and wounds. But there was one spell I didn't know. Valintinian. It was too far away to read the exact wording on the label.

I rolled up my trouser leg. The cut was worse than I imagined. It was a deep gash that would leave a scar, the skin bruised and swollen. Exposed to air, the gash stung and oozed.

Indree's nose twitched. "Hold still. I'll have to clean it."

She applied the antiseptic potion with a cloth. I bit my lip to hold in a cry. Indree didn't look at my face, but I didn't miss the slight rise and fall at the corners of her lips. She was enjoying this. She dabbed antibiotic ointment over the wound with a cotton ball, applied a sterile bandage, and wrapped the injury with gauze.

She smiled, but in her eyes, there was nothing kind about it. "Pity. Looks like you won't be able to wear knee-length dresses anymore."

"Where would I get a chance to wear a dress? Indree, if you're going to try and insult me, make sure it matters." I leaned back against the cave wall. My leg protested from the strain.

Not too much longer. The spells will kick in and the pain will disappear.

Instead of leaving, Indree settled beside me against the wall.

I tensed like a dog with raised hackles. "What are you doing?"

"I thought that would be obvious." Lines of concentration formed on her forehead. "I want to talk about Jad."

I froze. The only thing that moved was the irritation inside me. "Okay."

"None of this is okay. Marek told me you've been seeing Jad in visions. What's the connection? Why are you seeing him?"

A muscle in my neck strained. "Honestly, Indree? You're acting like your boyfriend is cheating on you in a dream. I don't know why I see Jad. It's my necromancy connecting me."

Her mouth pressed into a threatening line. "Let's make something clear. Jad and I are engaged. When we rescue him, it will be me looking after him. Not you. Get it?"

My patience cracked. "Listen. I don't care if you and Jad run off into the sunset to live happily ever after. I'm doing this because Jad saved my life. I owe him."

She laughed—the dry, humourless kind. "Sorry if I don't believe you."

"What are you worried about? Jad is *your* fiancé. That means he's thinking about *you*. He's missing *you*."

And only the gods of old would ever understand why.

She flinched, as though my words had caused her pain.

I knew something fishy had been going on. Jad never mentioned Indree once to me. He never wanted to talk about her when I'd brought her up. That didn't scream love. And honestly, they were so completely opposite. If this were a preppy high school in a Free Zone, it would be like watching the Goth kid date the self-absorbed cheerleader. It just didn't make sense.

I looked at the potions still assembled in their neat line. Something about Valintinian bothered me. It certainly wasn't a common spell found in a first aid kit. Why did Indree have an unidentified potion in her possession?

She saw me looking and quickly packed up her ingredients. "We'll have to change the dressing tomorrow. Let's hope your wound doesn't fester." She picked up the bloody cloth she'd used to clean my wound. "I'll dispose of this."

She stood up too fast and sashayed away to the rest of the group.

I watched her leave, wishing I had a dartboard with a portrait of Indree's face on it.

When we started our search again for the portal and roamed

the tunnels, I caught up to Talina to pick her brain. "Have you heard of a potion called Valintinian?"

She frowned, her green eyes almost the colour of dark emerald in the restrained light. "Yes, but it's not a common spell. It's actually illegal to use. I hear it can still be purchased through the black market in the provinces."

A smug, self-satisfied feeling coursed through me. Precious little Indree had an illegal potion. But whatever for?

I kept my voice neutral. "Why would a healing potion be illegal? Is there something wrong with it?"

Talina shook her head. "No. You have it all wrong. Valintinian isn't a healing potion. It's a love spell."

I blinked, thrown off by what she revealed.

"Or at least it's the closest thing to a love spell. You can never use magic to actually make someone fall in love with you, but Valintinian creates a serious infatuation. It lasts a few weeks, maybe a month, and then it needs to be applied again." She studied me, eyebrows raised. "Why do you ask?"

"No reason."

Just curious why Indree would have a love potion in her first aid kit.

And now I knew why.

CHAPTER 31

W e explored the dark, obscure tunnels for what felt like hours. My body was as tense as wire, my muscles jittery. The sensation that we were being watched dug into the back of my head.

It's just ghosts. Nothing to worry about.

So why did I have to convince myself so very loudly?

The lava tubes expanded for kilometres, maybe even farther then the sea-battered peninsula. They seemed to lead us in a twisted game. Every turn, corner, and rock appeared the same, and I seriously fretted that we moved in circles. Confusion sparked anger, which in turn brought on accusations. Everyone blamed someone for something, but eventually it all led back to me.

Our surroundings not only had a negative effect on our emotions, but it took a physical toll too. Talina struggled to breathe, her gasps scratchy and gruff. Marek tugged at his shirt to reveal a flood of pink hives across his neck. Lainie's and Edric's eyes watered, their footsteps uncoordinated. A small, imperceptible fear clutched at my heart. When Indree glanced at me without so much as a scowl, my alarm enfolded into panic. Indree always had her shoulders back and her confidence dialled to full volume, but now she was slouched and struggled to keep up. Tusk paced behind her, his footsteps dull thumps on the dusty ground.

Something isn't right here.

Our movements, our breathing, our direction were languid and slow, like we were staggering in a nightmare.

This has to be the work of some kind of magic.

"Stop!" My voice came out choked. "Can anyone else hear that?"

I detected a burbling, sloshing noise that sounded very much like water.

Marek's eyes met mine. In the flashlight, they'd dilated with fear.

Thump. Swish. Guggle. Drip.

It was definitely water… but not quite.

We waited. The flashlights trembled in our hands, sending sporadic light into the dark.

A look of curious horror spread across Talina's face.

My eyes adjusted, taking in the object of terror that detached itself from the dark.

Objects.

Five chak-lorks emerged. Their bodies writhed and twitched, their heads cocked to the side as they snapped their jaws with malicious pleasure. Sodden, mangled skin hung off their bones, as supple as candlewax. Whenever they moved, droplets splashed from their bodies. My head groped for understanding.

Two more appeared.

Then three.

Four.

Each new chak-lork lumbered out of the darkness with their lips drawn back. Their last meals were still evident in their teeth. Whatever or *whoever* they'd snacked on must have been juicy, because the meat was still raw and bloody.

If they've found us down here, then that means….

I heard the hooves first, hurtling through the water with devilish swiftness. Then the waves appeared. The whitecaps surged beside the black horses, fuelling the creatures' powerful legs, their godlike riders a cavalry ready to bring destruction and doom on the earth. The Four Revenants were beautiful deathtraps, faces serene and luminous, bodies as strong and gentle as angels, but their eyes betrayed what they really were. They shone as red embers, lit with greed, hunger, and a hatred for anything that moved and breathed.

Their sole intent was me.

Morgomoth's first command would have been to capture me alive.

But my friends?

The Four Revenants would pulverise them to dust.

Fear pushed up through my chest. "Run!"

I didn't have to say it twice.

Why hadn't I paid attention to my instincts? I'd sensed something watch us.

Stupid. Stupid. Stupid.

The psychotic cries of our pursuers rose behind us, a dead army with a blood-curdling battle cry and a wall of fast-moving water stronger than any tsunami. Whatever spell had previously held us was gone, which was a blessing, but our legs were still sloppy, and in our haste, we barrelled into each other. Our flashlight beams crisscrossed left and right, the tunnel ahead confusing and ambiguous.

"Lunette? Adaline? Violetta?"

I tried to focus my mind, calling on the wraiths for help. But there was no answer. Even the earth spirits had abandoned me.

I snuck a glance over my shoulder and wished I hadn't.

The Four Revenants and their army of chak-lorks were closing the gap. They seemed to become part of the water, as though it was the only thing holding them together and keeping them solid.

I doubled my pace, ignoring the pain in my calf and the stitch in my side.

"Lunette? Violetta? Adaline?" I tried again. "Come on. Where are you?"

Nothing.

What was the point of having necromancy if my power failed me when I needed it the most?

"It hasn't failed you," a voice whispered into my ear.

It was vaguely familiar. No, not vaguely. I knew that voice. I couldn't believe he was here. He'd never wanted to offer his help before when he'd been alive.

"Open your eyes, Zaya."

I exhaled a frustrated breath. Even in death, Crawley was useless.

"My eyes are open," I communicated back.

"No they're not. Look at the walls. Really look at them."

"It's hard to do that when you're running your arse off."

But I did what spirit-Crawley instructed.

Is it just me, or are runes glowing through the stones?

I glanced at my friends' terrified faces. They were oblivious to everything but the horror that pursued us.

It was just me. I was the only one who could see the runes burning silvery-white like stars in the night sky, so bright that I no longer needed the flashlights to see where I was going.

I inhaled an excited breath.

The runes are lighting our direction ahead. They're showing the way to the portal.

The light twisted sharply to the passage on the right—a passage we had entirely missed.

"This way!" I demanded.

The sickening swell in my head might have abated, but there was no way I could ignore the choking, spitting cries of the chak-lorks, their laughter resonating down the lava tube like cackling hyenas.

Please… please let us reach the portal.

The terrain changed. The air became sultry and oppressive, as though we were running into an oven. Heat sweltered under my arms. Sweat licked my hairline. I tasted it on my upper lip too. The ground gave a terrible bellow, the tunnel erupting into convulsive shudders.

We were approaching something big.

Something powerful enough to affect our surroundings.

We must be close.

The tunnel expanded into a cavern. Thunder and lightning exploded from a pool of blistering white light.

The portal.

It was impossible not to be awestruck by the swirling maelstrom of energy and magic. High-pitched buzzing filled my ears, the light so intense it was as though I stared directly into the sun. Wind swept through our hair and clothes. The portal was practically a vacuum. It was exactly what I imagined a black hole would be like.

I reached for Talina, wrapping my fingers around hers. "Everyone hold hands."

We linked ourselves at the same time our bodies lifted off the ground. An image of early autumn leaves rustled off trees sprang to mind. We were the leaves now, tossed and swept in the hot gusts, weightless and no longer in control.

I think Talina might have screamed. Or maybe it had been Indree. The world was muddled and blurred, the light making everything hazy. It was only sheer terror that made me keep my eyes closed.

This is no ordinary portal, Zaya. This is a necromancer's portal. This crosses dimensions. Think about where we need to go.

Jad.

We need to find Jad.

Even with my eyes firmly closed, it didn't prevent a white-hot furnace of light leaking in, filling every particle of me until I was completely enveloped.

I'd become ethereal, insubstantial.

Gone.

CHAPTER 32

M y first conscious thought was air.

I needed it.

Something rippled against my skin, familiar yet, for the life of me, was foreign at that moment. My head screamed as a burning sensation climbed in my throat. I gasped for air and received a mouthful of water for my efforts. It spilled into my lungs, choking me.

I'm submerged!

And the water was freezing.

Fully alert now, instinct propelled me forward. I kicked, thrashing my arms about in an endeavour to reach the surface. Darkish spots hindered my vision as dizziness closed in.

Just a little farther.

But the lack of air wasn't my only problem.

Chak-lorks thrive in water.

And knowing my luck, the creatures had probably been teleported through the portal with me.

Summoning the little energy I had left, I sliced through the surface, my throat and lungs reprieved from suffering. I'd barely inhaled my first gasp when a hand crushed over my mouth. My scream became a mumbled cry. Long, nimble fingers pressed into my arm, wrenching me out of the water onto a grassy embankment. The hands were too strong. I dug my heels into the mud, scraped my nails through the moss, but nothing was going to stop my captor from seizing their prize.

It's a chak-lork!

A frigging chak-lork!

My cast-shooter was secure in my holster, but my arm lacked the momentum to reach it. I grabbed a solid branch and whacked it over my assailant's head.

Only it wasn't a chak-lork.

"Zaya, stop! It's me."

The whisper stunned me.

I spun around.

Marek had his hands raised in surrender, his eyes locked on the powerful branch that I'd just slammed against his head. He rubbed at what would inevitably become a bruise. Indree, Tusk, and Edric crouched behind him. They peered fearfully beyond the reeds.

Relief leapt in my chest, then cascaded back to worry. "What's happening? Why are we hiding? Why are we whispering?"

Marek answered by lifting a finger to his mouth. He swept some of the tall grass back, giving me a clear view to a bridge. Only it wasn't just a bridge. It was a drawbridge. A line of prisoners was being transported across in cages. My heart thundered. Lainie and Talina were among them.

Marek placed a gentle hand on my shoulder. "They were caught when they emerged from the river. The rest of us managed to hide in time."

Great. We'd escaped the Four Revenants only for some of us to be captured by dissent rebels.

I surveyed Lainie and Talina. Soaked and afraid, they were shipped in like livestock into a massive black castle. Unlike other castles which had been designed in the past to be picturesque, this monstrosity was a monument to evil. It was gargantuan, a dwarfing building that reduced us to the size of ants. Black stone. Black turrets. Black towers that pierced the night—if it even was night. It seemed as though all the life and colour had been drained from the sky, leaving a mass of gloomy clouds in its wake. Tarahik had been a gothic beauty victimised by age and disrepair, but this castle was a hulking beast.

The portal worked.

This is Jad's prison.

Darthmusk.

And now we've lost Lainie and Talina.

I pushed myself onto my knees to take a closer look.

Marek's brown eyebrows furrowed as he studied the mapographic. "This place is three days' walk to Port Serres. Weather dependent, of course." He swallowed, the strain evident in his voice. "Zaya, how are we going to get Jad, Talina, and Lainie out of there?"

Good frigging question.

I brushed a wet strand of my hair behind my ear. "What does it say about the history of this place? Architecture? Building blueprints?"

Marek's eyes flew across the screen. "Nothing much. This is ULD territory. The castle was built by them. There's no blueprints."

I bit down on my lip to prevent a frenzy of cuss words. My goal had been to get us to Darthmusk. There'd been no plan beyond that.

How the hell are we going to get inside?

Without being seen?

Without being caught?

I squeezed my eyes shut.

Think, think, think.

I'd known from the beginning that this obstacle would be a challenge, but I'd honestly hoped for a reprieve in our bad luck.

There has to be something.

And there is.

I gestured for the others to approach. They crept forward, working hard not to make a sound in the mud.

Knowing Marek wouldn't like my idea, I avoided looking at the lieutenant. "I want you to take everyone away from the castle and hide them somewhere close. We need to keep them away from the river in case of chak-lorks. I need to be alone. I have to contact the wraiths. They'll be able to get me inside Darthmusk."

Marek stared, quiet for a moment. "No frigging way. I'm not leaving you here. And I'm not hiding. Talina is inside that castle."

Despite our predicament, I wasn't able to keep a hint of a smile from my face. "That's why, after you've found a safe place for Indree and Tusk, I need you to come back."

I couldn't do this without Marek. I knew it and he knew it. This was a two-person job. Maybe three.

My eyes connected with Edric's. "What about you?"

He glanced away. His long, matted hair fell across his face. "Me?"

"Yeah. Lainie is inside that castle. She was going to marry you before you broke things off. Are you going to help us get her out of there or not?"

I was fed up with Edric's pessimistic attitude. Yes, he'd been through some shit. We all had. But he'd cherished Lainie once, and she had done everything in her power to look after him since Essida. He owed her.

He bowed his head.

So that's a no.

Marek straightened his shoulders. I knew he didn't like seeing what Edric had been reduced to. He took out his mapographic and pointed to a reference in the surrounding forest. "I can take them here. It's about a kilometre downriver. Cross portals. They're a network, each with a predetermined destination. It might be our only way of getting out of this land."

I nodded.

Marek gave my hand a reassuring squeeze. "I'll be back soon."

The four of them trekked through the reeds. The soft treads of their footsteps faded fast.

I stole another look at the castle. It seemed to have doubled in height and strength. Lycanthors patrolled the parapets. A chill scraped over my bones. Their monstrous wolflike forms were robust and strong as they stood poised to attack at every corner. They reminded me of the jackal gods of ancient Egypt. When the creatures did move, they were a blur of muscle and speed. Their low, guttural snarls resonated across the castle walls, filling the night sky with animalistic cries.

Maybe it was a good thing I was saturated in muddy river water. It would disguise the smell of caster. I crossed my legs, closed my eyes, and centred my focus on the otherworld.

"Lunette? Adaline? Can you hear me?"

Nothing.

"Please?"

"I can hear you."

The voice that answered was powerful and imperious. It wasn't the wraith I'd hoped for, but being picky wasn't an option.

I inhaled a breath. *"Violetta, can you transport me into Darthmusk?"*

She took a long time to answer. *"No. You need to preserve your magic. You will need it inside the castle."*

I silently swore.

A fleeting laugh. *"There's no need to be like that. I can show you a way in."*

Before I could respond, something wet clutched my arms.

Fingers.

Violetta's silky voice whispered in my ear, *"Let me take your mind, your body, your soul. I'll show you what you want to see."*

A blistery cold slammed into my body, knocking me flat into the mud. It didn't stop there. A vaporous cloud sank into my skin. It was what I imagined being doused in liquid nitrogen would feel like. My hands moved without any instruction from me. My legs stretched, bent, and lifted my body out of the mud. One step forward. Then another.

I had no control.

Violetta was possessing my body.

And she was taking me straight into the river.

CHAPTER 33

I might not have had control of my body, but that didn't stop the sensation surfacing over every inch of my skin. The air held a hint of the salty waters of the river, the breeze biting into my flesh. I tasted the horrible metallic tang of panic creep up from my gut, my brain warning that this was a bad idea and to stop immediately. But I couldn't. My feet stepped into the water, followed by my knees, my waist. Down and down into the murky water I went. The surface closed over my head, the swell embracing me into its dark depths. Violetta hadn't even let me catch a last breath.

She forced my arms and legs into a gentle stroke. It was so dark beneath the surface, I couldn't see my own hands in front of me. A dull, aching pain emerged at the back of my head, climbing to my scalp to settle behind my eyes. I wanted air so badly. Violetta no longer depended on oxygen, but she'd forgotten that I did.

"Please, Violetta. Let me float to the surface. Let me breathe."

She ignored my plea.

Violetta must have known where she was swimming to, because my hand closed around a lattice grille. It was an old portcullis, maybe the official gateway into the castle before Darthmusk had partly submerged into the river. The eroded metal had rusted and broken, or the castle had been attacked centuries ago and this was the work of cannonball fire. Whatever it was, the hole was large enough that a body could swim through it.

Violetta's voice was high-pitched and resonated in my head, reminding me of shattered glass. *"This is your entry."*

A strange sensation overtook my senses. Everything started to dull. The pain in my head pounded like drumbeats.

I'm losing consciousness.

The insurmountable force that spellbound my body disappeared. Violetta had extracted her soul from mine. I was free. I kicked to the surface, not caring that my first gasp of air burned my throat with cold. My chest expanded and deflated from shock, but the pain subsided.

Shivers racked my body. I could barely concentrate on the right words in my mind. *"Never do that again."*

"Then don't ask for something you don't understand."

It was Violetta's parting comment, the air empty around me. She was gone.

They sky must have opened its floodgates when I'd been in the river, because rain pounded the castle like icy bullets. It mingled with my wet hair and made a wintry chill dance across my scalp.

I remained close to the castle wall, too afraid to swim back to the bank in case I was seen by the lycanthors on watch. Besides, I knew I didn't have the energy to fight the current. Even if I did have the strength, I'd lose the battle and end up farther downstream.

I treaded water, kicking my legs in a scissor motion to keep afloat. The landscape around me was bleak and sinister, the forest lifeless. I honestly didn't believe any animal could survive in a place like this. Everything about this world was crooked and sharp angles, as though I'd stepped right into a gothic artwork. Even the air smelt of decay. Life had abandoned this place.

I examined the castle. From this angle it appeared as a vertical city that never ended, its towers disappearing into the empty darkness of the sky. Darthmusk had been built on an island in the middle of the vast river. I clung to the stonewall beside me, only there was something eerie about the shape of the rock. My entire body relapsed back to terror.

Teeth! I'm holding on to a jaw!

I hadn't noticed at first because the salty water had weathered its appearance, but up close, I knew it was definitely a skull. And not just one skull. Darthmusk wasn't made of stone but from millions of detached skulls and bones, the eye sockets rendered to featureless blobs.

This really is a castle of death.

Something rustled in the reeds at the riverbank. Marek crouched low, perhaps looking for evidence of footsteps. He must have thought I'd been captured.

"Marek! Over here. This way." My voice came out in a barely audible whisper, too afraid the lycanthors would hear me with their supersensitive hearing to shout.

Of course, the lieutenant remained examining the bank, oblivious that I was close.

I have to get his attention another way.

I intended to tear some teeth out from the decrepit skull but succeeded in yanking out the entire lower jaw. It was disgusting, but it would serve the purpose. I tossed the jaw over to the bank. Thanks to several months of target practice, my aim was perfect, and the piece collided with Marek's head—hopefully not where I'd hit him with the branch.

Marek stepped back in revulsion. He gazed over in my direction.

I waved, urging him to meet me in the river.

He stood still for a moment, his expression transmitting one clear thought: *Have you gone entirely mad?*

I probably had, but in my defence, who wanted to be sane in a world like this?

I gestured again with more urgency.

Marek meandered down the bank and submerged. I waited anxiously, knowing what a struggle it was to fight the current and to avoid the need to surface for breath. At last he rose, rubbing the water out of his eyes.

He shook his head at me. "Why do I keep finding you in the most unlikely of places?"

I explained what Violetta had shown me.

He stared in disbelief. "You and your ghosts."

"What would you do without us?"

He didn't laugh at the joke, just inhaled a breath and submerged again. I ducked after him, kicking and paddling my way into the deep. Bubbles floated behind me, constantly making me think something was in pursuit. Marek had his flashlight on. He examined the portcullis. When he touched the rusticles, they crumbled in his hand.

Neither of us knew what was on the other side of the portcullis, or if there even was an entry into the castle. For all we knew, an underwater entry could have been sealed. We were taking it on blind faith that Violetta was honest.

Merek crossed through the portcullis first. I switched my flashlight on and shimmied my way inside, careful to avoid anything sharp or serrated. I kept close to Marek, his feet my security blanket in this dark underwater world. We must have resembled scuba divers exploring a shipwreck or a sunken city, minus the oxygen tanks. My flashlight revealed statues of warlords overgrown with coral, archways spaced across the ceiling like tree canopies, and slits in the walls where crossbowmen would have once launched arrows. It was beautiful and haunting. Fish swam in and out of the light's beam, scales glistening. So long as it was just fish in here and nothing larger, I was okay.

But that didn't eliminate our biggest problem.

Air.

Casters could stay underwater longer than humans, but that didn't mean it was comfortable.

Marek spun around, hinting with his hand that he'd found something ahead. Dull, aching pain hammered my skull. I forced my lips together to impede the urge to breathe. But damn, I was getting tired. And damn, everything was cloudy. Marek grabbed my hand and forced me to kick upward. I broke through the surface, relishing the sensation of air in my lungs.

The hair on my arms rose as my eyes took in the new environment. The walls—or should I say skulls—were slick with whatever mossy fungus had grown over the centuries. What had once been their eyes were now sunken pockets filled with dirty river water. "What is this place?"

Marek examined what was visible on the surface. "This is an old fortified entry. The original drawbridge probably connected to the portcullis we entered through."

"Can you see a way into the castle?"

The lieutenant pointed behind me.

A narrow staircase—probably an old escape route designed to thwart an enemy from drawing a sword—curved thinly to the level above. It was so tight we'd barely be able to scrape our shoulders through.

I began the steep ascent, Marek close behind me. His shoulders were much larger than mine, his body broader, making his climb difficult and slow. A moment of déjà vu flashed before my eyes as I recalled the staircase to Nekros Manteia. Those stairs had led me to loss, ruin, and doom. I wondered if my ascension tonight would lead to redemption.

Up and up we went, the hewn rock slick and wet.

Geez, the tide must rise high.

Our shuffling feet were the only sounds, the absence of noise unsettling. Not even the river could be heard. Or the rain. Or the howling wind outside.

Why does something feel off?

We turned around a bend, surprised to be greeted with a stone passageway. A solid door with an iron handle waited for us at the end. I tore forward and rattled the handle.

Nothing.

The door wouldn't budge.

I tried again. "Shit. It's locked."

Marek's eyes gleamed in front of the flashlight. Worry lines formed across his brow. "Or it's sealed from the inside."

CHAPTER 34

I elbowed Marek in the stomach. "Don't say that."

A sealed door was the last thing we needed. I could blow it apart with my cast-shooter, but what if there was a spell on the other side? The repercussion promised to be dangerous, even deadly. We had no idea what waited on the other side of the door. Our best option was to sneak in like quiet mice, unnoticed.

We are totally frigging screwed.

I ran my fingers through my damp hair. The cold temperature that lingered around us caused goosebumps to pop over my exposed skin. The air reeked of mildew and malodorous rot, as though the bones of Darthmusk's very foundations had died. On a deeper level, I sensed evil, torment, pain. The sense of absolute desperation swept its icy fingers down my neck. This building had seen horror. The souls that remained trapped here unearthed it for me to feel. The ever-present wailing and muffled cries confirmed it.

Think, Zaya. Think.

Marek pursed his lips in confusion. He examined the door. "There's a lock. Look."

He was right. Concealed in the oxidized door was a small lock-shaped skull. The jaw gaped open in a creepy portrayal of a scream.

I imagined those teeth snapping on fingers, mauling down to the bone.

If there was only something I could use to pick the lock....

A tempting yet terrifying idea struck me.

Neathror.

Violetta had shown me that Neathror had various uses. It could be used as a skeleton key.

But Neathror no longer answers to me.

Or did it?

The athame-sabre had chosen to come to me when I needed it at Scarmouth.

Morgomoth had stolen it. If he could manipulate time and space and summon the blade, then why couldn't I?

I recalled the evening at the beach when he'd taken possession of Mayor Belov. He must have surrendered his mind to necromancy, because in an instant the blade had left my hand and been swept into his by an invisible force.

Now, I needed that invisible force on my side.

I stood in silence for a moment, deliberating what I should do. My addiction to the blade had subsided over the days, but if Neathror was back in my grasp, it would consume me all over again.

There's no other option.

My voice came out in a hoarse whisper. "Marek, I have a way in, but it might take me a minute or so, and... and I've never done this before. It could..."

Frighten you.

That's what I wanted to say. But really, it was me that was terrified.

Marek's eyebrows knitted together. "Zaya, what are you talking about?"

I closed my eyes and surrendered myself to the dark power that lived inside me. The magic broke free. It soared across my skin, through my hair, extending over me like an old friend welcoming me home. It was... liberating. A part of me that I'd hidden away for so long—that only came out when I was angry and out of control—was now free and under my command. Necromancers had used their magic for dark purposes in the past. It had made me afraid of what I was capable of. Now I understood it had never been something to fear. *I* decided what I did with my magic.

The wailing around me grew into screams. When I opened my eyes, dead faces bore down on me. Their wispy, tapering hands reached for my arms as they begged for salvation.

I witnessed what fear had always blinded me to before. These souls were lost. They meant no harm. They just wanted to move on. They had died in Darthmusk, and it had become their tomb. An overwhelming urge to help struck me. This was a necromancer's true purpose—to protect and ferry the souls of the dead to the otherworld. How had we lost our path?

"Focus on the blade, Zaya."

Violetta's voice ran deep and clear in my head.

So she hadn't left me after all.

"You are too inexperienced to save all these souls," she continued. *"The power it takes would kill you. Focus on your friends. You need Neathror."*

I withdrew from the hazy faces that moaned and invaded my personal bubble. Violetta was right. It broke my heart, but I couldn't and *didn't* know how to save the wraiths. A surge of fury rose into my cheeks. Necromancers had let the dead down. Their magic had taken them to dark, selfish places when they should have been protecting wraiths. It provoked and shamed me, because I was about to do the same thing for my friends—abandon these wraiths to save Lainie, Talina, and Jad.

I closed my eyes, hating myself for it as I blocked out their cries for help.

"Think of the blade," Violetta instructed.

I focused my energy on Neathror, remembering the way it had

felt in my hands, its texture, its weight, its colour. Even its scent. Blood. Metal. Sweat.

Those smells suddenly invaded my nostrils—and that's when the visualisation became real. I let out a long breath I didn't realise I'd been holding. Somehow, I'd teleported myself into an expansive chamber. Large columns shaded in gold and painted in crimson tiles circled the room, positioned around a dark mahogany coffin like sentinels. Standing at each column was a large statue of Anubis. The death dogs stood guard facing the coffin, which struck me as odd. Normally in the ancient funeral rites of casters, the jackals faced the other way, warding off anyone who intended harm to the deceased.

I wandered closer. A shaft of moonlight descended from an oculus in the ceiling, falling upon the face that rested in the casket. My heart pounded so violently that my vision swam in and out. The embalmed corpse inside was something beyond caster or human. The skin was stretched thin over the bones, the lips pulled back in a grisly smile. The ears were gone. The nose was practically a black gash in the face. The eyes were closed, lids sunken in and black. This thing was alien, leathery, and sodden in what must have been embalming fluid. Or maybe someone had soaked the body in gasoline with the intention of lighting up a good bonfire.

The corpse held a black dagger between its hands. I did a double take.

Neathror.

But if Morgomoth had taken the blade when he'd possessed Mayor Belov, then that meant....

I'm staring at Morgomoth.

Nothing about this chamber—this tomb—suggested the United League of Dissent. Anubis was a symbol of the Council of Founding Sovereigns. The discovery made my blood run icy. Vulcan hadn't retrieved Morgomoth from the Galvac ruins as I'd imagined. The Haxsan Guard had. Morgomoth was still a prisoner to the Council, half conscious while the rest of his mind and soul drifted in a sleeping curse.

It was a pity there were no torches in the chamber. I would have lit the bastard up myself and spared the world this evil, but even as I thought it, I knew it would take more than fire to kill Morgomoth. It was why he was kept hidden away in this chamber. He couldn't die. Not without the right tools.

Neathror takes life.

Could I destroy this monster?

I eagerly wrapped my fingers around the blade. Morgomoth's wrinkled hands were solid and inflexible. I tugged and a crack splintered the air, some of his fingers torn right off. Swallowing my disgust, I snatched the blade and aimed the sharp point above his head.

Farewell, Morgomoth. Enjoy your time in hell.

I drove the blade down at the same time his eyes opened. My hand froze, the weapon suspended. The eyes that stared back at me burned the colour of molten lava. A howl mixed with part rage, part hatred swept through the chamber. Morgomoth was screaming. Not literally, but in his head. Every unpleasant decibel resonated through my skull.

His wicked voice roared, more powerful than any stagma or lycanthor combined. *"Did you think it would be that easy?"*

My body was suffused in cold sweat. I couldn't move. His magic held me captive.

His lips pulled back to reveal gleaming black teeth. *"Did you think no one else had tried? Foolish girl. They met an unpleasant fate. And so will you. No one can stop me. My curse is diminishing. I am growing stronger."*

Nausea curdled in my throat.

Get out of this, Zaya.

Focus on teleporting out of here.

I shifted my attention back to Darthmusk, driving my magic forward, thinking about it propelling my body away. A violent eruption of wind tore at me. The force shattered Morgomoth's spell. I was flung back into the air, past Anubis, past the columns, into darkness.

The gale vanished, replaced with the earthy scent of mildew and decay. I opened my eyes.

Marek stared with his mouth open, his eyes wide with astonished horror. "What the hell just happened?"

I'd like to know that myself.

The lieutenant shook his head, baffled. "You were here, but you weren't here at the same time. It's like your mind left your body. I was terrified."

I opened my mouth and then closed it.

Astral projection. Is that what happened? Did my consciousness leave my body?

Marek's shoulders tensed. "And what is that you're holding?"

I looked down, only now realising something solid weighed in my hand.

Neathror had followed me on my journey.

CHAPTER 35

The blade was lighter than I remembered. The runes seemed to glitter with anticipation and eagerness. They lit the space around us in a white-sapphire glow, forcing the shadows away into the walls. Neathror's magic pulsed in my fingers, as though a heavy weight had lifted now that it was no longer in Morgomoth's presence.

Morgomoth.

We had to move quickly. That sociopathic monster could summon the weapon back at any moment.

Holding the blade as though it were tipped in poison, I inserted it in the lock and gave the sabre a hard twist. The door swung open, the absence of noise unnerving.

I expected a darkened room. A dungeon. A cell. Even a horde of dissent rebels about to swarm us. What I did not expect was a morgue. My entire body tensed with fear. Marek's face wrinkled in revulsion. This wasn't like Valdavar Tower when I'd performed necromancy on Lunette's body. That was a pleasant memory compared to this atrocity.

We stepped into the makeshift morgue. Dozens of dead bodies, some covered in white sheets, others half embalmed or left in states of autopsy, were laid out on stainless-steel tables. Various cutting instruments, saws, breadboards, and chemical test strips were haphazardly arranged on trolleys. My hand clenched the athame-sabre so hard it hurt.

Marek stiffly wandered from body to body, his shadow elongated and watery across the tiled floor. "These people are human. Look."

I nudged a little closer. "How can you tell?"

"Their skin. It's infected."

The light wasn't strong. The subtlest of blue tinges shone on the bodies, but Marek was right. The corpses reminded me of life-size china dolls, faces polished and cracked, like they'd been left out in the sun to sallow and break. On their arms and shoulders were horrific black burns. Radiation burns. Swollen, blotchy, and still oozy, the burns must have been excruciatingly painful. One of the bodies—a female with long dark hair and bare feet—had a curved needle inserted in her chest with the waxed string still attached. It did a poor job of keeping the flesh intact.

What would the ULD want with humans? And how did they get them?

Humans were protected in the Free Zones. They never went beyond the celestial shield because... well, the result was on these tables. They couldn't survive.

Marek inspected an older-looking man whose face had half burned off from radiation. He flung back in disgust. "These aren't autopsies. They're experiments."

A sour taste soared into my throat like toxic food rejected by my stomach. On one side of the room were freezers, and on the other, something labelled as drying ovens. I didn't even want to know what those were used for. Next to the ovens was a chalk-board scattered with calculations and accurate depictions of body parts.

What kind of twisted game did the ULD do to these humans? What would they need with human bodies?

I wanted to leave this dank, miserable place. "Let's move on."

We found another door beside the freezers. As I turned to slip out, I couldn't help but look back. It struck me as odd that there was no emotion in the morgue. Normally, I sensed a presence in a place with so much death, but this was just a cold, depressing room, bodies stretched across the steel tables, unknown and alone.

What's happened to their souls?

Guilt crept along my bones, making me cold all over.

This isn't our place. We need to focus on our friends.

I shut the door behind me.

DARTHMUSK WASN'T AN OLD CASTLE, but it hadn't had modifications either. We walked down long, unwelcoming passages that were chilly and damp. Fungus sprouted between the stones— or should I say skulls, because the theme of dead faces was a never- ending trend in this castle. I couldn't imagine how eccentric the building's designer must have been.

The passages twisted and wound. More than once we found ourselves ascending narrow stairs that went on and on. In one hand I had my cast-shooter, the other the athame-sabre. Marek had his weapon loaded and ready, opening doors with the tip of the shooter to inspect each room or hallway we passed. It turned out Darthmusk wasn't an overly occupied castle, but I didn't believe for a second that we would be lucky enough to find the dungeons without meeting a single rebel.

And we weren't.

A howl shook the walls, followed by another. The grisly chorus traversed down the passage like wolves howling to the moon.

Lycanthors.

The taunting patter of paws grew sharper. Claws scraped across stone. I imagined those talons scoring the wet floor. Worse, I imagined what those claws could do to skin. Grating, snuffling, snorting sounds announced their proximity.

Marek and I exchanged a fearful glance. Our only option was to turn back—fast. We sped around, sprinting past the slew of right and left turns, the winding passages seeming to have doubled in length.

If the lycanthors smelt us, we'd be doomed.

If the lycanthors heard my heartbeat—which pounded so loud I thought it would fracture my ears—we'd be doomed. Either way, we were a walking meat platter.

Marek grabbed my shoulder, caution in his stiff fingers. "In here."

We ducked inside a partially open door, my breath suspended by what we found on the other side. It was a grand baroque-style gallery. We must have previously walked through the servants' passages, because this was something else entirely. The floor was black-and-white-chequered marble, the ceiling an illustration of painted night stars. Along one wall, compositions depicted the ULD's military victories, and on the other, portraits of ULD leaders and dignitaries stared with disarming smiles. It was a ridiculous display of lavishness, dominance, and power.

Voices echoed at the end of the gallery, followed by quick, forceful steps. Someone approached. Marek and I snuck around a gilded bronze statue—some ghastly thing that looked half angel and half goblin—and hid. My heart pulsed. There were two of them now, their footsteps in unison. Now three. Four. Five. More kept coming.

There must be a whole bloody battalion out there by now.

The gallery was lit by only a few weak torches, but in that second, I saw how pallid and sweaty Marek was. His eyes stared at the trigger on his cast-shooter. His finger hovered over it with barely a margin of air to spare. Shooting a dissent rebel in a gallery of this size would be like blowing a foghorn. I shook my head, pleading with my eyes. A flicker of remorse crossed his face. He left the trigger alone.

The footsteps were nearly upon us. I held my breath, afraid that a sudden intake of air would give up our location.

A voice spoke, deep and commanding, the vindictive tone echoed through the entire gallery. "Send lycanthors to the dungeons. If she's here, that will be the first place she heads. Search this entire castle."

That lilting familiarity paralysed me.

Vulcan.

Hundreds of painful memories resurfaced, the night at the Asrath cliffs coming back to me with shocking precision. It was something I tried not to think about and hoped to forget, but the nausea that overwhelmed me, the way my body shook from sheer anger and resentment, told me that was a luxury not afforded right now.

It wasn't only me suffering. The fury on Marek's face was all too visible, his cheeks flushed, his mouth narrowed in a severe line. He'd never met the lieutenant of the ULD before, but I knew from the way his fingers curled into fists that he was aware of exactly who Vulcan was. His eyes found mine, and he silently squeezed my hand. I understood his tacit communication. *Don't do anything rash.*

It would have been so easy to fire my cast-shooter and melt Vulcan's sadistic brains, but it wasn't possible. Not unless Marek and I wanted to end up dead. For now, Vulcan was an unassailable opponent.

How does he know I'm here?

Marek and I kept very still and listened.

Another voice spoke, this one was more docile and obedient, maybe even a little nervous. "Sir, we don't have enough men to cover the entire castle. Most of them are still out raiding Lothlarkin. It will be hours before they return."

Vulcan's voice seeped with resentment. "You're here, Quintus.

And your men." He raised his voice. "Search the castle."

A scampering of footsteps set out into multiple directions and faded into the distance.

I snuck the tiniest peek.

Vulcan stood not an arm's length from the man I presumed was Quintus. His black eyes glittered in the torch light, appearing snake-like and demonic. He took a step closer. "The girls found in the river… where are they?"

"Hanging in the dungeons, sir."

Hanging?

"Find out what you can from them. Torture them if necessary. I want to know if they've been travelling with Zaya Wayward. I want to understand how strong she's becoming."

"Sir?"

"Zaya Wayward summoned the Neathror blade through astral projection. She stole it from our master just now. That means she's getting stronger." Vulcan flashed him a deadly glare. Quintus flinched and draw back. "Zaya is in the castle. She's here for my son. I expected her, but not like this. Not with the Neathror blade. Listen carefully. Take the back passages to the dungeon. The lycanthors have been instructed not to kill her. We need her blood if we're to awaken Morgomoth."

"But His Dark Highness is still missing, sir."

Vulcan's lips shifted into a wicked smile. "That's why we need to snare the rabbit now and skin it later."

The ULD lieutenant stormed out of the gallery, his hands tense at his sides with barely controlled anger. Quintus shifted on his feet, helplessly alone.

Marek and I exchanged a glance.

We needed to reach the dungeons.

And now we had a guide.

CHAPTER 36

A premeditated plan wasn't necessary. Marek and I leapt from our hiding place, launching ourselves onto Quintus. The poor rebel didn't have time to even scream. Marek drew a dagger, the razor-sharp edge dangerously close to Quintus's throat. Every part of my body was raw and trembled. Marek wouldn't hurt him. It wasn't his style, but the way the lieutenant's lips pulled back in a grisly smile made my heart take off at a gallop.

Quintus kicked out with his legs, wriggled his arms till he found traction, and elbowed Marek in the side. The lieutenant winced. His leg slipped beneath him. The blade fell in an unearthly clatter on the marble floor. Quintus took the opportunity and lunged on Marek. Fists connected. Muscle pummelled muscle. The pair dodged and slammed into each other. Left-right, left-right, right-right, left. They were a blur of movement, the gallery filled with slaps, whacks, and grunts.

We don't have time for this testosterone-fuelled violence.

Wham!

Marek received a blow to the jaw. The impact sent him sprawling to the floor with a sickening crunch. Quintus stood tall and firm, his breathing heavy. I couldn't see his face, but I knew from the way the muscles in his neck were taut that he was about to deliver a killing blow. His shadow towered over Marek like a looming monster.

I tapped his shoulder. "Excuse me."

The rebel spun around. Surprise lifted in his eyes. I slammed my fist into his nose, the force knocking his head back. Blood splattered onto his chin. I lashed out with my boot, kicking his stomach and sending him crashing to the floor. Marek swerved around the rebel and retrieved the dagger. He kneeled over Quintus, the blade hovering over the rebel's throat.

Rage glistened in Quintus's eyes, but judging by the way his face slackened, exhaustion won over. "Zaya Wayward, I assume."

He said my name like I was a common criminal who should be hung at the gallows.

My hand itched for my cast-shooter. I took the weapon out, cocked it, and aimed the barrel at his head. "Take us to the dungeons. Now."

"You're walking into a trap. You know that, right?"

I bit my lip to hold in my frustration. Quintus hadn't stopped talking from the moment we'd captured him. He'd lost fighting. Maybe he thought he could save himself with conversation.

Humph. Not a chance.

The back passages reeked of mildew and dust. I tasted it in my mouth and felt it clog my nose. An irritating tickle climbed in the back of my throat. I resisted coughing. Who knew how far sound travelled down here? It's why I wanted Quintus to shut up.

Marek pushed the dissent rebel ahead. Quintus was our guide, our compass, our navigation, but every so often, Marek had to inch the dagger closer to his neck to remind him who was in charge. I followed with the flashlight, my cast-shooter firm in my grasp, ready to pull the trigger at the first sight or sound of movement. Patchy light cut into the misty dark ahead, revealing little horrors in the walls. Lined in grime-caked stone were notched skulls, only these decrepit faces had been burnt before they'd been cemented into the walls. Ash flaked off the bones, looking weirdly like black snow. I wondered if that's what the rats survived on.

Quintus shivered in the chilly air. "There will be lycanthors swarming the dungeons by the time we reach it. You don't have a chance of finding him, you know. After everything Hadar has done to your precious captain, he won't want to leave. He's not the same."

Marek struck him on the head with the back of his hand so hard, I wondered how Quintus's head didn't roll off right there and then. "Shut up. Otherwise, I cut off your tongue."

I knew Quintus was only trying to dampen our confidence— I'd probably do the same if I had a knife to my throat—but his badgering only provoked my anxiety. What if Jad wasn't the same? Violetta said he didn't have long.

We're here, Jad. We're on our way. Hold on.

We came to a staircase, the rock hewn at uneven angles. Serrated stone jutted out in deliberate trip hazards. Anyone who traversed these stairs often would know where the dangers lurked, but for invaders like us, it meant we had to watch every footstep, which slowed our progress. Up and up we went.

We must be nearly at the top of the highest tower by now.

Marek stilled. "This is the most direct route to the dungeons, isn't it?" he hissed into Quintus's ear.

My heart pumped. The faster it went, the colder my blood seemed to drop. We might have Quintus at knifepoint, but that didn't stop him from leading us astray. Were we even headed to the dungeon? They were normally at the base of a castle, deep in the ground, not at the top of the highest tower.

Quintus didn't say anything for a long moment. "Of course. Why would I risk my life?"

He didn't sound convincing.

I climbed a step and stared down at him. "Where is the dungeon?"

His lips flicked upward in the corners. "It's at the end of these stairs."

The tips of my fingers tingled with nervous sweat. "Then we no longer need you."

I clubbed him over the head with my cast-shooter. A wet clomp echoed down the stairway, my own insides spinning from the revolting sound. Quintus's eyes unfocused. His legs buckled beneath him, his body and face slack. He would have fallen down the stairs if Marek hadn't been holding him.

The lieutenant stared, his face more pale than usual. "My threats were pretend. I didn't think we were actually going to hurt him."

The tightness in my body abated. "Hurt is something you can feel. This guy is unconscious, so it doesn't count. Besides, if the dungeon is upstairs and there are other rebels, we now have the element of surprise."

"If?"

"He could have been lying."

Marek gently set Quintus on the stairs and searched his uniform for weapons.

Black spots popped behind my eyes. I had to look away from Quintus's face, his expression fixed in a blank square. His hair was damp where the cast-shooter had knocked the daylight out of him. The bile in my throat threatened to choke me.

Marek took my arm and nudged me up the stairs. "Let's go."

We slogged the rest of the hike up the tower. My legs trembled with adrenaline when light flickered ahead, anaemic at first but brighter the closer we approached. Delicious warmth crept over my skin, a welcome reprieve from my wet clothes, but it was short-lived. We came to a stretch of hall lit with torches. The flames sent flickers of shadow and light along the walls. Bodies had been left to rot in hanging cages. They hung from the ceiling like pendant lights.

Geez, I love how they've decorated the place.

I made a frantic survey of the passage, but there were too many bodies to count. "Well, that's terrifying."

My voice echoed strangely off the walls.

Marek charged ahead. There was a door—or rather a barrier—of steel metal with the smallest grate in the centre. A little peephole to spy on prisoners inside.

This is it. We're here.

Marek's hands trembled as he tried the handle. "It's locked."

I dug my fingernails into my palms. *Of course it's locked. Should we really have expected anything else?*

I pushed Marek aside. "Let me."

Neathror had quivered in my pocket this entire time, its power stirring through my body. I shoved the tip of the blade into the lock.

Click.

The door swung open, the tarnished hinges giving in to a bone-shuddering rasp. We stepped into the dungeon. Door grates, aged and corroded, lined the walls, the cells beyond shrouded in shadow. It gave the impression of pitch-black pits. Marek and I stole a glance at each other. I think we both knew in that moment we were headed down a path neither of us could return from. Just how different would Jad be when we found him?

The floor was old, concave in the centre where thousands of prisoners had undoubtedly trodden. My flashlight cast sporadic light across the roughly textured stone. Each cell contained a wooden sleeping shelf, a bucket for waste—currently inhabited by rats—and discarded chains.

Where are the prisoners?

Marek's gaze found mine. The silent question hung between us.

We turned into another passage. This one widened out to a large room with a....

I leapt back.

A huge circular pit.

No. Not a pit. This mammoth hole was a shaft so deep I couldn't see anything beyond the darkness below, not even when I shone my light down it.

Marek nudged my arm. "Look."

He directed his flashlight onto the opposite wall. Words had been inscribed into the stone.

CHAMBER OF THE FORGOTTEN

A shiver that had nothing to do with the cold tiptoed across my skin. I imagined prisoners lowered down the shaft, trapped below in an eternal world of darkness. No food. No water. No light. It must have been a lonely and horrible way to die. What concerned me more than anything else was the lack of presence. Wraiths always made an impression. The dead haunted places they couldn't escape. This dungeon spoke of unspeakable torment and suffering. I sensed it in the walls, but the prison was empty of life and death.

"Marek. I don't like this. Something isn't right about this place, even for necromancy."

Water dripped from the ceiling. It fell in fat droplets into the shaft. A shriek tore from the dark below. It was followed by a hideous cackle. Lunatic giggles. Coughs. Spatters. The cacophony was like sandpaper scraped over my eardrums.

Chak-lorks.

A surge of panic bubbled inside me.

They're in the shaft. They're not up here. Stay calm.

But they can climb.

They can climb!

Marek swallowed, the sound audible in the vast dungeon. "Zaya, that isn't water."

I followed the beam of Marek's flashlight. He was right. Crimson drops fell into the shaft. One drop. Two drops. Drip.

Drip. Drip. There was a cadence to the way they plunged into the dark.

Marek tapped my arm, then gripped it with frantic alarm. He aimed his flashlight to the ceiling—only there was no ceiling. The tower extended high into the shadows.

All my organs pulled inward. The beginning of a scream formed in my throat.

Lainie and Talina hung from rope by their ankles, their throats slashed.

CHAPTER 37

A small gash had been cut into Talina's and Lainie's necks. At least, I hoped it was small. There was so much blood it really was hard to tell. It streaked over their lips and past their noses to mat into their dangling hair. Their eyes were closed, their faces sallow. It was a small mercy they were unconscious. Seeing themselves strung up like meat hooked up in an abattoir would have frightened them shitless.

It frightened me shitless.

A strange combination of acrid and sticky filled my mouth. "We have to get them down."

Marek's eyes unfocused for a moment, but then he fixed me in his hazel gaze. "Over there. Stairs."

I shone my flashlight behind me. He was right. A ridiculously narrow staircase had been cut into the rock, large enough for a child to step through. We darted toward it and began the uncomfortable ascent. The steps were twice the height of an average step, forcing me to use my arms to wrench myself through the tight gap. Marek struggled behind me. He had to shift his arms and shoulders at what must have been uncomfortable angles to climb.

This isn't a staircase. This is a frigging chute with a few steps thrown in for good measure.

Which meant there had to be another way up there, wherever *there* was. No way could someone have dragged Talina and Lainie up this excuse for a staircase.

An anxious thought attached itself in my mind.

What if this is a trap? What if we come out at the other end to be met by rebels and tossed into an even darker recess of the dungeon?

I pushed the negative thought aside. It was something we'd just have to accept and deal with if it happened.

At the landing, I unceremoniously freed myself from the chute. Nothing short of dread gripped me. What I stood in was an enormous space, the floor made up of great stone slabs that had darkened with age. There was nothing present in the chamber but a large platform that overlooked the shaft. Lainie's and Talina's chains were attached to a wooden gibbet—something modern operated by a winch that tugged and pushed the beam back and forth. Marek wriggled out of the chute and beelined toward it. He spun the winch handle, swearing when it gave a groan of protest from long disuse.

That means prisoners aren't often brought up here.

Every muscle in my body seemed to knot itself in fear.

Why does this feel like a ploy?

Marek's face scrunched in sheer exertion as he drew Lainie and Talina in like fish on a trawl line. The chains rattled and clinked. The sounds bounced off the walls.

We're making too much noise.

My heartbeat terrorised my ribs with rapid pounding.

Come on. Hurry up. Hurry up.

Talina and Lainie were nearly at the platform. I reached for their arms and dragged the girls across the last metre. I hated how limp and cold they were. Both were drenched from the river, their waterlogged bodies giving them the appearance of death. I swallowed hard. The gashes in their necks weren't deep and were relatively small. Indree would be able to heal the wounds. It was the blood loss I was worried about.

I inspected the manacles around the girls' ankles.

Keys. We need keys to unlock these restraints.

My fingers brushed air where Neathror should have been. A trickle of sweat crept down my back. The athame-sabre was no longer in my sheath.

Morgomoth has summoned the blade.

Marek's broad hand closed around my upper arm. His eyes locked on to something in the shadows. "Zaya. Keep still."

A dry chuckle broke from the darkness. "Looking for something?"

I recognised the voice. I'd heard it expressed with command, strength, authority, but never with the hostility that accented its tone now.

I shut my eyes briefly, giving in to despair. I wished it was a nightmare—a trick conjured by my exhausted mind—but I knew what my eyes found when I faced the newcomer was real. It went beyond the worst horror imaginable.

Jad.

Tall. Imposing. Eyes the colour of arterial blood. I drank in every feature. His dark hair curled under his chin, loose around his face, which was bruised and lacked compassion. He was so familiar yet… different. His tanned skin was alive with colour, only tonight it was layered in blood that I didn't think was his. His lips, which had always been so gentle when they smiled, were quirked in an amused smirk. There was something predatory about the way he stepped toward us. He was the black panther creeping through the night, the shadows working in his favour.

My whole assessment took place in an instant.

We're too late.

Jad was gone. What I was looking at was a monster—soulless and savage.

Vulcan had won.

Jad lifted a gold key with a mocking wave.

The key that would release Talina and Lainie.

HOT TEARS slid down my face. I couldn't breathe, couldn't move. The world spun beneath my feet.

I'm too late. I've lost him.

Marek's hand trembled in an effort not to grab his cast-shooter. Horror and revulsion spread across his handsome features, but it was quickly replaced with maddening rage. "You did this to them?" He pointed at Lainie and Talina with aghast horror.

Jad's face took on an expression of pure joy. "Of course. I recognised the necromancer's friends when they were brought in. This was my plan."

So it had been a trap. I stared at this person who I knew but also didn't, my heart conflicted. Jad had saved me that night at the Asrath cliffs, only to ironically capture me now. Those eyes that I had always loved focused on mine, only now there was nothing welcoming or familiar in them. They were red and burned brighter than hot coals, the skin swollen and shrouded by shadow. It was Hadar's spells that made him stronger. It twisted his mind. It forced him to become this repulsive demon.

If we can get him away from here... cleanse him from the curse... maybe he'll be all right.

Maybe we can still save him.

The idea filled me with irrational hope.

Desperately, I tried to think of a way we could win and get out of this dungeon alive.

Jad made a sound I couldn't decipher and zeroed in on me. Marek leapt forward. He unsheathed a sword and aimed both the blade and his cast-shooter to wedge a barrier between us.

Jad let out a breathy laugh. He raised his hands in mock

surrender, the key between his thumb and finger. "I only want to make a peace offering. The necromancer in exchange for the key. I'll even show you the path out of here. You and your unconscious friends can be on your merry way. It's not you the ULD are after. "

"Not happening," Marek shouted before I could get a word out.

I slapped the lieutenant's weapons out of the way. "Agreed."

It wasn't possible to escape the way we'd come. It would be swarming with rebels and lycanthors by now. A deal with the devil was the only option my friends had of getting out of Darthmusk alive.

Marek's face lit with bewilderment. "You can't trust him."

Jad tilted his head to study me. "You stand by my side, necromancer. I throw the key at your friend's feet. Understand?"

Ignoring the burning abhorrence I sensed in Marek's eyes, I nodded and stepped forward.

I was nearly by Jad's side when, in a blur of movement, the lieutenant lunged at him with a vigorous battle cry. I leapt back, watching in sheer terror as Marek aimed his cast-shooter. His finger seemed to curl around the trigger in slow motion.

A growl ripped from Jad's chest. He charged forward, too fast for eyes to comprehend. He knocked the lieutenant's weapon aside like he was swiping away an annoying fly. I flinched at his unassailable strength. Jad unsheathed his own blade and struck, the pair locked in a fierce duel. Metal flashed. Strong blows were exchanged, the clash of swords singing as the opponents swept forward and took up the defensive, back and forth, right and left. Marek was a capable fighter, but he didn't have the strength to win this. Jad wasn't even trying. He moved with ease. This was a game to him. He was teasing the lieutenant. If Jad really wanted Marek dead, he'd do it in a heartbeat.

He's a cat toying with a mouse. Jad will kill Marek. He's just savouring the moment.

Jad lunged forward and skilfully knocked Marek's blade aside with a strength that was astounding. The athame-sabre soared through the air, landing a few metres away from my feet.

I have to do something.

Something that involves necromancy.

Violetta had said I didn't have the strength to cross the other-worldly plane and project myself into Darthmusk. *"You need to preserve your magic. You will need it inside the castle."*

Is this what she meant? Did she foresee that this would happen?

Please let this work. Please let this work.

I closed my eyes, summoning my energy and magic. It rippled inside me, flowing through every vein and artery in my body. It danced over my skin, consuming me until I sensed nothing but power.

"Violetta. Adaline. Lunette. I need you. Please answer."

Cold, wispy fingers touched my face. I opened my eyes to find the ghosts hovering before me, pale and washed out, but there.

Three ghosts for three people. I could do this.

"Take my friends to the cross portals," I communicated. *"Get them out of here. Now!"*

Violetta and Adaline stared with dull eyes.

It was Lunette who answered. *"Your power will dwindle, Zaya. This is too much for you."*

She was right. My magic was dimming. It flickered in and out like a candle. I was losing control. My head throbbed in response, my legs weak in the knees. I clenched my teeth, wishing it was enough to drive away the pain.

I strained to keep my concentration focused. *"Just do it."*

Wind drowned with the cries of tormented souls swept through the dungeon. I sensed the gale-strong squall wrap around me like a black storm, extricating my magic and devouring it with hunger and thirst. I heard nothing except for the unbearable screech of wailing and screams.

The otherworld was here. A doorway had opened.

Yes! I did it!

A loud pop broke the spell. It sounded as though a light bulb had burst. The wind flattened in an instant, sucked back into the otherworld.

I opened my eyes.

Marek was gone.

Lainie's and Talina's chains hung limp, the manacles empty.

It worked. They'd been teleported to the cross portals.

A smile inched across my lips, but it disappeared the moment I was confronted with my own predicament.

Jad.

He stood there, face blazing with anger, eyes shining with murderous intent.

CHAPTER 38

That penetrating stare shattered my hope. Saving Jad had been my only source of consolation. But this wasn't Jad. I'd been fooling myself in thinking it was. This creature didn't need saving.

I was staring at Trajan Stormouth.

A monster created by his father.

Jad had succumbed to the twisted magic that had tortured him for weeks… months. The curses Hadar had injected into his body had rotted out his heart and bled into his soul, saturating everything with darkness. My legs stilled. The shock had paralysed me.

Trajan tilted his head, the corner of his lips curved high. It sent a wave of icy fear over my body that made me weak and defenceless.

How can someone still look the same yet be so different?

He must still be in there. He must.

I cringed. There was blood on his hands and sword—probably from some poor victim whose life he'd just snuffed out.

A cold lump of dread rose in my throat, but I forced myself to speak. "Jad."

"It's Trajan." His voice escalated into a roar.

I flinched.

Stay calm. Panic is only going to make you sloppy.

I dared a quick look at Marek's abandoned athame-sabre.

Trajan laughed. "Don't bother. You wouldn't reach it in time."

He stood in a defensive stance, his sword tip raised. His eyes examined me the way a wolverine watched a rabbit. "I don't want to hurt you, Zaya."

For one heart-stopping moment, I actually believed him, but then I remembered who it really was talking. My emotions became conflicted all over again.

Trajan's not attacking.

He's stalling.

He's…

Blocking my path!

It wouldn't have been physically possible for Trajan to drag Lainie and Talina up that narrow stairway, which meant there had to be another way out of this death trap. Trajan was barricading it. He was keeping me here until dissent rebels, lycanthors, and providence knew what other unsightly monsters could arrive.

Which means they need me alive.

Blood flowed thick and fast through my head. It was a crazy idea. An impossible idea, but I'd never been one to take the safe path.

I darted for the athame-sabre. At the same time, Trajan vaulted impossibly fast toward me. His blade sliced the air. I heard it sing as it passed my ear and approached dangerously close to my arm— no doubt its intended target. I tore Marek's weapon from the ground and spun around just in time to block Trajan's next vicious blow. An explosion of metal ripped through the dungeon. The runes along the athame-sabres shone alight, a kaleidoscope of colours that came alive to deflect the other blade's power. I was already weak from conjuring wraiths. I didn't think I'd be able to hold off Trajan's sword much longer.

His face twisted with rage. He effortlessly unlocked the blades and, just as fast, struck his hand across the side of my head. Sparks danced before my eyes. The stone spun beneath me, and I fought for traction to stay upright. Jad had taught me how to fight. Trajan might be the one in control right now, but I didn't think their fighting style would be much different. The only problem with that logic though was that Trajan would be able to predetermine my moves too.

He reached for my throat. I flung myself backward just in time. Trajan struck again, faster and stronger. I met each lunge, parry, and strike, barely having the strength to repel them. The runes crackled and flared with searing light. Our duel fuelled their intensity. Magic burned around us, the walls awash in their glow.

He doesn't want me dead. He's just toying with me.

His red eyes met mine, a portal to a darker part of his soul, and I knew in that instant I'd been wrong. His smile hardened at the edges, and the next second his boot was against my stomach. There was no time to comprehend the pain. My eyes went wide as I was flung through the air. I hit the ground hard, rolling, rolling, rolling, until—

My legs toppled over the edge of the shaft. I screamed and struggled to keep my entire body from plummeting into the deep. My feet kicked against the wall, as though I could somehow climb to safety. My fingers clung to the stone edge, agony surging across the ligaments. I was certain the strain would break each finger at the knuckles.

No! No! No!

I'd dropped the athame-sabre. It rested metres away, the runes dimmed out. Gritting my teeth, I closed my eyes as the pain in my arms deepened. My boots couldn't get grip.

Is the wall... wet?

A warm stickiness made it impossible for my feet to get traction.

I recalled the blood that had dripped from Talina's and Lainie's cut necks and decided I really didn't want to know why the shaft was damp. This was, after all, an instrument for execution.

A familiar shriek reverberated from below, followed by maddening laughter.

Chak-lorks!

Whispering, cackling voices drew near. The sound and smell of the creatures polluted the air with the stench of death, blood, and rot. I had a terrifying image of my body ripped apart to be feasted on, my bones left to age in the dark.

They're getting closer.

My head screamed at me to move, but it felt like I had concrete blocks strapped to my feet. A shadow loomed over me. A pair of perfect black boots blocked my view. Trajan crouched down, his lips set in a feral snarl. A sob erupted from my throat as he grabbed me by the back of my neck and hurled me across the chamber. I slammed into the wall. Agony blinded me, my body giving out to pain and exhaustion. Trajan might not have intended to kill me, but that didn't stop him from breaking me apart piece by piece.

I have to get out of here.

But I don't have a weapon.

I don't have strength.

All I had was a world plagued with fog as vertigo set in.

Or… was it something else?

Hundreds of pale, translucent faces appeared. Wraiths. Horrible acts of atrocity had been inflicted on them. Some were covered in blood, their throats torn, their bodies hacked at. Others were burnt and blistered. Their muffled screams filled my ears. Somehow, through my delirium, my mind had connected with the otherworld, allowing me to see the wraiths that had been tortured and killed in this very chamber.

And if I had my wraiths, then I had strength and a way out of here.

I shut my eyes to prevent my mind from see-sawing up and down and centred my concentration on the ghosts.

My words were thick and slow in my head. *"Attack Trajan, but don't hurt him. Don't kill him. Be a barricade. Don't let him near me."*

The wraiths swept toward him in an explosion of white light. My command gave them the power they'd desperately sought—vengeance. And boy, did they give it. Trajan was surrounded in a sea of luminescent silver as hundreds of decrepit faces stared down at him. Their translucent figures soared one after another in and out of his body. He swatted them away like mosquitos, but his hands simply went through them. The ghosts weren't harming him, but they were doing a great job of scaring Trajan witless.

Welcome to my world.

Trajan's cry splintered my heart, and for a moment I considered calling the entire thing off—but no, this was my only chance. Shakily, I got to my feet and headed toward the darkness that Trajan had obstructed

Please be an exit. Please be an exit.

Before, it had been a solid mass of pitch black, but now that the ghosts had arrived with their otherworldly power, the glow from their radiant forms lighted the way.

A passage.

I broke into a dead sprint, my strength returning in small bursts, my legs running faster and stronger. I didn't think this was my body naturally recovering. Aches and pains still throbbed in various parts of me, and my vision was hazy at the edges. No, this was necromancy. My magic was giving me the boost of energy I needed to escape.

The passage was long and shrouded in sheets of cobwebs and dust. I didn't want to think about what size spider could make webs that large. My feet pounded hard, my breath like a razor in the back of my throat.

If I could just reach the end of this passage. If I could just find a way out—

A wave of light shone ahead to illuminate a new terror. I dug my heels in. The sudden halt forced my knees to buckle. My body lurched, tumbled, rolled…

Toward a sheer vertical drop to nowhere.

CHAPTER 39

My fingers instinctively dug into the moist ground. I scrambled back from the edge, my fear so thick my vision blurred. My arms and legs trembled from the effort, but once I was a safe distance away, the panic in my stomach abated. My breathing returned to normal.

That was close.

And… what the hell?

The silver light that had warned me of the impending danger was still visible, only now that my eyes had adjusted, I realised it was the smooth outdoor glow of the world beyond the castle. The passage was a trap—a sudden drop that plunged unsuspecting prisoners to the river below. At this height, hitting the water would be like hitting concrete.

Moonlight fought to make its presence known against the vicious rainstorm, the wind damp and cold on my wet skin. Mountains were just visible in the distance, polluted by a green mist that gave the impression of a toxic wasteland. I covered my mouth. The stench of sulphur permeated everything. The entire world smelt of swamp gas.

What the hell happened to this place?

To my left, a white-sapphire glow emanated from the trees. It grew larger and brighter, the forest and surrounding sky lit in radiance. The cross portals. Marek had said they weren't far. It had to be at least a kilometre away. If my plan had worked, that's where my friends would be. I had to get there, but the decision part of my brain was split. If I left, it meant abandoning Jad. It meant accepting that he was gone. The knowledge tormented me, fractured me, sliced its blade into my soul. I had to accept that I had failed Jad.

I can't save him.

Because he doesn't want saving.

"Goodbye," I sobbed, so quiet not even the wind could drown it.

Struggling and shaking, I summoned the will to get off the ground. I wouldn't fail Marek, Lainie, and Talina. I'd get my friends to Port Serres and on a ship away from the continent. Vukovar was all that was left for us now.

"Zaya!"

The scream carried down the passage.

I stiffened.

No. Please, no.

My magic connection with the wraiths must have broken when I'd nearly toppled over the edge. The ghosts no longer obstructed Trajan.

He was coming after me.

At the other end of the passage, feet slapped the ground hard, louder and faster.

I examined my surroundings. Fear and despair played tug of war in my head, forcing me into full-scale panic.

There has to be a way out of here. There has to be.

Trajan had brought Talina and Lainie through this passage to the chamber. The stairway had been far too narrow, which meant there had to be another entry somewhere close. I ran my fingers over the walls, feeling for a latch, a handle, a trapdoor... anything.

The skulls cemented into the stone walls seemed to smile at me with knowing smirks. I peered through the crevices and gaps of their teeth. Nothing.

"Zaya!"

Trajan's voice reverberated down the passage. He sounded as though he'd eat me alive.

I kicked at the wall in frustration, surprised when my foot slid right through it.

What the fu—

A glamour!

A frigging glamour!

Of course the ULD would use magic to disguise a doorway. I leapt forward, the stone and skulls malleable as my body slid through. The consistency was like black sludge, sucking me in as fast as quicksand. I emerged on the other side of the castle. Rain pelted me with relentless strength. Darthmusk's towers, keeps, and turrets were lit on-again off-again in the blinding flashes of lightning, the spires ending at such thin points they appeared to be needles piercing the sky. I shivered. Cold and fear soaked into my skin. My only escape were the winding staircases that connected each tower, which were absent of handrails.

Damn the ULD and their insane architecture.

I ran along the parapet. Puddles played havoc with my feet, the stone slick beneath my boots. The intermittent lightning was the only thing that guided my way as I descended a stairway. Down and down I went, one staircase after another, praying to whatever high entity was out there that I made progress toward an exit. The steps were tight and high, a capable trip hazard even without the rain. A bolt of pure hot light struck the nearest tower. Shock made me lose my footing. I flailed my arms, but gravity had already latched hold of me. I fell onto the roof below, failing to swallow my scream in time.

Great. Now Trajan knows where I am.

It hadn't been a long drop, only about five metres, but panic was making me sloppy.

"Zaya!"

I tossed a terrified glance over my shoulder.

Trajan was leaping from one stairway to another. He ran across roofs and jumped the flying buttresses like a jaguar through trees.

Of course he knows parkour.

My night was just getting better and better.

I took off at as fast a run as was possible, my muscles still weak from the exertion of my escape.

It wasn't enough.

Trajan's body slammed into mine, the force knocking us both from the roof. Wind tore at me, my arms and legs tangled as I plummeted like a stone. We hit the ridge of a turret, the impact bursting through my side and shoulder. Tiles came loose beneath us, slipping down and over the edge. I scrambled onto my hands and feet. Mercifully, Trajan had rolled when he'd landed, which had provided distance between us. He was bleeding from a cut in his upper arm. Blood oozed from the wound like a black toxic sludge. His gaze was fixed on me, and in his eyes, I saw madness.

I moved—too quickly. The tile beneath my foot slackened, and I slammed hard on my stomach.

No! No! No!

In a domino effect, the tiles went out from beneath me, pulling me down with them like a leaf caught in rapids. My scream rang into the night. I plunged over the edge, striking a monstrous gargoyle-looking stone. It broke my fall, but the collision tossed me onto the castle's battlement. My ungainly position made the impact more painful. I must have fallen at least seven metres, my body experiencing every acute ache, twinge, and throb imaginable.

Breathe.

Get up. Don't give in.

Trajan would reach me in less than a minute.

I forced myself to stand. Exhaustion threatened to tear me down again, but damn if I would let it succeed.

The battlement stretched far ahead with a parapet that overlooked the river. It must have been designed with the intention of protecting the castle from enemies that invaded from the water. It was a long drop below. Definitely not survivable. I strained my eyes to see through the mist and rain. A waterfall, about a kilometre ahead. If I miraculously survived the jump from the parapet, I was certain the waterfall would wait for me with open arms to finish me off.

There has to be another way.

I tore down the path that aligned with the parapet, sensing in my bones that I was being followed.

CHAPTER 40

My feet wouldn't move fast enough. I snuck a glance over my shoulder and had to close my eyes to suppress another dizzy spell. Trajan loped behind me, his lycanthor strength spurring him on with speed and agility. I tried frantically to run faster, but a hand closed around the collar of my jacket, jerking me backward. I screamed. Kicked. Lurched. Anything to fight him off.

Trajan's hot breath caressed the back of my neck. "Stop fighting me." His voice teemed with fury. "You can't escape. You belong to the ULD now."

I responded with a fierce elbow-punch to his gut. He cried out, probably more from shock than physical pain. The force loosened his grip enough that I wriggled free—but now there was another problem. At the other end of the battlement wall stood Vulcan—and he wasn't alone. Lycanthors larger than any wolf prowled beside him as he advanced. The creatures' red eyes glittered hungrily, their black fur sleek in the rain, exposing muscle and powerful muzzles. Veined lightning streaked across the sky, revealing dissent rebels behind the pack. Vulcan had brought a small army to prevent my escape.

Trajan's hand latched around my neck with enough force that he'd easily snap it if I struggled. "Move."

In case I needed more convincing, he nudged me forward by punching his fist into my lower back. I blinked the pain away and began walking. My inner voice screamed at me to do something, but my mind came up with nothing.

I'm totally screwed.

We met Vulcan and his entourage at the centre of the battlement wall. He gave me a scolding wag of his head, his grin insufferable. I recalled the way Vulcan had looked when he'd been young and handsome like his son, but there was nothing left of that boy. Vulcan had been cruel back then, but now he'd grown into something far more twisted and sinister, his physical appearance marred by his obsession to cleanse the earth of humans. His skin was sallow, his hair long and matted in the rain. It cast shadows across his eyes so that they appeared sunken in his face. His lips curled in amusement. To him, I was an ant he could squish with a boot.

Emotion I didn't realise I'd been holding broke loose at the realisation that Vulcan's path would become Trajan's path too.

The lieutenant of the ULD examined me with a curt shake of his head. "So predictable. It was almost too easy to bring you to Darthmusk."

I resisted the urge to sneer. "I came to rescue your son from this madness. What you've done to him… it's inhuman."

Vulcan cast a bored look at the sky. "Inhuman? That word has always bothered me. We are not human and therefore cannot be *inhuman*. The *word* is extinct." His black eyes glistened silver in the lightning. "Trajan is where he should be. As are you."

"Your cause is evil," I spat. I was cold all over, but what made me shake had nothing to do with the temperature. "You're not saving the world by ridding it of humans. It's genocide."

He glared at me with disdain. "We've had this conversation before, and it's tiresome. I don't want to kill you, Zaya. You'd be an asset to the ULD. Since our little *scene* at the Asrath cliffs, I've had time to study the sleeping curse that binds Morgomoth. You need to be alive when your necromancer blood is transferred to his body. The hex won't break otherwise. We can't kill you."

Trajan's fingers pressed tighter around my neck, making it difficult to speak, but I managed a smirk. "Good to know."

Vulcan's lips lifted into another cunning smile. "That doesn't mean we can't hurt you. You're at my mercy now, Zaya. I can lock you away. Torture you. Make everyone you care about die." His voice rose, unctuous and cruel. "I will break you. You will join the ULD and give your blood willingly to Morgomoth."

"I'll kill myself before you can try." It wasn't an idle threat. Since the moment I'd lost Jad at Galvac Tower, I'd come to terms with death and accepted it. I'd done what I could to survive for my friends and to save Jad, but on a deeper level, I'd known death was a very real possibility. There was no way I'd help the ULD. If dying meant Morgomoth would never be resurrected, so be it.

Vulcan laughed, a heinous cackle that echoed in time with the crackling thunder. His eyes connected with Trajan's. Something tacit was communicated between them, because suddenly Trajan thrust me over the parapet wall, my legs bicycling through air. Trajan stood on the parapet, his arm stretched out, holding me by the throat. I grabbed his arm to hoist my weight and relieve the pressure on my neck. I panted hard through my nose, but my airways were blocked. Not enough oxygen reached my lungs.

He's going to break me.

My eyes drifted downward. This side of the river was a black snake through the landscape. Odd rock formations peered in and out of the current, the water powerful as it dipped and crashed against them. It was a blackwater power storm that threatened to rip everything apart in its rapids.

Vulcan took a swift step forward. "I can make you feel pain, Zaya. Pain that should kill you but won't. The ULD has the ability to take you to hell and back. Just think about that."

Hadar emerged in her white lab coat, her streaked black-and-white hair tangled in the pouring rain. She limped toward Vulcan, her damaged hip protruding at a crooked angle. She lifted a glass vial from her pocket and held it up to the subdued moonlight. Something inside it glowed hot green. The liquid blended together in bubbles like a lava lamp.

Vulcan's voice was drenched with exaggerated cynicism. "Hadar has been working on a spell that allows an individual to experience excruciating pain but prevents them from dying."

Hadar extracted a syringe from her lab coat with a wicked-looking needle attached. She pumped the spell inside it. Her eyes locked on mine.

I couldn't tell what were tears and what was rainwater down my cheeks. It wouldn't matter if Trajan dropped me into the river. With that foul curse in my system, the plunge would maim, paralyse, or damage me... but it wouldn't kill me. They had to keep me alive, but that didn't mean my body had to work.

Hadar crept forward. All she had to do was lean over the parapet and jab the syringe in my arm. The ULD would win. I'd be under their control.

I can't let this happen.

I won't let this happen.

Death is better than this.

Trajan dragged me back toward the parapet. I thrashed and struggled for release, but it was like trying to fight a concrete wall. He was too strong.

I need something to hinder him.

That's when I remembered the silver bullet in my pocket—the very bullet Vulcan had shot Jad with and I had kept as a sort of keepsake. A plan both brilliant and stupid formed in my head. I dug into my pocket and wedged the bullet between my fingers.

Here goes nothing.

I swung my arm forward, my hand pressing the bullet into Trajan's wrist. Silver was a lycanthor's worst nightmare. He screamed a grisly roar. Steam wafted from the flaming burn in his skin.

He let go.

Of me.

Time slowed down, every second dragged out.

I saw real fear in Trajan's eyes, and for a moment I questioned whether I was staring at Trajan or Jad. He reached out for me with that insane lycanthor speed and caught my hand, but gravity had already started its process, and no one, no matter how strong, could thwart that. My weight caused him to topple. I heard Vulcan's anguished cry, heard the intake of breath from the rebels as their greatest weapon went over the parapet. Trajan and I tumbled down the castle wall, the river waiting for us like a great gaping mouth.

We fell.

Into the mist.

Into the unknown.

Our hands still linked.

CHAPTER 41

I didn't know how it happened.

Somehow, whether by gravity, weight, or magic, Trajan and I became intertwined, legs and arms tangled. It felt like we fell forever. The wind tore at our clothes and hair, my whirling head unable to distinguish any direction. The only thing I knew for certain was down.

Trajan hit the water first. His body cushioned my fall, the light fading out of his eyes as we submerged.

No. No!

I tried to hold on to him, but the current ripped us apart. His unconscious body, maybe his dead body, floated farther downstream. The scream in my head was so loud it reverberated through my skull, but there was nothing I could do except watch him fade away into the dark, farther and farther away until he was gone.

I reminded myself that he was no longer Jad. After everything that had happened to him, this was probably sweet mercy, but it still didn't prevent heartache from piercing every inch of me.

Goodbye.

I had told myself—convinced myself—on the battlement that I'd been ready to die, but I guess some primeval response in me wanted to survive after all, because my legs kicked toward the surface.

The river had other ideas. The current held me in its embrace, dragging me through the rapids. I surfaced. Went under again. Up, down. Up, down. The river couldn't decide what it wanted to do with me. Rocks scraped my arms and legs, and for a moment, everything dimmed as my head took a serious whack to the side. I caught a brief glimpse of Darthmusk castle, farther away than I would have thought possible in the time I'd been in the river. The massive edifice disappeared in a swirl of mist, as though a stage curtain had theatrically shut. Production over. Please vacate your seat.

Darthmusk has to be a kilometre away, which means—

A roar of water, more terrifying than any sound a fighter jet could ever make, thundered in my ears. Through the mist ahead, the river surged and plunged. My stomach contracted. The waterfall loomed twenty metres away. Nineteen metres away.

No! Noooo!

I tried to latch on to rocks, reeds, anything that felt secure, but the current ripped me away. I'd survived the fall at Darthmusk, only to be killed at the next sheer drop. Irony was a bitch.

Fifteen metres away.

Fourteen metres.

I braced for the inevitable.

Can people survive waterfalls?

I guessed it depended on the height and whether there were rocks below.

Ten metres.

Something grabbed my side. I went under, my mouth and nose assaulted by volumes of water.

Am I... drifting the other way?

Something—no, someone was tugging me from the surface's bounding, erratic current, diving deeper where they had the propulsion to swim. They were either super strong or part amphibian. We reached shallow water. My feet and legs were dragged over a sandbank before I was unceremoniously dropped onto the shore. My throat and chest burned from the cold and something even more painful. I rolled onto my side and vomited. Water was expelled from my mouth. I had no idea I'd swallowed so much.

"Did you forget everything I trained you for?"

The voice lacked empathy. Instead, it sounded faintly amused.

I was shivering—possibly suffering from hypoxia—and delirious. My head was too heavy for my body, as though it had shattered into hefty pieces that hung somewhere behind me. But that *voice*... everything had been worth it for that voice.

I turned, unable to suppress my elation. Jad stared back. Not Trajan, Jad! Hadar's curse had deteriorated from his blood. His eyes had returned to that familiar dark chocolate shade I'd always admired, his face no longer animalistic but achingly handsome and rugged. Raven-black hair floated past his jawline. It looked twice as long now that it was damp.

No wonder Indree used the Valintinian spell on him.

Indree!

My hands balled into fists. There was unfinished business between Indree and Jad, business that would continue now that he was saved. I'd wanted to wrap my arms around him, embrace him for every week, day, and hour I'd missed. Instead, I slapped his shoulder and forced my lips into a mocking grin. "Took you long enough."

"It's nice to see you too. The reunion will have to wait. We need to get to the cross portals." His gaze lingered on the forest. "They'll be tracking us. Lycanthors will be on their way." He took my arm and lifted me off the ground as though I weighed nothing. "Can you walk?"

The reason I was ungainly on my feet had nothing to do with plunging into a river and nearly drowning, but I was grateful I had it for an excuse. It was difficult not to stare at him. Jad might have returned, but he still carried the lycanthor curse, namely in his strength. Maybe that part would never disappear.

Grisly, blood-curdling howls rippled across the night. Dread sliced into me. I imagined the lycanthor pack tearing and snarling, clawed paws crashing into the ground as their animal gaze targeted us.

My head swam. "Forget walking. Run!"

We broke into a sprint, weaving through the trees, the thick fog making it impossible to see ahead. The only thing I was certain of was the direction of the cross portals. Powerful, silver-blue light lit the sky about a kilometre away, pinpointing the portals' exact location. Not even the fog was a match for its luminous glow.

Branches snapped behind us. Deep, resonating growls carried through the air and fog.

They're getting closer.

Jad snatched my hand in his and forced me to keep up with his pace. My lungs burned, and my legs were leaden. My waterlogged clothes made me miserably cold.

I don't think I can do this much longer.

My knees buckled, the ground tilting at an impossible angle. My head met it with jarring impact. Everything became an impossible blur of dark and mist that threatened to swallow me whole.

Strong arms lifted me off the ground. A part of me was conscious enough to be ashamed by my weakness as Jad carried me the rest of the way.

I'll never live this down.

If I live.

Because seriously, this had to be death. My arms and legs had no feeling. My heartbeat slowed like a clock on its final tick. The pain and affliction started to dim. I welcomed it.

This is it. The end.

Searing blue light flooded my eyes, refusing to let me slip away. Shapes appeared ahead—people silhouetted against the azure glow that lit the forest. The light was beautiful. Radiant. Warm.

The cross portals. We've made it.

So why were we travelling toward the dark? Why were we headed toward a deep, jaded crack in the centre of the cross portals? Smoke and shadowy wisps extended from the fissure. It widened like a cavernous mouth. The stench of sulphur and flames permeated the air. My friends were running toward it. In it. How could they not see what was there? Were they blind? I wanted to scream that they were going the wrong way, but all I managed was a whimper.

Don't go in there. Don't go in there!

But I was limp and useless in Jad's arms and couldn't warn him.

He ran inside the void. Steam whipped at my face, the light from the cross portals hazier and more distant the farther we entered the dark. I craned my neck to see the aperture close behind us.

What have you done?

The last thing I was aware of was the sound of my own panicked heartbeat before the darkness enveloped us.

CHAPTER 42

I woke to deafening gunshots. Vague impressions of orange-gold caster fire flashed in and out of my vision, the roar of explosions amplified in my semi-conscious state.

Magic. Someone's fighting with magic.

I jolted upright, so quickly my head risked losing its small grasp on reality again.

Where are we?

Steam sizzled off the road I sat on, scalding my skin through my wet clothes. The asphalt was as much rubble as it was tarmac, disjointed and strewn with potholes. Weeds hung limp among the cracks. White-hot sun blazed down. All around me stood enormous tall buildings in a ramshackle of structures. Windows broken. Doors rusted. Walls half crumbled from their foundations. It was a freeze-frame of an urban landscape left to rot and ruin. The hazy outline of skyscrapers in the distance blurred with the ocean. At some point in history, part of this once magnificent city had collapsed into the sea.

What the hell is this place?

A howl crackled around me. Ahead, the monstrous forms of lycanthors appeared in the black aperture. Their paws scraped onto the broken asphalt as the pack tried to wrench themselves through the portal.

They've followed us.

Marek fired his cast-shooter, round after round, his muffled shouts outweighed by shrieks and vicious snarls. Each time a lycanthor fell, another was there to replace it, gnashing its teeth, haunches in a low crouch as it prepared to launch itself out of the aperture.

I should have remained unconscious.

My brain felt as though it were sitting in my head unattached, my feet and legs struggling to stand.

Talina appeared, her face ashen and tear-stained. "Don't get up." She pushed my shoulders back and forced me to lie down again. "You can't help them. Let them do this."

Them?

I swatted her hands away and looked over her shoulder. On the road ahead, Jad emerged in a cloud of vaporous smoke. He approached the aperture with a looming firestorm behind. The inferno was so powerful it obstructed the sunlight. Darkness and shadow closed in, heat and humidity making the air intolerable. Sweat popped out on my skin as ash fell from the sky. I'd never seen magic like this. Jad was a skilled fire wielder before Hadar's medical experimentations, but now his magic was triple the strength. He could literally cast firestorms.

The lycanthors snapped their jaws, eyes centred on their new target. Gusts of strong wind carried their foul stench. They broke through the aperture, arching across the air in giant leaps, bounding toward Jad.

Marek.

Lainie.

Edric.

Indree.

Tusk.

One of the beasts charged toward Talina and me. Talina closed her eyes, accepting the inevitable as the lupine creature arrived with a formidable roar, muzzle ready to rip us apart. I pushed myself in front of Talina at the same time stabbing light, as strong and radiant as the sun, blazed around us. I blinked spots out of my eyes. In the centre of the firestorm stood Jad. He conjured flames into his hands and shot them forward like arrows of red fire. It struck the wolves with perfect precision. Charred meat reeked in the air. I almost felt sorry for the lycanthors as flame tendrils leapt over their bodies, their grisly moans short-lived. The rest of the pack bounded back into the aperture. The large slit closed with a thunderous crack.

Everything went silent.

Talina scrambled out from underneath me, her blonde hair stained with soot. She stared aghast at the blood-red rings that stained Jad's eyes. Lainie collapsed onto the ground and threw up everything in her stomach. Marek trained his cast-shooter at his former captain, but the barrel wasn't quite in line. At his range, he might shoot an arm. Indree, Edric, and Tusk stared. Their ashen faces projected disbelief.

Blood pounded through my legs when I surveyed Jad. The firestorm, smoke, and shadows had evaporated now that he'd calmed down, the rings in his eyes gone. My fear abated with it. Whatever madness had taken over Jad had vanished. He looked like... well, Jad again.

Before I could move, Indree hurtled toward him. She wrapped her arms around his neck and enveloped him in a possessive hug. She kissed his cheek, his forehead, his lips. I looked away, not wanting to imagine the private words she whispered into his ear.

The initial confusion over, everyone greeted and welcomed him back. From the way they all acted, a passer-by might have thought Jad had been on a long overseas journey, not suffering at the hands of the ULD. He did look well. The abrasions, bruises, and sores were gone, healed by his lycanthor magic. He was stronger and fitter than any of us. But how long would it last? How long until the monster returned?

I pushed back onto my knees, still shaky as I stood. The first thing that struck me as odd was why the ground was wet. Had the entire ocean been sucked into a cloud and strewn as rain across the abandoned city? The buildings were damp, but only as far as thirteen stories. Beyond that was dry and weathered. Not one white or dark cloud tarnished the blue sky.

Not rain.

But what else could have drenched the lower part of the city. Half the potholes in the road were filled with water.

And what is this place?

I jumped, not expecting to turn around and find Jad standing in front of me. Even though I'd chosen not to be a part of that little reunion, it still annoyed me that no one had asked me to come over. I had been the one to risk life and limb to bring Jad back, after all. I crossed my arms, unable to keep the annoyance from my voice. "Happy to see Indree?"

Jad didn't respond. His eyes trailed over the buildings, the cracked pavements, the waterlogged roads. His forehead creased in puzzlement. "Something isn't right about this place."

"Yeah, no shit. It's abandoned."

He spun around to observe the rest of our location. The glow of sunlight brightened the worry in his eyes.

A savage snort tore from my throat. Our luck had deteriorated, and if I didn't laugh about it, I'd surely curl up into a ball and cry. "Why did the cross portal bring us here?"

It was ironic that we had left one wasteland only to end up in another.

Footsteps drew our attention. Marek appeared with the mapographic. His eyes darted frantically over the terrain. "This place is Gonzavree. It used to be a human settlement... destroyed hundreds of years ago by a galactic storm that burnt the city's celestial shield to the ground."

I shook my head, not quite believing what I heard. "I didn't think anything could obliterate a celestial shield."

Except for the Four Revenants.

Jad's handsome face almost appeared brutish as he looked at me. "Their magic needs to be replenished on a regular schedule. Miss that opportunity and a powerful galactic storm could bring a celestial shield down with a lightning strike."

I arched an eyebrow. "But an entire city?"

"It's happened before."

"So again, why would the cross portal bring us here?"

Marek shifted beside me. "It's my fault. A black portal means a dead end. They don't stay open for long, and I saw that ours was starting to close. I thought if we snuck through in time, it would shut and the lycanthors wouldn't be able to follow us. I should have led us through a blue cross portal. I'm sorry."

"Yeah, damn right you should have." The accusation flew out of my throat before I could stop it.

"Zaya.'" Jad's frustrated voice surprised me. Just like that, we were back to being instructor and cadet. Not equals. It hurt more than I wanted to admit.

Jad turned his attention to the lieutenant. His voice was deliberately expressionless. "Blue cross portals don't close. The lycanthors would have caught us. You did the right thing."

Marek nodded but didn't look convinced. His upper tooth bit into his lower lip. "The mapographic has highlighted another black portal east of here. This city is large. It might take us a day to reach it, and even then the portal could be closed. We'd have to wait for it to open... but it might be our only way out of here."

I glared at him through my overwhelmed eyes. "And where does that portal lead?"

Jad stepped in front of me, his face unforgivably cold. "Leave it, Zaya. Everyone is tired, and this isn't the place to play the blame game."

"I'm not blaming anyone."

Why was I so angry all of a sudden?

Why was Jad staring at me with such… dislike?

Indree watched us from a distance, her eyes narrowed. Had she said something to him?

Jad's lips tightened at the corners. His gaze was heavy on my own, and there was nothing kind in it. "No one knows where black portals lead. That's why they're called black portals."

His hand closed around the hilt of his athame-sabre—the same sabre he'd tried to hurt me with only an hour ago. He called out to the group. "I suggest we start moving and look for the portal. Keep your eyes open for shelter. We may need it."

He marched ahead. The group followed his lead.

I shut my eyes, light-headed again. I plodded heavily after the group, keeping a watchful eye on the potholes. The water inside them made me nervous.

There are no chak-lorks here. There are no chak-lorks here.

But even as I thought it, I didn't believe it.

CHAPTER 43

Gonzavree was a post-apocalyptic wasteland. Buildings stood together like abandoned boxes, windows black and empty. The burnt-out husks of old vehicles cluttered the road, every street, alley, and highway long and lonely. We'd been walking for an hour, block after block, building after building, kicking our way through crumbled debris and wreckage. Even nature had abandoned this place. No animals scavenged for food in the ruins. No birds flew overhead in the sky. No trees. No plant life. This place was a ghost city, a graveyard, a frozen place in time.

Jad led the way. Indree sauntered beside him like a loyal dog brushing up for attention. I didn't know if they talked. I'd kept my distance to protect myself from the jealous, raging monster in my heart. My guess was that they would wait for somewhere more private to rekindle their relationship. I really wished I had my cast-shooter on me. The target practice would have been therapeutic.

Marek, Lainie, and Edric were next in the line, followed by Tusk and Talina. I meandered at the back. Dusk was closing in, the air cooling fast, but it did nothing for my pounding headache, which started to snake its way down my neck into my shoulders. Twice I had to stop to empty my stomach. The third time I dry-heaved for a full three minutes. My body felt as though it had been twisted, knifed, and pulled apart by a horrific torture device. When Jad saw me on my hands and knees, I guess he didn't have any other choice but to insist we find somewhere to rest.

I sat against the crusted remains of a car while the others searched for shelter that wasn't wet, rotten, or eaten away with mould. I heard them talk among each other, heard the disappointment in their voices as they found, yet again, another unsuitable building, but honestly I didn't care. My head hurt too bad.

Someone sat down beside me. I opened my eyes and blinked away the dwindling sunset. Talina's green eyes stood out against the pink sunburnt splotches that covered her face. Her lips were chapped, her honey-blonde hair practically straw.

"How are you feeling?" She winced as she spoke. The cut on her neck had stopped bleeding, but the blood had dried on her skin in streaks down to her chest. She slapped a hand over it.

I elbowed her gently in the side. "You should know better than to touch it. You'll get it infected."

Her lips shaped into a sad smile. "It's itchy. There's a curse in it somewhere. Lainie feels it in her too."

"Why haven't you healed yourselves?"

An apologetic look sprang across her face. "The spell will fade and the cut will heal on its own. Besides, the ULD took our rucksacks and all our medical supplies when they captured us. All we have left is Indree's. We need to conserve what we have in case of...."

In case something more serious happens.

I swallowed the bitter taste in my mouth. "Jad's right. We need to rest, but this place, it's.... Something isn't normal about this city. It's—"

The ground lurched. A terrible boom erupted below, the asphalt seeming to crack apart and rise like ant mounds from the roads. Buildings shook. Red dust tumbled from the roofs in crimson waterfalls, the city enveloped in brown fog.

Talina grabbed my arm. "It's an earthquake."

I hung on to her. The earth was violent and angry. I imagined the buildings uprooted like trees and cringed at the thought of them falling in an unstoppable domino effect around us.

Breathe, Zaya. It will pass. We're in the provinces. These things happen in the provinces. It will pass.

At last it ended, but somehow the silence that followed was worse.

Is everyone okay?

Jad?

Lainie?

Marek?

For a long time, I couldn't hear anything.

Movement caught my eye. Tusk emerged from around a pile of rubble, his face coated in dust. "No wonder this place was bloody forsaken. It's on a frigging fault line."

The rest of the group appeared. Except for a few scratches and cuts, no one was seriously hurt. They were more shocked than anything. Jad helped Talina and me off the ground. My head spun, but something about Jad's presence settled me, which was annoying because I wanted to be mad at him. I lifted my gaze to his face and found his eyes on mine. He didn't say anything, but he assessed me for injuries, relieved when he saw none.

"I'm fine," I snapped and walked away.

He'd spent all his time with Indree and hadn't said boo to me. I didn't need his help, thank you very much.

"Hey, guys?" Marek's hands were trembling as he held the monographic to his pale face. "We need to get out of this place. Everything here is unstable."

Yeah, no shit.

Lainie frowned at the buildings' upper levels. "Pity we can't rest up there. It looks dry. It would have been nice to have just stopped for a while."

I halted. What she said raised a perturbed thought in me.

The upper levels are dry.
The ground is wet.
The buildings are decayed from sea corrosion.

Jad must have seen the colour drain from my face, because he moved toward me with quick strides. "What is it?"

I studied the upturned vehicles around us. Their peeling, tarnished husks weren't burnt out like I'd previously thought. They weren't covered in rust but rusticles—the very same kind of icicle-like formations that appeared deep underwater.

But that doesn't make sense.

Jad's sudden gasp sparked my own fear. He'd worked it out at the same time I had.

A scream rippled through the hot winds, sending a shiver of foreboding through my body. I spun around. Lainie's mouth was open in terror, her eyes directed toward the sky. On the edge of the city, blocking out the horizon, was a wall of ocean water.

A tsunami.

And it was coming straight for us.

CHAPTER 44

I didn't know what was worse, seeing the massive swell of water or the hopeless, terrified expressions that crossed everyone's faces. An onslaught of cries erupted from Tusk, and for a moment, it may have taken us all a fraction of a second to compute that we had to run. Again.

Jad grabbed my shoulder, but his shout was directed at everyone. "Move. Find a building that's stable and get to high ground."

We ran toward what must have once been a grand hotel, its lavish exterior tarnished in green-and-brown stains, the large Romanesque arches to the front door damaged down to stumps. They reminded me of trees snapped in half. Out of every building around us though, the hotel was definitely the most durable.

I tossed a glance over my shoulder and understood why Gonzavree was completely abandoned, why no one had made a shelter out of its ruins, why no animals or scavengers frequented the crumbled site for food. The earthquake and tsunami weren't a one-off event. They were frequent, scheduled like clockwork, occurring over and over again. No wonder the portal to this place had been coloured black. It was a warning not to come here.

Too late now.

A mountain-sized shadow loomed over us. It extended across the street ahead, reminding me of a cloud of locusts blocking out the fraying sunlight. I stole another peek at the wave. The water rose in an impenetrable wall of darkness.

It's going to—

It crested like the jaw of a hungry animal snapping down. The disrupted ocean slammed into the buildings, the impact sending geysers into the sky. Foam and spray upturned anything that wasn't secure—vehicles, benches, loose bricks, tiles. They were all swept up in the surge, barrelling toward us in a flood of liquid, debris, and mud. Buildings groaned, suddenly as stable as the Jenga towers I'd played with when I was twelve. Ripped metal, thrashing waves, and the horror-struck cries of my friends rattled my ears.

This is madness. We'll never outrun it.

Jad reached the hotel's once impressive glass door, smashed out the remaining fragments with his elbow, and waved everyone through. He'd been putting on a brave face, but the moment our eyes locked, I saw what was really going on behind that valiant mask. Confusion, despair, angst. He was just as frightened as the rest of us, and that really drove it home that we were in trouble.

I was about a metre away from the door when a cry tore through the air behind me.

Marek!

Some of the ground had uprooted in the earthquake, and in the searing hot winds, a small anchor bolt had impaled the fleshy part of his thigh. He couldn't run, at least not fast. I moved toward him, but a hand firm on my shoulder yanked me backward.

Jad's voice was laced with urgency. "Get inside and lead the others to safety. I'll get Marek."

Before I could say anything, he'd raced forward, his lycanthor strength fuelling his speed. For a moment I could have sworn his eyes glowed like molten lava again, but now wasn't the time to worry about whether the monster inside him would take over. That would have to wait.

I sprinted into the hotel's lobby. The lavish mosaic floor was choked with seaweed, the elegant brass fixtures smoothed down from years of water damage. I weaved around the gold-leaf columns, dodging showers of plaster that fell from the ceiling. The tiled lobby, the rotten wood-panelled walls, and what was left of the floor-to-ceiling windows shook violently in the powerful tremors that preceded the water. Talina, Lainie, and Edric were ahead. They ascended the spiral staircase that snaked around the lobby to the upper levels.

It took all my vigour to shout up to them, "Get above floor thirteen. Don't stop for anything."

I was nearly at the stairs myself when I was forced to pause. I blinked, unable to believe it. Indree and Tusk were waiting by the elevator. They hit the button, once, twice, and stared at the doors in outrage when they refused to open.

Are they frigging serious?

I slapped Indree's shoulder hard—an immensely satisfying experience. "There's no power, you idiots. Run!"

The lobby's windows exploded. Water cascaded, surging, rippling, flooding the entire length of the room and nearly halfway to the stairs. Jad carried an unconscious Marek over his shoulder, only a few metres in front of the gigantic swell. Despair welled up in me, as swift and ruthless as the water rushing behind them.

Please make it. Please make it.

I wanted to run to him, help him, do what I could to save him and Marek, but the firm glare in his eyes told me that was the last thing he wanted me to do. Thank providence for his lycanthor strength, because he made it to the staircase and started the ascent, catching up to us with swift strides. But now we had a bigger problem. The stairs were damaged and strewn with holes, making our climb treacherous. A part of the banister broke off in my hand when I grabbed it, nearly toppling me into the rising water. I stumbled back, continued to run, slipped, got back up again. On and on we went, past level two, three, four.

Thirteen floors. Thirteen floors.
We're never going to make it.
Five, six, seven.
The water roared after us, approaching like a yawning, hungry mouth.
Eight. Nine.
A screeching cry broke out somewhere behind me. Water had sloshed over the railing and saturated Tusk. For a second, I couldn't understand why he flailed his arms and bawled like he'd been doused in fire. Then I saw it. Not water. At least not anymore. The liquid had taken on a solid form, morphing into hands, arms, legs, and feet. It had a head and a body—a putrid, slimy, sopping mess of something that had once been human or caster. Ringing filled my ears.
Chak-lork.
The creature wrapped itself—no, it *fused* itself with Tusk, commingling mind, body, and water. I watched with open-mouthed horror as the monster trained a malicious smile on me and burst like a ruptured water balloon. Tusk's skin, muscle, and bone went with it, meaty chunks skittering across the water. The pieces liquified into a bloody paste to make a gruesome red stain on the surface.
I scrambled away from the mess that used to be Tusk.
He's dead. He's dead!
Indree screamed and wouldn't stop.
She was annoying at the worst of times, but I grabbed her hand and forced her to continue up the stairs. Jad carried the unconscious Marek behind us, neither surprised nor traumatised by Tusk's death. I didn't think it was because he disliked the cadet. No, Jad had seen this before. He was desensitised.
Level ten.
Did that really just happen? Is that how chak-lorks kill? By going inside you and….

I didn't want to think about it. Couldn't think about it. The image had been too gruesome.

Eleven.

I couldn't help it. I looked over my shoulder. It had to be my exhaustion playing tricks, right? But no. Heads dipped in and out of the lapping water. They bobbed like floating apples, then rose. Necks. Shoulders. Chests. Torsos and arms appeared, fish-eaten and clumpy. Chak-lorks. Hundreds of them.

And if they're here, then that means....

The Four Revenants are close.

Twelve.

Thirteen.

We whipped up the last steps to level fourteen, down the guest corridor, past sealed doors coated in cobwebs, right to the end at door 1482. The water had reached its peak and no longer chased us, but now we had chak-lorks on our heels—and unlike the water, the creatures wouldn't stop. They flew down the corridor, some of them skittering toward us on all fours, others climbing the walls and ceiling, leaving damp, oily stains on the plaster.

Every horror novel I'd read in the orphanage came back to me. This was exactly like a scene from a zombie apocalypse.

Talina opened the door to 1482. We all piled into the hotel room.

"Shut the door!"

"Lock it!"

"Find something heavy to block it."

The door slammed.

Grunts and manic shrieks rose outside the room.

I didn't know who shouted or did what. The pressure in my head became too much.

We'd lost Crawley.

We'd lost Tusk.

Was it my fault?

Yes, it was.

Everything was spinning, my vision fading. The buzzing in my ears grew to a deafening ring.

"Zaya."

I looked up. Violetta was there, the only thing clear in the chaos. She smiled at me, but it lacked warmth. *"You're exhausted. You need to rest."*

Rest. Yes. That sounds nice.

The world tilted into a blurry grey, dimming toward dark. I dropped too suddenly on my head and saw...

Nothing.

CHAPTER 45

"Zaya! Can you hear me? Zaya!"

The voice floated in and out, the darkness refusing to let me go. I didn't know how long I'd drifted in this obscure, shadowy world. It felt like hours, maybe days. The pain in my head, the agony in my body, the torment that my mind subjected me to were… gone. I blinked. My lids peeled back with difficulty, as though the sleep in my eyes had melded them with glue.

Wake up, Zaya. Wake up.

I did, and the memories returned. Panic cinched my chest. I struggled to sit, tossing away pillows and blankets as my defences kicked in.

There has to be something I can use as a weapon. Anything to fight off those heinous monsters.

"Zaya, calm down. It's okay. It's over. Everything is okay."

The voice was soothing and very out of place.

Talina sat in a chair beside my bed, a book in her hand. The sight of her reading was an image that confused me more than anything else I'd been through over the last few weeks. Slowing down and putting our feet up was not a luxury afforded to us— ever. I stared, damning her with my blank stare.

She smiled. "Relax. Everything's okay. You've been asleep for five days. We have our situation under control… for the most part."

Five days?

I knew it had been a while, but… five days? I should have won an award for most unconscious person on the planet.

"We can't afford a time out," I insisted. "We have to keep moving. Have you all gone completely insane?"

Talina's shoulders sagged with a hint of indignation. "You needed rest. So did Marek. We all did."

My eyes swept around the room. I was sitting in an enormous bed in a darkened apartment, the curtains drawn to close out the day. A single candle on the dresser lit the surroundings. The bed sheets were satin, no longer white but stained yellow from age, the ceiling high enough that not even the candlelight flicked over it. Just like the rest of the hotel, this room would have been luxurious and opulent once, but now the soft shades of white wall paint had peeled and appeared grey, and the burgundy carpet was threadbare and eaten away in places by the sun.

I pressed my fingers against my throat, my voice hoarse. "What happened? The chak-lorks…."

"Are gone for now." Talina clenched and unclenched her right hand on her book.

"For now?"

She didn't answer.

"Talina, what is happening?"

She motioned her head toward the ceiling as though to say 'Why me?' and gave a loud sigh. "It appears that the chak-lorks are dependent on water and need to remain close to it. This place… the curse on it, it's on some kind of schedule. Every evening before the sun sets, the earthquake occurs, followed by the tsunami. At sunrise the water recedes. Gonzavree is flooded only at night."

I put two and two together. "And the chak-lorks go with the water."

"Yes, but they're back as soon as that wave crests. They know we're here somewhere in the building, but they can't venture too far from the water to find us. Some of them have come close, but for now... we're safe."

"There's those two words again that I hate. *For now.* Where are we, exactly?"

"The penthouse. Well, what's left of it. It's the highest room in this tower. We moved here on the second day. Captain Arden... I mean Jad thought it would be best to get us to as high ground as possible."

"I don't disagree with Captain Arden on that one, but if the water has receded, then we need to move and find that portal. Or better yet, just get the hell out of this city."

"We can't."

"Excuse me?"

Talina flinched. "We can't leave this place. We're smack in the middle of the city. We'd never get out in time before the next wave. Our only option is to find that portal and... that's proving difficult."

I stared incredulously. "What is Captain Arden doing about it?"

Talina's mouth parted. Her eyes drifted down to her hands and back again. "He doesn't want to be referred to as captain anymore. He said he's not fit to be one and no longer deserves the title."

"That's bullshit."

"I know but he's... different."

I had no argument for that. I'd experienced first-hand how *different* Jad was. The lycanthor inside him pushed out everything that made him who he was and replaced it with violence and rage. He'd been a soldier, an assassin—a brainwashed killing machine for the ULD. So long as Hadar and her curse were out of his system, we weren't in any real danger, but it was the unseen changes, the ones we had yet to learn about, that frightened me. We really had no idea what Jad was capable of.

The horrors I'd encountered with him at Darthmusk returned, shoving me back into that wretched world of despair. My eyes threatened to break into tears, the discomfort in my throat as sharp and painful as a wedged piece of glass. I breathed hard, refusing to let the emotion out. If I couldn't be strong, how could I expect anyone else to be?

I swallowed, unsure if I really wanted to know the answer to the question I was about to ask. "How is he?"

Talina brushed a delicate curl behind her ear. Five days' respite had been good for her. She looked healthier, stronger, her skin smooth and healed. Maybe rest hadn't been such a bad idea.

She discarded the book she'd been reading and leaned back in her chair. "Jad's sad. He's grieving, maybe even feeling guilty. Marek's tried to ask him what happened in Darthmusk, but Jad won't say. He hasn't talked much about anything, which is driving Indree insane. It's good to have a fire wielder among us though. Jad's managed to cast flames around the apartment, so there's no risk of chak-lorks getting in. It keeps us warm too." Her face lifted into a brief smile, then fell again. "He's been searching for the portal with Marek. Lainie and Edric go with them. They're out during the day and return at sunset, before the wave."

I relaxed back into my pillow.

At least Jad is… partly okay.

Alarm flooded me again. "Marek!"

The last thing I remembered was an anchor bolt wedged through his thigh.

Talina dipped her head. "That's partly the reason why you took so long to recover. I'm sorry." The tears in her green eyes conferred her shame. "I gave what was left of our asith potion to Marek. I was able to clean and cauterize the wound. He needed the healing potion more than you. And you did recover on your own. It just took time."

I drummed my fingertips on my dusty bed sheet. "I would have done the same."

And honestly, I did feel better. Sleep had healed the aches in my body. My migraine was gone. I could think clearly, which was more than I'd been capable of for days. I conceded defeat. If everyone looked half as good as Talina, then Jad's decision to stay put had been the right one.

Talina stood and wandered to a partly open door. Inside was a bathroom. I could just make out a marble bathtub. Steam wafted from it, and condensation trickled down the mirror.

Talina turned to look at me. Her voice was soft but insistent. "We've come up with a few inventions while you were asleep. Behold, your bath. Sorry to say it, but you stink."

Ignoring the insult, I slid off the bed. In the doorway, I wasn't sure what to make of their so-called invention. "Are you trying to boil me?"

What I stared at was a portable steel bathtub, something they'd obviously found because it was worn and scratched. Underneath the tub, sticks and branches had been lit in fire—probably ignited by Jad's magic—keeping the water warm and inviting. A block of soap waited for me on the basin.

I could barely suppress my delighted laughter. "How did you do this?"

Talina beamed. "Marek and I came up with it. We found the tub. The building must have had a roof garden at one stage, but everything was dead. We collected what we could for firewood. There was a storm three nights ago, and we were able to find some old cleaning buckets that weren't too badly damaged. We have enough water to drink and obviously"—she pointed to the tub—"some to spare. But this will be your only bath. We only have enough water to keep us going to Port Serres."

I stared. "Isn't Port Serres days away?"

She did a little jump of excitement. "Marek has been studying the mapographic. If we can find this portal, it should take us to Baglash. That means we'll only be a day south of Port Serres."

My heart lifted, lighter than it had been in weeks. I had

forgotten what it felt like to have hope. "I think I'll enjoy my bath now," I said, almost in happy tears.

I reached for the soap. That's when I saw the drain in the basin. It was filled with dirt and stones. Someone had jammed them inside. "What's that about?"

The shower and sink had been filled too. Even the drain in the floor.

Talina grabbed the door handle and stood at the threshold. "That's to stop Chak-lorks from getting in through the pipes. I told you, they can go anywhere water can."

With that unsettling news, she shut the door behind her.

CHAPTER 46

Despite Talina's alarming revelation, I did manage to relax in the bath, soaking until my fingers were pruned and the water was practically black. I'd had a cringeworthy amount of dirt in places I hadn't even known existed, and parts of my hair fell out in knotted clumps when I brushed it. The rucksack I'd stolen had a small amount of body wash and shampoo in its toiletry compartment, which I put to good use. I was glad I'd kept it. There'd been times where I thought tossing it would be more practical. It had only been adding weight to my back and shoulders, after all.

I'm soooo glad I kept you, I thought, massaging shampoo into my scalp.

When I'd finished in the bath and towel-dried my hair, I changed into a spare set of clothes Talina had laid out for me—it looked like they'd been raiding wardrobes too—and entered the living area. The cream couches were covered in thin sheets of grime, the wooden floors rotted out in places, all the light fixtures broken. The huge holographic screen would have been nice once—real nice. I could imagine a family sitting in this room enjoying each other's company while they looked out at the sunset through the wide windows. Life must have been pleasant back then.

In the centre of the room, where a coffee table once stood, was another magic-lit fire, a frypan on top. Something sizzled inside it.

Great. Fish.

"Hungry?" Talina emerged from the kitchen, which was so broken and scattered with mould it was a serious health hazard. "Took forever to clean the pans and pots. Here." She sat down with a spatula and scooped the fish onto a plate.

Fish was one of my least favourite foods, but I was so hungry I'd probably eat a fried rat if it was served to me. I sat down by the fire and ate gratefully.

I pushed my plate toward Talina. "You don't want some?"

She shook her head. "No, thank you. Fish is the only thing that's been on the menu, and I am over it. Don't get me wrong. I appreciate Marek catching our food all the time, and it is saving what's left of our food supply for the last leg of the trip, but I don't think I could eat another fish again in my life."

"Fair enough." I shoved more of the fried—if not pleasant, at least filling—goodness into my mouth. "Where is everyone?"

"Looking for the portal. They'll be back soon. Sunset is in an hour."

The warning in her tone was undeniable.

With the sunset came the wave.

And that meant chak-lorks.

It had been nice to just relax for a while, but now worry closed in all over again.

Talina must have been familiar with the routine, because she tossed another five pieces of fish into the pan. Ten minutes later, the rest of the group arrived. They were tired, the strain evident in the way they held their shoulders, which were slouched and tight, but like Talina, the five days of rest had invigorated them. They were exhausted from the day's work. Not from weeks of running, fighting, and struggling to survive.

Marek pulled me into a hug when he saw me. Lainie and Edric embraced me too, but it was brief and lacked warmth. I told myself it didn't mean anything. They were tired and hungry. Indree sat by the fire and didn't look at me, just scrunched up her nose at the fish on her plate.

Everything faded away when I saw Jad. His tanned skin seemed to glow in the flickering firelight. I'd done a superb job of detaching my feelings for him since Darthmusk, or so I'd thought, but now every mixed emotion came back—hope, courage, faith, relief, and... jealousy when he took a seat beside Indree. He bent over and whispered in her ear. She nodded. The pair left our makeshift campsite and wandered into a spare room, which I was pretty sure was a bedroom. Scratching my eyes out would have been nicer than seeing that.

Get over it, Zaya. Accept it and get over it. Focus on what's important: getting to Port Serres.

Jad hadn't so much as looked at me when he'd entered the penthouse. Me, who'd saved him from Darthmusk. Not her. He might have considered me like a little sister, maybe even nothing more than a friend, but he could have at least taken the time to thank me.

A cheer broke from Talina. She grabbed my arm happily. "Isn't that great news?"

I blinked away my heartbroken confusion. "What?"

I hadn't been listening to a word any of them had said.

Marek gawked, a piece of fish halfway to his mouth. "We found the portal. We leave when the sun rises tomorrow. Gather your things, because Jad's keen to get moving." The corners of his mouth lifted in an elated smile. "We're nearly there, Zaya. Port Serres isn't far."

"Nearly there," I repeated, as though saying the words would somehow make me believe it.

But we're not.

There was still a day's journey north to Port Serres, and literally anything could prevent or delay us. At this point, I wouldn't bat an eye if a tornado arrived to wipe us off the face of the earth. We were in the provinces. Unpredictable weather came with the territory. I was all for optimism, but seriously, Marek should have known better.

I sighed and put my plate down. "I'm sorry. I'm still tired. I think I'll go get some more sleep."

Anything to get me away from these confused and disappointed feelings.

Talina rubbed her hands, keeping them close to the fire. "That's probably for the best. That earthquake will strike soon. It always makes me queasy."

Earthquakes, tsunamis, galactic storms.

Just your average evening.

I wandered back into my room, ready to drown myself in sheets and pillows.

UNSURPRISINGLY, I couldn't sleep because… well, I'd slept for five days and nights and had more vigour in me than a caffeinated energy drink. I tossed and turned when the earthquake struck. The tremors weren't nearly as bad in this tower as they'd been down at ground level, which I suspected was because of reinforced concrete. Magic might have abandoned this place, but at least the original architects had made some sensible decisions. That was probably why half of Gonzavree remained standing, even if it was partially destroyed.

I got out of bed and stood on shaky legs.

When was the last time I had fresh air?

Deciding I needed to walk off my weird mood, I left my room on tiptoes, my feet soft on the frayed carpet, and slipped out of the apartment. The hallway was long and deserted except for the flames that licked the floor. The fires rose in wispy tendrils. They made the passage overly warm, but they worked in barricading the exits to the lower levels, so I wasn't complaining.

Jad's protective spells working at their finest.

I suppose that was something I should have been grateful for, but honestly, I didn't want any reminders of him.

Talina had said there was once a garden roof. I found a staircase that led to the roof and climbed out into the night. The air was warm and humid but much cooler than the suffocating heat in the hallway. I straightened my shoulders and took a look around. The rooftop must have once been an observatory that provided stunning views—a touch of nature in what would otherwise have been a grey urban sprawl. Only now it was all dead. The tree branches were empty of leaves and splintered. Whatever grass was here had long died off, and the garden statues were so soiled and black they appeared burnt. Even the bench chairs had collapsed, now only good for firewood.

A dead garden for a necromancer. How fitting.

I wanted a place for peace and quiet, a place where I could let it all out and just reflect over everything I'd been through without disruption or trouble.

But someone else had the same idea.

At the far end of the roof was Jad. He stood by the rail. He didn't turn, not even when I'd started backing away. My head screamed, *Abort, abort, abort.*

I reached the door and congratulated myself on being sneaky enough to get away unnoticed. That was until Jad's voice floated out across the night.

"Come here, Zaya. We need to talk."

Damn.

CHAPTER 47

J ad didn't look at me. He was staring out at the city, a black
outline against the purple-streaked twilight, which seemed to
last much longer in this part of Navask than anywhere else. I
could imagine what Gonzavree must have looked like when the
city was alive and bustled with noise, the streets teeming with vehicles and crowds, windows lit to reveal small glimpses into people's
lives. I pictured the bars and clubs crammed with dancers. Music
playing. Dogs barking. Children's laughter. It was a dream, a
memory of something that could never return, and infinitely sad.

Just standing beside Jad made my heart pulse in chaotic
rhythm. "What do you want to talk about?" My voice was distant
and cool. I prided myself that I could keep my dignity when all I
wanted to do was scream.

Jad gripped the railing with both hands. His knuckles
whitened. "I wanted to thank you for what you did at Darthmusk.
That took real bravery… to face me the way I was."

He wouldn't look at me, but this time I knew it wasn't from
dislike. Had I gotten it entirely wrong from the beginning?

Stupid, idiotic fool.

Jad hadn't ignored me because he saw me as something inferior and annoying. Guilt had made him avoid me. I saw it in the way his eyes stared at the landscape ahead, in the way the line of his throat moved as he swallowed. He'd recovered physically, yes, but he couldn't forgive himself for the lives he'd taken when he'd been under the influence of Hadar's curse—for the terrible thing he had nearly done to me.

I closed my eyes, urging myself to stay calm. It would be so easy to screw this up. "We're friends. Friends look out for each other. I wasn't about to leave you there. And that wasn't you. I know what you did in those towns, Jad. That was the curse. It was all Vulcan and Hadar. Not you."

His voice sounded strained. "But I still did it."

"Trajan Stormouth did it, and he's gone."

"He's not."

I raised my eyes to him, confused.

"I always had lycanthor blood in me," he confessed. "What Hadar did… she increased it. I can feel the lycanthor inside me now, all the time. Whenever I'm angry or afraid… it's there." He laughed, a chuckle filled with irony. "My father got what he wanted after all. I'm a monster."

"You're not a monster."

He shook his head in despair. "Tell that to my victims."

My body quaked with nerves, afraid by how truly hurt he was. I couldn't deal with another Edric. I couldn't lose another friend to remorse. Even the strongest, bravest, fiercest casters had weak moments, but this was different. Jad was spiralling. He was no longer able to distinguish his own actions from those of the ULD's. He was losing part of himself.

I grabbed his arm, willing him to look at me. "Listen. It's not your fault. The ULD turned you into a weapon. Your father didn't make you that way because he wanted you on his side. He did it to punish you. To punish me."

Collateral to ensure I would walk straight into the hands of the ULD.

Jad studied me with the saddest expression. His eyes communicated a world of pain, but the faintest trace of an indebted smile hinted I'd succeeded in pulling him from the darkness.

Seeing it nearly made me weep with joy.

The smile faded. "I'm still capable of terrible things."

My elation deflated. I admired Jad, but sometimes I could have strangled him. "We're all capable of terrible things. People are afraid of necromancers. I'm afraid of the magic inside me, but I choose what I do with my power. I'd never hurt anyone with it... not intentionally. You're the same. You have a second chance. And now you have incredible strength and agility. I know you, Jad. You'll use your power to help others, not destroy them."

He stared at the lifeless city, the warm breeze sweeping his hair back. "It's good to have you here, Zaya."

I offered him a crooked smile. "I think you mean it's good for us to have you here. We've missed you." My cheery mood evaporated. "Indree missed you."

His eyes closed. I suspected from the way he tensed his jaw that he gritted his teeth.

Uncertainty provoked my need for answers. "Why did you never talk about her? All that time when we were training, you never mentioned Indree once."

I leaned against the balustrade and waited for an answer, annoyed when one didn't follow.

He stared at the moon, his tan skin almost golden in the light. "Indree and I are over. We have been for a long time. She knows it, but for whatever reason, she's decided not to believe it. I talked to her privately tonight to reinforce the fact. She didn't take it well. Indree's always been—"

He stopped himself and looked at his feet.

I gave a nervous laugh. "Wow. Sounded like you were about to hit relationship-blasphemy territory. What were you about to say? She's a real pain in the arse? Possessive? Spiteful? Manipulative? A real bitch—"

"That's enough." Jad's expression was both fierce and disappointed, his facial muscles tight, but it was the agonised tone in his voice that caught me off guard. "Being petty is beneath you."

I tried to subdue the jealousy inside me. "Then tell me, please. I'm fascinated to know what you saw in her. You must have liked her once... and I mean *really* liked her to be engaged."

He waved his dark hair out of his eyes. "Not that it's any of your business, but I did like her once, yes. I loved her."

I drew back. Hearing that was like someone had doused me in gasoline and lit a match.

I cleared my throat. "I was just teasing. You don't have to tell me anything, really. I'll head back now."

I've heard quite enough, thank you.

I turned back to the door, but Jad's voice stopped me. "Indree and I met when we were teenagers. Back then we had common interests. We were friends, and it grew into something more. Her father donated his time and money to the Ludovitch orphanage where I grew up. He kept an eye out for me, got me a place at Tarahik. Otherwise, I would have been sent to a base of no consequence. He even helped Marek. I practically begged him for that. It was Mr Raminorf's wish to see Indree and me united. I owed him, so I agreed."

"Wait. You owed him—in marriage?"

That didn't seem like the Jad I knew. But then, this was teenager Jad. When I reached his age, I doubted I'd be the same as I was now. Experience and maturity had a way of changing one's attitude... and mind.

I approached the subject carefully. "So you and Indree just... drifted apart?"

"I did. She didn't. That's why I never told you... and because it was none of your business."

I raised my hands in surrender. "Okay. I heard you the first time, and I get it. No more questions."

"No more prying."

I flinched. "I wasn't prying. Everything I asked was purely out of concern."

Jad shook his head and looked the other way.

Even though I despised her, I actually felt a little sorry for Indree. It couldn't have been easy knowing the person you loved didn't feel the same about you.

Oh. Wait. I know exactly how it feels.

I tried hard to fight back the blush in my cheeks. "I should get back. We have a long hike tomorrow to Port Serres."

I started moving toward the door, wishing I'd never left the apartment.

His voice followed me. "You have a long hike. I'm not going with you."

The strange quality in Jad's tone made me spin around. "What?" My legs were suddenly much heavier walking back to him. "What do you mean?"

His shoulders drooped. His face now lacked colour, as pale and fragile as the bloom of a moonflower. "I mean what I just said. I'm not going with you."

The lump in my throat threatened to overpower my voice. "We just got you back. I didn't risk—*we* didn't risk everything just to lose you now."

"And I'm grateful for that. But it's just as you said before. I have the ability to help people. The commander and colonel need my help."

Commander Macaslan and Colonel Harper? I hadn't thought about them once since I'd left Scarmouth, which riddled me with guilt. "Darius is working on that."

Jad's lips pressed into a thin line. "He can't if he doesn't know where they are."

For the second time, I found myself confounded. "What are you talking about? Macaslan and Harper are imprisoned at Yukovslar."

"Not anymore. At Darthmusk I learned that someone working

for the Council—a double agent—sent word that Macaslan and Harper had been moved and imprisoned at Stazika Palace. They're awaiting trial there and will likely be burned at the stake. That's the price for betrayal. In the eyes of the Council, that's what they are. Traitors." Small tendrils of flame flared from Jad's fingers. Red glittered in his eyes. I stepped back. His anger had sparked his power again.

I must have looked afraid, because he waved his hand to extinguish the flames. His eyes returned to jet black. "Stazika Palace is also where Morgomoth is being concealed."

I grappled with what he revealed. So General Kravis had been the one to retrieve Morgomoth's body. He'd locked that monster away yet again in another tomb, intending to do who knew what with Morgomoth's power this time—and the commander and the colonel were there, waiting for their inevitable deaths.

Was I partly to blame? Macaslan and Harper had been captured so I could flee.

Remorse drove its double-edged sword through my gut. Yes. It was my fault.

The moon went behind a cloud, as though it sensed my shame and wanted to shroud me in shadows. A salty, nervous taste filled my mouth. "How do you know all this?"

Jad turned to me, his eyes so much darker now that the light had faded. They practically looked hollow. "Because I was the one who was meant to lead the attack. Vulcan plans to strike Stazika Palace in two days. He wants to retrieve Morgomoth's body. Once the ULD has Morgomoth, they'll come for you… by sending the Four Revenants."

I took a moment to catch my breath and absorb what Jad revealed. I had always known it would come down to this. That's why Lunette had wanted me to flee, to leave Navask and make the long journey to Vukovar. The ULD had all their chess pieces in the right places, closing in move after stealthy move. I'd told myself the right thing to do was leave and make a new life for myself in

Vukovar. And maybe one day that would happen. But it wasn't today.

"I'm coming with you to Stazika Palace."

Jad flinched at my announcement. The moon came back out, revealing the growing anxiety on his face. "No. Absolutely not. You at Stazika Palace would be like leading a lamb to slaughter. You need to get to Port Serres and far away. If you do that, the ULD will never have a chance of obtaining your blood. Morgomoth will remain a victim to the sleeping curse." He raked his fingers through his black hair. "Macaslan, Harper, Darius, and I will reconvene our plans to defeat the ULD. You need to stay out of the picture."

He couldn't be serious. "The ULD will find me," I insisted. "They'll come looking for me and drag me back. I can't run from this. Not anymore." I stepped closer, expecting him to edge back, but his feet remained planted where he stood. "Marek can lead the others to Port Serres. I'm coming with you. We'll rescue Macaslan and Harper together."

"Why are you so insistent on putting yourself in danger?"

Now my irritation really escalated. Without thinking, I drew so close that only the thinnest margin of air stood between us. Anger provoked the words out of my mouth. "Isn't it obvious? I care about you, you idiot. I just got you back, and I don't—"

Oh shit!

What is wrong with me?

What am I doing?

My emotions had taken control. I'd revealed a truth that I shouldn't have.

Jad actually looked unnerved, like a startled deer in headlights. The expression was gone in an instant. I'd expected revulsion, shock, disbelief. Hell, I wouldn't have been surprised if Jad ran for the hills. But he didn't do any of that. The way his eyes stared into mine, with just the subtlest hint of desire, brought heat into my face and tightened every nerve in my chest. He was so close that I could see the traces of scars that spotted his tanned skin, a reminder of all the fights and combats he'd endured. I was petrified to do it but fought the instinct to shy away. My spellbound moment acted on its own accord. I pressed my lips against his. Warmth radiated through my body. The delicate, feather-light touch of our lips connected us, and then… nothing.

Jad pulled away, his face a perfect display of astonishment.

Uh-oh.

The sensation that I'd been snuggled tightly in a warm bed, only to have someone yank the sheets off, left me cold and exposed. My face went red for an entirely different reason. "I'm sorry. That was incredibly wrong of—"

His mouth met mine, warm and intoxicating. The soft brush of our lips fuelled my yearning, and I intensified our kiss, as though he were my lifeline and I'd surely drown without him. Jad's arms circled my waist, pinning me closer, our hips pressed into each other. I thought it would be too much to ask for Jad to need me the same way I needed him, but apparently he did. The kiss turned hungry, driven by a passion neither of us could control. I didn't believe in heaven, but surely this must have been it.

Jad's lips traced the curve of my jaw and down my neck, his voice a whisper against my skin. "You're still going to Port Serres."

"Not a chance." I returned my lips to his.

Rather than arguing, our mouths pressed hotly together again. The walls, the barriers—whatever you wanted to call them—were down. His hand tangled in my hair, which the breeze swept in a curtain around our faces, cocooning us in our own private world.

A voice broke the spell. "Jad?"

I pushed away, recognising that intrusive whine.

Indree stood by the rooftop door, her mouth open in abhorrence. It couldn't have been easy to have had the person you loved tell you it was over, only to then find them locked in a passionate embrace with someone else—on the same night. Murderous rage crept in Indree's eyes when she looked at me. It was her signature

queen-bee stare-down, a glare that had most girls wanting to evap-
orate into thin air. It just made me want to strangle her.

Jad didn't put distance between us as I expected. He reached
for my hand. The tips of our fingers barely touched. "Indree—"

She didn't stick around to hear what he'd say. She bolted back
through the door, her cries soaking away whatever happiness I'd
found.

Jad's troubled expression grew dark. "Let me go talk to her."

He left the rooftop, his sudden absence making my body cold
and heavy.

What the hell just happened?

I kissed Jad!

He kissed me!

Confusion.

Relief.

Happiness.

Astoundment.

Round and round the emotions went.

I looked over the balustrade and stared at the midnight-blue
water that lapped against the building below. Maybe the waves
would soothe my frazzled mind.

What might Indree and Jad talk about? How could he be
expected to console her after this?

Then I remembered the love potion Indree had tucked away in
her rucksack. I couldn't help but wonder if Indree's bad timing had
been more than just *bad timing*.

CHAPTER 48

At sunrise we waited outside the lobby doors, dismayed that the ocean surge hadn't gone down. The street was ankle-deep in water, and while wading through the flood wasn't an issue, the threat of chak-lorks was an alarming possibility. I hadn't forgotten what happened to Tusk. Judging by everyone's pallid faces, no one else had either. Marek stared with his mouth slightly ajar. Lainie and Edric hung back with their arms crossed. Indree stared at her feet to avoid eye contact with everyone. Talina waited by my side, her good humour from the previous night replaced with disappointment. Sweat dampened her upper lip.

Jad took a cautious step toward the water, no doubt to assess it for chak-lorks. Tension built around the group. No one wanted to bring up the dangerous topic that was so evident before us—we were marooned.

Marek dropped his hands helplessly by his sides. "I can't believe it. It's never been like this before. The water always recedes at sunrise. Why change now?"

A frosty smile crossed Lainie's mouth. "Because it knows we want to leave."

Jad stepped into the water, which made Talina gasp and my

insides unravel. "It's a king tide. It will be deeper farther out near the city's outskirts. And we are leaving. There are no chak-lorks here. I can sense when they're near."

I stared, surprised by what he revealed. Was this another side effect of his lycanthor abilities? If it was, I wasn't complaining. We needed all the help we could get against those creatures, but it still worried me.

Jad strode farther into the water. Lapping ripples splashed up his boots to stain his trousers. We hadn't spoken to each other since the kiss. He hadn't so much as even looked at me all morning. Did he regret it? Was Jad ashamed that he'd let things get too far between us? Or was he trying to spare Indree pain and humiliation? I had no idea what happened between them after Jad left. For all I knew, Indree could have doused the love potion all over Jad.

Stop it. You're being paranoid.

And paranoia was the last thing I needed. Chak-lorks weren't present now, but situations changed, and being caught off guard was all the difference between staying alive and ending up like Tusk.

We trudged through the drowned streets. The sun rose, bringing an intense wave of heat over my clothes and skin. My boots were heavy in the water, my progress slow. Even the ground was soft and sticky. The combination of sun and hot water had partly melted the tarmac. Every time I looked ahead, the hazy mirage on the horizon made me balk. Blood raced through my body as though it were running a marathon. I couldn't help it. The mirage appeared so much like a wave coming to inundate us.

At noon we arrived at a Parthenon-like structure, its remains standing firm on a rocky outcrop above the water. The rectangular building must have once been the central station for all portal activity in the city, because glorious blue light immersed the edifice from within, streaming out between the marble columns. It rippled onto the surrounding buildings and gave the impression that we were in an underwater cavern. It was incredibly beautiful and powerful, and amazing that after all the damage and ruin that Gonzavree had suffered, the portal had somehow managed to survive.

A spark of hope fired through me. "I thought you found a black portal."

Jad's eyes drifted toward me, but they were cold and aloof. "Don't get too excited. A blue portal means this city is still in the network. Haxsan Guard soldiers must come here, probably for training. We could be tracked through the portal."

The bad news didn't seem to bother anyone, or it hadn't entirely sunk in. Talina practically choked on her happy tears. The beaming smile on Marek's face made my own lips split into a grin. Even Lainie and Edric, who had been miserable and bitter for days, had a twinkle in their eyes.

Lainie exhaled a grateful sigh. "Who cares? Let's get out of this shithole."

We made our way toward the portal. Jad remained behind, which jolted me like a current of electricity. He watched us in silence. I thought his gaze lingered a little longer on me, but I was strung so tight at that moment I could have imagined it.

The back of my throat tasted sticky. "Aren't you coming?"

Surely he wasn't leaving us now. Not after everything that had happened last night.

Didn't he listen to anything I said?

I was going to Stazika Palace with him. He didn't have a choice in the matter.

My legs moved toward Jad with a will of their own, but the silent shake of his head froze me. He focused on the water, his shoulders strained, every muscle in his face tense. It made my heart thunder behind my ribcage. Jad listened intently to something the rest of us couldn't hear. Something was happening. Something big.

He fixed his eyes on me at the same time the water bubbled and hissed. Fish floated to the surface, their scaly bodies burned beyond recognition. It looked like they'd been eaten away at by acid.

Jad's lips pulled back in a cry. "They're coming!"

At the end of the street, fast-moving water jetted toward us. The Four Revenants barrelled through the waves on their horses, eyes burning amber-red, their army of chak-lorks spreading out like black poison as the creatures leapt and scurried along the broken buildings. Hideous shrieks erupted from their mouths. It reminded me of a wild fox hunt, only instead of hounds, there was the undead.

And we're the foxes.

Everyone gunned it for the portal. My boots hit the ground hard. Sizzling water splashed around my legs, staining through the thick fabric of my trousers. Any second now, the water would rise and we'd all be ripped off our feet. The current tugged on my legs, growing more powerful every second.

It's a rip!

It's working against me.

It's trying to pull me toward—

The thought was knocked out of my head as a hand firmly took hold of my own. I stared, amazed to find Jad at my side. He'd moved that fast? His hair clung to the sides of his face, either by water or the sheen of sweat. "Keep moving." His voice was urgent and afraid.

My heart felt like it would explode from the exertion, but I kept up with his pace. The water climbed over our knees, threatening to reach our thighs. Ahead, Marek arrived at the portal. It was practically a vacuum, a wind-drain sucking in everything that approached. He reached for Talina at the same time he was lifted off the ground. The pair were suspended for a moment in a superb azure glow, the way I imagined angels looked in heavenly light, and were then swept away. Edric and Lainie went next, their bodies sucked into the vacuity. All that remained was Indree. She waited just out of reach of the portal. Her blonde hair whipped around her face, her eyes intent on Jad. Perhaps she was pleading to some higher power that he'd make it.

And probably praying I don't.

Jad stared back at her in disbelief. "Get inside the portal. Now!"

We were only a few metres away.

But it didn't matter.

A chak-lork leapt onto Indree. The creature flattened her into the water. Her cries were swallowed by a colossal clash as Jad lunged onto the heinous monster, the impact tossing the chak-lork aside. It screamed an ear-splitting screech and burst into thousands of tiny droplets that dissipated in the water. Jad was the closest to the portal now. The wind clung to him, ripping him away from Indree.

Away from me!

Our eyes locked at the same time he was flung backward. Immersed in the solid blue light, Jad vanished.

For a moment, my own heart felt like it had been sucked right out of me, but then a cry so painful and coarse drove my senses back inside. Indree rose from the water, her skin pink and blistered. A tiny crack splintered my hatred. I'd rather put an entire world of distance between us, but I took the higher ground and laced my arm around her. "We need to get inside the portal. Come on."

Maybe I should have focused on myself for once instead of helping others. Maybe I should have paid more attention to what was happening behind me. Indree's eyes widened at the same time the chak-lork grabbed my legs—the same creature that had exploded in beads of water only moments ago—knocking me flat on my stomach. Indree clasped my hand, but the portal's hurricane winds had captured hold of her now too. It wrenched her back with effortless strength. I was the rope caught in a fierce game of tug of war.

I let out all the air in my lungs, my voice fighting to overcome the agony from my arms and legs. "Don't let go. Please."

Something happened on Indree's face then—a realisation that sent icy fear straight into my chest. She had a problem she wanted solved. And now she had a way to eliminate that problem. All she had to do was—

My voice was frantic. "No, Indree. No! Please don't!"

She let go.

I screamed as she was towed away by the portal, disappearing in a heartbeat.

She let me go!

She let me go!

The chak-lork dragged me through the water, its strength unparalleled now that it had no opponent. I struggled, kicked, thrashed, anything to free myself, but nothing worked. The surge burned my skin. It was like being in a broiling hot spring. I had a knife in my sheath which I reached for, but another chak-lork kicked it out of my hand.

The *click-click-click* of horses' hooves approached. Panic flooded in. The Four Revenants stared down at me, their faces no longer angelic but demonic and twisted, their skin scaly and wet. Some of it peeled in places so I could see right past their meaty flesh to the bone. One of them took out a war horn and blew a deep, hair-raising note that resonated through every fibre of me. It wasn't the sound of impending battle. It was the announcement of a victory.

Their hunt was over. They'd triumphed and won.

My head was struck with something hard. The blinding force propelled my face into the water again. I tasted salt on my lips and sucked in a mouthful of hot seawater as I gasped from the shock and pain.

I was conscious briefly, aware of the chak-lorks' screeching laughter, before the world went dark.

CHAPTER 49

I woke with the sensation that my head was hanging somewhere behind me, scrambled and detached. Cold air tickled my skin, the icy wind frigid and biting. The burns and blisters I sustained from the hot seawater were gone. Someone had healed me. It didn't stimulate my gratitude. If anything, it made me more afraid. I blinked, my vision aligning itself into focus. Leafless branches stretched toward a dark sky, the tips ending in wooden points, as though someone had deliberately filed them down to impale passers-by.

Woods. I'm in a wood.

The knowledge wasn't helpful. There were literally thousands of woodlands across Navask.

The insides of my thighs were chaffed, my back and shoulders stiff. The more my consciousness woke from its hazy sleep, the more sensation drove deep into my body.

Providence help me, my backside is in pain.

The tangy smell of horsehair crept in my nose. I sat up straight, the memories surfacing like bubbles up a well. I was sitting in a saddle. On a horse. The creature's coat and mane were an unearthly black. Gilded hooves moved in a rhythmic, almost mechanical amble. This creature wasn't just a horse. It was something other-worldly and unnatural.

The Four Revenants.

They caught me!

I shifted to jump from the horse and make a run for it in the dark forest, but something solid pressed into my back.

A rider.

Long skeletal arms circled my sides, closing around me in an inescapable embrace. What was left of my captor's flesh was banded with black stitches. Bony fingers curled around the reins. Knuckles gleamed white in the moonlight. The rider was twice my height. I tilted my head, unsure if I really wanted to see the creature's face. The surface was nothing more than a milky membrane of skin stretched over bones. Empty black sockets replaced his eyes. Veins snaked out and streaked across his cheeks. It looked as though he'd bled black tears.

Revenant.

Paranoia swirled through me. This wasn't a hysterical hallucination. It wasn't a nightmare. Two revenants rode beside me on my left, the other on my right, their black-and-crimson cloaks falling in a rippling wave around them. Embroidered across their shoulders was the ULD insignia, the swastika like a blood-red stain against the dark material.

If they're wearing new cloaks, then that means....

I twisted my head and shoulders at an uncomfortable angle. We weren't alone. Behind us was a large company of dissent rebels on horseback, and farther beyond that, tanks and armoured fighting vehicles equipped with machine guns, missiles, and rocket launchers. The tanks' solid chain tracks crunched snow and ice, taking down whatever small or large foliage stood in their way.

It's a cavalry.

Anxiety drowned my confusion.

A cavalry strikes at detected weak points.

The company rode at a brisk trot into a large clearing. My fears multiplied, the hairs on my arms rising in aversion. Thousands of dissent rebels and lycanthors had assembled together in efficient, organised ranks. Horns and drums accompanied the raging battle chant, no doubt striking fear into the hearts of their opponent. The rumbling seemed to make the ground quake. Tremors rippled through the horse into my body, clamping like a fist on my heart.

A choked cry broke from my throat, my eyes unable to believe what waited ahead. A rioting, churning storm loomed in the sky. It stretched out in all directions across the night, enfolding itself around what was left of the moon. No, not a storm—but not far from one either. Smoke and lightning and swirling, apocalyptic shadows.

What is that?

A familiar voice called out behind me. "Beautiful, isn't it?"

Vulcan.

He approached on a trotting horse and halted beside me. His black cloak and armour were already speckled with blood, his lips stretched in an appeased smile.

I wished I could have punched that poisonous smirk off his face. "It's a bit medieval."

His eyes gleamed with enjoyment. "Do you prefer I use fighter jets and stagma? I have both on standby."

I bristled at his maddening sarcasm. "What is this?"

"This is our attack on Stazika Palace."

As though he'd spoken a command, wind swept through the black shadows ahead, which curdled like oil on water as it took shape, allowing flecks of the other side to appear through its smoky form.

Every nerve in my body tingled. Stazika Palace would have been a structure of beauty once, and perhaps even the crown jewel of the entire land. It was a gargantuan building of white brick and stone. Monolithic columns adorned the marble frieze, the doors painted gold, the windows lit from the inside by what was probably glass chandeliers.

Now it was under attack and resembled an ancient edifice that slowly crumbled to the ground. I imagined ornately decorated chambers on fire, courtyards and gardens shrouded in ash, prized artworks melted down, sculptures toppled and defaced. The rebels had turned the lawn and gardens into a battlefield of blood and carnage. From the look of things, anyone who tried to flee—men, women, or children—was cut down in a flicker of an eyelid. I squinted through the smoke and haze. Chak-lorks stood over the bodies. Their vicious shrieks sliced into the night like an acoustic device straight from hell.

Vulcan watched the display with a sharp laugh. "They thought the celestial shield would protect them."

Celestial shields!

They brought it down.

The dome-shaped storm that blew havoc and devastation all around us was what was left of it.

But how is that possible? Celestial shields can't be destroyed.

Hadar appeared on a chestnut mare. She watched the bloodshed with bored eyes. Her swollen hip bulged out on the side, and I wondered how many rebels it had taken to get her on the horse. "I told you it would work."

Vulcan didn't acknowledge her. He continued to stare at the atrocity before him. "I never doubted it wouldn't. Celestial shields are powerful, but their one flaw is the access they provide to shelter humans."

Humans!

I remembered the deformed creatures that Marek and I had encountered in Darthmusk, cut up, burnt, and stitched back together like frogs in a science experiment. I shuddered at the recollection of how those dead humans had resembled chak-lorks.

Chak-lorks!

Panic, slimy and acidic, made a nasty taste in the back of my throat. Theories that shouldn't have been possible swept through my mind.

Chak-lorks were once casters.

Casters with human DNA.

And any human who required shelter only had to plea for help and the celestial shields would open.

That's how the ULD had coordinated such an easy attack.

Chak-lorks could enter celestial shields.

They could destroy them from the inside.

CHAPTER 50

The implications for this were staggering. The United League of Dissent had the power, the tools, and the motive to destroy every Free Zone on the planet. They had an army of chaklorks, possibly thousands more, and the Four Revenants to lead that army—an evil that would devour the entire world. No human stood a chance. No caster stood a chance.

Forget Vulcan's smile. My fists ached to bash his teeth down his throat. "All this for one caster?"

He shut his eyes, slow and lazy, as though I had interrupted an important moment. "I could hardly knock on the front door and ask them to kindly hand Morgomoth over, now could I?"

His black eyes fixed me in place. The colour was so like Jad's, only Vulcan's were filled with hunger and an endless, ageless obsession for power. "The Four Revenants will take you to Morgomoth to complete the ritual. There's still time for you to join the United League of Dissent, Zaya. Awaken Morgomoth, and he'll make you an equal at his side. Two necromancers hand in hand, bringing justice to all casters, annihilating the filth they call humans. Together, you will be the casters' salvation."

"Very poetic, but I'd rather not."

He made an exaggerated face of disappointment. I knew that was exactly what he wanted to hear. I'd caused enough trouble. Vulcan wanted me out of the picture.

Thunderous rumbles tore through the night. The monstrous black deformity in the sky stirred and bled outward, a living, breathing organism hungry to devour everything in its path. Magic and energy crackled. Lightning flashed across the ghostly landscape, illuminating the horror of the battle below. Terror and sorrow seized me, strong enough to suck the very warmth from my bones.

Hadar stroked her horse's mane in an effort to keep the beast calm. "It is a pity that such a beautiful place had to be destroyed." She said it with about as much sentiment as someone cutting down a flower.

Vulcan's dark brows rose. "Beautiful place? Do you know how many wars have been fought over this land? Stazika is a graveyard. Thousands of soldiers' bodies have been left to rot in this forsaken pit. All in an endeavour to protect humans. This place is no more beautiful than a wasteland."

"Sir." A young dissent rebel, probably only a couple years older than me, appeared. He was out of breath, his face sticky from sweat. "Haxsan Guard soldiers have been spotted in the woods. He's with them."

He's with them?

The lieutenant of the ULD tightened his grip on the reins. Unadulterated rage lit in his eyes. "That boy is such a disappointment."

Jad!

Jad's here!

But how?

How long was I unconscious?

Vulcan turned his glare from the battle and focused on his men. The commanding rebels drew near, the ULD insignia embroidered proudly on the breast of their red-and-black uniforms. They waited for their superior's next order, weapons brandished in eager excitement. Warpaint made them look like tribal leaders from another age, hungry for blood.

Vulcan held his chin high as he barked orders. "The Haxsan Guard are attempting a flanking manoeuvre. Once their troops arrive, attack. They think they can take us by surprise, but it is the ULD who will trap them."

I wanted to summon the strength to stay strong, but my heart had already split in despair. Jad and the troops would never see the ULD coming. The mass of black darkness shielded the rebels from sight. It would be a bloodbath.

Vulcan turned a satisfied smile on me. His smug face revealed that victory had come quicker and easier than he'd expected. "Time to go, Zaya. Morgomoth awaits your arrival."

He clicked his tongue and jabbed his heels into the sides of his stallion, wrenching the reins with a force that sent the creature into a gallop. The Four Revenants rode behind him, flanked by Hadar and several other rebels. The sound of the horses riding into the thick of battle boomed like rolling thunder. We must have resembled Norse gods barrelling straight out of the gates of Asgard.

The revenant behind me hunched forward, reminding me of an animal springing for attack. He snapped the reins. The horse doubled its speed, its hooves leaving deep imprints in the blood-soaked ground. Battle raged all around us. High-pitched screams were dwarfed by explosions, the ash-riddled air making it difficult to breathe. I tried not to look at the discarded victims stabbed, torn, and bleeding out in the slush.

Blinding gold flashes erupted through the smoke on either side of us. My vision spotted, as though I'd stared into a fire. The miasma cleared, or rather the figures that emerged from the black cloud became apparent. The Haxsan Guard. They'd arrived—and were shooting at us.

I struggled in my captor's arms, desperate to break free, but the revenant squeezed harder. We'd halved the distance to Stazika Palace. The building loomed ahead, its white walls now blanketed in a powdery black residue that I recognised as soot. Fire had engulfed part of the roof. Plumes of thick smoke belched from the windows. Had the Haxsan Guard burnt the palace down themselves? A last, desperate attempt to keep Morgomoth's body out of the hands of the enemy?

Macaslan and Harper are in there!

The thought of the pair chained in a cell and watching the flames reach its fiery tendrils toward them made my stomach cramp. I had to get off this damn horse. I needed something to throw the revenant off, but I had no weapon.

Or did I?

The last time I'd conjured the Neathror blade, it had nearly spent all my energy. I'd only just escaped the ULD alive. Could I risk that again?

If you want to get out of this alive, yes, you can.

I shut my eyes, imagining the blade in my hand, sensing my fingers ripping it from the clutches of Morgomoth's hold. I didn't look at him in his stone coffin, just focused on Neathror. If I did anything else, my concentration would break. My fear of him would consume me.

Mine, I thought, with every intention of getting what I wanted.

I opened my eyes.

Neathror gleamed in my hand. I leaned to the side and impaled the dagger straight into the revenant's stomach—if the creature even had a stomach. A horrible, screeched wail exploded from its gaping mouth, more powerful than any ghostly banshee. Its hold loosened, and with my weight so unbalanced, I toppled to the frozen ground so hard my breath was sucked out of me. I rolled out of the way, barely missing the horse's powerful kick, and sprang onto my feet, running fast through the battle. What direction? I had no idea. So long as I wasn't anywhere close to Vulcan and the Four Revenants.

I snuck a glance over my shoulder.

Panic smothered the small light of hope in my chest.

They'd turned around.

The cavalry headed straight for me.

CHAPTER 51

Explosions pummelled the earth, fracturing the ground and shooting snow and ice into the air like geysers. Not even the damp, savage chill of the wind could prevent fires igniting. If anything, the wind seemed to invigorate the flames. I ducked, weaved, and leapt out of the way of the one-on-one attacks between Haxsan Guard soldiers and chak-lorks. Screams and agonising cries rose in a deafening crescendo, but somehow—maybe I was more in tune to it—all I heard was the intensifying rumble of horses' hooves. I swept a terrified glance behind me. The Four Revenants surged through the battle like a powerful storm, only instead of a wall of water behind them, it was a rapidly rising wave of fire and cinders.

Great. They've upgraded!

Fatalities mounted rapidly around the four monstrosities, the victims' armour and weapons reduced to molten metal. The revenants didn't seem to care about the chak-lorks that fought at their side as the creatures melted into boiling liquid in the snow. My vision reeled, the sight enough to make me nauseated. I tripped, hit the ground hard, and remained curled in a foetal ball.

Streams of caster-shooter fire soared over me. Their sonic booms resonated in my ears and teeth.

The Haxsan Guard reinforcements are here.

Which means....

I snuck a peek at the black vaporous cloud that had once been the celestial shield. The second wave of attack came tearing out of the thick folds of darkness. Dissent rebels and lycanthors tore forward, swarming the battlefield like a plague of locusts. I couldn't let them destroy the reinforcements. I couldn't let myself be captured by the Four Revenants. I couldn't let Macaslan and Harper burn in a fiery prison while Stazika Palace tumbled to ruins.

I have to do something.

But what?

There was a ringing in my ears, something that had always been there since the moment I'd fled into this terrible war scene, something I had thought was the result of too many explosions and gunfire but now increased in strength and volume.

Not ringing.

Whispers.

It came from the ground, eerily melodic, and reminded me of the aged and ruined church bells I'd hear toll in the wind back at the Brendlash orphanage. The whispers weren't in a language I recognised but were breathy and gasping, as though the people it came from couldn't catch enough air.

The dead!

Vulcan had said that armies fought over this land for centuries. *"Thousands of soldiers' bodies have been left to rot in this forsaken pit."*

I knew what I had to do, it was just a matter of figuring out how to do it.

I pressed my hands into the ground. Snow and blood covered my fingers, my palms brushing over grass and the thick tangle of roots beneath the surface. I sensed energy pulse from the wet soil.

It soaked into my fingers and up my arms, coursing through my entire body. It was a power that connected with me, a magic I could tap into and make my own.

I shut my eyes, blocking out the scenes of the surrounding battle, focusing on the world that waited below.

"Rise and help me," I commanded softly in my head.

The ground lurched, then split. I crawled away, fearful I'd be swallowed in the ever-expanding fissure. Soil and snow collapsed. The yawning hole was about grave size. A fleshless hand tore out of the black chasm. The moist soil that clung to its fingers made the bones appear as white and pale as moonlight in comparison. The hand was followed by a body, half-eaten by the earth, worms and maggots still feasting on what was left. It climbed out of the grave like a crab out of sand and rose onto its legs, which were bent at odd angles. I stifled a scream, more shocked by what I had done than the actual fact that I was staring at a dead soldier. The creature twitched and stumbled. Bones clicked back into place. Socket joints popped as they realigned. It stared down at me with a wicked grin, teeth—or what was left of them—sharp as metal.

High-pitched screams resonated from every direction, no longer a result of the violence and rage of battle but from disbelief and panic. I flicked my eyes desperately around the battlefield. I hadn't just resurrected one dead soldier. I'd conjured an army of them. Even the Haxsan Guard soldiers who had died only minutes ago were standing, eyes lifeless, faces streaked with blood. The army of the dead looked down at me, this pathetic little thing bunched in a foetal position in the snow, and waited...

For my orders.

My head swayed. It was powerful necromancy, something I hadn't even thought I was capable of, and my energy was dwindling. I had expended my magic, too much and too fast. Vertigo rippled through my body, but I fought the wave of dizziness away and forced my communication into the minds of the dead.

"Fight with the Haxsan Guard! Oppose the ULD!"

I wouldn't win first prize for valiant war speech, but it was enough. The dead army moved like an activated mechanical device and charged toward the oncoming ULD. Their war cry was a howling, fiendish screech. Their feet pulsed like drumbeats over the earth.

There wasn't time to see how the ULD reacted. The two opposing forces collided in a relentless wave of chaos and destruction. Sparring. Jousting. Brawling. Shooting. Stabbing. It sounded like the entire universe had exploded and ripped away.

Stop watching, Zaya. Run!

The Four Revenants may have been hindered, but that wouldn't stop them from pursuing me. I scrambled onto my feet and ran—straight into the arms of an assailant. My body instinctively went into defence mode. I raised Neathror, intending to cut down my captor.

"Zaya. Stop. Stop! It's me."

I pulled the blade back. Relieved tears sprang in my eyes.

Jad.

There were new bruises and cuts on his face, and I wondered what he'd been through to get here. Marek, Talina, Lainie, and Edric stood behind him, staring at the atrocity of the battle with wide, dumb-founded eyes. Soot and ash streaked their clothes. It pained me to see them. They should have been at Port Serres, or on a ship far away from here.

My voice sounded desperate. "How…?"

Jad touched the side of my face. His fingers were light on my cheek. "With great difficulty, but I'll explain later. Right now, we need to get inside Stazika Palace. There are tunnels under the palace—passages that lead to carrier-hornets."

We'll be able to flee.

We'll be able to find Macaslan and Harper and leave this place.

Marek appeared at our side. His troubled expression grew darker. "Getting to the palace might be easier said than done."

Battle continued around us. Cast-shooter fire spilled through the air, the world smelling of melted metal and burnt flesh. We'd never make it to Stazika's front doors. Not without help.

I shut my eyes, concentrating hard to express my command. *"Cover us."*

The dead surged forward. Their decrepit bodies stood tall, as though they'd suddenly been pulled taut by string, and made a barrier wall directly to the palace. It wasn't the safest path. Gun- and cast-shooter fire still rained down, but it kept the dissent rebels, lycanthors, and chak-lorks out.

If Jad and the others were surprised, they didn't show it. We ran. Our feet hit the ground hard, our bodies turned inward to protect ourselves from the hot bullets that whipped past.

We're nearly there. We're nearly there.

The palace's golden doors weren't far.

We're going to make it.

Lainie's scream crushed my hope.

A rebel had managed to cut through the barrier and had knocked Edric to the ground. They grappled, fists slamming into each other. Each blow was racking and intense on the other's body. Edric raised his eyes at us. In them I saw not fear, not conviction, not bravery—just numb acceptance. He'd been depressed for weeks, the guilt of what he'd done at Essida eating away at him. It had filled his heart with suffering, something none of us were qualified to heal.

He turned back to the rebel. "We both deserve this."

I realised too late what he intended to do.

Edric took out a hex-grenade from his pocket, something I wasn't aware he even had, and yanked the safety pin. There was an impossibly bright light that happened almost too fast to register, and then the spot where Edric and the rebel stood erupted into a blast of emerald fire.

Lainie screamed so loud, I didn't understand how her lungs hadn't ruptured.

The flames and smoke dissipated.
Edric was gone.

CHAPTER 52

I barrelled toward Lainie. "Don't look. Don't look."

I wrenched her away from the scene. If there was anything left of Edric… well, it wasn't something I wanted her to see.

I'm sorry, Lainie. I'm so sorry.

It had all happened so fast that it had been impossible to intervene.

Horrible racking sobs threatened to overcome her, her body heavy against me. Her knees buckled. Marek grabbed Lainie before she could hit the ground and carried her the rest of the way. She'd passed out. That was probably a good thing. Half her soul had died in that explosion too.

We reached the palace. Up close, it was a sprawling and majestic complex, the three levels perfectly symmetrical with arched windows and a gold balustrade that lined the flat roof. It was a symbol of power and authority. Even with flames and ash bellowing from the gaping holes that had been blown into it, the building still seemed to be as impregnable as ever.

We ran inside. Jad led the way through suites of large and airy rooms. Unlike the palace's exterior, there was not a hint of white inside. The walls were painted in bold red, the furniture the deepest brown mahogany, chairs and sofas upholstered in burgundy velvet. Even the chandeliers that hung from the enormously high ceilings glistened with rosy-gold light. Fruit and what would have been exquisite cake had been left half-eaten on plates. Tea and coffee had gone cold. I flinched. The wealthy politician casters who lived here had been caught unprepared. They must have all fled through the tunnels.

Jad padded down one of the walls. His fingers brushed across the paintwork in a frenzy. There was a click. Part of the wall sprang open, revealing a hewn rock stairwell that led to a tunnel deep in the ground.

I gawped. "How did you know that was there?"

He smiled, but it was brief. "Captain, remember? I've accompanied the politicians and dignitaries in this palace as a security escort more times than I care to remember. I know all the building's secrets."

And that's why Vulcan wanted you to lead the ULD's attack.

It all made terrible sense.

Jad directed his gaze at Marek. "Get Talina and Lainie out of here. Follow the tunnel until you reach the underground hangar. There are twice as many carrier-hornets down there than this palace requires. Zaya and I will find Macaslan and Harper." He grabbed Marek's shoulder. "Don't wait for us. We'll meet you at Port Serres."

Marek shook his head. "No one is splitting up. We stick together."

When his eyes focused on Talina and saw how pale and frightened she appeared, there was a change in his countenance. He looked at me. He looked at Jad. A world of indecision crossed his already pained expression. Lainie hung limp in his arms. Her white skin gave her the appearance of a fragile china doll that could break at any second.

Marek exhaled a frustrated sigh. "I'll wait five minutes."

Talina swept forward and enveloped me in a hug. "I don't want us to separate. I don't have a good feeling about it. Why can't we all leave together?"

I blinked away a fresh wave of tears. "Macaslan and Harper are in the palace. We need to get them out." I took her hand and gave her fingers an encouraging squeeze. "Look after Lainie. She needs her best friend."

Talina sniffled. "She needs both her best friends."

"And she'll have that, but not yet. I'll see you in Port Serres."

She backed away in defeat, silently nodding.

Jad and Marek exchanged a handshake and did one of those pat-on-the-shoulder things all guys did. I hugged Marek goodbye and wiped some of the soot out of Lainie's hair. Grief had her heavily sedated. She hadn't even stirred once in Marek's arms.

I bent down to whisper in her ear. "Talina and I will take care of you. I promise."

Marek carried Lainie down the stairs. Talina followed, peering back at me with tearful eyes. They'd barely faded into the darkness below when the door sealed. It blended back into the wall as though it had never been there.

I crossed my arms with a sly look, intrigued by Jad's decision. "You didn't force me to go with them."

He raised his eyebrows. "I understand you too well and know any order I give would be disobeyed. Come on. The prisons are this way."

"Jad, wait."

He turned, agitation evident in his stiff shoulders. He was anxious to get moving.

I licked my dry lips, nervous from what I was about to reveal. "Indree let me go. She let me be captured by the Four Revenants."

Everything we're experiencing now, it's her fault.

I expected him to be irritated, wretched, enraged. I did not expect calm disappointment. His face remained blank, but his eyes stared into mine with the tiniest hint of sadness. "I know." He stepped forward and took my hand in his. Our fingers laced together. "Indree said the portal sucked her away. She had everyone convinced."

"But not you?"

"I know when she lies."

"She despises me. She has ever since I stepped into Tarahik."

Indree was a parasite. I hated how she always managed to get under my skin, but if our situations had been reversed, I'd never have let her fall into the hands of the Four Revenants. It still astounded me that her jealousy could have driven her to do something so cruel.

Jad's lips pressed softly against mine. "You won't see her again. After the portal, we met a camp of refugees who were making their way to Port Serres. I told Indree to go with them. I told everyone to go with them." Guilt racked his face. I knew he was thinking about Edric. "Indree's gone. It's just you and me now."

It's just you and me.

Surely if angels existed, they had to be singing "Hallelujah" in my ears. That or my heartbeat had climbed so high it was pounding blood and warmth in my head.

It's just you and me.

Words I never thought I be lucky enough to hear.

I squeezed his hand in return. "To the prison, then."

We swept past rooms abundant with lavish furniture and gilt-framed mirrors, past private business and reception chambers large enough to fit tables for thirty people, through a huge open gallery with a vaulted ceiling. The decorative busts seemed to watch me as we slipped past. Stazika Palace really was a maze of highly decorative and theatrical tastes. I was glad Jad knew his way, because honestly, I was lost.

Just when I thought things couldn't get any grander, the palace's décor took an altered change. Jad led me down a stairwell into the dungeons. The Haxsan Guard on duty either fled or had gone to join the battle. I coughed damp, musty odour out of my lungs. This dungeon was a place of gruelling misery. The tiny cells were lit by a single oil lamp, the rusted bars hard and unyielding. The only ventilation in this place came from the staircase. Every narrow corridor ended in a thick slab of rock. My spine tingled. Mournful, wailing cries wept from every surface. Ghosts were trapped down here, countless victims who'd suffered from neglect or mistreatment. They weren't aware of me or Jad. They were too far gone in their purgatory, not able to cross over.

A lump caught in my throat. This was what necromancers were meant to prevent. It was our responsibility to ferry the dead to the otherworld, to send them to peace and ease. How had everything gone so wrong?

"Zaya?"

Jad watched me. Uncertainty flicked across his face.

I drew a deep breath and followed him down a corridor lined with metal grates. A flare of light lit in Jad's hand. Flames sparked from his fingers. He was about to melt the cast-iron lock on a door so old and oxidized that the cell number was unreadable.

I slapped his arm away. "Let me."

For some miracle reason, I still had Neathror in my possession, and it was better that Jad saved his energy. An awful feeling in my gut told me we'd need his magic for later.

I twisted the tip of Neathror's blade into the lock. The door opened, the cell beyond veiled with the thick gloom of oppression. Only a few candles lit the miserable scenery. The ground was buried in an endless amount of dust, the stonework solid enough to make it impossible to escape but thin enough that cold air rushed in. There were two wooden sleeping shelves, a tarnished basin, and a chair with a partly splintered leg.

It was depressing, but it was still way more than anything I had in Gosheniene.

This must be for the more noble prisoners.

Sitting on a sleeping shelf and wrapped in a blanket was a hunched woman. I recognised her but at the same time gaped at how much she had changed. Commander Macaslan's hair had always been neatly pulled back in an immaculate bun on the top of her head, but now it was loose and tumbled past her shoulders in a tangled mess. Dirt was smeared across her face, the candlelight making the hard lines more pronounced. She looked like she'd aged ten years. Thin, wrinkled, and stooped, for the first time she resembled her sister, Macha.

Her grey eyes pinned me in place, as though she'd sensed what I'd thought. "What are you waiting for, girl? Get us out of here. There's a war happening."

I rolled my eyes. "It's nice to see you too."

In the corner of the prison stood Colonel Harper. The purple marks on his face indicated he'd met someone's fist, more than once. I didn't think I'd ever seen the Colonel smile, but he practically glowed at the sight of us. Colour sprang back into his blue eyes, which had been downcast and hooded. I recognised it as hope. And maybe... a little bit of pride.

I stepped toward Macaslan. Her high cheekbones appeared sharper through her frail skin. "Still haughty as ever, I see."

"Of course. I'm the commander." Her authoritative voice still made me uneasy, but a hint of a smile crept over her mouth. She was pleased to see me.

I used Neathror to unfasten the chains that bound her to the sleeping shelf.

She stared at the blade. I knew from the way her lips suddenly thinned that she wasn't happy I had it.

I tried to keep my composure but failed. "It just saved your arse. Deal with it."

Her gaze raked sharply over me. "You were meant to stop the Four Revenants, not let them cause this terrible carnage across Navask."

Anger flared heat in my face. "A little clue for next time. Tell me what the plan is from the beginning. Don't throw me into a portal and hope for the best."

"I thought you would have been smart enough to work it out."

I shook my head in exasperation. "Do you want me to chain you back up?"

She said nothing.

Didn't think so.

I unlocked the shackles from Colonel Harper's wrists, freeing him from the wall.

Jad was already out the door, assessing our surroundings. "We need to go through the tunnels and into a carrier-hornet. This entire palace is about to crash to the ground."

He wasn't wrong. We sped out of the dungeon, only to find that fire and smoke obstructed the way we'd come.

"Down here." Jad ran in the opposite direction, his body hazy as he fought through the thickening curtain of smoke.

"No." Macaslan's shout dominated the room. Even in her tattered dress, which had practically been reduced to rags, she appeared powerful and stern—a queen about to take back her rightful throne. She was definitely not the kind of woman you would want to mess with or double-cross. "There's something we need before we leave. Something worth saving from these fires."

Yeah, but is it worth our lives?

Freedom had seemed to renew Macaslan's energy. "This way."

She hurried through the building, leading us through various burning chambers and suites. Jad kept the flames at bay. They seemed to meet an invisible wall as we drew near, igniting the carpet and tapestries instead. I wondered how long Jad would be able to hold the flames. He was strong. He was powerful. But he couldn't stop an entire palace from burning to the ground.

I scurried after Macaslan. "This is crazy. We need to get out of here."

She stepped into an office chamber. "We need to find it before we leave."

"Find what?"

She didn't answer me. Her eyes connected with Jad's. "We need to find *it*."

Understanding lit across his face. He joined Macaslan, rummaging through drawers and cabinets. Colonel Harper searched the bookcases, hands reckless as books were strewn across the floor.

I shook my head in exasperation. "No, no, no. You do remember what happened last time you three left me out of the loop, right?"

None of them answered, too involved in their hunt.

Only the near-frigging apocalypse occurred and the Four Revenants rose.

Unbelievable.

They really aren't listening to me.

I slouched against the door frame, arms crossed. Something rushed past me in the corner of my eye. I leapt back, expecting a chak-lork. A rebel. A ghost. But it wasn't any of them. Someone ran up a flight of stairs a few metres ahead. They snuck a glance over their shoulder and then disappeared into the smoke beyond. I sucked in a breath, not sure if I'd hallucinated it.

No one should have been in the palace.

So why had I seen Indree?

CHAPTER 53

That was Indree, right?

   No. It couldn't have been. Jad said she was halfway to Port Serres.

I spun around to go ask him, but the door was sealed.

No! Noooo!

A thick black cloud barricaded me from Jad and the others. It wasn't smoke but something else. It ebbed and flowed. Bursts of light streaked through the churning haze, as though it were reaching out and trying to wrap me in a tight cocoon.

I took an awkward step back. Despite the suffocating heat that consumed the palace, a chill emanated from the dark cloud. It crept through my boots, up my legs, over my spine.

"Jad? Jad?"

No answer.

"Jad?"

A cold whisper of breath touched my neck. "He can't hear you. None of them can."

I flinched, startled by Lunette's sudden appearance. Her skin was icy white and veined. Her feet hovered above the ground with a disturbing twitch, as though she were hanging from an invisible noose.

The worst part was her eyes. They were horrified and wide. Her voice turned into a prolonged scream in my head. *"Stop her. Otherwise we are all headed for the Dark Divide."*

Dark Divide?

Lunette pointed to the stairwell with a long crooked finger. *"Stop her. Stop her. Stop her."*

I wasn't one to question Lunette's ghostly presence. If she was afraid, she had good reason to be. I ran to the staircase and took two steps at a time to the next level. This girl, whoever she was, was obviously a threat to have Lunette so psyched out.

It can't be Indree. It can't possibly be.

I pictured Indree's face and how similar it had been to the girl's.

It can't be.

Floor two of the palace hadn't fared much better than floor one. Flames sent waves of sparks skidding in all directions, the furniture and once velvety curtains burned to char. The smoke hurt to breathe. Every room I ran past was ablaze with orange light.

I tugged the collar of my jacket over my nose and clambered into a hallway on my right—the one with less smoke. The girl was at the other end. She slipped around the corner and out of reach. I sprinted after the mysterious girl, around the bend and up another flight of stairs to the third level. The fires hadn't yet reached this part of the palace, but the roar and blast of the flames below made parts of the floor feel as supple as butter. A splintering crash tore behind me. I leapt out of the way as a section of the floor collapsed in an epic shower of timber, marble, and soot. I hung back a moment, fear threatening to choke me. The air was so hot, it saturated my skin with sweat and ash. I tasted it on my lips and felt it send pinpricks of itchiness across my scalp.

This better be worth it, Lunette.

I cast an uneasy glance at the hole in the floor, grateful I wasn't in it, and continued down the hall. The girl seemed to know where she was going. She entered a set of intricately carved double doors and didn't close them behind her. Was that an invitation? Did she know I was in pursuit?

Lunette's voice echoed in a slow, melancholy cry in my mind. *"Be careful, Zaya."*

I approached the doorway. Images and sounds flooded my mind as I stepped into a round, circular room. Memories surfaced from every direction.

I've been here before.

The chamber was exactly as I remembered it. Monolithic columns shaded in golds and reds held an incredible vaulted ceiling. A large oculus in the centre permitted rays of moonlight to descend on a mahogany casket. Standing at each column were the statues of Anubis, the death dogs facing the coffin in a symbolic gesture to ward off evil.

I'm here.

The place where the Four Revenants had intended to bring me.

Morgomoth's burial chamber.

And standing behind his casket was Indree.

For a moment all I could do was stare, not quite believing what my eyes revealed. Her hair was a dirty mess of tangled knots, her face streaked in ash and grime, the whites of her eyes shockingly bright from tears and heat. She looked like a woman resurrected from her own cremation, brought back to seek revenge on the world.

She stared at me with hatred. "Hello, Zaya."

I met her cold gaze with equal wrath. She had let me go to the Four Revenants. She had hurt and betrayed me. And she'd lied to my friends about it.

My voice shook out of my throat. "Indree… what are you doing here? This palace is burning to the ground."

What I really wanted to do was cut her down with Neathror,

but instead I raised my hand in what I hoped she'd perceive as a kind gesture. "We need to get out of the palace. Whatever it is you're here for, we can work it out on a carrier-hornet."

Yeah right. She's here for Jad. She's obsessed with him.

She flinched. Accusation settled deep in her eyes. "You ruined everything."

Resentment flared inside. I trembled so bad even my teeth chattered. "Listen. We don't have time to play 'he likes me best.' We need to get out of here… this chamber especially."

My eyes darted to the casket. Was Morgomoth listening? Of all the things that could have brought me to this chamber, he probably couldn't believe it was a jealous girl.

My hand clasped Neathror tighter. Why hadn't Morgomoth attempted to seize the blade back?

Indree's face lit in a nasty smile. "What's wrong, Zaya? You look frightened."

"And you would be too if you understood where we are."

Why did Indree run into this chamber? What purpose did she have to—

She lifted a dry, bloodstained cloth. "Remember this?"

The chamber walls felt as though they were closing in, the air thin and difficult to breathe. I remembered the way Indree had healed my wound in the Otturin Cave, the way she'd picked up the cloth with a satisfied smirk when she'd finished. *"I'll dispose of this."*

Only she hadn't disposed of it. She'd kept it.

And she was parading it over Morgomoth's open casket like a pet owner with a treat for a dog.

Panic ballooned inside me.

Indree tilted her head to the side and pouted her lips in a mock display of empathy. "Every last drop of your blood is required to resurrect Morgomoth to his full glory and strength, but only one drop is required to actually awaken him. He'll be weak, of course, but if he keeps you by his side—his own little blood bag—his power will resume."

I stared, unable to believe what she was saying. "Indree, I understand you're angry about me and Jad, but this… if this is your revenge, you're making a terrible mistake."

I moved closer. Neathror was so tight in my grasp that I felt the hilt dig into my skin. Would I use the blade on her? I wasn't sure. But I couldn't let her do this.

Indree lifted the cloth and held it loosely between her index finger and thumb. "Step any closer and I'll drop this right now."

I stiffened. My jaw hung stupidly agape. "Indree, don't do this because you're upset. This isn't right. You have no idea what you're about to unleash."

"Yes I do." Her voice echoed through the chamber with poorly acted conviction. Flames licked the windows. The glass splintered in spiderweb cracks. We were running out of time.

Indree's eyes were puffy from crying. "Jad was meant to be mine. They promised me he would be mine."

"Promised he would be mine"?

Her breathing turned choppy. "My father, Count Raminorf, is part of the ULD. He kept an eye on Jad in the orphanage because that's what Vulcan Stormouth asked him to do. I befriended Jad because that was what I was asked to do." She slammed her palm against her chest, emphasising a point. "It was my duty. I didn't expect to end up loving Jad, but that's what happened. I was meant to bring him back to the ULD. We were meant to be together."

I shut my eyes, soaking in the hard truth.

There had always been a traitor working against us at Tarahik. Someone who had communicated with Melvina. Someone who had tipped off the ULD about Jad's mission in Essida. Someone who had led Lunette into the woods to meet her horrific death. Now I understood why Indree had conveniently run into us in the marshes. She hadn't been trying to flee the chak-lorks. She'd joined us to keep an eye on me. That's how Vulcan knew I was coming to Darthmusk. She'd clued him in.

Indree was the traitor.

How did I miss this?

Indree must have contacted the ULD when Jad and the others thought she'd left for Port Serres. It was the only explanation for why she was here. Indree was Vulcan's backup plan.

I looked at the bloodied cloth in her hand.

I'd been such a fool.

A voice, cold and muted, slipped in my ear. *"Don't let her do it. Only a necromancer can awaken Morgomoth with their blood. If she does it, she'll die."*

Lunette hovered beside me. She faded in and out like a flickering light. If she had any resentment for Indree, she didn't show it. A soft tear streaked down her cheek. *"Indree doesn't know. They never told her."*

I stared back at the incensed girl who stood by Morgomoth's coffin. Frustration sharpened my tone. "Indree, you're being used. Can't you see that? You don't matter to the ULD. If you do this, it will kill you."

She spat out a laugh. Cold rage bubbled from deep in her throat. "You'd say anything to stop me."

"Indree, I'm not—"

"Shut up. I do this and Jad's mine. They promised me."

Her crazed, overwrought expression told me there was no convincing her.

"Zaya!"

The voice threw me off. My fear clicked into double time.

Jad.

No. Don't come in here!

But it was too late.

He appeared in the doorway, his eyes registering what was before him in stunned disbelief. "Indree?"

Her face lit up, but it disappeared the moment his gaze moved to me. Terror. Worry. Desire. Longing. It was all there in the way his eyes connected with mine.

And that's all it took.

Indree dropped the cloth.

"No!" I sprinted forward, determined to stop it somehow, knowing it wasn't possible.

An explosion of white light flared from the coffin, so glorious and strong it must have outshone the sun. The force flung me across the marble floor. Agony wrenched my spine. My neck was crammed at an uncomfortable angle, but I forced myself to look up. Indree's body had slumped onto the floor, a corpse too burnt and bloody to recognise. I sensed a horrified cry in the back of my throat, but revulsion paralysed me. The explosion had killed her.

Why didn't she listen?

Stupid, stupid fool.

The coffin remained encased in a bright, pulsing glow, as though the fires from hell had erupted straight from it. The walls rumbled. The Anubis statues melted to the ground, reminding me of wax figurines. Plaster fell from the ceiling. The searing luminosity never faded. It grew stronger, a high-pitched ringing accompanying the sparks and blaze that crept in tendrils out of the light.

He's... awake.

He's awake!

"Zaya!" Jad appeared at my side, his hands strong on my arms as he tried to coax me upright. "Come on. We have to go. Come on."

Pain raced through my body. "He's back. He's back! I have to stop him."

I scanned the floor. *Where is Neathror?* Had I dropped it? Where had it gone?

Jad's hands cupped my face. He forced me to look at him. "Zaya. The blade's gone. It's with *him*. It's over. We need to leave."

I shut my eyes. I'd failed Lunette. I'd failed Macaslan.

Harper.

Darius.

Jad.

I'd failed everyone.

My eyes turned back to the casket. Something else rose in the flames and smoke. It was a featureless body. Part liquid, part slime, it broke down in slippery blobs and reinvented itself like water in a fountain, becoming more solid as the fires intensified around it.

I took Jad's hand and ran.

CHAPTER 54

Light consumed the palace, a tremendous pressure that seemed to expand and flood every room. Accompanying it was a savage wind that invigorated the fires. It forced the flames to rise. They obstructed our path and were too powerful even for Jad to diminish. The floor shuddered beneath us. The light fixtures swung violently. Jad kept his hand firm around mine. My own fingers pressed against his equally hard, my only lifeline in this nightmare. We raced down hallways, past parlour rooms set ablaze, descended flights of stairs so narrow they could only have possibly been used by servants. I wondered how the palace still stood with the amount of damage sustained, and how much longer we had until its foundations finally gave way.

If Jad was upset about Indree, he didn't show it. His face was a mask, emotions buried. "This way."

We ran through a set of double doors and into a marble courtyard paved with black-and-white tiles in a geometric pattern. The night sky was obstructed by smoke and haze. Not even the moon or stars could be seen. At the opposite end of the courtyard was a white staircase that led into the gardens.

My sigh of relief was cut short. The Four Revenants barricaded it.

And not just the Four Revenants.

Dissent rebels were stationed at every exit. Lycanthors paraded around them, grunting and snorting. Large drops of saliva dripped from their jaws, which they snapped with hungry menace.

The ULD had us trapped from every angle. There was no way we could retrace our steps back into the palace again. The fires had made sure of that.

A fresh sheen of sweat danced across my skin. I looked at Jad. He looked at me. It was all either of us could do.

I'd been so focused on the ULD that I'd failed to see beyond the smoky maelstrom that obstructed the courtyard. Hot, howling wind swept the choking fumes into the sky, revealing the full situation before us. The courtyard was crammed with Haxsan Guard survivors—men and women who'd been captured and dragged into this barbarism. They were on their knees, forced into surrender or servitude. I didn't know which. My eyes locked on some familiar faces. I covered my mouth to hold in a cry.

Marek.

Talina.

Lainie.

Macaslan.

Harper.

They'd never escaped.

Marek had a nasty gash on the side of his face. Talina's jaw was bruised. I was relieved to see Lainie had regained consciousness but was concerned by the sunken skin around her eyes. Her lower lip bled, her chin swollen. Someone had hit her. The skin at the back of my neck tingled. I hated seeing my friends beaten down and afraid. Beside them, Macaslan resembled a queen about to be beheaded. Colonel Harper had blood running down his face and nose, probably one too many blows to the head. The pair's shoulders were slouched, but there was fight in their eyes, a determination to not give in.

I don't think we have a choice in the matter.

A dissent rebel grabbed me. His hold on my arms was so strong I knew he'd been injected with lycanthor magic. His foul breath wheezed into my ear. "They your friends, huh?" He ripped me away from Jad—who was ambushed by four dissent rebels simultaneously—and hauled me across the courtyard. The rebel struck a fist into my spine, which was already aching and sensitive. The force knocked me onto my knees among my friends. He leaned forward and growled into my face, "Then you can either surrender with them, or die with them."

I didn't answer, dizzy with the need to be sick.

The rebel sneered and left to join the other dissidents. A snicker moved through the group as they surrounded Jad. Their teeth gleamed when they smiled. I drew both hands over my mouth, transfixed by horror as Jad was kicked, punched, and thrown onto his knees on the other side of the courtyard. There wasn't much distance between us, but it felt like an entire world.

"Zaya." Talina's voice was a frightened whisper at my side. "What is happening? What are they going to do?"

I didn't answer. I wasn't capable of talking.

The fear in the air became a tangible essence, like a lightning storm about to bring ruin and destruction. The prisoners shivered and cringed as blistering white light appeared in the palace doorway that Jad and I had stood in only moments ago. Everyone sensed that something unnatural had occurred in the palace.

No. No. Please, not this.

Cries of horror filled the nightscape.

In the doorway, the white-hot furnace took on a new form. It flowed and rippled into a foreboding black cloud, as though the very light had burnt to ash and darkness. That same high-pitched ring I experienced in the chamber sliced the night again, growing so loud and intense it was like static reverberating through my brain. I knew the others sensed it from the way they clutched their ears.

Hot tears leaked from my eyes. The shadows coalesced into a silhouette, then a figure, something that was alive and breathed—a creature that should have remained in the dark and the deep. Surely only nightmares could create something so atrocious. It was a skeletal horror. The skin was black and polished as a raven's wings. Whenever the creature moved, those fat slippery drops made a steaming paste on the ground. Bones protruded at odd angles, so blackened they appeared burnt. What I had mistaken for a dark cloak was smoke. No, not even smoke. Faces. Translucent souls that writhed and struggled, trapped into making this one corporeal body. My chest heaved as I dry-retched, my chest consumed by an all familiar terror.

Morgomoth.

His bloodshot eyes singled me out, as though I were a magnet he was drawn to. His face was scabbed and thin, his cheeks sunken. He had half a nose, which was crooked and burnt. The other half was a black hole where the nostril had either rotted away or imploded. He was truly one of the vilest things I'd ever had the misfortune to look upon.

His lips broke into a grotesque smile. Even his mouth and saliva were black, his stubbed teeth gleaming yellow in the firelight. His eyes settled on the crowd. "Do not be afraid. I know my appearance is… frightening. But I assure you I am not here to cause you harm, merely to provide you with a choice."

His powerful voice caused people to shudder. It was high-pitched and scratchy but at the same time pervasive. He lifted his hands in a placating gesture, a signal to urge everyone to stay calm. "I am Morgomoth. I was never dead. The Council cursed me to an eternal sleeping hex and used my powers for their own purpose and gain… much like the way they are using you."

There was a murmur of apprehension through the crowd. My legs shook with nervous adrenaline.

What game is he playing?

Morgomoth tilted his neck and took a good look at what he

obviously saw as his disciples beneath him. "I never believed in the Council's ways. Protecting humans. Giving them our resources. Our food. Our lands. Keeping humans safe in the Free Zones while the rest of us struggle in the provinces. The Council steal caster children and train them for the Haxsan Guard. How many of you were taken from your families?"

Empty silence settled through the crowd. The air was no longer saturated with fear or panic. I saw it in the way people's faces hardened, in the way their lips thinned and their eyes stared ahead. Morgomoth had their attention.

The leader of the ULD fixed his steel-like gaze on the crowd. "I tried to change the Council. I tried to make them see how evil their ways were… and for that, they did this to me." He stretched his arms, revealing the horror of what he'd become. Bone, smoke, and shadows. "The Council tear caster families apart. How many of you have lost loved ones, family, friends to this war? Protecting humans, letting casters be ruled by humans, it all goes against nature. We need to claim back what is ours. We are the dominant species on this planet. Not the humans. Not the Council. Us."

My eyes found Jad's in the crowd. So much was communicated in that silent stare. He wanted me to stay calm and not to draw attention to myself. I nodded, a promise to do my best, but somehow I doubted Morgomoth would let me stay hidden for long. Would he spare my friends?

I stole a fearful glance at them. Talina cried beside me. Marek stared at the crowd with confoundment. It was Lainie's reaction that struck me the hardest. Her demeanour had changed, her tears gone. Her eyes were alight with purpose and resolve.

Is she… actually listening to him?

Morgomoth continued like a preacher giving a sermon. "Join the United League of Dissent and reclaim what is yours."

He struck his hands forward. A black slit appeared in the centre of the courtyard. It expanded thicker and larger, wispy tendrils dripping like glue. It was the same formless darkness that Morgomoth was made of.

It's a portal.

Where it led I didn't know. No one could possibly know except for its creator.

He created a portal out of nothing!

I strained to breathe. It was another testament to Morgomoth's power and strength.

But he's meant to be weak.

Morgomoth raised his hand in the air. "Do not be afraid. This is old magic."

"It's necromancer magic," someone shouted from the crowd.

Morgomoth blinked like a satisfied cat. "Yes it is. I am a necromancer. But I am not something to be feared. I can save you all. Once we rid this world of humans, I can return your loved ones to you."

And just like that, he had them hooked. The crowd needed no proof. No explanation. They were told exactly what they'd always wanted to hear—the return of the people they'd loved and lost. People stood, cried, cupped their hands over their mouths. Morgomoth was their miracle worker and their one stop to salvation. They were tired of war. Tired of death. They just wanted it to be over.

Morgomoth's voice rolled through the night, a king commanding the respect and gratitude of his subjects. "Join the United League of Dissent." He pointed to the rippling black portal.

No! No!

People were actually doing it.

Are you all frigging sheep?

One by one, people who were captives only a minute ago walked willingly into the portal. Some ran into it. Each time a caster crossed, the portal expanded. It was like a beast that doubled in height and strength after devouring a long-awaited meal.

Macaslan was the first one to come to her senses. She rose from the ground faster than I would have thought possible for a woman of her age and grabbed my arm. "We need to leave. Now"

My heart thundered in my chest. "How? The courtyard is barricaded."

"Not anymore. The rebels and lycanthors have already left. Once that portal times out, it will explode. It's a ticking time bomb. You didn't really think Morgomoth would let those who remained behind live, did you?"

"And the people inside?"

"They've crossed over. Who knows where?"

Judging by the tremor in her voice, Macaslan knew exactly where the portal led. She just wasn't going to tell me.

"Come on," she barked.

I looked over my shoulder. Marek, Talina, and Harper were right behind us, and to my relief, Jad had skirted through the crowd straight toward me. He took hold of my hand and did a quick once-over, checking if I was hurt.

I offered him a weak smile. "I'm okay."

But I wasn't. How could anyone be okay with this happening around them?

Flames sent a wave of scorching heat through the air, and I wondered how we didn't all blister right there. The palace window-panes exploded, glass splinters raining across us in a hailstorm.

Jad raised his hand, using his magic to keep the flames at bay, but the ferocious gale from the portal continued to send scalding heat toward us. Macaslan was right. We had to get out of this chaos. But we couldn't leave yet. Not without—

I scanned the courtyard. "Where's Lainie?"

The thick haze made it difficult to see as my gaze wandered inadvertently to the portal.

My jaw dropped.

Lainie wasn't hurrying away. She walked toward it.

CHAPTER 55

A strangled cry burst from my throat. "Lainie! Lainie!"

Not caring if I drew attention to myself, I barrelled through the crowd, weaving my way through the converted casters. Some of them were looking down at their hands with joyful tears. The Infinite Eye had disappeared, their loyalty crushed with only a few simple words from Morgomoth. I didn't know how he did it, but somehow Morgomoth had managed to break through that seal that kept Haxsan Guard soldiers devoted to the Council. It had taken days for my friends to lose their marks. How had Morgomoth managed it so fast? How could these people not see that they were walking away from one tyranny only to be stepping right into another?

I had to stop Lainie from making the same mistake. "Lainie! Lainie!"

Her shoulders were hunched like those of someone in pain, but she turned around to face me. Shadows lined her face. Dark hair obscured her eyes. "Don't try to stop me, Zaya. I want this. I've wanted this for a long time."

My blood seemed to have suddenly stopped flowing, every part of me shocked by her confession. "Lainie, Morgomoth is ev—"

"No. You listen to me for once." Her mouth pinched into an ugly line. "Morgomoth is the answer. I've lost so much. My brother... my family... Edric." She gasped, her voice muted and thin. "Morgomoth can bring them back. He's right. Humans have taken everything from us." She shut her eyes and cried. "I need Edric back. You have the ability to do it. And you won't."

"Lain—"

"You wouldn't bring Edric back if I asked you to, would you?"

A glimmer of hope flashed in her eyes. She was testing me.

Doubt tugged my emotions, unravelling everything inside. "I can't. That's not how necromancy works. What Morgomoth is doing to the undead is not natural. His magic is animating their bodies. The soul is gone. Morgomoth can't return these people's loved ones. He's lying."

Furious tears leaked down her cheeks. "No. *You're* lying."

I retreated a step. I didn't recognise Lainie anymore.

A foreign thought spread through my mind. *Or maybe you never really knew Lainie from the beginning.*

I reached my hand out to her. "Please. Come back with us. We can figure this out."

She stepped away, as though I were contaminated. "No we can't. Stay away from me, Zaya. Run if you have to. Just remember that you're on the wrong side."

The venom in her voice stunned me. She sped away through the crowd. For a moment I lost sight of her, but then I saw her run into the portal. A second later, she was enveloped by the thick swirl of darkness.

Lainie, what have you done?

"Zaya!" Jad tore toward me, or tried to. The crowd knocked him back and forth like a paddler in the surf. "This place is about to blow," he shouted.

He was right. The high-pitched buzz that filled the air had increased in cadence and pressure. The entire courtyard was about to erupt in a shower of marble fragments, smoke, and fire. No wonder the dissent rebels and lycanthors had retreated.

A voice, cool and imposing, sent shivers over my skin. "What is the opposite of a beating heart?"

I flinched, startled to find Morgomoth behind me.

Smoke and bone, I reminded myself. His earthly presence wasn't natural. That's how he'd snuck up on me.

Like a wraith.

His lips quirked up at the corners. "Don't know the answer? Let me show you."

He clicked his fingers. In an instant, everyone around us slumped to the ground. I screamed so loud my lungs hurt. Jad had been running toward me, but he wasn't immune to Morgomoth's power either. He clutched at his chest. Confusion registered on his face as he sank to his knees. A moment later, he sagged to the ground. Marek and Talina had collapsed in each other's arms, faces white as stone. Macaslan and Harper were sprawled on the tiles, their skin sallow and sweaty.

Whatever thin semblance of control I had left vanished. I sprang at Morgomoth, ready to punch my fist straight into his triumphant smirk. "What did you do?"

The madman grabbed my wrists. Smoke and bone wrapped around my arms, preventing me from moving. Morgomoth wasn't weak. He was stronger and more powerful than I could ever have imagined. "I've bought us some time." The icy spite in his voice sent a gush of poison to my gut. "Your friends aren't dead. I lowered their heart rates, slowing them down enough that they'd lose consciousness. It gives us a chance to talk."

I shook my head vigorously, struggling to flee his strong grip. It was like trying to fight myself out of a concrete wall. "I don't want to talk to you."

"And I don't want to kill you."

My voice seethed with sarcasm. "Oh really? Sorry, but the evidence says otherwise."

"I don't want to kill anyone, Zaya. Unlike the Council, I can be merciful."

"You call this merciful?"

He leant forward, his face—or what was left of it—close to mine. "I'm going to let you and your friends go because I know in time you will join the ULD. There will not be a corner on this earth where anyone can hide." His breath was syrupy and sweet, a strange combination for a man who probably hadn't brushed his teeth in several years, but it also made me want to retch. "You are a powerful necromancer, Zaya. You don't realise it, but you and I can be powerful allies. You could be a queen."

I tried to look away from his glittering black gaze, but the shadows that made up his body forced me to look at him. All I had for defence were words. "I don't want to be a queen."

Especially if that made you my king.

He cocked his head to the side, as though he were truly disappointed. "Then I have no choice but to slow you down, make sure we are evenly matched in our weakness until you decide to pledge allegiance to the ULD... until you decide to swear loyalty to me."

He brought his wrist to his mouth and drove his stubbed teeth down. Revulsion swam through me. He tore out a remnant of rotting flesh and spat it on the ground. Black blood flowed thick and fast across the marble. His other hand snaked around my back. He dug his fingers into my neck and forced my head back. I was immobile to my own commands. Somehow, he'd taken control of my body.

Dizziness closed in. My heartbeat had slowed down, just enough that I didn't lose consciousness but enough to make me limp. My body felt as though pins and needles were striking at every point.

Morgomoth raised his bleeding wrist inches from my mouth. "Drink."

I watched wide-eyed, like a child terrified by a dark

pantomime. My head pounded. I managed to twist my head away, but only slightly.

This was a game to Morgomoth. He could crush me right now. Break me so there was nothing left but dust. Instead, he chose to torment me.

Make me as weak as him?

I'm already weak.

Or was I?

If Morgomoth wanted me as an ally, then that meant I was a stronger threat than I'd initially thought. He wasn't about to kill me. This was something far worse.

His eyes lit with rage. "Drink."

This time he accompanied his command with a ruthless jerk to my neck. Pain stabbed through my scalp into my throat. My lips parted with a distracted cry—

Which was Morgomoth's intention all along.

Drops of the foul-tasting blood dripped onto my lips. It seeped into my mouth like slow-moving honey. I attempted to cough it out, but the metallic taste in the back of my throat told me it had entered my system.

Morgomoth trailed his finger down my cheek. "My curse is now your curse. The Dark Divide awaits you."

He dropped me. I tumbled to the ground in a boneless heap, my arms and legs numb. I fought through the oppressive haze that suffocated my brain.

Breathe, Zaya.

Breathe!

My heart soared to a regular beat. Sensation returned to my body. I spat out whatever blood was left in my mouth, determined that I would no longer be tainted with Morgomoth's poison. But it was too late. I knew it. *He* knew it.

What has he done to me?

I trembled with fear as he stared down at me. He had Neathror in his bony hand. The blade had switched allegiance again. Morgomoth could so easily kill me, but he kept his word. He discarded me like a toy he no longer had use for and headed toward the portal.

"I'll come back for you, Zaya. And soon."

Smoke and shadows followed him. Wispy tendrils curled into the air wherever he trod. He stepped into the black mass of swirling darkness and disappeared. The portal seemed to expand in response, doubling in strength and magnitude. Hot, scorching wind threatened to rip me away. It was sucking everything in, a vortex that was hungry for anything it could capture.

Hands grabbed me. "Come on. Let's move."

Jad.

He must have regained consciousness when Morgomoth left the courtyard.

He helped me from the ground. "Come on, Zaya! We need to move."

My brain still felt scattered, but I shook the fog clear, determined to find strength. Together we ran to the stairwell that led down to the gardens. Macaslan, Harper, Marek, and Talina were already ahead of us, shouting for anyone who was alive to flee. I was glad they were all right. The smell of ash was thick in the air. Firelight extended across the gardens, lighting our way to the thick fold of trees that had probably been planted to offer shade but was now our refuge.

I looked over my shoulder at the same time the portal erupted with an unfathomable boom. It flared too bright to watch. The ground trembled, throwing each of us off balance. A wave of energy swept through the gardens, stripping leaves from their trees and toppling statues. I held on to Jad's hand so tight, I didn't think I'd ever be capable of letting him go again. The world grew brighter, a purifying white almost as powerful as the sun.

And then, as fast as a speeding bullet, everything went dark.

CHAPTER 56

S tazika Palace had collapsed to the ground in a charred heap.
Almost nothing remained except for a few reinforced walls
that had refused to be torn down and now stood like crooked
gravestones. The night sky was filled with the thick haze of smoke.
Not even the horizon could be seen. That made me afraid. It
wouldn't be long till the Council sent Haxsan Guard reinforcements to comb the area. We needed to be far away when that
happened. In the eyes of the Council, we were traitors.

Commander Macaslan—if I could still call her that—settled
her grey eyes on Jad in strict authoritative mode. "Captain Arden,
is there any chance you and Lieutenant Spiers could commandeer
an aircraft?"

Jad's eyes flashed with anxiety. "We can if there are any carrier-
hornets left."

Marek released a conflicted sigh. "There is. In the underground
hangar. I'd just fuelled a carrier-hornet when we…." He stopped
and swallowed discreetly. "When we were captured."

Talina stiffened. She dropped her gaze to the ground and
refused to look at anyone.

A coppery taste filled my mouth. Lainie's decision had been

hurtful. For Talina, it must have been excruciating. She'd known Lainie since they were little. Unimaginable betrayal must have been foremost in Talina's mind at that moment. I shut my eyes, knowing eventually we were going to have to talk about Lainie and what to do next—if there even was anything we could do. She'd made her choice pretty clear.

Everyone was tired and suffering the effects of Morgomoth's magic. My pulse still didn't feel quite right. It seemed to thump too loud one minute, then not at all. I swallowed a deep breath. I was crazy sleepy all of a sudden, my thoughts barely stringing together. I fought to keep my eyes awake. It was just exhaustion. And stress. And shock.

Get through this. You can sleep on the plane.

After much deliberation over where to go and what our choices were, we strode across the gardens to a cave covered in thick climbing ivy. Only it wasn't just a cave. It was a good thing Jad had been a security escort in the past, because hidden in the rock wall was a glamour. He led us through the murky stone into a secret passage beyond. It must have been another underground escape route from the palace. We followed the captain through the twisting network of tunnels and eventually come out to the hangar. There were only three aircraft left. A part of me was happy to see that. It meant most of Stazika's residents had escaped.

The only people who are dead are the Haxsan Guard and the rebels who fought them.

My good mood evaporated.

The carrier-hornet must have been for the elite, because the first thing I did was raid the restroom, which was bigger than my entire bedroom at Tarahik, and cleanse my mouth with mouthwash. I spat out the acidic taste of blood, repeating the process five times until I was satisfied it was gone. I stared at myself in the mirror, aghast by the shocking sight. My skin was washed out and covered in dirt. Ash and snow peppered my hair. The worst was my eyes. The blue irises were a sea of tears, the whites now red and swollen. Fatigue threatened to tear me down. I could have gone to sleep right on the bathroom floor.

Inside the cabin, I settled into a comfy chair, but no amount of luxury leather could dampen the anxiety inside me. Through the door to the cockpit, I saw Jad and Marek pull themselves into the pilot seats and familiarise themselves with the controls. A memory surfaced. My first meeting with Jad had been in a carrier-hornet, back when he and Marek had volunteered to collect me from Gosheniene. Jad and I had been rude and obtuse and practically loathed each other from the beginning, but now we were... well, I didn't know what we were.

But I'm keen to find out.

The cabin lurched as the carrier-hornet ascended out of the underground hanger. I stared out the window, questioning whether fire-crusaders were speeding in to blow us out of the sky. Fine layers of ash fell like gentle rain on the spongy earth below, and then the aircraft accelerated so high that I saw nothing but cloud.

I settled back in my seat. Macaslan and Harper were in the cockpit, no doubt discussing our options.

Where would we go?

Port Serres?

The commander and the colonel weren't the type of casters to flee Navask. No, they would find Darius. They would rebuild their strength and forces. Jad and Marek would follow. So would I. But what about Talina?

She sat on a chair with her legs curled together, her arms wrapped around herself. She saw me staring. Cold fury burned in her eyes, but I didn't think it was directed at me. She wiped at her mouth. "I can't believe she left like that. I thought... I thought I knew Lainie. She's my best friend. Was my best friend. How could she side with the ULD?"

I blinked to keep my eyes awake. "Morgomoth preached exactly what everyone wanted to hear. They'll realise that when he can't deliver."

"You really think so?"

I hope so.

But I wasn't sure I believed it.

Talina massaged her temples, perhaps soothing a headache. "Honestly, I don't know why I'm so surprised."

"What do you mean?"

She bit her lip. "You know what I'm talking about. There was always a darkness in Lainie... and not just in the way she dressed. She honestly hated the Council and the Haxsan Guard. She lost her brother. Then Edric. I guess she just couldn't...."

Talina didn't have to finish for me to know what she'd been about to say. Lainie had lost so much because the Council and the Haxsan Guard had taken away her choices. We'd all lost so much, but it had been different for Lainie. She'd lost loved ones. I understood why she sided with the ULD. I really did. It was the same reason everyone else had. The chance for change and freedom. But Morgomoth would never offer that. If the Council of Founding Sovereigns fell and the United League of Dissent rose to power, the world would have just swapped one dictatorship for another.

Macaslan strode in and dropped into a seat. It was the first time I'd ever seen her do something without grace or style.

I flexed my hands open and closed in my lap. "Where are we going?"

She shut her eyes. "I need to decide on that. Let me think. I need to rest."

I contemplated interrupting her respite. Lunette's warning still filled my veins with icy terror, and I needed someone with some understanding about necromancy to talk to.

"Stop her. Otherwise, we are all headed for the Dark Divide."

What was the Dark Divide?

I'd deliberated whether I should wake Macaslan or not for too long, and by the time I had the courage, the commander had drifted into a deep slumber. Talina had also shut her eyes, her face serene and peaceful, even though inside she was probably troubled and hurting.

Exhaustion raked down my body. I squeezed my eyes shut, but my brain wouldn't switch off. Instead, it was plagued by troubled thoughts.

Four lives lost.

One friend siding with the enemy.

This was not how I imagined things would end.

It hasn't ended, Zaya. It's just beginning.

Morgomoth is awake!

What was he doing now? What was he planning?

The Dark Divide.

What is the Dark Divide?

"You okay?'

I jumped at the voice.

Jad sat beside me.

I tried to shake off the guilt, but who was I kidding? Jad knew me. He'd see straight through a lie. "Is this my fault?"

"No."

"Then why does it feel like it is?"

"Because you're a decent person, and you want the best for people."

I took a moment to reflect on those words. "Do you... resent me?"

His eyes focused on mine, sharp and a little surprised. Concern slipped into his tone when he asked, "Why would I resent you?"

I dropped my head, unable to bear the disappointment that would surely surface on his face. "Because of what happened to Indree."

He was silent for a moment. "Indree made her choice. I don't think anyone could have stopped her."

I didn't want to cause Jad pain, but I didn't want to hide the truth from him either. "There's more."

I told him about Count Raminorf's true allegiance and how

Indree had simply been a tool to spy on the Haxsan Guard and, eventually, convince Jad to return to the ULD.

I had expected him to be angry, upset, livid, but the expression on his face went from disappointment to dull acceptance.

I tipped my chin up. "You already knew?"

"I suspected. It's why I kept my distance from Indree and never mentioned her to you. Now that I look back on it, perhaps that was a mistake."

I chewed on the inside of my cheek. "What were you, Macaslan, and Harper looking for in that office chamber?"

Instead of answering, Jad pressed his lips against mine. A warmth I had thought would be impossible to ever feel again spread through me. He took me by the shoulders and pulled me closer. The kiss deepened, growing more powerful and hungry. I'd never felt stronger or more alive, as though a stranger had taken over my body.

Forget sleep.

I twisted my fingers into his dark hair, kissing him with passionate urgency.

Thank the higher entity I used mouthwash.

A heat that became incredibly unpleasant built in my chest. I gasped and sprang back. Jad's eyes widened. I knew he was afraid he must have hurt me, but this was something beyond physical discomfort. His magic didn't do this. This was the work of my own body. The burning sensation expanded into my shoulders and arms. It drove down my legs into my feet.

What the hell is happening to me?

My body felt as though it were on fire. I screamed and collapsed in a pathetic heap on the floor.

"Zaya! Zaya!" Jad's voice was frantic.

I couldn't respond. My throat, voice, mouth—everything was paralysed. The only sensation was that terrible, scorching heat. My vision clouded. A buzzing drowned out Jad's voice. The gentle vibrations of the plane disappeared.

Jad, I'm scared.

"*He can't hear you,*" a voice echoed in my head, deep and resonating.

And familiar.

Morgomoth.

Somehow, he was communicating with me.

I imagined the cold smile that must have inched across Morgomoth's face as he linked our minds. "*I told you I'd equal the playing field. I am weak, Zaya. And now you're weak too. My curse is now your curse. The Dark Divide awaits you.*"

The same words he'd used when he'd pinned me in a crushing embrace and forced his disgusting blood down my throat.

No!

Realisation dawned on me.

Morgomoth's voice swept through my body, the heat forcing sweat to pop out on my skin. "*Pleasant dreams, Zaya.*"

The sleeping hex that had kept him in an eternal sleep.

He'd transferred it into me through his blood.

What is the Dark Divide?

What is happening?

I had brief movement and sensation in my fingers. I felt Jad's hand in mine and squeezed, but even that took effort. Everything was dying inside me, shutting down and readying itself for hibernation.

"*Please. Don't do this.*"

But there was no response at the other end of the mind link.

Jad.

He was my last thought.

My lids closed, the darkness complete.

THE STORY CONTINUES

THE
DARK
DIVIDE

THE WAYWARD HAUNT SERIES

THE DARK DIVIDE

GET THE BOOK AT THE LINK BELOW

https://books2read.com/u/baqWPv

Zaya faces a terrifying new reality.

Morgomoth has trapped her in a sleeping curse, and Zaya's soul has been dragged into the nightmarish underworld of the Dark Divide—a place of endless, shifting tunnels filled with lost, raging ghosts.

There is only one way out. A door that, if opened, will unleash the Dark Divide into the living world.

Morgomoth has given Zaya a choice. Open the door, join him and his evil forces, or remain trapped for eternity.

Zaya must do the impossible. Escape from the Dark Divide, save Jad and her friends from Morgomoth's horrors on the world, and learn to defeat him using necromancy.

But it won't come without sacrifices... or betrayal.

ACKNOWLEDGMENTS

A big thank you to the Brisbane Night Writers; Tom, Stuart, Sandy, Poet Pete, Phillip, Shannon, and our fearless leader Gillian, who read and critiqued various chapters of The Four Revenants. Thanks for your honest opinions and instructions, and for offering incredible support to all writers in our little group.

An enormous thank you to author Shan L. Scott, who read the completed draft of the novel and provided support and advice during this writing marathon. I benefited greatly from her insight, and will always appreciate the positivity that she brought to The Four Revenants.

Thanks are due to Tom Jones, who tirelessly proofread the draft and found those silly mistakes that all writers make. I think he got a good laugh out of some of the very funny blunders I made. I did too.

A tremendous thank you to my editor Kristin Scearce from Hot Tree Editing, who has been on the journey for The Wayward Haunt and The Four Revenants from the very start. She improved the writing in both novels astronomically and is a truly talented woman with words. Thank you too to Barbara Hoover for the final edit and proofread. You made this story shine.

A huge thank you to the bookworms out there who took a chance on a new author and read The Wayward Haunt and The Four Revenants. This new author truly appreciates it.

And finally, thanks to my mum, who encouraged me to pursue my writing dream.

I offer my heartfelt thanks to you all XOXO.

ABOUT THE AUTHOR

Cas E. Crowe is an admirer of all things spooky, quirky, and witchy. She enjoys writing YA and NA dark fantasy, horror, and romantasy stories filled with magic and adventure. Cas lives in Brisbane, Australia and, when she is not reading or writing, is often daydreaming about her next story or creating art with Photoshop.

www.casecrowe.com

BB bookbub.com/authors/cas-e-crowe?

a amazon.com/author/cascrowe

g goodreads.com/casecrowe

o instagram.com/casecroweauthor

X x.com/CroweCas

f facebook.com/casecroweauthor

d tiktok.com/@casecroweauthor

p pinterest.com/casecroweauthor

LEAVE A REVIEW

If you enjoyed The Four Revenants, please consider leaving a review on Amazon and Goodreads through the links below. Authors depend on reviews to get the word out about their books.

Amazon
https://books2read.com/u/4Xe0Eg

Goodreads
https://www.goodreads.com/book/show/122779060-the-four-revenants

NEWSLETTER

Sign up for Cas E. Crowe's Author Newsletter

Get access to
Author Interviews
Sample Chapters
Bonus Book Material
Book Recommendations
WIP (Writing in Progress)
Book Reviews
News and Social Events
Reading Lists
Exclusive Reveals
Upcoming Events
https://casecrowe.com/contact/

BOOKBUB

Follow Cas on BookBub to get notifications about upcoming releases, preorder availability, new book launches, and limited-time discounts.

bookbub.com/authors/cas-e-crowe?